PRAISE ...

JA...

WI...

"Enough plot and a ... side."

DARK JUSTICE

"High-speed narration." —*Publishers Weekly*

"A mesmerizing tale . . . Higgins cements readers to the pages." —*Times Colonist* (Victoria, B.C.)

BAD COMPANY

"Higgins writes with spare velocity, racing through a complex plot . . . [and] has no equal in the realm of ex-Nazis wreaking havoc." —*St. Louis Post-Dispatch*

"Fans will find enough gnarly action and sentiment here to make them anticipate [Higgins's] next."
—*Publishers Weekly*

MIDNIGHT RUNNER

"The fun comes from the wisecracking band of dangerous but bighearted secret soldiers Higgins wheels out to save the world—and his galloping Hollywood-ready pace."
—*People*

"Swift and coursing with dark passion . . . as credible and steel-hearted as Higgins's best." —*Publishers Weekly*

EDGE OF DANGER

"This is Higgins near the top of his game . . . another winner." —*Publishers Weekly*

"The action is non-stop." —*Minneapolis Star Tribune*

continued . . .

DAY OF RECKONING

"The action is sleek and intensely absorbing, but the supreme pleasure is in those Higgins celebrates—tarnished warriors who value honor over life and who get the job done no matter what the cost." —*Publishers Weekly*

THE WHITE HOUSE CONNECTION

"*The White House Connection* has one heckuva heroine . . . [who] begins a one-woman assassination spree that will keep you turning the pages." —Larry King, *USA Today*

"Masterful . . . a satisfying, suspense-filled book."
—*Roanoke Times & World News*

"[A] page-turning thriller." —*The Indianapolis Star*

THE PRESIDENT'S DAUGHTER

"A tight story with plenty of action."
—*Chattanooga Free Press*

NIGHT JUDGEMENT AT SINOS

"This is one you won't put down." —*The New York Times*

DRINK WITH THE DEVIL

"A most intoxicating thriller." —The Associated Press

"It is Dillon's likability and the author's adroitness in giving his character the room he needs that make Higgins's novels so readable." —*Washington Times*

YEAR OF THE TIGER

"Higgins spins as mean a tale as Ludlum, Forsythe, or any of them." —*Philadelphia Daily News*

ANGEL OF DEATH

"Pulsing excitement . . . Higgins makes the pages fly."
—*New York Daily News*

"The action never stops." —*The San Francisco Examiner*

EYE OF THE STORM

Also published as *Midnight Man*

"Heart-stopping . . . spectacular and surprising."
—*Abilene Reporter-News*

"Razor-edged . . . will give you an adrenaline high. It's a winner."
—*Tulsa World*

ON DANGEROUS GROUND

"A whirlwind of action, with a hero who can out-Bond old James. It's told in the author's best style, with never a pause for breath."
—*The New York Times Book Review*

SHEBA

"When it comes to thriller writers, one name stands well above the crowd—Jack Higgins." —The Associated Press

THUNDER POINT

"Dramatic . . . authentic . . . one of the author's best."
—*The New York Times*

"A rollicking adventure that twists and turns."
—*The San Diego Union-Tribune*

TITLES BY JACK HIGGINS

Rough Justice
The Killing Ground
A Fine Night for Dying
The Bormann Testament
Without Mercy
Dark Justice
Hell Is Always Today
Bad Company
Midnight Runner
The Graveyard Shift
Edge of Danger
Day of Reckoning
The Keys of Hell
The White House Connection
In the Hour Before Midnight
East of Desolation
The President's Daughter
Pay the Devil
Flight of Eagles
Year of the Tiger
Drink with the Devil
Night Judgement at Sinos
Angel of Death
Sheba
On Dangerous Ground
Thunder Point
Eye of the Storm
(also published as *Midnight Man*)
The Eagle Has Flown
Cold Harbour
Memories of a Dance-Hall Romeo
A Season in Hell
Night of the Fox
Confessional
Exocet
Touch the Devil
Luciano's Luck
Solo
Day of Judgment
Storm Warning
The Last Place God Made
A Prayer for the Dying
The Eagle Has Landed
The Run to Morning
Dillinger
To Catch a King
The Valhalla Exchange
The Khufra Run
A Game for Heroes
The Wrath of God

ROUGH JUSTICE

Jack Higgins

BERKLEY BOOKS, NEW YORK

THE BERKLEY PUBLISHING GROUP
Published by the Penguin Group
Penguin Group (USA) Inc.
375 Hudson Street, New York, New York 10014, USA
Penguin Group (Canada), 90 Eglinton Avenue East, Suite 700, Toronto, Ontario M4P 2Y3, Canada
(a division of Pearson Penguin Canada Inc.)
Penguin Books Ltd., 80 Strand, London WC2R 0RL, England
Penguin Group Ireland, 25 St. Stephen's Green, Dublin 2, Ireland (a division of Penguin Books Ltd.)
Penguin Group (Australia), 250 Camberwell Road, Camberwell, Victoria 3124, Australia
(a division of Pearson Australia Group Pty. Ltd.)
Penguin Books India Pvt. Ltd., 11 Community Centre, Panchsheel Park, New Delhi—110 017, India
Penguin Group (NZ), 67 Apollo Drive, Rosedale, North Shore 0632, New Zealand
(a division of Pearson New Zealand Ltd.)
Penguin Books (South Africa) (Pty.) Ltd., 24 Sturdee Avenue, Rosebank, Johannesburg 2196,
South Africa

Penguin Books Ltd., Registered Offices: 80 Strand, London WC2R 0RL, England

ROUGH JUSTICE

A Berkley Book / published by arrangement with HarperCollins Publishers Ltd.

PRINTING HISTORY
G. P. Putnam's Sons hardcover edition / August 2008
Berkley international edition / November 2008

For information, address: The Berkley Publishing Group,
a division of Penguin Group (USA) Inc.,
375 Hudson Street, New York, New York 10014.

ISBN: 978-0-425-22480-9

BERKLEY®
Berkley Books are published by The Berkley Publishing Group,
a division of Penguin Group (USA) Inc.,
375 Hudson Street, New York, New York 10014.
BERKLEY® is a registered trademark of Penguin Group (USA) Inc.
The "B" design is a trademark of Penguin Group (USA) Inc.

PRINTED IN THE UNITED STATES OF AMERICA

10 9 8 7 6 5 4 3 2 1

To Ian Haydn Smith—a good friend

We sleep safe in our beds because rough men stand ready to visit violence on those who would do us harm.

—*George Orwell*

Nantucket

The President

1

There was no place President Jake Cazalet wanted to be more right now than this Nantucket beach, the sea thundering in to the shore in the strange luminous light of early evening, the wind tasting of salt.

The President had been delivered there by helicopter from the White House only an hour before, and here he was, walking with his favorite Secret Service man, Clancy Smith; his beloved flatcoat retriever, Murchison, dashing in and out of the incoming waves.

"He'll need a good hosing," Cazalet said. "Silly old boy. You'd think he'd have learned by now that the salt is bad for his skin."

"I'll see to it, Mr. President."

"I'll have a cigarette now."

Clancy offered him a Marlboro and flicked his Zippo lighter, which flared in the wind. Cazalet smiled. "I know, Clancy, what would the voters think? It's the curse of old soldiers."

"We've all been there, Mr. President."

"Harper on communications as usual?"

"Yes. The only other person in the house is Mrs. Boulder, cooking dinner."

"Amen to that." Cazalet smiled. "I love this place, Clancy. Iraq, Afghanistan, our friends in Moscow—if we can call them that—they could all be on another planet when I'm here." He sighed. "At least until that damned helicopter picks us up and deposits me back at the White House."

Clancy's cell phone rang and he answered, listened for a few moments, then turned to Cazalet. "Blake Johnson, Mr. President. He's arrived back from Kosovo sooner than he thought."

"Well, that's great. Is he coming down?"

"By helicopter. And he also ran into General Charles Ferguson, who was passing through Washington on his way to London after some business at the United Nations. He thought you might like to meet with him, so he's bringing him down, too."

"Excellent." Cazalet smiled. "It's always good to see Ferguson, find out what the Prime Minister's up to. It'd be interesting to get his take on Blake's report, too."

They continued walking. "I thought Kosovo was history, Mr. President," Clancy said.

"Not really. After what the Serbs did to them, they want their independence. The Muslims are in the majority now, Serbs the minority. It's still a problem. The Kosovo Protection Corps the UN set up in 2004 is still operating—troops from various countries, a British general coordinating the situation—but when you get into the backcountry, things happen. There've been reports of outside influence, rumors of the presence of Russian troops."

"And they were always for the Serbs," Clancy pointed out.

"Exactly, which is why I decided to send in Blake to scout around and see what's happening." There was the sound of a helicopter in the distance. "That must be them. We'd better get back."

Cazalet called to Murchison, turned to the beach house, and Clancy followed.

BLAKE AND FERGUSON sat together on one of the leather sofas beside the open fire, the coffee table between them and the President. Clancy served drinks, whiskey, and branch water for both of them. Cazalet toasted them.

"Here's to both of you. It's a real bonus having you here, Charles."

Ferguson said, "You look well, Mr. President, and you, Clancy."

"We get by," Cazalet said. "How is the Prime Minister?"

"I saw him three days ago and he seemed to be coping. Iraq hasn't helped, and Afghanistan is a major problem. There's combat of the most savage kind there—we haven't seen its like since the hand-to-hand fighting against the Chinese on the Hook during the Korean War. Most of our infantry and paratroops are nineteen or twenty. Boys, when you think about it. They're winning the battles, but perhaps losing the war."

Cazalet nodded, remembering his time in Vietnam. "War has always been a young man's game. So tell me—what did the Prime Minister send his private security adviser to the UN for? Can you tell us, or is it for his eyes only?"

"I can certainly tell you, Mr. President. I'm keeping an eye on the Russian Federation. I sat in on two committees also attended by Moscow and Iran. *Supposedly,* they were trade delegations."

"Why am I laughing?" Cazalet asked.

"I listened, drifted around. Putin was the name on everyone's lips."

"What would you say he's after?" Cazalet raised his hand. "No, let me put this in another way. What's his purpose?"

"I need hardly tell you, Mr. President—to make the Russian Federation a power in the world again. And he's using the riches of Russia's gas and oil fields, networked throughout Europe as far as Scandinavia and Scotland, to do it."

Blake said, "And once Europe signs up, if he wants to bring them to heel, all he has to do is turn off the taps."

There was silence. Cazalet said, "He knows he couldn't win anything militarily. One of our Nimitz aircraft carriers alone, plus its battle group, is the equivalent of the present Russian navy."

"And we certainly have enough of them," Blake put in.

Ferguson said, "He wouldn't be so foolish as to imagine he could take those on and succeed."

"So what is he after?" Cazalet asked.

"A return to the Cold War," Ferguson said. "With certain differences. His personal experiences in Chechnya, Afghanistan, and Iraq give him considerable insight into the Muslim mind. Extremist Muslims hate America in an almost paranoid way. Putin recognizes that and uses it."

"How do you mean?" Cazalet asked.

"The favorite weapon of the IRA was the bomb, and the influence of the IRA on revolutionary movements throughout the world has been enormous. Only a handful of years ago, they virtually brought London to a standstill, blew up the Baltic Exchange, almost wiped out the entire British Cabinet at Brighton."

Cazalet nodded. "So what's your point?"

"Putin wants disorder, chaos, anarchy, a breakdown in the social order, particularly with countries dealing with America. In instructing his intelligence people to cultivate Muslims, he is actually getting them to do his dirty work for him. The terrorists' favorite weapon is the bomb, too, which means increased civilian casualties, which means a growing hatred of all things Muslim. We hate them, they hate us—chaos."

There was silence. Cazalet sighed and turned to Clancy. "I really could do with another drink. In fact, I think we all could."

"As you say, Mr. President."

Cazalet said, "After that, I could also do with some good news, Blake. Somehow I doubt I'm going to get it."

"Well, Kosovo could be worse, Mr. President, but it also could be better. The United Nations troops are in place, but

Bosnia intends to hang in there for as long as possible. The Serbian government in Belgrade has been urging the Serbs in Kosovo to boycott the November elections."

"And what's the Muslim opinion on that in Kosovo?"

"The memory of what the Serbs did in the war, the shocking butchery of the Muslims, will never go away. The Muslims want total independence, nothing less. And there are outside influences at work, which aren't helping the situation."

"Such as?" Cazalet demanded.

"Well, when you go out into the boonies, you find villages, market towns that aren't exactly twenty-first century, very old-fashioned people, Muslims on the whole. When I traveled to that part of the country, I found interlopers close to the borders. Russians."

There was silence. Cazalet said, "What kind of Russians?"

"Soldiers in uniform, not freebooters."

"Can you describe them? Which unit, that sort of thing?"

"Actually, I can. The ones I met were Siberians. I know that because their commanding officer identified himself as a Captain Igor Zorin of a regiment called the Fifteenth Siberian Storm Guards. I checked them on my laptop, and the unit exists. It's a reconnaissance outfit, special ops, that sort of thing. They were apparently based over the border in Bulgaria, and their mission was to visit a village called Banu that was supposed to be a center for Muslim extremists crossing the border and creating merry hell in Bulgaria."

Ferguson said, "This fellow Zorin—did you find him on the regimental roster?"

"Oh, yes, he was there all right. But here's the interesting thing—just as I was checking him out . . . he disappeared."

"What do you mean?"

"My screen went blank. He might as well never have existed."

There was a pause. Cazalet said, "Something you did, perhaps? You know what computers can be like."

"No, Mr. President, I swear to you. What happened in

Banu was shaping up to be pretty nasty, and I witnessed it—and they clearly wanted no record of it."

Ferguson nodded. "But except for your word in the matter, there's no proof. Accuse the Russian government, they'll simply deny it ever happened. I see the game they are playing."

"The cunning bastards," Cazalet said. "Somewhere in the Bulgarian mountains is a unit that doesn't exist, commanded by a man who doesn't exist named Igor Zorin."

Blake said, "Actually, not quite, Mr. President." He turned to Ferguson. "General, do you by any chance know a British Member of Parliament named Miller—Major Harry Miller?"

Ferguson frowned. "Why, was he involved in some way?"

"You could say that. He shot Igor Zorin between the eyes. I've never seen anything like it."

"And he's a Member of Parliament? What was he doing there in the first place?" Cazalet demanded.

"He was doing what I was doing, Mr. President, checking out things in the backcountry. We met by chance at a country inn about twenty miles from Banu. We stayed overnight, got talking, and each of us discovered who we were. Decided to carry on together the following day."

Cazalet turned to Ferguson. "Charles, this Major Harry Miller, do you know him?"

"I know of him, but keep my distance, and by design. You know what I do for the Prime Minister—with my team, we provide a distinctly hands-on approach to any problems of security or terrorism. Most of what we do is illegal."

"Which means you dispose of bad guys without troubling the rule of law. I've no trouble with that, it's the times we live in. Blake does the same for me, as you know. So what about Major Miller?"

"I don't fraternize with the Major, because I try to keep out of the political side of things, and he has a political relationship with the Prime Minister. Before he became a Member of Parliament, though, he was a career soldier in the army, Intelligence Corps, retired some years ago."

"Quite a change," Cazalet said.

"You could say that. He became an under secretary of state in the Northern Ireland Office, a desk man helping to develop the peace process."

"A troubleshooter?" Cazalet asked.

"Exactly, but since the changes in Northern Ireland, the Prime Minister has found uses for him elsewhere."

"Again as a troubleshooter?"

"The Prime Minister's eyes and ears. Sent to Lebanon, Iraq, the Gulf States—places like that."

"And Kosovo," Cazalet said. "He must be quite a guy."

"He is, Mr. President. People are very wary of him because of his privileged position. Even members of the Cabinet tread carefully. He is also modestly wealthy from family money, and married to a lovely, intelligent woman, an actress named Olivia Hunt, Boston born. In fact, her father is a senator."

"Good Lord," Cazalet said. "George Hunt. I know him well."

There was silence now for a while and then Cazalet said, "Blake, old friend, I think it's about time you told us exactly what happened in Banu that day."

Blake reached for the shot glass in front of him, swallowed the whiskey in it, and leaned back. "It was like this. It was lousy weather, Mr. President, and I'd just about had enough of it. I was driving myself in a jeep through a forest and over miserable terrain, and toward evening, I came to an inn near Kuman. The landlord appeared, and we were making arrangements for my stay when suddenly another jeep appeared out of the forest and the rain. It gave me quite a turn."

"Why was that?"

Blake considered. "It was strange, strange country, like some old movie taking place in Transylvania. There was rain, mist, darkness falling, and suddenly the jeep emerged from all that. It was kind of spooky."

He accepted another whiskey from Clancy, and Cazalet said, "Major Harry Miller?"

"Yes, Mr. President. I hadn't expected anyone, not in a place like that, and there he was at the back end of nowhere."

Cazalet nodded. "Tell us what happened, Blake, as you remember it, the whole business. Take your time."

"I'll do my best, Mr. President." Blake sat back thinking about it, and suddenly, it was as if he was there.

The Village of Banu

Kosovo

2

HARRY MILLER WAS A LITTLE UNDER SIX FEET, WITH SATURnine, gray eyes, a slight scar tracing his left cheek, which Blake was old soldier enough to recognize as a shrapnel scar. He had a face that gave nothing away, that showed only a man, calm and confident in himself. Also, someone who'd known command, unless Blake was much mistaken. He wore an old-fashioned long military trench coat over basic camouflage field overalls, the kind any ordinary soldier might wear, and paratroop boots. A crumpled combat hat guarded him against the rain, as he ran across to the steps to the inn, a canvas holdall in his left hand.

He stood on the porch, beat his hat against his leg. "Bloody rain, god-awful country." And then he held out his hand to Blake and smiled, for the moment totally charming. "Harry Miller. Who might you be?"

Blake had never liked anyone so much so quickly. "Blake Johnson."

Something showed in Miller's face, a change of expression. "Good heavens, I know who you are. You run the Basement for Cazalet."

His announcement was received by Blake with astonishment. "How in the hell do you know that?"

"Work for the Prime Minister. Poke my nose in odd places when he orders and report back. That's what I'm doing now. What about you?"

"Doing exactly the same thing for the President. I had to see someone in Zagreb, and I thought I'd check out Kosovo before I went back."

"Excellent. Let's freshen up and compare notes over dinner."

WHEN BLAKE CAME DOWN from his room a little while later, he found the innkeeper, one Tomas, behind the bar. The room was pleasant, a beamed ceiling, a log fire burning.

"I'll have a beer. It's very quiet."

"You and the Major are the only guests."

"Major?" Blake said.

"So it says in his passport, sir." He poured the beer. "We don't get many guests these days."

"Why not?"

"Bad things can happen, just like in the war. People are afraid."

At that moment, Miller came down the stairs into the great lounge and found him.

"Beer?" Blake asked.

"Perfect. What's happening?"

"I was just asking him why there's no one here. He says people are afraid."

"Of what?" Miller asked.

Tomas pushed two large flagons of beer across the bar. "Between here and the Bulgarian border is not a good place. I would leave, but the inn is all I have."

Miller said, "So what gives you the problem?"

"Those who cross the border and attack the villages."

"And who are they?"

"People who don't like Muslims. But sit by the fire, gentlemen, and enjoy your drink. We have good bread, sausages, and a lamb stew. I'll bring your beer over."

They did as he suggested, taking a chair each on either side of a great log fire. There was a small table next to each chair, and he put the beer down carefully. "The food will be ready soon."

He turned away and paused as Miller said, "But the soldiers of the Kosovo Protection Corps—what about them?"

The innkeeper nodded. "They are good people, but their effect is minimal. Small patrols, jeeps, sometimes a warrior or two. They appear and then go away again, which leaves us at the mercy of those who would harm us."

"Again, who are they?" Blake asked.

"Sometimes Russians."

Miller said to the innkeeper, "Are you saying uniformed soldiers from the Russian Army?"

"Oh, yes, sir. Usually they stay close to the border." He shrugged. "They have even been as far as this inn. Maybe a dozen men, all in uniform."

Miller said, "So how did they treat you?"

"The food in my inn is excellent and I sell good beer. They ate, they drank, and they went. Their captain even paid me, and in American dollars."

Blake said, "So they did you no harm?"

The innkeeper shrugged. "Why should they? The captain said they'd see me again. To burn me down would be to penalize themselves. On the other hand, there were bad things happening elsewhere. Several people died in a village called Pazar. There was a small mosque. They burned that and killed seven people."

Miller said, "Just a minute. I was at the Protection Corps headquarters the day before yesterday. I asked to see their file on incident reports for the past six months, and there was one on this place Pazar. It said that, yes, the small village mosque had been burned down, but when the Protection Corps sent a patrol to check it out, the village mayor and his elders said it was an accidental fire, and there was no mention of seven dead people, certainly no mention of Russian soldiers."

"The village council decided it was not in their best interests to make an official complaint. The Russian authorities would always deny it, and some bad night, the villagers would find themselves going through it all over again." The innkeeper bowed slightly. "And now please excuse me. I must see to your dinner."

He disappeared through a green baize door leading to the kitchen. Blake said, "What do you think?"

"I suspect what he said about the villagers at Pazar taking the easy way out is true."

"You were in the military?" Blake asked.

"Yes, Intelligence Corps."

"So when you became a Member of Parliament, the Prime Minister decided that your special talents could be put to good use?"

"Whenever he sees what appears to be a problem, he sends me. I'm classed as an under secretary of state, although not attached to any particular ministry. It gives me a little muscle when I need it." He drank some of his beer. "And what about you?"

"To a certain degree, I'm in a similar situation. The President's man."

Miller smiled gently. "I've heard about what you do. Only whispers, of course."

"Which is the way we like it." Blake stood up. "I think they're ready for us now. Let's eat."

"Excellent," Miller said, and followed him out.

AFTERWARD, the meal having proved excellent, they returned to their seats by the fire and the innkeeper brought coffee.

Blake said, "I've been thinking. I'm only here for another couple of days, traveling south, visiting a few villages, getting the feel of things."

"From here to the border?" Miller said. "That makes sense. I checked it all out on the maps. A lot of forest, villages from a bygone age. The people go nowhere, only to market, they keep to themselves."

"Peasants who keep their heads down and don't want trouble." Blake nodded. "Have you anywhere in mind?"

"There's a place called Banu, deep in the forest, about ten miles from the border."

"How far from here?"

"Thirty miles or so, dirt roads, but it could be worthwhile. We could leave your jeep here and travel in mine—that's if you favor the idea of us going together?"

"Favor it?" Blake said. "I'd welcome it. What time do you suggest in the morning?"

"No need to rush. Let's enjoy a decent breakfast and get away about nine to nine-thirty."

"Excellent," Blake told him. "I think I'll get an early night."

Miller glanced at his watch. "It's later than you think. Half past ten. I'll hang on, enjoy a nightcap, and arrange things with the innkeeper."

Blake left him there and mounted the wide stairway. There was something about Miller, a calmness that seemed to distance him from other people, a self-assurance that was obvious, and yet no arrogance there at all.

In the bedroom, he sat at a small dressing table, took out his laptop, entered "Harry Miller" and found him without difficulty. He was forty-five, married, wife Olivia, thirty-three, maiden name Hunt, actress by profession. No children.

His military career was dealt with so sparsely that to the trained eye it was obviously classified. From Sandhurst Military Academy he had joined the Army Intelligence Corps. He experienced war very quickly, only three months later, as a second lieutenant attached to 42 Commando. Afterward, his posting was to Army Intelligence Corps headquarters in London, where he had served for the rest of his career, retiring in the rank of major in 2003, before being elected a Member of Parliament for a place called Stokely that same year. As he had indicated, he enjoyed the rank of under secretary of state, although in no special ministry. Nothing but mystery piling on mystery here.

"Who in the hell is he?" Blake murmured to himself. "Or, more to the point, what is he?"

No answer, so he closed his laptop down and went to bed.

On the following day, Blake was doing the driving. Miller had a military canvas holdall beside them, and he rummaged in it and produced a map. It was a gray and misty morning, dark because of the pine trees crowding in.

"Looks as if there's been no upkeep on this road since the war," Blake said. "What's between here and Banu?"

"Not much at all." Miller put the map back in his holdall. "Depressing sort of place, isn't it? You'd wonder why anyone would want to live here."

"I suppose so."

"Are you married?"

"For a few years, but it didn't work out, mainly because of the demands of my job. She was a journalist."

"Do you still see her?"

"No, she's dead, murdered actually, by some rather bad people."

"My God." Miller shook his head. "That's terrible. I can only hope there was some kind of closure."

"The courts, you mean?" Blake shook his head. "No time for that, not in today's world, not in my world. The rules are no rules. The people concerned were taken care of with the help of some very good friends of mine." He shrugged. "It was a long time ago, Major."

"Why do you call me that?"

"Tomas, the innkeeper. You had to show him your passport."

"You were military yourself, I think?"

"Yes, I was also a major at the early age of twenty-three, but that was Vietnam for you. All my friends seemed to die around me, but I never managed it. Are you married?"

Although he knew the answer, it might seem strange to Miller not to ask, and he got an instant response. "Very much so. Olivia. American, actually. She's an actress. Twelve years younger than me, so she's in her prime. Gets plenty of work in London."

"Children?"

"Not possible, I'm afraid."

Blake didn't say he was sorry. There just didn't seem any point, and at that moment, there was the sound of shooting and they went over a rise and saw a young peasant riding a cycle toward them. He was swaying from side to side, his mouth gaping, panic stricken. Blake braked to a halt. The man on the cycle slewed onto his side and fell over. Miller got out, approached him, and pulled him up.

"Are you all right? What's wrong?" He spoke in English. The man seemed bewildered, and there was blood matting his hair on the left side of the head. "Banu?" Miller tried.

The man nodded energetically. "Banu," he said hoarsely, and pointed along the road. There were a couple more shots.

"I'll try Russian," Miller said, and turned to the man. "Are you from Banu?"

His question was met by a look of horror, and the man was immediately terrified, turned and stumbled away into the trees.

Miller got back in the jeep and said to Blake, "So much for Russian."

"It frightened him to death," Blake said. "That was obvious. I speak it a certain amount myself, as it happens."

"Excellent. Then I suggest we go down to Banu and find out what's going on, don't you think?"

Miller leaned back and Blake drove away.

THEY PAUSED on a rise, the village below. It wasn't much of a place: houses of wood mainly on either side of the road, scattered dwellings that looked like farm buildings extending downward, a stream that was crossed by a wooden bridge supported by large blocks of granite. There was a wooden building with a crescent above it, obviously what passed as a small mosque, and an inn of the traditional kind.

A sizable light armored vehicle was parked outside the inn. "What the hell is that?" Blake asked.

"It's Russian, all right," Miller told him. "An armored troop carrier called a Storm Cruiser. Reconnaissance units use them. They can handle up to twelve soldiers." He opened his holdall and took out a pair of binoculars. "Street's clear. I'd say the locals are keeping their heads down. Two soldiers on the porch, supposedly guarding the entrance, drinking beer, a couple of girls in head scarves crouched beside them. The shooting was probably somebody having fun inside the inn."

"So what do we do?"

"Well, to a certain extent I represent United Nations interests here. We should go down and take a look at what's happening."

Blake took a deep breath. "If you say so."

"Oh, I do, but I like to be prepared." Miller produced a Browning from the holdall. "I know it might seem a little old-fashioned, but it's an old friend and I've always found it gets the job done." He produced a Carswell silencer and screwed it in place.

"I wouldn't argue with that," Blake said, and took the jeep down into the village street, his stomach hollow. There were people peering out of windows on each side as they drove down and braked to a halt outside the inn. The two soldiers were totally astonished. One of them, his machine pistol on the floor, stared stupidly, his beer in his hand. The other had been fondling one of the girls, his weapon across his knees.

Miller opened the jeep door and stepped out into the rain, his right hand behind him holding the Browning. "Put her down," he said in excellent Russian. "I mean, she doesn't know where you've been."

The man's rage was immediate and he shoved the girl away, knocking her to one side against her friend, started to get up, clutching his machine pistol, and Miller shot him in the right knee. In the same moment, Miller swung to meet the other soldier as he stood up and struck him across the side of the head with the Browning.

The two girls ran across the road, where a door opened to receive them. Blake came around the jeep fast and picked up the machine pistol on the porch floor.

"Now what?"

"I'm going in. You take the alley and find the rear entrance."

Blake, on fire in a way he hadn't been in years, did as he was told, and Miller crossed to the door, opened it, and went in, his right hand once again behind his back holding the Browning.

THE INN was old-fashioned in a way to be expected deep in such countryside: a beamed ceiling, wooden floors, a scattering of tables, and a long bar, bottles ranged on shelves behind it. There were about fifteen men crouched on the floor by the bar, hands on heads, two Russian soldiers guarding them. A sergeant stood behind the bar drinking from a bottle, a machine pistol on the counter by his hand. Two other soldiers sat on a bench opposite, two women crouched on the floor beside them, one of them sobbing.

The officer in command, a captain from his rank tabs, sat at a table in the center of the room. He was very young, handsome enough, a certain arrogance there. That the muted sound of Miller's silenced pistol had not been heard inside the inn was obvious enough, but considering the circumstances, he seemed to take the sudden appearance of this strange apparition in combat overalls and old-fashioned trench coat with astonishing calm. He had a young girl on his knee who didn't even bother to struggle as he fondled her, so terrified was she.

He spoke in Russian. "And who are you?"

"My name is Major Harry Miller, British Army, attached to the United Nations." His Russian was excellent.

"Show me your papers."

"No. You're the one who should be answering questions. You've no business this side of the border. Identify yourself."

The reply came as a kind of reflex. "I am Captain Igor Zorin of the Fifteenth Siberian Storm Guards, and we have every right to be here. These Muslim dogs swarm over the border to Bulgaria to rape and pillage." He pushed the girl off his knee and sent her staggering toward the bar and his sergeant. "Give this bitch another bottle of vodka. I'm thirsty."

She returned with the bottle, and Zorin dragged her back on his knee, totally ignoring Miller, then pulled the cork in the bottle with his teeth. But instead of drinking the vodka, he forced it on the girl, who struggled, choking.

"So what do you want, Englishman?"

A door opened at the rear of the room and Blake stepped in cautiously, machine pistol ready.

"Well, I've already disposed of your two guards on the porch, and now my friend who's just come in behind you would like to demonstrate what he can do."

Blake put a quick burst into the ceiling, which certainly got everybody's attention, and called in Russian, "Drop your weapons!"

There was a moment's hesitation, and he fired into the ceiling again. All of them, including the sergeant at the bar, raised their hands. It was Zorin who did the unexpected, dragging the girl across his lap in front of him, drawing his pistol, and pushing it into her side.

"Drop your weapon or she dies."

Without hesitation, Miller shot him twice in the side of the skull, sending him backward over the chair. There was total silence, the Muslims getting to their feet. Everyone waited. He spoke to the sergeant in Russian.

"You take the body with you, put it in the Storm Cruiser, and wait for us with your men. See they do it, Blake." He turned to the Muslims. "Who speaks English?"

A man moved forward and the girl turned to him. "I am the mayor, sir, I speak good English. This is my youngest daughter. Allah's blessing on you. My name is Yusuf Birka."

The Russians were moving out, supervised by Blake, two of them carrying Zorin's body, followed by the sergeant.

Miller said to Birka, "Keep the weapons. They may be of use to you in the future."

Birka turned and spoke to the others, and Miller went outside. Blake was standing at the rear of the Storm Cruiser, supervising the Russians loading Zorin's body and the wounded man. There was an ammunition box on the ground.

"Semtex and timer pencils. I suppose that would be for the mosque," Blake said.

The soldiers all scrambled in and the sergeant waited, looking bewildered. "If these people had their way, they'd shoot the lot of you," Miller told him.

To his surprise, the sergeant replied in reasonable English. "I must warn you. The death of Captain Zorin won't sit well with my superiors. He was young and foolish, but well connected in Moscow."

"I can't help that, but I have a suggestion for your commanding officer when you get back. Tell him from me that since you shouldn't have been here in the first place, we'll treat the whole incident as if it didn't happen. Now get moving."

"As you say." The sergeant looked unhappy, but climbed up behind the wheel and drove the Storm Cruiser away, to the cheers of the villagers.

People milled around in the street, staring curiously. Some of the men arrived now, but they kept their distance as Miller and Blake talked with the mayor, who said, "How can we thank you?"

"By taking my advice. Keep quiet about this. If they come again, you have arms. I don't think they will, though. It's better for them to pretend it never happened, and better if you do, too. I won't report any of this to the Protection Corps."

The mayor said, "I will be guided by you. Will you break bread with us?"

Miller smiled. "No, my friend, because we aren't here. We never were." He turned to Blake. "Let's get going. I'll drive this time."

As they moved away, Blake said, "Do you think the villagers will do as you say?"

"I don't see why not. It's entirely to their advantage, and I don't think it's worth us mentioning it to the Corps because of, shall we say, the peculiar circumstances of the matter."

"I've no problem with that," Blake said. "But I'll have to report back to the President."

"I agree. I'll do the same with the PM. It wouldn't be the first time he's been informed of this sort of thing. Meanwhile, you've got your laptop there, and the information pack you were given by the Protection Corps people includes Russian military field service codes for the area. See what they have on Captain Igor Zorin and the Fifteenth Siberian Storm Guards."

Blake opened his laptop on his knees, got to work, and found it in a matter of minutes. "Here it is," he said. "Forward Field Center, Lazlo, Bulgaria. Igor Zorin, twenty-five, decorated in Chechnya. Listings for the unit, home base near Moscow."

"Sounds good," Miller said.

And then a magic hand wiped it clean, and the screen went dark. "Dammit." Blake punched keys desperately. "It's all gone. What have I done?"

"Nothing," Miller told him. "I imagine the sergeant called in and gave his masters the bad news within minutes of his leaving us. It didn't happen, you see, just like I told you. Except the Russians are being even more than usually thorough. So is it back to Zagreb for you?"

"No, Pristina. I'm hitching a lift from there back to the States with the Air Force. How about you?"

"Belgrade for me, and then London. Olivia's opening on Friday in the West End. An old Noël Coward play, *Private Lives*. I hope I can make it. I disappoint her too often."

"Let's hope you do." Blake hesitated, awkward. "It's been great meeting you. What you did back there was remarkable."

"But necessary. That's what soldiers do, the nasty things from which the rest of society turns away. Zorin was something that needed stepping on, that's all." And he increased speed as they went over the next rise.

Nantucket

London

3

•

Seated by the fire in the beach house, Blake finished his account of what had taken place at Banu. There was silence for a while, and it was Cazalet who spoke first.

"Well, it beats anything I've heard in years. What do you think, Charles?"

"It's certainly given the Russians a black eye. No wonder they wiped the screen clean," Ferguson replied. "It's the smart way to deal with it."

"And you think it could stay that way? A non-event?"

"As regards any important repercussions. How could the Kremlin complain while at the same time denying any involvement? Okay, these things sometimes leak, Chinese whispers as they say, but that's all. Miller will mention it to the PM, but it's no different from the kind of things I have to tell him on a regular basis these days. We're at war, whether we like it or not, and I don't mean just Iraq and Afghanistan."

"One thing does interest me," Blake said. "According to his entry on the computer, except for the Falklands as a boy out of Sandhurst, Miller spent his eighteen years behind a desk at Army Intelligence headquarters in London."

"What's your point?" Cazalet said.

"That was no desk jockey at that inn in Banu."

Ferguson smiled gently. "All it does is show you how unreliable information on computers can be. I should imagine there are many things people don't know about Harry Miller." He turned to Cazalet. "With your permission, I'll retire."

"Sleep well, Charles. We'll share the helicopter back to Washington tomorrow afternoon. I'll see you for breakfast."

"Of course, Mr. President."

Ferguson moved to the door, which Clancy held open for him, and Cazalet added, "And, Charles, the redoubtable Major Miller. I really would appreciate learning some of those 'many things' people don't know about him, if that were possible, of course."

"I'll see what I can do, Mr. President."

FERGUSON LAY on the bed in the pleasant guest room provided for him, propped up against the pillows. Ten o'clock London time was six hours ahead, but he didn't worry that no one would be in. He called the Holland Park safe house and got an instant response.

"Who is this?"

"Don't play silly buggers, Major, you know very well who it is."

"What I do know is that it's four o'clock in the morning," Roper told him.

"And if it's business as usual, you're right now sitting ensconced in your wheelchair in front of those damned computer screens exploring cyberspace on your usual diet of bacon sandwiches, whiskey, and cigarettes."

"Yes, isn't life hell?"

He was doing exactly what Ferguson had said he was. He put the telephone system on speaker, ran his hands over his bomb scarred face, poured a generous measure of scotch into a glass, and tossed it down.

"How were things at the United Nations?"

"Just what you'd expect—the Russians are stirring the pot."

"Well, they would, wouldn't they? I thought you'd be back today. Where are you, Washington?"

"I was. Briefed the Ambassador here and bumped into Blake Johnson just back from a fact finding mission to Kosovo. He brought me to Nantucket to see Cazalet."

"And?"

"And Kosovo turned out to be rather interesting for our good friend Blake, let me tell you."

WHEN FERGUSON WAS FINISHED, he said, "What do you think?"

"That it's a hell of a good story to enliven a rather dull London morning. But what do you want me to do with it? Miller's a troubleshooter for the Prime Minister, and you've always said to avoid politicians like the plague. They stick their noses in where they aren't wanted and ask too many questions."

"I agree, but I don't like being in the dark. Miller's supposed to have spent most of his career behind a desk, but that doesn't fit the man Blake described in this Banu place."

"You have a point," Roper admitted.

"So see what you can come up with. If that means breaking a few rules, do so."

"When do you want it, on your return?"

"You've got until tomorrow morning, American time. That's when I'm having breakfast with the President."

"Then I'd better get on with it," Roper said.

He clicked off, poured another whiskey, drank it, lit a cigarette, then entered Harry Miller's details. He found the basic stuff without difficulty, but after that it was rather thin on the ground.

The outer door opened and Doyle, the Military Police sergeant who was on night duty, peered in. A soldier for twenty years, Doyle was of Jamaican ancestry although born in the east end of London, with six tours of duty in Northern Ireland

and two in Iraq. He was a fervent admirer of Roper, the greatest bomb-disposal expert in the business during the Troubles, a true hero in Doyle's eyes.

"I heard the speaker, sir. You aren't at it again, are you? It's four o'clock in the bleeding morning."

"Actually, it's four-thirty and I've just had the General on. Would you believe he's with the President in Nantucket?"

"He certainly gets around."

"Yes, well, he's given me a request for information he wants to have available for breakfast."

"Anything special, sir?"

"He wants a background on a Major Harry Miller, a general fixer for the Prime Minister."

Doyle suddenly stopped smiling. "A bit more than that, I'd have thought."

"Why do you say that? How would you know him? You don't exactly get to Downing Street much these days."

"No, of course not, sir. I'm sorry if I'm speaking out of turn."

"He looks pretty straightforward to me. Sandhurst, saw what war was like in the Falklands for a few months, then spent the rest of his career in Army Intelligence Corps Headquarters in London."

Doyle looked uncomfortable. "Yes, of course, sir, if you say so. I'll get your breakfast. Bacon and egg sandwich coming up."

He turned and Roper said, "Don't go, Tony. We've known each other a long time, so don't mess around. You've known him somewhere. Come on—tell me."

Doyle said, "Okay, it was over the water in Derry during my third tour." Funny how the old hands never called it Londonderry, just like the IRA.

"What were you up to?"

"Part of a team manning a safe house down by the docks. We weren't supposed to know what it was all about, but you know how things leak. You did enough tours over there."

"So tell me."

"Operation Titan."

"God in heaven," Roper said. "Unit Sixteen. The ultimate disposal outfit." He shook his head. "And you met him? When was this?"

"Fourteen years ago. He was received, that's what we called it, plus a younger officer badly wounded. Their motor was riddled. An SAS snatch squad came in within the hour and took them away."

"They weren't in uniform?"

"Unit Sixteen didn't operate in uniform."

"And you don't know what happened?"

"Four Provos shot dead on River Street is what happened. It hit the news the following day. The IRA said it was an SAS atrocity."

"Well, they would." Roper nodded. "And when did you see him again?"

"Years later on television when he became an MP and was working for Northern Ireland Office."

"It gets worse." Roper nodded. "So, a bacon-and-egg sandwich and a pot of tea, and bring me another bottle of scotch. Be prepared to hang around. I may need your expertise on this one."

HARRY MILLER had been born in Stokely in Kent in the country house in which the family had lived since the eighteenth century. His father, George, had served in the Grenadier Guards in the Second World War, there was family money, and after the war he became a barrister and eventually Member of Parliament for Stokely and the general area. Harry was born in 1962, his sister Monica five years later, and tragically her mother had died giving birth to her.

George Miller's sister Mary, a widow, moved in to hold the fort, as it were. It worked well enough, particularly as the two children went to boarding school at an early age, Winchester for Harry and Sedgefield for Monica, who was only fourteen when he went to Sandhurst. She was a scholar by nature, which eventually took her to New Hall College at Cambridge to study archaeology, and when Roper checked on her, he found she was still there, a lecturer and a Fellow of the College, married to a professor, Sir John Starling, who had died of cancer the previous year.

According to the screen, Miller's career with the Intelligence Corps had been a non-event, and yet the Prime Minister had made him an under secretary of state at the Northern Ireland Office, which obviously meant that the PM was aware of Miller's past and was making use of his expertise.

Roper was starting to go to town on Unit 16 and Operation Titan, when Doyle came in with a tray.

"Smells good," Roper said. "Draw up a chair, Tony, pour me a nice cup of tea, and I'll show you what genius can do to a computer."

HIS FIRST PROBINGS produced a perfect hearts-and-minds operation out of Intelligence Headquarters in London, in which Miller was heavily involved, full of visits to committees, appeals to common sense, and an effort to provide the things that it seemed the nationalists wanted. It was a civilized discussion, providing the possibility of seeing each other's points of view, and physical force didn't figure into the agenda.

Miller met and discussed with Sinn Fein and the Provos, everything sweetly reasonable. Then came a Remembrance Day, with assembled Army veterans and their families, and a bomb that killed fourteen people and injured many more. A few days later, a hit squad ambushed a local authority van carrying ten Protestant laborers who were there to do a road repair. They were lined up on the edge of a ditch and machine-gunned.

Finally, a roadside bomb destined for two Land Rover army patrols was late, and the vehicle that came along was a bus carrying schoolgirls.

It was that which had changed Miller's views drastically. Summary justice was the only way to deal with such people, and his superiors accepted his plans. No more hearts and minds, only Operation Titan and disposal by Unit 16, the bullet leading to a crematorium. All very efficient, a corpse turned into six pounds of gray ash within a couple of hours. It was the ultimate answer to any terrorist problem, and Roper was fascinated to see that many hard men in the Protestant UVF had also suffered the same fate when necessary.

He found the names of members of Unit 16 and the details of some who had fallen by the wayside. Miller had been tagged as a systems analyst and later as a personnel recruiter at Army Intelligence Headquarters in London, and then, a captain, was put in charge of what was described as the Overseas Intelligence Organization Department. A harmless enough description that was obviously a front.

Unit 16 itself consisted of twenty individuals, three of them women. Each had a number, with no particular logic to it. Miller was seven. The casualty reports were minimal on the whole: the briefest of descriptions, names of victims, location of the event, not much more. Miller's number figured on twelve occasions over the years, but the River Street affair was covered in more detail than usual.

Miller had been detailed to extract a young lieutenant named Harper who'd been working undercover and had called in that his cover had been blown. When Miller picked him up, their car was immediately cut off in River Street by the docks, one vehicle in front, another behind.

A burst of firing wounded Harper, and Miller was ordered at gunpoint to get out of his vehicle. Fortunately, he had armed himself with an unusual weapon, a Browning with a twenty-round magazine. He had killed two Provos by shooting them through the door of his car as he opened it, turned and disposed of the two men in the vehicle behind through their windscreen. As Doyle had mentioned, they'd reached the safe house later and been retrieved by the SAS.

"My God, Major," Doyle said in awe. "I never knew the truth of it, just the IRA making those wild claims. You'd have thought he'd have got a medal."

Roper shook his head. "They couldn't do that—it would lead to questions, give the game away. By the way, Lieutenant Harper died the following day at the Royal Victoria Hospital in Belfast."

Doyle shook his head, genuinely distressed. "After all that."

"Name of the game, Tony, and I don't need to remind you that this is all top secret at the highest level."

"I've worked for General Ferguson long enough to know my place, and it isn't in Afghanistan, it's right here at Holland Park. I wouldn't jeopardize that for anything."

"Sensible man. Let me get on with this report for Ferguson."

"I'll check on you later." Doyle hesitated. "Excuse me asking, but is Major Miller in some kind of trouble?"

"No, but old habits die hard. It would appear he's been handing out his original version of justice in Kosovo, in company with Blake Johnson, of all people."

Doyle took a deep breath. "I'm sure he had his reasons. From what I've heard, the Prime Minister seems to think a lot of him."

He went out and Roper sat considering it, then tapped "No. 10 Downing Street" into his computer, punched Ferguson's private link code, checked the names of those admitted during the past twenty-four hours, and there was Miller, booked in at five the previous evening, admitted to the Prime Minister's study at five-forty.

"My goodness," Roper said softly. "He doesn't let the grass grow under his feet. I wonder what the Prime Minister had to say?"

MILLER HADN'T BOTHERED with Belgrade. A call to an RAF source had indicated a Hercules leaving Pristina Airport after he and Blake had parted. There had been an unlooked-for delay of a couple of hours, but they had landed at RAF Croydon in the late afternoon, where his credentials had assured him of a fast staff car to Downing Street.

He didn't phone his wife. He'd promised to try and make her opening night, and still might, but duty called him to speak to the Prime Minister on his return and that had to be his priority. There was a meeting, of course, there always was. He kicked his heels in the outer office, accepted a coffee from one of the secretaries, and waited. Finally, the magic moment came and he was admitted.

The Prime Minister, scribbling something at his desk, looked up and smiled. "So good to have you back, Harry, and good to see you. How did it go? Sit down and tell me."

Which Miller did.

When he was finished, the Prime Minister said, "Well, you have been busy. I would remind you, however, that this isn't Northern Ireland and the Troubles are over. We have to be more circumspect."

"Yes, Prime Minister."

"Having said that, I'm a practical man. The Russians shouldn't have been in this Banu place in the first place. They'll let it go. Whatever else he is, Putin's no fool. As far as I can see, shooting this wretched Zorin chap probably prevented a serious atrocity. It must have enlivened things for Blake Johnson, though. I'm sure President Cazalet will find his report interesting."

"It's good of you to take such a view in the matter, Prime Minister."

"Let's be frank, Harry, I've heard worse. Charles Ferguson's people—their activities are beyond belief sometimes. For that matter . . ." He paused. "I know you've always kept out of his way, but it might make sense if you two talked. You've got a lot of interests in common."

"If you wish, Prime Minister. Now, if there's nothing else, may I be excused? It's Olivia's opening night."

The Prime Minister smiled. "Give her my love, Harry, and get going. It'll be curtain up before you know it."

Curtain up was seven-thirty, and he arrived at the stage door at ten past seven to find Marcus, the ancient doorman, at his desk reading the *Standard*. Marcus was delighted to see him.

"Good God, Major, she'll be thrilled. And your sister's

with her, Lady Starling. Your wife's been prepping an understudy. They thought you was still in Kosovo. Anthony Vere broke a bone in his right foot, so you've got Colin Carlton. He's a little young for the part, but then, Madame looks ten years younger than she is."

"Tell her that and you'll have a friend for life."

"You haven't got long, sir. Front row, dress circle. House seats. I got them myself."

Miller was at the door of his wife's dressing room in seconds, knocked and entered, and was greeted with enormous excitement. His wife had her stage makeup beautifully applied, her red hair superb, and was being zipped up in her dress by his sister Monica, who looked lovely, as usual, her blond hair beautifully cut, looking younger than her forty years.

They were thrilled, Olivia actually crying a little. "Damn you, Harry, you're ruining my makeup. I didn't expect you'd make it. You usually don't."

They kissed gently, and his sister said, "Come on, move it. We won't even have time for a drink at the bar."

He kissed her on the forehead. "Never mind, we'll make up for it afterwards. You're staying over at Dover Street, I hope?"

"Of course."

Monica had rooms at the University in Cambridge, but the London townhouse had been the family home since Victorian times. It was close to South Audley Street, convenient to the Dorchester Hotel, Park Lane, and Hyde Park, and it was spacious enough for her to have her own suite. She also had shared use of Stokely Hall in the Kent countryside, where Aunt Mary led a gentle life, supported by Sarah Grant, the housekeeper, and her husband, Fergus, who chauffeured the old Rolls and turned his hand to most things. They lived in the lodge, and a Mrs. Trumper came in from the village to cook.

In a strange way, all this was going through Miller's mind as he and Monica made tracks for the dress circle. It was a reaction to what had happened, the violence of Kosovo, the prospect of a weekend in the peace of the countryside in the company of loved ones. He and Olivia had no children, Monica had no children, and dear old Aunt Mary would have been totally alone without them all. As he and Monica settled into their seats, he felt relaxed and happy, back with the close-knit family members who were so important. Love, kindness, concern—these were the people dearest to him in his life and yet totally unaware of the dark secrets, the death business behind his apparently quiet service in the Intelligence Corps.

So many times over the years, family friends had congratulated him on his desk job with Intelligence. He had only two medals to show for eighteen years in the Army: the South Atlantic ribbon for the Falklands Campaign and the Campaign Medal for Northern Ireland that all soldiers who'd served there received. It was ironic when you thought of River Street in Derry, the four dead Provos, and the many similar occasions for Unit 16, and yet the two people closest to him, his sister and his wife, didn't have even the slightest hint of that part of his life. He'd never go away for more than a week at a time and was always supposed to be at Catterick, Salisbury Plain, Sandhurst, or Germany, somewhere like that.

He took a deep breath, squeezed Monica's hand, the music started to play, and then the lights dimmed and the curtains parted. It was the old, wonderful excitement, just what he needed, and then his wife entered stage left looking fantastic, the woman with whom he had fallen hopelessly in love on their first meeting so many years before, and his heart lifted.

THE PERFORMANCE was a triumph, earning four curtain calls; young Carlton was more than adequate, and Olivia, superb. She'd booked a late dinner at a favorite French bistro in Shepherd's Market, and the three of them, she and Miller and Monica, thoroughly indulged themselves, sharing a bottle of Dom Perignon champagne.

"Oh, I'm very pleased with myself," Olivia announced.

"And you've got tomorrow to look forward to," Monica told her. "Saturday night and a full house."

"I've been thinking," Miller put in. "I'll arrange a car from the Cabinet Office. After the show tomorrow, we'll go straight down to Stokely, the three of us. Chill out on Sunday, then come back for Monday evening's performance."

"Oh, you two lovebirds don't want me around," Monica told them. "I'll stay the night at Dover Street and go back to Cambridge tomorrow."

"Nonsense," Olivia said. "It'll be nice to be together for a change, and Aunt Mary will be thrilled." She put her hand on Monica's. "Just to be together. It's so important. And imagine. We've actually got him to ourselves for a change. You and I can go shopping tomorrow."

She kissed her husband on the cheek, and Monica said, "I bumped into Charley Faversham at a function last week, Harry. He called you the Prime Minister's Rottweiler and asked after you. I said I understood you were visiting Kosovo. He was there during the war covering it for the *Times* when the Serbs were killing all those Muslims. He said it was as bad as anything he'd ever seen in all his years as a war correspondent. It's different now, I suppose?"

"Completely," Miller told her. "And Olivia's right. You must come down to Stokely with us. After all, there is no one in this life I am more indebted to than the sister who argued and begged me all those years ago to take her down to Chichester Festival Theatre to see Chekhov's *A Month in the Country*. As you well know, I was never a Chekhov person until the girl from Boston walked in through the French windows." He reached for Olivia's right hand and kissed it. "And after that, nothing in my life was ever the same."

She glowed as she squeezed his hand. "I know, darling, same for me."

Monica laughed. "I used to despair of him. Women just didn't seem to be part of his agenda."

"Well, I was hardly exciting enough, not Household Cavalry or Three Para, no red beret and a row of medals. Pretty staid, a Whitehall Warrior. No real soldiering, I've heard that mentioned enough."

"And thank God for it," Olivia told him. "Let's have the bill and go home."

AFTERWARD AT DOVER STREET when they'd retired, he and Olivia made love very quickly, genuine passion still there. Not much was said, but the joy was there so strongly. She fell asleep very quickly and he lay there listening to her gentle breathing, unable to sleep himself, and finally slipped from the bed, found his dressing gown, and went downstairs.

The sitting room was his favorite in the entire house. He didn't need to switch on the lights, because there was enough drifting in from the street outside. It was raining, the occasional car swishing by, and he went to the drinks cabinet, poured himself a very large scotch and did something he only did at times of stress. He opened a silver cigarette box and lit a Benson & Hedges. It was Kosovo, of course, and what had happened, and it made him think back four years to what had got him out of the Army.

The lies, the pretense, the deceit of it all, had been giving him a problem. He was two people: the man his wife and sister thought he was, and the dealer in death and secrets. A new dimension had entered his life, a new kind of terror, just when things were looking hopeful in Northern Ireland. It was called Muslim fundamentalism. It had become apparent to him that this was where his future would unfold, and the prospect filled him with a kind of despair, because he didn't want to be involved.

But fate intervened, giving him a solution. His father died of an unexpected heart attack and they buried him on a wet and miserable day at Stokely Parish Church. Afterward there was a wake at Stokely Hall, and champagne, his father's favorite drink, was poured, a great deal of it, in honor of a much-loved man.

Miller was standing at an open window, smoking a cigarette and considering his lot, when he was approached by his father's political agent, Harold Bell.

"What are you thinking about, Harry?"

"Contemplating my future. If I stay with the Corps, I'll make lieutenant-colonel, but that's it. If I leave, what do I have to offer? When I was at Sandhurst, they taught me the seven ways of sorting someone out with my bare hands. I became a weapons expert, acquired reasonable Arabic, Russian, and French. But what do I do with all that out of the Army?"

Olivia had heard as she approached and gave him a gin and tonic. "Cheer up, darling, someone might offer you a nice job in the City."

"That someone is me," Bell told them, savoring his drink. "But it's not the City. The Party wants you to come forward as a candidate for your father's seat. The local committee is completely behind you. Harry Miller, Member of Parliament."

Miller was shocked and couldn't think of a thing to say, so his wife did all the talking. "Does that mean I get him home nights?"

"Absolutely," Bell assured her.

She'd immediately announced it to the entire room, and he was kissed on the cheek and slapped on the back many times. "Better than Iraq or Afghanistan, old man," someone said. "You're well out of that."

He resigned his commission and was duly elected, suddenly free of what had haunted him all those years, but he should have remembered that nothing ever worked out as expected. The Prime Minister was privy to his Army record and appointed him to the Northern Ireland Office, and when the Irish situation was finally settled, started sending him from one trouble spot to another.

The Prime Minister's Rottweiler—that was a good one, and any guarantee he would be home nights had long since gone with the wind, and Olivia didn't like it at all.

That was one thing, but this—the events at Banu—it was like a return to the past. It could have been a Unit 16 operation. The shooting of the sentry, the instant execution of Zorin. The fact that he'd taken the Browning with him in the first place, using his political clout to circumvent security—what was that supposed to mean?

He said softly, "For God's sake, Harry, what in the hell happened to you?"

Maybe the genie had escaped from the bottle, but that didn't make sense. He'd always understood the genie was a supernatural creature who did one's bidding. In Kosovo, perhaps it was the other way around. Maybe it was he who had done the genie's bidding.

He shook his head, unable to accept such a thought, even for a moment, and went back to bed.

AT HOLLAND PARK, Roper had worked through into the middle of Saturday morning, had put together as much information on Miller as he could find. Around ten o'clock, Luther Henderson, the day sergeant, came in.

"Tony told me you'd been at it all night, Major. I asked him if it was anything special and he suddenly turned into Mr. Mystery."

"You'll find out at the right time, Luther. What's new?"

"Levin, Chomsky, and Major Novikova have all begun that induction course at Kingsmere Hall now, trying to turn MI6 agents into good little Russians."

"With all their years in Russian Military Intelligence, if anybody can do it, they can." He shook his head. "Still—they're supposed to be down at Kingsmere for a month, which means we don't have them. I hope Ferguson doesn't regret saying yes when Simon Carter asked."

"It's difficult to say no to Mr. Carter, Major, especially when he had the Prime Minister's backing."

"I suppose." Simon Carter was not popular with many people, but he was, unfortunately, Deputy Director of the Security Services, and that was difficult to argue with.

"Is Mr. Dillon in, by any chance?"

"He called about an hour ago, sir, from Stable Mews. Said he'd be in later." He glanced at the main screen. "What a lovely lady, sir, who might she be?"

"That's Olivia Hunt, the actress," Roper told him. "She's married to Major Harry Miller, who works out of the Cabinet Office for the Prime Minister."

"Is that a fact, sir?"

"Tell me something. Did you ever come across him, maybe in Belfast or somewhere like that? You did enough Irish time."

"Five tours. Nothing like you, Major. You were never out of the bloody place. God, but you saved some lives. And that big one at the Grand Hotel in Belfast? Six bloody hours on your own. No wonder they gave you the George Cross."

"Yes, I was rather good, wasn't I? Peed myself several times because there was nowhere else to go." Roper was mocking the whole business now. "King of the castle until the little red Toyota turned up with the supermarket bag on the passenger seat. No big deal, only it was, and here I am. Whiskey and cigarettes, but no wild, wild women like the song said."

"Fuck them, Major, the bastards who did that to you."

"Nicely put, Luther, but alas, there's no possibility of that with anyone, so I'll settle for an invigorating shower in the wet room and would welcome your assistance."

"My pleasure, sir," and as Henderson wheeled him out, he added, "As to your question about Major Miller, sir, no, I never did come across him over there."

THERE WAS NO SIGN of Roper when Sean Dillon arrived at Holland Park. He wore black velvet cords and a black bomber jacket; a small man, his hair was pale as straw. Once a feared enforcer for the IRA, he was now Ferguson's strong right hand. He was sitting in one of the swivel chairs examining Roper's screens when Henderson entered.

"Where's the Major?" Dillon asked.

"I just helped him shower in the wet room, and now he's dressing. He'll be along directly." He nodded to Olivia Hunt on the screen. "A lovely lady. Know who she is?"

Roper entered in his wheelchair. "Of course he does. Mr.

Dillon was involved with the theater himself once upon a time. Who is she, Sean?"

"Olivia Hunt. Born in Boston and she's illuminated the British stage for years. That's her in Chekhov's *Three Sisters*. A National Theatre production a year ago."

"Told you," said Roper. "We'll have a pot of tea, Luther," and Henderson went out.

"What's she doing there?"

"I'm investigating her husband for Ferguson. Harry Miller, he works out of the Cabinet Office, a kind of troubleshooter for the Prime Minister. Used to be Army Intelligence. A headquarters man only, supposedly, but now it seems there's been more to him for some time." Henderson came in with the tea. Roper said, "Leave us, Luther. I'll call you if I need you."

Henderson went out. Dillon said, "What kind of more?"

"Have a hefty swig of that tea, Sean. I think you're going to be interested in what I've found out about Major Harry Miller."

WHEN HE WAS FINISHED, Dillon said, "And after that, I think I could do with something stronger."

"You can pour one for me while you're at it."

"So you say Ferguson wants this for breakfast, American time, with Cazalet?"

"That's it."

"Jesus and Mary." Dillon poured the drinks. "It must have been a hell of a thing, he and Blake together."

"You can say that again. Come on, do you have any input?"

"I heard whispers about Titan, but I don't think anyone in the movement took it too seriously, or Unit Sixteen. We had enough to deal with. You were there, Roper, you know what I'm talking about. So many people got killed, far more than the dear old British public ever realized. I remember the River Street affair, though. It's true the Chief of Staff put it out as an SAS atrocity."

"Gallant freedom fighters gunned down without mercy?"

"That's right. So Miller left the Army four years ago, becomes an MP, helps the Prime Minister get Ian Paisley and Martin McGuiness running the government together. A decent job there, actually. I'm not sure I can help you too much, Giles. I left the Provos in 'eighty-nine to do my own thing."

"Which included the mortar attack on John Major's war cabinet at Downing Street in February 'ninety-one."

"Never proved." Dillon shook his head.

"Bugger off, Sean, it was a hell of a payday for you, but never mind. Is there anything you can add to Miller's story?"

"Not a word."

"All right, then. I'll send it straight to Ferguson. We'll see what he makes of it."

AFTER BREAKFAST at the beach house on Nantucket, Clancy passed around the coffee, and Cazalet said, "So, what do you have for me, Charles?"

"Something so extraordinary, I'm surprised my laptop didn't catch fire, Mr. President."

"I see." Cazalet stirred his coffee. "So tell us."

Ferguson started to do just that.

When he was finished, there was silence and then the President turned to Clancy, "Well?"

"That's one hell of a soldier."

Blake said, "I knew there was something special about him the moment we met."

"And you, Charles?" Cazalet asked.

"Obviously, I knew a certain amount about him," Ferguson answered. "But I'm stunned to hear the full story."

"It would certainly shock his father-in-law, Senator Hunt. Very old-fashioned conservative guy, Hunt."

"So how do you want to handle this, Mr. President?"

"I think I'd like to meet Miller. He could be a useful recruit on certain missions for you and me, Charles. Discuss it with the Prime Minister and Miller first, of course. What do you think, Blake?"

"I think that could be beneficial to all parties, Mr. President."

"Excellent. Now, why don't we all go for a walk on the beach, take the sea air? The surf is particularly fine this morning."

THE SATURDAY-NIGHT performance of *Private Lives* was another triumph for Olivia Hunt, and she drove down in the Mercedes afterward to Stokely with Harry and Monica and Miller's usual driver, Ellis Vaughan. He had provided a hamper, sandwiches, some caviar, and a couple of bottles of champagne.

"You've excelled yourself, Ellis," Monica told him.

"We do our best, my lady," he said.

The truth was that as an ex-paratrooper, he enjoyed working for Miller. During these overnight stops at Stokely, he stayed in the spare bedroom at the Grants' cottage.

Olivia was on a high. Miller, on the other hand, felt strangely lifeless, a reaction to his trip, he told himself. They didn't arrive until one-thirty in the morning, and went to bed almost at once, where he spent a disturbed night.

They had a family breakfast on Sunday morning, with Aunt Mary later than usual. She was eighty-two now, white haired, but with a healthy glow to her cheeks, and her vagueness was, in a way, quite charming.

"Don't mind me, you three. Go for a walk, if you like. I always read the *Sunday Mail* at this time."

Mrs. Grant brought it in. "There you are, Madame. I'll clear the table if you're all finished."

Miller was wearing a sweater, jeans, and a pair of short boots. "I feel like a gallop round the paddock. I asked Fergus to saddle Doubtfire."

Olivia said, "Are you sure, darling? You look tired."

"Nonsense." He was restless and impatient, a nerviness there.

Monica said, "Off you go. Be a good boy. We'll watch, you can't complain about that."

He hesitated, then forced a smile. "Of course not."

He went out through the French windows, and it was Aunt Mary who put it in perspective. "I think it must have been a difficult trip. He looks tired and he's not himself."

"Well, you would know," Monica said. "You've known him long enough."

They took their time walking down to the paddock, and he was already in the saddle when they got there, Fergus standing by the stables, watching.

Miller cantered around for a while and then started taking the hedge jumps. He was angry with himself for allowing things to get on top of him, realized now that what had happened in Kosovo had really touched a nerve and he was damned if he was going to allow that to happen.

He urged Doubtfire over several of the jumps, then swung the plucky little mare around and, on an impulse, urged her toward the rear fence's forbiddingly tall five-barred gate.

"Good girl," he said, "We can do it," and he pushed her into a gallop.

His wife cried out, "No, Harry, no!"

But Doubtfire sailed over into the meadow, and just as Olivia caught her breath in relief, Miller galloped a few yards on the other side, swung Doubtfire around, and once again tackled the gate.

Olivia's voice rose in a scream. "No, Harry!" Monica flung an arm around her shoulders. Miller took the jump perfectly, however, cantered over to Fergus, and dismounted. "Give her a good rubdown and oats. She's earned it."

Fergus took the reins and said, "If you'll excuse me, Major, but I've the right to say after all these years that—"

"I know, Fergus, it was bloody stupid. Just get on with it."

He walked toward the two women, and Olivia said, "Damn you, Harry Miller, damn you for frightening me like that. It will take some forgiving. I'm going in."

She walked away. Monica stood looking at him, then produced a cigarette case from her handbag, offered him one, and took one herself. She gave him a light from her Zippo.

He inhaled with conscious pleasure. "We're not supposed to do this these days."

She said, "Harry, I've known you for forty years, you are my dearly loved brother, but sometimes I feel I don't know you at all. What you did just now was an act of utter madness."

"You're quite right."

"You used to do things like that a lot when you were in the Army, but for the last four years, working for the Prime Minister, you've seemed different. Something's happened to you, hasn't it? Kosovo, that trip there?" She nodded. "What was it? Come on, Harry, I know Kosovo is a hell of a place. People were butchered in the thousands there."

"That was then, this is now, Monica, my love." He suddenly gave her the Harry smile and kissed her on the cheek. "I'm tired, a bit wound up, that's all. Now, be a good girl, come up to the house and help me with Olivia."

And so she went—reluctantly, but she went.

The Kremlin

London

4

THERE WAS A HINT OF SLEET IN THE RAIN FALLING IN MOSCOW as Max Chekhov's limousine transported him from his hotel to the Kremlin. It was a miserable day, and to be perfectly frank, he'd have preferred to have stayed in Monaco, where one of the best clinics in Europe had been providing him with essential therapy to his seriously damaged left leg. But when you received a call demanding your appearance at the Kremlin from General Ivan Volkov, the personal security adviser to the President of the Russian Federation, you hardly said no.

The limousine swept past the massive entrance to the Kremlin and negotiated the side streets and checkpoints until they reached an obscure rear entrance. Chekhov got out and mounted a flight of stone steps with some difficulty, making heavy use of the walking stick in his left hand. His approach was obviously under scrutiny, for the door opened just before he reached it.

A tough-looking young man in the uniform of a lieutenant in the GRU greeted him. "Do you require assistance?"

"I'm all right if we stay on the ground floor."

"We will. Follow me."

Chekhov stumped after him along a series incredibly quiet, quite dull corridors that seemed to stretch into infinity, and then his guide opened a door leading to a much more ornate passageway lined with paintings and antiques. At the far end, a burly man in a dark suit, his head shaven, sat outside a door, a machine pistol across his knees. The GRU officer ignored him, opened the door, and motioned Chekhov inside.

Chekhov moved past him and the door closed behind. The room was fantastic, decorated in a kind of seventeenth-century French style, beautiful paintings everywhere, a superb carpet on the floor, and a marble fireplace on the wall with what at least looked like a real fire. There was a desk, three chairs in front of it and General Ivan Volkov behind it. There was nothing military about him at all. In his sixties with thinning hair, wearing a neat dark blue suit and conservative tie, he could have been the manager of some bank branch, not one of the most powerful men in the Russian Federation.

He wore old-fashioned wire spectacles and removed them as he glanced up. "My dear Chekhov." His voice was curiously soft. "It's good to see you on your feet again."

"Only just, Comrade General." Chekhov stuck to the old titles still popular with older party members. It was better to be safe than sorry. "May I sit down?"

"Of course." Chekhov settled himself. "Your stay in Monaco has been beneficial?"

"I'm better than I was." Chekhov decided to bite the bullet. "May I ask why I'm here, Comrade?"

"The President has expressed an interest in your personal welfare."

Such news filled Chekhov with a certain foreboding, but he forced a smile. "I'm naturally touched."

"Good, you can tell him yourself." Volkov glanced at his watch. "I anticipate his arrival in approximately two minutes."

Chekhov waited in some trepidation, and was thrown when a secret door in the paneled wall behind Volkov's desk swung open and President Putin walked in. He was in a tracksuit, a white towel around his neck. Chekhov struggled to his feet.

"My dear Chekhov, good to see you up and about again. You must excuse my appearance, but I look upon my gym time as the most important hour in the day."

"Comrade President," Chekhov gabbled. "So wonderful to see you."

"Sit down, man," Putin urged him, and sat on the edge of Volkov's desk. "So they've saved the leg and the word is you're almost as good as new."

Volkov put in, "Which must confound that animal, this London gangster, Harry Salter, who ordered the shooting."

"I must say General Charles Ferguson employs some unlikely help." Putin smiled. "Perhaps he's getting hard up for the right kind of people these days. Afghanistan must be taking its toll. So, Chekhov, you're ready to get back to work? I'm delighted to hear it."

As it was the first thing Chekhov had heard on the matter, he made the mistake of hesitating. "Well, I'm not sure about that, Comrade President."

"Nonsense. You must get back in the saddle. Best thing for you! Besides, you have that wonderful apartment in London going to waste. And as the CEO of Belov International, you have a lot of responsibilities to the company—and to us."

"Responsibilities that I've had to take care of while you've been recovering," Volkov pointed out.

"Which obviously can't go on," Putin said. "I suggest you move back within the next few days. Any further therapy you need can obviously be found in London. Once established, you will ease yourself back in harness and liaise with General Volkov."

Chekhov didn't even try to resist. "Of course, Comrade President."

As if by magic, the door by which Chekhov had entered opened again, revealing the GRU lieutenant. Chekhov understood that he was being dismissed. As he stood up again, Volkov said, "One more thing. I know you're angry about being shot. But I don't want you going off on any personal revenge mission against Salter or Ferguson's people when you get back. That's our job. They'll be taken care of eventually."

"I hope so," Chekhov said with some feeling, and went out.

Putin turned to Volkov. "Keep an eye on him, Volkov. He's all right for now, but he strikes me as a weak link. Just like those traitors we lost: Igor Levin, a decorated war hero, of all things, a captain in the GRU; Major Greta Novikova; even this Sergeant Chomsky of the GRU. I still can't understand what happened with them. What are the British doing with them?"

"Our people at the London Embassy inform me that all three have been transferred for the moment to teach a total-immersion course in Russian to agents of MI6. Ferguson was reluctant to let them, but Simon Carter, Deputy Director of the Security Services, persuaded the Prime Minister to order it."

"Did he indeed?" Putin's smile was enigmatic. "Well, much good it'll do them. So, Ivan, anything else? Otherwise, I'll get to the gym."

"As a matter of fact, there is, Comrade President. An unfortunate incident has just taken place in Kosovo, involving the death of an officer commanding a special ops patrol from the Fifteenth Siberian Storm Guards . . . ."

WHEN HE WAS FINISHED, Putin sat there, thinking. Finally, he said, "You are absolutely certain it was this Miller, no possibility of error?"

"He announced his identity when he challenged Captain Zorin. Zorin's sergeant confirms it."

"And you can definitely confirm the other man was Blake Johnson?"

"The sergeant heard Miller call him Blake, and people on the ground traced the inn where they'd spent the previous night. The landlord had taken their passport details. He told our people that they didn't arrive together, but seemed to meet by chance."

"That doesn't sound too plausible." Putin shook his head. "Blake Johnson, the President's man."

"And Harry Miller, the Prime Minister's. What do we do?"

"Nothing. Zorin's unit wasn't supposed to be there and so we can't very well complain, and if anybody says they were there, we'd have to strenuously deny it. I don't think we need to worry about the wretched Muslim peasants in those parts. They'll keep their heads down. And as for the U.S. and Britain, their attitude will be the same as mine. It's not worth World War Three."

"A pity about Zorin. He was a good man, decorated in Chechnya. His mother is a widow in poor health, but his uncle . . ." Here Volkov looked at his papers. ". . . is Sergei Zorin. Investment companies in Geneva, Paris, and London. What do I do about him?"

"Just explain to him that for the good of the State we can't take it further. As for the mother, say Zorin was killed in action, died valiantly, the usual nonsense. Tell her we'll arrange a splendid funeral. And make sure the regimental commander confirms our story."

He stood. "We should do something about Miller, though. Are you still in contact with this mystery man of yours, the Broker?"

"Our link with Osama? Certainly."

"You might want to give him a call." And he left.

An excellent idea, Volkov thought. He dialed a coded number and had a quick conversation. Then he phoned Colonel Bagirova of the Fifteenth Siberians and gave him his orders, which left him with Sergei Zorin. He phoned the great man's office and was informed that he couldn't possibly see anyone else that day, his appointment book was full. Volkov didn't argue, simply told the secretary to inform Zorin that President Putin's chief security adviser expected to meet him at the Troika restaurant in forty-five minutes, and put the phone down.

Sergei Zorin was already there when Volkov arrived, and squirming like all of them, frightened to death that he'd done something wrong. "General Volkov, such an honor. Unfortunately, the headwaiter says they don't have a table available, only stools at the bar."

"Really." Volkov turned as the individual concerned approached in total panic.

"General Volkov—please. I had no idea you were joining us today."

"Neither had I. We'll sit by the window. Caviar and all that goes with it, and your very finest vodka."

They were seated at the necessary table, Zorin terrified. Volkov said, "Calm yourself, my friend. People always treat me like Death in a black hood, like something from a Bergman film, but I can assure you that you are guilty of nothing." The vodka arrived in pointed glasses stuck in crushed ice. "Drink up and then another. You're going to need it. The news is not good, but you will have the satisfaction of knowing you have been part of something that has served Mother Russia well."

Zorin looked bewildered. "But what would that be?"

"Your nephew, Captain Igor Zorin, has died in action while taking part in a highly dangerous and most secret covert operation. I had the unhappy duty of conveying this news to our President a short while ago. He sends his condolences."

"Oh, my God." Zorin tossed back the vodka, then poured another. But was that a certain relief on his face? Yes, thought Volkov. "What terrible news. When did this happen?"

"Within the last few days. His body is already here in Moscow at the military morgue."

"Where did it happen?"

"I'm afraid I cannot divulge that information. However, he died honorably, I can assure you of that. There may even be another medal."

"That won't help my sister. She's been widowed for years and her health isn't good." The caviar arrived, and more vodka.

"Try some of this. A man must live, my friend." Volkov spooned some of the caviar himself. "Your sister is here in town at the moment?"

"Yes, she lives alone with her maid."

"Would you like me to be with you when you go to see her?"

The relief on Zorin's face was even greater. "That would be too much to expect, General."

"Nonsense, I'm happy to do it. Now eat up. It will do you good. Then you can take me to your sister's house and we'll break the bad news."

Zorin was pathetically grateful, strange when you considered his stature, and yet dealing with such a wealthy man gave Volkov no problem at all. The oligarchs, the billionaires, those Russians who preferred the delights of English public schools for their children and townhouses in Mayfair for their residences, still had enough to contend with back in Moscow. In the old days, the KGB had kept Russians of every level in line, and now it was the FSB, Putin's old outfit. Putin was hugely popular as President—which meant that he, Ivan Volkov, didn't need to be. Fear was enough.

THE ZORIN APARTMENT was in a grand old block with views over the river and looked as if it hailed from tsarist times. The bell echoed hollowly and the door was opened by an old woman who answered to Tasha, grim and rather forbidding, her hair bound by a scarf, her face like a stone, dressed in a peasant blouse and a long skirt.

"Where is she?" Zorin demanded.

"In the parlor," she said, and with the privilege of an old servant asked, "Forgive me, but is this bad news?"

"It couldn't be worse. This is General Volkov from the President himself to tell us of her son's glorious death in action against our country's enemies."

His sense of theater was poorly received. She glanced at Volkov briefly, obviously not particularly impressed, but then she looked as if she had lived forever. She had probably been born during the Great Patriotic War, the kind of woman who had seen it all.

"I will speak to her first," she said. "If you gentlemen would wait here."

Simple, direct, it brooked no denial. She opened a mahogany door with a gold handle, went in, and closed it behind her. Zorin shifted from foot to foot, very uncomfortable.

"She's very direct, Tasha," he said. "Peasant stock from the family estate."

"So I can see." There was a dreadful keening from inside the room, a wailing that was quite disturbing, followed by sobbing. After a while, Tasha opened the door. "She will see you now, both of you."

They entered, and Volkov found himself in a room that was a time capsule from another age: tall French windows to a terrace outside, a distant view of the river, old-fashioned mahogany furniture, wallpaper with paintings of rare birds, an Indian carpet, the grand piano covered with family photos. There were green velvet curtains, a musty smell to everything. It was as if nothing had changed since the 1920s, and even the clothes that the brokenhearted mother wore seemed antique.

She was sitting in a chair clutching a photo in a silver frame, her hair bound with a gold scarf, and Zorin embraced her.

"Now then, Olga, you mustn't fret. He wanted only to be a soldier since his youth, no one knows that better than you. See, look who I have brought you. General Ivan Volkov, with words from President Putin himself extolling the bravery of Igor."

She stared vacantly at Volkov, who said, "He died for the Motherland. There's talk of a medal."

She shook her head, bewildered. "A medal? He's got medals. I don't understand. Where are we at war?" She clutched at Zorin. "Where was he killed?"

Volkov said, "On a mission of the greatest importance to the State, that's all I can say. You may remember him with pride."

She held up the photo of Igor Zorin in a bemedaled uniform, and Volkov took in the handsome face, the arrogance, the look of cruelty. Then she seemed to come to life.

"That's no good to me, General. I want my son alive again, and he's dead. It's turned my heart to stone already."

She burst into a torrent of weeping. Tasha held her close and nodded to Zorin and Volkov. “Go now,” she said. “I’ll see to her.”

They did as they were told, went out into the street, and paused beside their two limousines.

“I can’t thank you enough for coming with me,” Zorin said.

“When I spoke to Colonel Bagirova of the Fifteenth Siberians, we agreed on the funeral for the day after tomorrow, ten o’clock in the morning, the Minsky Park Military Cemetery, so your nephew will be laid to rest with some of Russia’s finest soldiers. We will see what we can do about the medal. I can certainly promise a letter with Putin’s name on it.”

“I doubt whether even that will cheer her.” Zorin got in his limousine and was driven away.

“Just another day at the office,” Volkov murmured, got into his own limousine and was driven back to the Kremlin.

THE FUNERAL at Minsky Park was all that could be desired. There was a company of soldiers from the Fifteenth Siberian’s training camp outside Moscow, plenty of mourners in black, family and friends. The coffin was delivered on a gun carriage, lowered into the prepared grave, and twenty soldiers delivered the correct volley at Colonel Bagirova’s shouted command.

Olga Zorin stood with her brother, a few relatives behind, Tasha on the end of a line. Zorin held an umbrella, his sister sobbed, the regimental bugler played a final salute. Volkov stood some distance away wearing a military coat of finest leather and a black fedora, an umbrella over his head. The crowd dispersed to their various cars and Zorin came toward him.

“It was good of you to come. The family are very grateful.”

Volkov, who had observed the furtive glances coming his way, smiled. “Oh, I don’t know. I think they’re more worried than anything else. This coat always makes me look as if the Gestapo actually got to Moscow.”

Zorin obviously couldn't handle such levity. "The reception is at the Grand. You're very welcome."

"Duty calls, I'm afraid. You must make my excuses."

"The letter from the President, which came yesterday, was a great comfort to her after all."

"Yes, it was intended to be." In truth, he'd signed it himself, but that was no matter.

Olga Zorin sobbed as relatives helped her into the backseat of one of the funeral cars and Tasha followed her.

"A mother's love," Zorin said piously. "I'm a widower with no children, you know. Igor was my only heir."

"Well, he isn't now," Volkov said brutally. "You'll get over it. We know what you oligarchs get up to in London. That bar at the Dorchester, the delights of Mayfair, the ladies of the night. Oh, you'll cheer yourself up in no time."

He walked away smiling, leaving Zorin with his mouth gaping.

SHORTLY AFTER HIS RETURN from America, Ferguson received a call to visit the Prime Minister, where they discussed Miller and the Kosovo affair at length.

"So what do you think, Charles?"

"I've no quarrel with Miller's actions regarding Zorin. But I'll be frank with you, Prime Minister, I thought I knew him and I find I didn't. The stuff he was engaged in all those years, Titan and Unit Sixteen. Remarkable."

"Especially when you consider that even people as knowledgeable as you had no idea. No, I'm very impressed with Harry Miller." He got up and paced around. "Miller has done many excellent things for me, great on-the-ground reporting. He has a brilliant eye and a gift for a tactical approach to difficult situations. You'd find him very useful, Charles."

Ferguson could see how things were going. "Are you saying you think we should get together?"

"Yes. I know there's always been a fine line between what you do and his more political approach."

"And the fact that the two might clash," Ferguson said.

"Yes, but I believe Harry Miller is a kind of hybrid, a mixture of the two."

"I've no argument with that. So what are your orders?"

"To get together and sort things out, Charles." The Prime Minister shook his head. "What a world. Fear, uncertainty, chaos. It's a war in itself. So let's try and do something about it."

THE FOLLOWING DAY, Roper had Doyle drive him down to the Dark Man on Cable Wharf in Wapping, the first pub Harry Salter had owned and one still dear to his heart. When they arrived, Doyle parked the van and extracted Roper from the rear, using the lift, and they went inside.

Harry Salter and his nephew, Billy, were at the table in the corner booth, his two minders, Joe Baxter and Sam Hall, having a beer at the bar. Ruby Moon served drinks and Mary O'Toole beside her handled food orders from the kitchen. Roper joined the table and nodded to Ruby, who immediately sent him a large scotch by way of Joe Baxter.

Harry Salter and Billy were reading a file between them. Roper said, "Is that the stuff I sent you on Miller?"

"It certainly is," Harry said. "Where have they been keeping this guy all these years?"

"In plain sight," Billy told him. "He's been around. We just didn't know the other side of him."

Harry, a gangster most of his life, said to his nephew, "And what an other side. His past is incredible."

"I wouldn't argue with that." As Billy leaned over, his jacket gaped, revealing a shoulder holster and the butt of a Walther PPK.

"I've told you before," his uncle said. "A shooter under your arm when we're about to have our lunch—is that necessary? I mean, there are ladies present."

"God bless you, Harry," Ruby called.

"As an agent in Her Majesty's Secret Service, I'm licensed to use it, Harry, and in this wicked world we live in, you never know when."

"Give it a rest, Billy," Harry told him, and Ferguson walked in. "Thank God it's you, General, perhaps we can have some sanity round here. Where's Dillon?"

"He got a call last night from Levin, down at Kingsmere Hall. They've asked Dillon to give them a day for some reason. He'll be back this evening."

At that moment, a man walked in behind him. A light navy blue raincoat hung from his shoulders, over a smart suit of the same color, a white shirt, and regimental tie.

"I had to park by the river," he told Ferguson. "Had to run for it." He slipped off the raincoat. "It's started to pour."

That his suit was Savile Row stood out a mile. There was a slight silence and Harry said, "Who's this?"

"Sorry," Ferguson told him. "I'm forgetting my manners. Meet Major Harry Miller. You could be seeing him from time to time in the future. He's thinking of joining us."

The silence was total. It was Billy who said, "Now, that's a showstopper if ever I heard one." He stood up and held out his hand.

THERE WAS ONLY a certain amount of truth in what Ferguson had said. He'd spoken to the Major as the Prime Minister had asked him, and Miller in his turn had had his orders from the great man, which he'd accepted with some reluctance. On the other hand, after looking at the file Ferguson had given him, with details of his unit's activities and personnel, he'd warmed to the idea.

"A drink, Major?" Harry asked. "Best pint of beer in London."

"Scotch and water," Miller said.

"A man after my own heart," Roper told him, and called to Ruby, "Another here, love, for Major Miller, and a repeat for me."

Billy said to Ferguson, "So what's Dillon doing at Kingsmere? I know he speaks Russian, but Levin, Greta, and Chomsky are the real thing."

"Maybe they're supposed to be encouraged by how well

Dillon copes with the language," Roper said. "After all, he is still a Belfast boy at heart."

"Anyway, Simon Carter sanctioned it, and I wasn't about to argue it," Ferguson said.

Miller surprised them all by saying, "You have to understand his logic. All Irish are bogtrotters, with a face like a dog and broken boots. By displaying Dillon with his Russian ability, his argument probably runs something like: *If this animal can do it, so can you.*"

"Jesus, Major, that's really putting the boot in old Carter."

"Who isn't popular in our society," Roper told him. "And he loathes Dillon."

"Why, particularly?"

"It goes a long way back, to when John Major was PM. Major was hosting an affair on the terrace of the House of Commons for President Clinton, and Simon Carter was responsible for security. Dillon told Carter the security was crap, and he laid a bet that no matter what Carter did, sometime during the affair, he would appear on the terrace, dressed as a waiter, and serve the two great men canapés."

"And did he?"

It was Ferguson who said, "Yes. He got in from the river. Harry and Billy dropped him off overnight in a wet suit."

"Me being the biggest expert in London on the Thames," Harry said modestly. "You've got to get the tide just right, and the current can be a killer."

"President Clinton was very amused," Ferguson said.

"But Simon Carter wasn't." That was Miller.

"No." Roper laughed. "Hates him beyond reason, perhaps because Dillon is what Carter can never be."

"And what's that?"

"Carter is the ultimate desk man," Ferguson put in. "He's never been in the field in his life. Sean is someone quite beyond his understanding. He will kill at the drop of a hat if he thinks it's necessary."

"And on the other side of his coin, he has an enormous flair for languages, a scholar and poet by inclination," Harry said. "Plays great piano, if you like Cole Porter, and flies a plane."

"And don't forget, a bloody good actor in his day," Roper said. "A student at RADA, even performed with the National Theatre."

"And gave it all up, as he once said to me," Ferguson put in, "for the theater of the street."

Miller nodded, a strange alertness there. "Is that what he said?"

"I remember it well. We have what you might call a special relationship. At a stage when he was no longer with the IRA, I was responsible for him ending up in the hands of Serbs and facing the possibility of a firing squad."

"And what was the alternative?"

"A little judicious blackmail led him to work for me." Ferguson shrugged. "It's the name of the game, but then no one knows that better than you."

Miller smiled. "If you say so. I look forward to meeting him."

"He's often found at the Holland Park safe house. You're welcome there anytime."

"I look forward to it."

Harry Salter interrupted. "That's enough chat. We've got some of the best pub grub in London here, so let's get started."

LATER IN THE AFTERNOON, Miller looked in at Dover Street and found his wife preparing for the evening performance. She was in the kitchen in a terry-cloth robe, her hair up, preparing cucumber sandwiches, her personal fetish and absolute good-luck charm before every performance. He stole one and she admonished him.

"Don't you dare." The kettle boiled and she made green tea. "I'm going for my bath after this. Are you looking in on the show tonight? You don't need to, I don't expect you to be there every night, Harry. And anyway, I'm having a drink with the cast afterwards."

"I should check in at Westminster. There's a foreign policy debate and I do have things to do. The PM's asked me to interest myself in General Charles Ferguson's security unit, just as an adviser."

"Oh, I didn't tell you! I came home on the tube last night, and something truly strange happened."

"What was it?"

"It was reasonably busy, quite a few people, and this man got on, a real thug and horribly drunk. He started working his way along, leering at women and putting his arm about one or two of the young ones. Of course, everybody, including the men, buried themselves in books and newspapers or looked the other way."

Miller felt anger stirring inside. "Did he bother you?"

"I think he was going to, because he looked at me and started forward, but then he was distracted by a terribly young girl, and he went over and put his arm round her, and she was crying and struggling."

"What happened?"

"There was a young black man who'd been reading an *Evening Standard*. He wore a raincoat over a very nice suit, gold-rimmed glasses. He looked like an office worker. He suddenly sort of rolled up the newspaper, then doubled it. He got up, holding it in his right hand, and tapped the drunk on the shoulder. He said: 'Excuse me, she doesn't like you.' And you've no idea what happened next."

"Yes, I have. When you do that with a newspaper, it becomes brick hard, like a weapon. I should imagine he rammed it up under the drunk's chin."

She was amazed. "How on earth did you know that? He went down like a stone and lay there vomiting. The train came into the station a few minutes later and we all got off and left him."

"And the young man?"

"He smiled at me, Harry, and said, 'I've already seen *Private Lives,* Miss Hunt, you were wonderful. Sorry about what just happened. What terrible times we live in.' And then he just walked off and disappeared up the escalator. But how did you know about the newspaper trick?"

He shrugged. "Someone told me once. Have a great performance, darling." And he went out the door. Olivia's eyes followed him as he left.

At Westminster, he parked the Mini in the underground car park, walked up to his office, and found far more paperwork than he had expected. Two hours flew by, then he went into the Chamber and took his usual seat on the end of one of the aisles. The debate concerned the secondment of British troops to Darfur to back up the United Nations force. It was difficult, with Afghanistan still a drain on military forces. As usual at that time in the evening, the Chamber was barely a quarter full. Still, it was always useful to hear informed opinion, and if Miller had learned anything about politics in his four years as an MP, it was that these evening debates were often attended by people who took their politics seriously.

He finally left, dropped in at a nearby restaurant and had a simple meal, fish pie and a salad with sparkling water. By the time he got back to the underground car park, it was nine-thirty.

He drove out and up the slope between the walls, and as always it made him remember Airey Neave, the first Englishman to escape from Colditz in World War II—a decorated war hero, and another casualty of the Irish Troubles, who had met his end driving out of this very car park, the victim of a car bomb from the Irish National Liberation Army, the same organization that had taken care of Mountbatten and members of his family.

"What a world," Miller said softly, as he moved into the road and paused, uncertain where to go. Olivia wouldn't be home yet and she was having a drink with the cast, so what to do? And then he remembered Ferguson's invitation for him to familiarize himself with the Holland Park safe house.

It looked more like a private nursing home or some similar establishment, but his practiced eye noted the electronics on the high wall—certain to give any intruder a shock requiring medical attention—the massive security gates, the cameras.

He wound down the window and pressed the button on the camera entry post. Sergeant Henderson was on duty and his voice was calm and remote, obviously following procedure.

"Who is it?"

"Major Harry Miller, on General Charles Ferguson's invitation."

The gates opened in slow motion and he passed inside. Henderson came down the entrance-door steps.

"Sergeant Luther Henderson, Royal Military Police. You've already been placed on our regular roster. A pleasure to meet you, sir. If you'd like to get out, I'll park the Mini. General Ferguson isn't with us this evening, and Major Roper's having a shower in the wet room."

"The wet room? What's that?"

"Special facilities, nonslip floor, seats on the walls that turn down. The Major has to take his shower that way. A car bomb left him in a very bad way, nearly every bone in his body broken, his skull, spine, and pelvis all fractured. It's a miracle he still has two arms and legs."

"Incredible," Miller said.

"The bravest man I ever knew, sir, and his brain still works like he was Einstein. Straight through the entrance, armored door last on the left, and you're in the computer room. I'll let the Major know you're here. He'll be along in a while, but you'll find Mr. Dillon in the computer room having a drink. He'll look after you, sir."

He got in the Mini and drove away around the corner. Miller went up the steps and along the corridor, paused at the armored door, and opened it.

DILLON WAS SITTING in one of the swivel chairs in front of the screens, a glass in his right hand. He turned to look and Miller said, "You're Sean Dillon, I believe. I'm Harry Miller." Dillon had been smiling slightly, but now he looked puzzled, and shook hands.

"I know all about you," he said. "Quite a file."

"Well, your own reputation certainly goes before you."

Dillon said, "I was thinking about you, actually. Have a look at this. It was on Moscow television."

He pressed a button and there was Minsky Park Military Cemetery, and Igor Zorin's funeral. "See the one at the back in the black leather coat and black fedora? That's President Putin's favorite security adviser, General Ivan Volkov."

"I've heard of him, of course."

"A right old bastard, and not exactly our best friend. He was behind a Russian-sponsored plot to put us all in harm's way. Unfortunately, it succeeded with one of us." His face went grim.

"Hannah Bernstein," said Miller.

"You know about that? Well, of course you do. Volkov was behind it, with some help." He shook his head. "A great lady, and sorely missed."

"An IRA involvement, you say. I thought that was behind us."

"Nineteen sixty-nine was the start of the Troubles, and thirty-eight years later we're supposed to have peace in Ireland. But what about all those for whom it was a way of life, those who've been used to having a gun in their hand for years? What's the future for them?"

"Plenty of demand for mercenaries, I'd have thought." Miller shrugged. "Always enough opportunities for killing in the world today."

"It's a point of view." Dillon poured himself another whiskey. "Join me?"

"I think I will."

"I hear your wife's in *Private Lives* at the moment. I won't ask if she's doing well, because she always does. I saw her in Brendan Behan's *The Hostage* at the National. He'd have jumped out of his grave for her, the old bastard. A great play, and she got it just right."

There was genuine enthusiasm in his voice, and Miller had a strange, excited smile on his face. "And you would know because you were once an actor yourself, but gave it all up for the theater of the street."

"Where the hell did you hear that?"

"You told me yourself, running for it through a sewer from the Shankill into the Ardoyne, one bad night in Belfast in 1986."

"My God," Dillon said. "I knew there was something about you, but I couldn't put my finger on it."

"Twenty-one years ago," Miller said.

Dillon nodded. "Long and bloody years, and where did they all go? What in the hell was it all about?"

Belfast

March 1986

5

LOOKING BACK, HARRY MILLER REMEMBERED THAT YEAR well, not just because of the bad March weather in London and the constant rain, but because what happened proved a turning point in his life. He was a full lieutenant in the Intelligence Corps at twenty-four and nothing much seemed to be happening. He shared an office with a young second lieutenant named Alice Tilsey, and she'd beaten him to it that morning. He took off his trench coat, revealing a tweed country suit, uniforms being out that year as the IRA had announced that men in uniform on London streets were a legitimate target.

Alice said brightly, "Thank God you're wearing a decent suit. Colonel Baxter called for you five minutes ago."

"What have I done?"

"I lied and said you were getting the post downstairs."

"You're an angel."

He hurried up to the next floor and reported to Baxter's receptionist, a staff sergeant he knew well. "Am I in trouble, Mary?"

"Search me, love, but he certainly wants you right now. In you go. Captain Glover's with him."

BAXTER GLANCED UP. "There you are, Miller. Just sit down for a moment."

He and Glover had their heads together and enjoyed a brief conversation that made no sense to Miller, and then Baxter said, "Still living at Dover Street with your father?"

"Yes, sir."

"He's certainly the sort of MP we can rely on. Always has a good word for the Army in his speeches in Parliament."

"Old soldier, sir."

"Captain Glover would like a word."

"Of course, sir."

Glover had a file open. "You were on the Falklands Campaign seconded to 42 Commando, which of course was invaluable experience of war at the sharp end. Since then, you've been seconded once to the Intelligence Desk at Infantry Headquarters at the Grand Hotel in Belfast. What did you make of that?"

"Interesting, sir, but it was only six weeks."

Glover said, "Looking at your personal details, I see you're a Roman Catholic, Miller. If I ask if your faith is important to you, please don't be offended. It could be crucial to why you're here."

Uncertain what Glover was getting at, Miller said, "I was raised in the faith, I was a choirboy, I'm obviously familiar with the liturgy, and so on. Having said that, I must admit that, like many people, my religion is not at the forefront of my life."

Baxter intervened. "So you'd be capable of going to Belfast for us as a Catholic?"

There was a distinct pause, Miller totally astonished, and it was Glover who explained. "Think of it as one of those old black-and-white British war films where SOE sends you to go to Occupied France as an undercover agent."

"Which is what we want you to do in Belfast for us." Baxter smiled. "Are you up for it?"

Miller's stomach was churning. It was the same rush of adrenaline he'd experienced in the landings at San Carlos in the Falklands with those Argentine Skyhawks coming in.

"I certainly am. Just one thing, sir. Having visited Belfast, I know that the Northern Irish accent is unique, and I don't know if—"

"No problem. You'll stay English," Glover told him.

"Then I'm at your command, sir."

"Excellent. You're in Captain Glover's hands."

IN THE PLANNING ROOM, Glover laid out a map of Belfast. "The River Lagan runs into Belfast Lough and the docks; it's a busy area." He pushed a manila file across. "Everything you need is in there, but I'll go through it anyway. Boats go backwards and forwards from Glasgow, trawlers, freighters."

"Illegal cargoes, sir?"

"Sometimes. Arms, for example, and people. There's a pub in the dock area we're interested in, the Sailor. The owner is a man named Slim Kelly."

"IRA, sir?"

"Certainly. Did time in the Maze Prison and was released, so there's good photos of him in your file. He's supposedly clean these days, but he's certainly killed many times. Our understanding is that he's fallen out of favor with the Provos. Lately he's been involved with a man named Liam Ryan, a psychopath who murders for fun. He's another one the IRA want to dispose of. Our information is that he's done a deal to supply Kelly with Stinger missiles. These things can be operated by one man and they'll bring down a helicopter. We understand they'll be delivered to Kelly by Ryan next week in a trawler called the *Lost Hope*. The moment you can confirm the meet, you call your contact number in Belfast, which will bring in an SAS team on the run. It sounds simple, but who knows? Whatever happens, don't use the contact number unless you are positive you have Kelly and Ryan in the frame."

"What exactly is my cover, sir?"

"You're employed by St. Mary's Hospice in Wapping.

There's a branch in Belfast close to the Sailor, an old priory run by nuns that provides for the deserving poor and so forth. It needs renovating, and it's already had a building surveyor from London come in. You're an ordinand, whatever that is."

"Someone who's considering the priesthood."

"Perfect cover, I should have thought. You're from the London estate office. You've got all the documents on what needs doing. The story is you're there to confirm it. You're the man from head office, in a way."

"Where do I stay?"

"The priory. It's all arranged by the mother superior, a Sister Maria Brosnan. To her, you're the genuine article."

Which in some strange way made Miller slightly uncomfortable. "Can I ask how you've been able to make these arrangements, sir?"

"As it happens, Colonel Baxter's younger brother is Monsignor Hilary Baxter in the Bishop of London's Office. St. Mary's Hospice in Wapping was facing closure because their lease was coming to an end. We've been able to resolve their problem."

To that, there was no answer. "I see, sir."

"If you call round to Wapping this afternoon with the documents in your file, there's an old boy called Frobisher who'll go through them with you. All the necessary work's been done. You just pretend at the hospice and look busy. Sister Maria Brosnan expects you Monday."

"What about my identity?"

"It's all in the file, Harry, courtesy of the forgery department of MI6."

"And weaponry?"

"I'm afraid you're expecting too much there. After all, you're a traveling civilian heading into the war zone. There's no way you could go armed."

"I see, sir, it's we-who-are-about-to-die-salute-you time." It was a statement, not a question, and Miller carried on. "What you really want aren't the Stingers on that boat. This is all about Kelly, the publican of the Sailor who has fallen out of favor with the Provos, and this Liam Ryan who you say is a psychopath."

"Two years ago, he formed a breakaway group, no more than a dozen people, calling it the Irish Liberation Movement. Wholesale butchery, torture, kidnap—his favorite pastime is removing his victims' fingers with bolt cutters. Bad news for the Republican movement as a whole. The word is the Provos put their best enforcer on the case. Eight of Ryan's people are known to have been executed for certain, but perhaps more."

"But not Ryan?"

"A will-o'-the-wisp with all the cunning of a beast. He's one of the few big players who's never been arrested, so there aren't prison photos. He's always avoided cameras like the plague, a bit like Michael Collins in the old days, but we have one anyway."

"How is that, sir?"

"He took out an Irish passport five years ago under a false name. There's a copy of the passport photo in the file."

Miller had a look at it. The face was very ordinary, cheeks hollow, the whole thing desperately stilted, the face of some little man for whom life had always been a disappointment. Miller replaced it.

"Thanks very much, sir. Would you have told me all this if I hadn't asked?"

"It's the name of the game." Glover shrugged. "I'd get on with it if I were you." He patted the file. "I'll put the word out that you're off on a spot of leave."

THE OFFICE WAS EMPTY when Miller went in, so he sat at the desk and checked out the contents of the file. There was a passport in the name of Mark Blunt, aged twenty-four, a surveyor by profession, a London address in Highbury. He'd been to Italy once, France twice, and Holland on a day trip from Harwich. The photo had the usual hunted look and made him look thinner.

He worked his way through the survey reports referring to various parts of the priory in Belfast. It was all laid out simply and made perfect sense. There was also a Belfast street map, some photos of the priory and the docks.

So far so good. He put the file in his briefcase and pulled on his raincoat, tense and slightly worked up. The door opened and Alice Tilsey came in.

"You clever bastard," she said. "Off on leave, are we? How in the hell did you work that?"

"For God's sake, Alice," he said. "After a year in the Corps, I'd have thought you'd have learned when to keep your mouth shut and mind your own business."

A look of total contrition and horror spread over her face. "Oh, my God, Harry, you're going in-country, aren't you? I'm so bloody sorry."

"So am I, actually," he said, and left.

MR. FROBISHER at St. Mary's Hospice in Wapping was in his early seventies and looked it. Even his office seemed like something out of Dickens. He stood at a drawing table and went through documents with Harry, in the kind of faded voice that seemed to come from another time and place.

"I produced these plans after a visit to Belfast a year ago. I thought we'd never be able to attempt the necessary work, but Monsignor Baxter's explained that everything's changed. We have money now. You aren't a trained surveyor, of course. He told me he was sending you for what he termed a layman's opinion."

"I'm that, all right," Miller said.

"Yes, well, it's all detailed very clearly. The cellars extend along the whole waterfront, and in places there is flooding. It's the docks, you see."

"Thanks for the warning."

"You're an ordinand, I understand. Monsignor Baxter said you might enter the priesthood."

"Perhaps," Miller told him. "I'm not certain."

"Belfast was not good during my visit. Bombs at night, some shooting. A godless place these days."

"The world we live in," Miller said piously.

"I would warn you of the pub next door to the priory, the Sailor. I had luncheon there on occasion, but didn't like it. The people who frequented it were very offensive when they heard my English accent, particularly the landlord, an absolute lout called Kelly."

"I'll remember that."

"Take care," Frobisher said, "and give my regards to Sister Maria Brosnan, the mother superior. She comes from Kerry in the Republic, a beautiful county."

Miller left him and walked up to Wapping High Street. He happened to pass a barbershop, and on impulse went in and had his hair cut quite short. It emphasized his gauntness, so that he resembled the man in the passport photo more than ever.

His Savile Row suit was totally out of place, so he searched and found a downmarket men's outfitters where he bought a single-breasted black suit, three cheap shirts, and a black tie. He also invested in a shabby fawn raincoat, much to the surprise of the salesman he dealt with, as he'd gone in wearing a Burberry. Spectacles were not possible, because they would have had to be clear glass, a giveaway in the wrong situation.

He walked on, reaching the Tower of London, adjusting to thoughts of his new persona: someone of no importance, the sort of downtrodden individual who sat in the corner of some musty office, not to be taken seriously at all. Finally, he hailed a taxi and told the driver to take him to Dover Street.

When he arrived, opening the front door, Monica appeared from the kitchen at the end of the hall. "Guess who?"

He dropped his bags. "Why aren't you at Cambridge?"

"I decided, purely on impulse, to spend a weekend with my dear old dad and my loving brother." She kissed him and pushed the bag containing the clothes with her foot. "What have you been buying, anything interesting?"

"No, nothing special." He put the bag in the cloakroom and took off his decent trench coat. "Regarding the weekend,

I'm afraid I'm only good for tonight. I'll be going north on the train tomorrow."

"Oh, dear, where?"

"Catterick Camp, Paratroop headquarters." The lies came smoothly, the deceit. He was surprised how easy it was. "A week at least, perhaps more. I report Sunday morning."

She was disappointed, and it showed. "I'll just have to hope that Dad's not doing anything. Come on into the kitchen. I'll make you a cup of tea."

THERE IS an old saying that in Belfast it rains five days out of seven, and it certainly was on the following Monday morning when Miller went down the gangway of the overnight boat from Glasgow. He carried a canvas holdall that contained his file and the barest of necessities: pajamas, underwear, a spare shirt, and a small folding umbrella. He raised the umbrella and proceeded along the quay in the cheap raincoat and suit, making exactly the impression he had wanted. Having examined the street map thoroughly, he knew where he was going and found St. Mary's Priory with no difficulty at all.

It looked out over the harbor as it had done since the late nineteenth century; he knew that from the documents in his file and because that was the period when Catholics were allowed to build churches again. It had a medieval look to it, but that was fake, and rose three stories high, with narrow stained-glass windows, some of them broken and badly repaired. It had the look of some kind of church, which the pub down the street from it didn't. A sign swung with the breeze, a painting of a sailor from a bygone age on it wearing a faded yellow oilskin and sou'wester. A long window was etched in acid *Kelly's Select Bar.* In spite of the early hour, two customers emerged, talking loudly and drunkenly, and one of them turned and urinated against the wall. It was enough, and Miller crossed the road.

THE SIGN READ: *St. Mary's Priory, Little Sisters of Pity. Mother Superior: Sister Maria Brosnan.*

Miller pushed open the great oaken door and went in. A young nun was at a reception desk writing in some sort of register. A large notice promised soup and bread in the kitchen at noon. There was also a supper in the canteen at six. There were times for mass in the chapel noted, and also for confession. These matters were in the hands of a Father Martin Sharkey.

"Can I help you?" the young nun asked.

"My name is Blunt, Mark Blunt. I'm from London. I believe the mother superior is expecting me."

The girl sparkled. "You're from Wapping? I'm Sister Bridget. I did my novitiate there last year. How is the mother superior?"

Miller's hard work reading the files paid off. "Oh, you mean Sister Mary Michael? She's well, I believe, but I'm working out of Monsignor Baxter's office at the Bishop's Palace."

A door to the paneled wall at one side of her, labeled *Sacristy,* had been standing ajar, and now it opened and a priest in a black cassock stepped through.

"Do you have to bother the boy with idle chatter, Bridget, my love, when it's the mother superior he's needing?"

She was slightly confused. "I'm sorry, Father."

He was a small man, fair haired, with an intelligent face alive with good humor. "You'll be the young man with the plans for the improvements we've been waiting for, Mr. Blunt, isn't it?"

"Mark Blunt." He held out his hand, and the priest took it.

"Martin Sharkey. You know what women are like, all agog at the thought that the old place is going to be finally put to rights." There was only a hint of an Ulster accent in his voice, which was fluent and quite vibrant in a way. "I'm in and out of the place at the moment, but if there's anything I can do, let me know. You'll find the lady you seek through the end door there, which leads to the chapel." He turned and went back into the sacristy.

THE CHAPEL WAS everything Miller expected. Incense, candles, and holy water, the Virgin and child floating in semidarkness, the confessional boxes to one side, the altar with the sanctuary lamp. Sister Maria Brosnan was on her knees scrubbing the floor with a brush. To perform such a basic task was to remind her to show proper humility. She stopped and glanced up.

"Mark Blunt, Sister."

"Of course." She smiled, a small woman with a contented face. "You must excuse me. I have a weakness for pride. I need to remind myself on a daily basis."

She put the brush and a cloth in her bucket, and he gave her his hand and pulled her up. "I was talking to Mr. Frobisher the other day. He asked to be remembered to you."

"A good and kind man. He saw what was needed here a year ago and doubted the order could find the money." She led the way into the darkness, opened a door to reveal a very ordered office, a desk, but also a bed in the corner. "But all that has changed, thanks to Monsignor Baxter in London. It's wonderful for all of us that the money has been made available."

"As always, it oils the wheels."

She went behind her desk. "Take a seat for a moment," she said, which he did. "As I understand it, you will examine everything referring to Mr. Frobisher's original findings and report back to Monsignor Baxter?"

"That's it exactly, but let me stress that I don't think you have the slightest need to worry. There is a very firm intention to proceed. I just need a few days to check things out. I understand I can stay here?"

"Absolutely. I'll show you around now."

"I met Father Sharkey on my way in," Miller told her.

"A great man—a Jesuit, no less."

"Soldier of Christ."

"Of course. We are fortunate to have him. Father Murphy, our regular priest, was struck down the other week with pneumonia. The diocese managed to find Father Sharkey for us. He was due at the English College at the Vatican, a great scholar, I understand, but he's helping out until Father Murphy is fit again. Now let's do the grand tour."

SHE SHOWED HIM everything, starting with the top floor, where there was dormitory space for twenty nuns, then the second floor, with special accommodations for nursing cases of one kind or another, a theater for medical attention. There were half a dozen patients, nuns in attendance.

"Do you get people in and out on a regular basis?"

"Of course—we are, after all, a nursing order. Five of the people on this floor have cancer of one kind or another. I'm a doctor, didn't you know that?"

All Miller could do was say, "Actually, I didn't. Sorry."

The doors stood open for easy access, and a couple of the nuns moved serenely in and out, offering help as it was needed. Some patients were draped in a festoon of needles and tubes, drips of one kind or another. Sister Maria Brosnan murmured a few words of comfort as she passed. The end room had a man in a wheelchair, what appeared to be plaster of Paris supporting his head, a strip of bandage covering his left eye. He was drinking through a straw from a plastic container of orange juice.

"Now then, Mr. Fallon, you're doing well, but try a little walk. It will strengthen you."

His reply was garbled and they moved to the next room, where a woman, looking pale as death, lay propped up against a pillow, eyes closed. Sister Maria Brosnan stroked her forehead, and the woman's tired eyes opened.

"You're very good to me," she whispered.

"Go to sleep, dear, don't resist it."

They walked out. Miller said, "She's dying, isn't she?"

"Oh, yes, and very soon now. Each is different. A time comes when radiotherapy and drugs have done their best and failed. To ease the patient's journey into the next world then becomes one of our most important duties."

"And Fallon?"

"He's different. According to his notes, he has a cancer biting deep into the left eye and it also affects his speech. He's only been with us for two days, waiting for a bed at the Ardmore Institute. You see, radiotherapy is beyond our powers here. Up at Ardmore, they do wonderful things."

"So there could still be hope for him?"

"Young man, there is hope for all of us. God willing. With cancer, I've seen total remission in some cases."

"A miracle?" Miller said.

"Perhaps, Mr. Blunt." Her simple faith shone out of her. "Our Lord performed them."

They were on the ground floor: kitchens, canteen, a dormitory for twenty-five with a divider, women one side, men the other.

"Street people. They queue to get a bed for the night."

"Amazing," Miller said. "You really do good work."

"I like to think so." They were back in the entrance hall, Bridget at her desk.

She produced a parcel. There was a bright label that read *Glover Hi-Speed Deliveries.*

"For you, Mr. Blunt," she said. "A young man on a motorcycle—I had to sign for it."

Miller took it and managed to smile. "Something I needed to help me in my work," he said to the mother superior.

She accepted that. "Just come this way." He followed her toward the chapel entrance, and she turned into a short corridor with a door that said *Washroom* and two doors opposite.

"Father Sharkey has one room, now you, the other." She turned the key in the door and opened it. There was a locker, a desk, and a small bed in the corner.

"This will be fine," Miller told her.

"Good. Obviously, you're free to go anywhere you want. If you need me, just call. One thing—do keep your room locked. Some of our guests can be light-fingered."

She went out. Miller locked the door, sat on the bed, and tore open the package. Inside in a cardboard box was a soft leather ankle holder, a Colt .25 with a silencer and a box containing twenty hollow-point cartridges, a lethal package if ever there was one. There was no message; the name Glover Hi-Speed Deliveries said it all, the deliveryman on the motorcycle probably SAS.

"So it begins," he said softly, and unpacked his holdall.

THERE WAS A CRYPT beneath the chapel, he knew that from Frobisher's plans. He found the entrance in the dark shadows and noticed a couple of nuns sitting on one of the benches by the confessional boxes. The door opened behind him, he turned, and Father Sharkey entered the chapel, a violet stole around his neck.

"Confession about to start. Are you interested?"

"Actually, I'm about to examine the crypt."

"There is electric light in the crypt itself, but once you move on from there, it's a creepy old place."

"I've had a look at Frobisher's plans."

Sharkey was speaking softly because there was a murmur of prayer from the nuns. "It's an underworld down there, extending not only under the Sailor but along the quay itself. Go poking your nose in there and it's tricky. No lights. There's a battery lantern on the shelf at the top of the crypt steps for emergencies."

"Thanks. I'll take care."

Sharkey crossed to the confessional boxes and entered one of them, and Miller opened the crypt door and entered. It was cold and damp, and he switched on the light, found the lantern, and took it with him when he ventured down the steps. There was an arched entrance into a cellar, a sound of dripping water, and he moved on. A single bulb, and through another entrance, only darkness.

He switched on the lantern and kept going, aware of noise somewhere near at hand. Some of it was overhead, voices, laughter, and then he came to a wooden door secured by massive bolts. When he opened it, the light from his lantern disclosed a large cellar, barrels, crates of beer bottles, wine racks. There was a table, chairs, a door on the far side with a wooden cupboard beside it.

He opened the door to a stairway and the voices seemed clearer from up above. He closed it again, opened the cupboard door, and found six AK-47 assault rifles above a khaki-painted ammunition box. So Kelly was still in business? He turned to go back to the other door and noticed a grille in the wall, originally a Victorian innovation to allow air to circulate, and then he heard somebody calling through the other door, hurried back, bolted the door, and turned off his lantern.

He waited. The other door opened and the light was switched on, shining fingers stabbing through the grille. He could hear perfectly, managed to peer through, and recognized Kelly at once. The other man was one of the two he'd seen coming out of the bar that morning.

Kelly was speaking. "Well, God's been good to us and the weather's not held the *Lost Hope* up too much, Flannery."

"Tomorrow evening, is it?" Flannery asked.

"If we're lucky. Reach over and get a couple of bottles of the Beaujolais. They'll see to lunch for us."

There was the clink of bottles. "So, we'll get a chance to meet the man himself, the great Liam Ryan, and me never having even clapped eyes on him," Flannery said.

"And neither have I. A man to avoid, and that's a fact. He's been known to remove fingers with bolt cutters and make his victims swallow them."

"Mother Mary, what kind of a man would do that?"

"A monster, if all they say about him is true. So the boat comes in, but he won't be on it. He always covers his back, you see. When he's satisfied it's safe, he'll be in touch and check that I've paid up in Geneva. Only then do we unload the Stingers. We'll hide them down here for the time being."

"And he's away out of it when the boat leaves?"

"I've no idea, and I don't care as long as he goes. . . . That's enough of the talking now. I'm parched. Let's get back upstairs and sample the wine."

The light went out, and the door shut with a hollow boom. Miller switched on the lantern, turned, and made his way back to the crypt. A stroke of luck, hearing all that. It certainly clarified a few things, and the fact that Ryan wouldn't be on the boat when it came was important. So where would he be? He thought about that as he went back up to the chapel.

SISTER BRIDGET at her reception desk smiled at him. "Can I help in any way?"

"I could do with a bite. Can I eat here?"

"Certainly, but for lunch we only do bread and vegetable soup. It's very nourishing, but the Sailor does burgers and pies and Irish stew." She hesitated. "They're a rough lot in there."

"So Mr. Frobisher told me in London."

"Father Sharkey goes there sometimes. He's just left, so I expect he's gone."

Miller thought about it. In a way, it was necessary for him to step into the circle of danger that was the Sailor. Given that, it seemed to him that he had a better hope of survival if the priest was present.

"I'll take my chances," he told Bridget, who was looking worried. "Don't fret."

HE OPENED the front door of the pub, stepped inside, and found himself in a bar typical of the kind to be found on the Belfast waterfront and dating from the beginning of the nineteenth century. There were mahogany cubicles for privacy, iron tables with tiled tops, a long bar with a brass rail to put a foot on, ornate mirrors of the Victorian period. Behind the bar, bottles of every kind of drink ranged before the pub's patrons.

There were perhaps a couple of dozen men propping up the bar, talking, laughing, sailors and dockworkers. Kelly stood at the end with Flannery, enjoying the wine.

Father Sharkey sat in a window seat, reading the *Belfast Telegraph* and smoking a cigarette. He had no drink in front of him.

"Hello, Father," Miller said. "Can I get you something?"

Sharkey looked up and smiled. "That's kind of you. A Guinness wouldn't be a burden."

There was something of a silence, and men turned to stare with unfriendly looks as Miller approached the bar. The barman had cropped hair and a hard face. He wore a black waistcoat, and his shirtsleeves were rolled up above muscular arms.

Miller said cheerfully, "Guinness twice, please."

The barman said, "English, is it?"

"That's right. I'm working at the priory."

"The wrong part of the waterfront for you, Sunshine," the barman told him. "The English aren't exactly popular here."

Kelly intervened. "Now then, Dolan, don't let's be hard on the young man. It's not his fault his mother spawned a Brit. Give him his Guinness now and serve it properly in a bottle. How many times do I have to tell you? Manners, boy, manners."

"I see what you mean, Mr. Kelly, I do indeed." Dolan produced a bottle, flicked off the cap, walked all the way around the bar, and approached Miller. "Your drink, sir."

He started pouring it on Miller's left shoulder, then down the front of his raincoat. He was smiling as he said, "Would that be satisfactory?"

Somebody cheered, and there was genuine laughter. Miller was trapped. The character he was playing was not supposed to be able to handle a brute like Dolan. As it happened, he didn't need to. Father Sharkey was on his feet and approaching.

"You'll excuse me, Mr. Kelly, if I have words with your man here." He smiled at Dolan. "Did I ever tell you my uncle was a bare-knuckle boxer? I was up to Belfast from County Down for my schooling, and I came home the worse for wear after what they did to me in the yard. Timing and hitting, that's what you must learn, he said, like this."

He drove his left into Dolan's stomach, his right into the side of the barman's face as the man keeled over, turned him around to fall across the bar, delivered a double blow to the kidneys, then bent and grabbed an ankle and heaved him over headfirst.

It was like an execution, the sheer brutal savagery almost beyond belief. The bar was reduced to total silence. Sharkey turned to Kelly and Flannery.

"My God, you see, is a God of wrath. Think about that, Mr. Kelly, I'd strongly advise it. As for Mr. Blunt, remember he works for the Church. I'd see to your man if I was you, he doesn't look too well. We'll dine at Molly Malone's place today. Her Irish stew is better than yours anyway."

LATER, sitting at a window table in the café along the front after the meal, sharing a pot of tea, Miller said, "A hard lot, Kelly's people."

"A hard life for them here, the Troubles year after year and things never getting any better. Where do you live in London?"

The lies again, the deceit. "Highbury," Miller told him. "It's near Islington."

"I know where it is. I lived in London for years when I was at college. Kilburn."

"Why was that?"

"There was no work here when I was a boy, and my mother died when I was born, so we crossed the water, lived there for years, and then my father died in an accident. So I came home, back to my uncle, and the religious life beckoned." He took out a packet of Gallaghers and lit one. "The only trouble is I have a terrible temper."

"Well, you certainly don't mess about," Miller said.

"I have a personal philosophy, a kind of existential thing. Life should be lived to the full. If you feel it, then do it, it's quite simple. You create your own values."

"It sounds great, but I think there are times when that wouldn't be very practical."

"O ye, of little faith. We'd better get back. I have another session in the confessional box and then a mass."

FOR THE REST of the day, he tried to look busy, starting on the top floor, always with one of Frobisher's plans under his arm and a note board at the ready. Life carried on around him, the nuns busying themselves with their nursing duties on the second floor. There was a brooding atmosphere there, the thought of death waiting in the wings, the occasional moan of pain.

And one macabre sight: Fallon with the cancer-ravaged face, out of his room in a cardigan and trousers, taking a turn along the long corridor in slow motion, leaning on a walking stick. It was like something out of a horror movie, the decay of flesh under the plaster of Paris, and the smell as Miller eased past, sickly sweet like rotting flowers.

It made him feel desperately uneasy, and he went downstairs to his room. He'd washed his raincoat in the shower to remove the Guinness and hung it over a central heating radiator to dry, so it wasn't available when he decided to go out and explore the waterfront. Raining it was, but there were some umbrellas in a stand next to the door, and he took one and went out. It was early evening now, darkness not far away.

There were boats of every description, large ferryboats lined up in the outer harbor with freighters and cargo ships. Closer to home lay a variety of smaller craft and several trawlers, plus a couple of rust-streaked freighters with Glasgow registrations.

He walked along slowly, thinking. According to Kelly, there was a fair chance the *Lost Hope* would dock tomorrow evening, but Glover's orders had been explicit. On no account was he to use his contact number for backup unless Kelly and Ryan were in the frame together. So the boat was due in, the Stingers on board, but where was Ryan?

He paused to light a cigarette under the umbrella. There was a small supermarket beside a warehouse on the other side of the road, and Sister Bridget emerged with a grocery cart and paused to put up an umbrella.

"Just doing my chores," she called. "How are you?"

"Fine," he replied.

She crossed the road, her umbrella in one hand shielding the groceries. "Having a look round, are you? Do you like the boats?"

"I suppose so."

"I grew up in a fishing village in Galway. My father and three brothers were all fishermen. I used to love the trawlers, drifting into harbor when they'd been away a few days, like that one there."

Miller turned, and sure enough there was a large deep-sea trawler nosing in, festooned with nets, men in oilskins working the decks.

"The *Lost Hope,*" she said. "I like that name. I don't know why." Her face was shining. "It's been in several times since I've been at the priory."

"Is that a fact?" Miller said calmly.

"I must be getting back, they're waiting for these things in the kitchen. I'll see you later."

"Of course."

He watched as the *Lost Hope* eased in toward a berth where a couple of dockworkers waited on the quay to catch thrown lines, and for a moment there was a flurry of movement from the men on deck. Only one thing was certain now. The early arrival changed everything. But whatever he did had to be carefully considered. He was aware of a woman's raised voice, and turned. On the other side of the quay a little farther along, a white van had stopped. Flannery was beside it, the driver's door open and Sister Bridget's trolley on its side, her packages spilling as she wrestled with him.

"Would you leave me alone?" There was anger in her voice.

Miller arrived on the run, pulled Flannery away, and swung him around. The stink of alcohol permeated everything and the man was obviously drunk.

Miller shoved him back against the van. "Leave her."

"Put your hands on me, would you?" Flannery swung at him. "I'll show you, you English bastard."

The Sergeant-Major in charge of what the Intelligence Corps called the self-defense with extreme prejudice course would have been proud of him. Miller kicked Flannery with precision under his left kneecap, jabbed the knuckles of his right hand into the stomach, and when Flannery doubled over, raised a knee into his face, breaking his nose, then turned him and ran him headfirst into the cab.

Suddenly, there was Kelly running toward him from the pub door and, beyond, Father Sharkey outside the priory, watching. Miller gathered Sister Bridget's groceries and packages and put them in her trolley.

"There you go, Sister."

Kelly arrived. "What in the hell's going on?"

"Oh, just teaching your man here some manners." Miller turned to the girl. "I'll see you back."

"I'm so grateful. He won't leave me alone."

As they neared the priory, Sharkey moved toward them. "Are you all right, Bridget?"

"Thanks to Mr. Blunt, I am." She went in.

"I'm impressed," Sharkey said.

"Yes, well, I'm like you, Father. I lose my temper."

"Strange, I didn't get that impression. It seemed to me you knew exactly what you were doing. Kelly won't be pleased. I'd take care from now on. You're certainly an interesting kind of surveyor."

"Thanks for the advice, Father."

Miller followed Bridget inside, cursing silently. What a stupid thing to do. In a way, he'd blown his cover. There had been a question in Sharkey's eyes, and he'd put it there, and then he suddenly thought of the girl and decided he didn't give a damn.

HE WENT to his room, sat on the bed thinking about it, and went outside and looked out along the quay at the *Lost Hope,* lights all over her as darkness eased in. No speaking to his contact unless he could guarantee a meet between Kelly and Ryan: Those were his orders. On the other hand, there was the *Lost Hope,* which he knew from the overheard conversation in the cellar with Kelly and Flannery definitely had the Stingers on board. Perhaps half a loaf was better than none?

He opened his locker, lifted a piece of plywood in the bottom, and took out the box. He'd loaded the Colt earlier, and now he strapped the holster around his right ankle, screwed on the silencer and seated the Colt in the holster. His raincoat was dry now, so he put it on and went out. Bridget wasn't at the reception desk. He could hear voices in the chapel, and he eased the door open and listened. It was Father Sharkey talking to some young woman.

"I'll have words with the mother superior in the morning and see if we can help."

Miller took his chance, opened the sacristy door, stepped inside, and reached for the phone on Sharkey's desk. He dialed the contact number, and the answer was instantaneous.

"Who is this?" The voice was calm, controlled.

"Lieutenant Harry Miller. The *Lost Hope* has arrived early. I can confirm Stinger missiles are on board. I can also confirm AK-47s in Kelly's pub cellar."

"And Ryan?"

"I've no idea. No sign of him. I thought something was better than nothing. What do I do? I'm in the priory."

"Go outside, keep the *Lost Hope* under observation, and we'll come quickly. That means not in uniform."

Miller replaced the receiver, opened the door carefully, and stepped out to find Bridget at her desk.

"Oh, it's you, Mr. Blunt. I thought the Father was in there."

"No, he's in the chapel. I was just borrowing the phone." He walked to the door, which stood open for the street people who would be there for their supper later on.

He stood outside for a moment, there was a strange clicking, and Mr. Fallon appeared from the shadows leaning on his walking stick. Miller said, "Taking some exercise, Mr. Fallon?"

"Not really," Fallon told him. "What I'm doing is checking up on you, you bastard." He produced a Smith & Wesson .38 revolver from his left raincoat pocket.

Flannery slipped up behind him, his face battered, the nose broken. He was clutching a sawn-off shotgun. "There's him, Mr. Ryan, and you can see what he did to me."

He ran his hand over Miller, checked the pockets. "Nothing, Mr. Ryan." He slapped Miller across the face. "Who are you?"

"More important, what are you?" Ryan said. "All that clever unarmed-combat stuff."

"Maybe he's SAS," Flannery said.

"Whatever he is, through the side door of the pub with him

and down to the cellars, where he'll talk fast enough. I've got my cutters with me."

Flannery jammed his sawn-off in Miller's back and urged him to the pub, and Ryan followed.

INSIDE, flattened against the wall by the open door, Bridget had heard everything and was terrified. That bad things happened was a way of life in Belfast, but Sharkey solved it for her, following the young woman he'd been talking to out of the chapel. He was still wearing his violet stole from confession.

"Good night to you," he told the woman, who brushed past Bridget and went out.

Sharkey was smiling as he came to Bridget, but he stopped when he saw her face. "What is it, girl?"

"It's Mr. Blunt," she said. "Mr. Fallon isn't called that at all. His real name is Ryan, and he and Flannery have taken Mr. Blunt down to the cellars next door. I believe something terrible is going to happen to him."

"Well, we can't have that, can we?" Sharkey's face was completely calm. He opened the sacristy door, led her inside. "Sit down, there's a good girl."

She did as she was told, and he put a Gladstone bag on the table, took out a Walther, and quickly fitted a silencer on the end. He slipped it into the right-hand pocket of his cassock with another magazine.

"Stay there, my darling, and don't tell a soul."

"But what are you going to do?"

"As a priest, I would say I'm about God's work, but all is not what it seems."

He hurried out, through into the chapel, got the door open to the crypt, found the lantern, and descended.

MILLER, forced down the stairs, found Dolan waiting at the open door at the bottom, holding a Browning. He slapped Miller across the face and shoved him into the cellar where Kelly waited by the table. Ryan entered, tearing at his face, ripping away the bandages and plaster of Paris. "Christ, am I glad to be rid of that stuff. It's been hell. Sit him down."

He removed his raincoat and took out a cloth bundle and unwrapped it, revealing bolt cutters and a pair of pliers. He sat opposite Miller, such an ordinary-looking little man who was, in fact, a monster. There was still the sickly-sweet smell to him.

Miller flinched in spite of himself, and Ryan said, "You like the way I smell? I didn't. The wrong kind of perfume, but it was essential, you see, to smell that way. That's what I told the Paki doctor I used to prepare my file and the medical notes. Everything had to be right, and it even fooled the mother superior. The truly good are so easy."

"The doctor? You killed him?" Miller said.

"Now, how would you be knowing that? You're quite right. He ended up in a canning factory in South Armagh."

"Well, he would, wouldn't he, after being stupid enough to trust a creature like you."

He leaned on the table on his left arm and eased down his right hand, trying to find the butt of the Colt. Ryan said cheerfully, "There's the bolt cutter, they're for fingers, then the pliers for fingernails. You can take your choice. Hold his arms, boys," and Dolan and Flannery did, which was exactly the moment that Sharkey, having eased back the bolts on the other side of the door, hurled it open and came through, the Walther extended.

He shot Dolan in the side of the head and Kelly in the throat, and as the hands slipped from him, Miller found the Colt, pulled it out of the ankle holster, and shot Ryan between the eyes, the hollow-point bullet penetrating the skull so that the back disintegrated and the force hurled Ryan backward in his chair. Flannery turned in a panic, making for the door, and Sharkey shot him twice in the back, then leaned over to Kelly, who was choking, and finished him off with a head shot. The silenced weapons had made only the usual muted sounds, but suddenly through the ceiling there was the sound of stamping feet and shouted commands.

"Would you happen to know who that would be?" Sharkey demanded.

"SAS retrieval squad. They might have expected to find me dead."

"Well, you're not, and as I just saved your life, you owe me, so let's get out of here."

He turned and went through the door, and Miller went after him and shot the bolts. They started through toward the crypt. "They're bound to hit the priory—they knew I was there."

Sharkey turned, holding the lantern. "You can go that way if you want, and no hard feelings, but I've got my own exit."

He turned to the far corner, where it was dark and wet. There was an old Victorian manhole cover, and when he removed it, the smell was powerful and yet Miller made an instant decision.

"I'm with you."

"Then down you go."

Miller descended a steel ladder and Sharkey followed, pulling the manhole cover over his head. Miller found the tunnel so small he had to crouch, but emerged on the bank of a large tunnel, a brown stream coursing through it.

"The main sewer," Sharkey told him. "Don't worry, we'll pass right through all the Protestant shit from the Shankhill and come up in the Ardoyne."

They emerged some time later behind a wall on a factory yard. It was still raining, and fog crouched at the end of the street.

"Quite a show," Miller said. "How did all that happen?"

"It was dear little Bridget. She saw Ryan and Flannery lift you, heard everything."

"God bless her indeed. Where are we?"

"The Ardoyne, all friends here."

"You mean your kind of friends?"

"And who would that be?"

"Oh, the sort of people who found Liam Ryan a bad advertisement for the Republican movement, and a chief of staff who called in a top enforcer to take care of things."

"And that would be me?"

"Well, you're no priest, that's for sure, but you gave a good performance as one."

"Funny you should say that. I used to be an actor, then I gave it up for the theater of the street when the Troubles started."

"No chance of your name?"

"Which one? It certainly isn't Martin Sharkey, any more than yours is Mark Blunt. Who are you with?"

"Intelligence Corps."

"I didn't think you were SAS. Too clever by half. Turn round, walk straight down two hundred yards, and you'll find the main road into the town center if you're lucky. I'm away now. One piece of advice. Make sure you're playing the game in future and it isn't playing you."

He walked away, and so did Miller. After a while, he turned to look, but there was no sign of the man he'd known as Martin Sharkey, only the fog at the end of the street. It was as if he'd never been.

London

Washington

6

The meeting in the Prime Minister's study at Downing Street was composed of Ferguson, Simon Carter, and Harry Miller. At the Prime Minister's request, Ferguson had provided a breakdown of his department's activities in the previous couple of months, and Carter and Miller had both been provided with copies.

"I'm impressed with the way you and your people handled this Rashid affair," said the Prime Minister. "The Hammer of God—such a theatrical title! But responsible for so many deaths. Excellent work, General." He turned to Carter. "Wouldn't you agree?"

"The outcome of the whole affair was reasonably satisfactory," said Carter, "although I still find it difficult to accept the actions of Dillon and the Salters."

"It would appear they got the job done," the Prime Minister said mildly.

"Of course, Prime Minister, but there are loose ends," Carter told him.

Oddly enough, it was Miller who spoke up. "I've read the report, and I think it quite excellent. What loose ends?"

"The leader of this Army of God we discovered in London, Professor Drecq Khan—he could have been apprehended, but instead I understand the Salters allowed him to flee the country."

"General?" the Prime Minister asked.

"Khan gave us important information that was crucial to the successful completion of the whole operation—and he's no good to us in a prison cell. We know exactly where he is—in Beirut—and we have people watching him. I assure you, Prime Minister, we'll know his next move before he does. He's the gift that keeps on giving."

"And this man the Broker, the mystery man who gives him orders?" the Prime Minister said.

Carter cut in. "You don't seem to be any closer to discovering his identity."

"But we do know a lot more about his associates now."

Again, Miller cut in. "And we know that he deals at the very highest level of Russian intelligence—with General Ivan Volkov."

"Which is as close as one can get to President Putin," the Prime Minister remarked. "No, I think it's an excellent result, General. And I assume thc two of you have now discussed liaising as appropriate?" He glanced at Miller.

"Absolutely."

The Prime Minister turned to Carter. "All right, Simon?"

"As always, you have my full support."

"Good." The Prime Minister turned to Miller. "There's a meeting at the United Nations tomorrow that I can't go to. I'd like you to attend on my behalf, and President Cazalet would like you to call in and see him in Washington on the way back. My staff will give you the details." He grinned. "Sorry if it disturbs your social life."

"No problem, Prime Minister."

They departed and went downstairs. As they went out of the door to Ferguson's Daimler, Carter said softly, "Watch yourself with this man, Major, he could get you into trouble."

"Oh, I think I'm a big boy now," Miller told him.

Ferguson said, "Can I give you a lift, Simon?"

"No, thank you, Charles, it would be a lift with the devil. I'll walk." He started down to the security gates.

"Miserable sod, always was," Ferguson said. "And all those years sitting behind a desk haven't improved him. What about lunch? Are you up for it?"

"My pleasure."

"Dillon and Roper were intending to take a break at the Dark Man. Let's join them. It would give you a chance to get to know them better and meet the Salters, and for me to tell everybody what a hell of a job we did on the Rashid affair."

"Well, you did." Miller followed him into the Daimler. "You have some remarkable people on your team."

They drove out of the security gates into Whitehall. Ferguson said, "Yes, well, you've done some pretty remarkable things yourself. Roper showed me your original report on your trip to Belfast in 1986." He shook his head. "Dillon as a priest." He chuckled. "Always the actor. I spoke to him late last night and he filled in even more."

"It was an excellent performance."

Ferguson said carefully, "But not for you, I think."

"Not a performance at all, I'm afraid. I surprised myself, but it was the start of something. Nothing was ever the same after that."

His face was bleak, a hint of sadness there as they turned onto Cable Wharf and stopped at the Dark Man in time to see Dillon standing by the van and Doyle off-loading Roper.

"Out we get," Ferguson told him. "At least you're amongst friends here, I can guarantee that."

RETURNING FROM LUNCH IN MOSCOW, Volkov found some interesting trace material on his desk fresh from the computer department, which constantly searched for VIP travel information. Miller was on his way to New York, and then to Washington, he noted. He was staying one night at the Hay-Adams Hotel—which likely meant a visit to the White House.

He sat there thinking about it. Miller's actions in Kosovo

had been unacceptable, a direct attack on the Russian State. A rough town at night, Washington. Muggings, street crimes . . . it was too good a chance to miss. He called the Broker.

MICHAEL QUINN was in his early fifties, powerful, well-dressed, the head of Scamrock Security in Dublin. He offered expertise in the field of international private security, which was a multimillion-pound business, especially since the advent of the Iraq war. In his day, he'd been Chief of Staff of the Provisional IRA, and now was exactly the right man to provide mercenaries and security men of every description, men with their skills honed by service in the Provisional IRA over more than thirty years of the Troubles, men who didn't know what to do with themselves after the peace settlement in Northern Ireland. When he answered his phone and found the Broker at the other end, he was immediately excited.

"What can I do for you?" he asked.

And the Broker told him, emphasizing that it came from General Volkov, who was very good to Quinn in the past, even arranging for him to take charge of security for Belov International. "Can this be arranged?"

"No problem. I've got a good friend from the old days, Tod Kelly, who has a sizable operation in Washington. Everything from drugs to protection and most things in between. Tell General Volkov I'll arrange it. My gift to him."

AT HIS HOUSE IN GEORGETOWN, Tod Kelly was checking his accountant's entry book when the phone rang. He'd worked under Quinn in Londonderry at the height of the Troubles and was delighted to hear from him. He listened patiently while Quinn explained in detail.

"No problem."

"It's of real importance, from a special client, so no slipups."

"Anyone I would know, this client?"

"He's strictly a middleman—a broker, you could say."

"Consider it done."

OLIVIA ARRIVED HOME to shower and change around four-thirty and found Miller packing. "What on earth's going on?" she demanded.

"Sorry, love, it's New York for me. The Prime Minister wants me to sit in on a meeting tomorrow at the United Nations."

"He's really piling it on with you these days. What time do you have to be at Heathrow?"

"I'm not going from Heathrow. I'm flying from Farley Field."

"Where on earth is that?"

"Oh, it's a private field, VIPs in and out, that sort of thing. I'm going by Gulfstream."

"Who with?"

"Just me."

"In a Gulfstream?" She was amazed. "Harry, what's going on?"

"I'm standing in for the PM at the United Nations tomorrow, so they want to make sure I get there safely, that's all."

"So you'll be back tomorrow night?"

"No. I've got to stop off in Washington to see the President."

"Cazalet? What for?"

"That's an unanswerable question, my love."

She shook her head and looked so unhappy. "Harry, somehow you're drifting away from me. I'm left on the shore waving good-bye."

He laughed out loud. "What a performance. You're such a wonderful actress, and you know I'm your greatest fan. Now, I've got to go. You probably noticed Ellis waiting downstairs for me in the Merc. After he drops me at Farley, I've told him to come straight back here and he's yours to command until

I'm back." He kissed her. "God bless," and then he grabbed his traveling bag and a dark raincoat and was gone.

She sat there for a moment, shaking her head and feeling pushed to one side. "Oh, Harry," she said softly. "What's happening to you?"

IT WAS RAINING HARD in Washington that Friday night. Tod Kelly waited in an ordinary black Ford sedan across from the Hay-Adams Hotel. Kelly was well-dressed in an expensive gray flannel suit because he'd been inside the hotel itself earlier. He'd seen Miller arrive, sign in, and then go up to his room, after greeting the doorman cheerfully. Surprisingly, the doorman had addressed him as "Major," although doormen, when you thought of it, made it their business to know who their customers were.

Next to Kelly was a passenger, a bruiser named Regan from one of his clubs, dressed roughly in boots, jeans, a black leather bomber jacket, and a dark tweed cap. He was pulling on black leather gloves with some sort of studs in the knuckles.

"What do you intend to do, kill him?" Kelly joked.

"I thought that was the idea."

"I don't want it to look like it was premeditated," Kelly told him. "It should look like it could have happened to anybody, just another tragic mugging. Take his wallet, cards, watch, mobile—everything."

"What if he doesn't walk? Maybe he gets a taxi."

"I heard him ask how long it took to walk to the White House from the hotel. The doorman said it was raining and Miller said he liked the rain, it would freshen him up and clear his head and he'd been traveling too long."

At that moment, Miller appeared in the hotel entrance. The doorman said, "I thought you'd at least like a hotel umbrella, Major."

"That's kind. What was your war?"

"Vietnam, infantry sergeant, best forgotten. If I may say so, muggers have been known to frequent even this neighborhood."

"Oh, I'll be all right." Miller gestured across to the lights of the White House. "I've an appointment with the President."

"You mean that, Major?"

"As you say in America, I sure do." He went down the steps, and on the other side, Kelly started the engine of the sedan and said, "Out you get, and hurry. Get well ahead. I'll drive round to the other side and wait for you."

He drove away, and Regan dodged into the darkness, moving fast. Miller walked toward the statue of President Andrew Jackson and paused, ostensibly looking at it. He had excellent vision coupled with a trained eye, and all those years in and out of Northern Ireland had left an indelible mark. Everywhere was like a crime scene, everything and everybody had to have a reason for being there. He'd noted Tod Kelly when he entered the hotel because he was interesting, a certain kind of man. Just now, standing talking to the doorman, Miller had looked across, alerted by the car suddenly starting up, recognized Kelly behind the wheel, and had even sensed the figure of Regan jumping out and vanishing into the dark.

It was a skill, honed over the years, the thing that had kept him alive for so long. As Dillon had said all those long years ago, you always had to make sure the game wasn't playing you, that you were playing the game.

He lowered the umbrella, rolled it tightly and fastened it, then suddenly he slipped away from the park, through the bushes and trees, making his way to the other side, the rush of the falling rain hiding any sound of movement.

Regan was totally outfoxed. He waited behind a tree, looking back toward Andrew Jackson, and started to worry. Perhaps Miller had slipped into another path. He felt for the backup in the waist of his jeans at the rear, the one he hadn't mentioned to Kelly, a short-barreled Smith & Wesson that used to be known as a Banker's Special in the trade. He held it ready in his right hand as he moved to the edge of the trees and paused. Miller simply stepped in behind him and rammed the end of the umbrella into his spine.

"I wouldn't move if I were you." Regan froze, and Miller reached over and relieved him of the Smith & Wesson. "That's better. A little old-fashioned, but it does the job, I'm sure." Regan started to move. "No, don't turn round, I told you. Who are you working for?"

"Go fuck yourself."

"An impossibility. Now you have two choices. If you don't tell me what I want to know, I'll stick the barrel in the back of your knee and blow it off. I'm not calling the police, I wouldn't waste my time, I'll just leave you screaming your head off and walk away. No? All right, here we go." There was a distinctive click as he cocked the weapon.

Regan said, "Jesus, no—I work for Tod Kelly."

"And he was the man with you in the black Ford sedan?"

"Yes."

"What did he tell you about me?"

"That you were English, you were named Miller, and he was doing a big favor for a friend who wanted you dead."

"And who would that be?"

"I haven't the slightest idea." Bitterness overflowed. "You could always ask him yourself. He's supposed to pick me up on this side of the square."

It was so obviously true that Miller didn't even argue. He slammed the Smith & Wesson with brutal force into the nape of Regan's neck, sending him down, first on his knees, then headfirst into the bushes. There was no railing at that point, and keeping out of sight in the trees, Miller waited. The Ford sedan coasted by slowly and pulled in at the curb. Miller kept to the trees on his approach, moving fast once he got behind the vehicle, and at the last minute wrenching the passenger door open and sliding in.

"Harry Miller, and you'd be Tod Kelly."

The usual bluster began. "What the hell is this?"

"Shut up. I've left your friend back there in the bushes in a poor way. He tried to pull a gun on me, would you believe that, but as you can see, I have the gun now. Your chum told me you were doing a favor for someone, so tell me all about it."

"Like hell I will."

"From the sound of you, you hail from Belfast, Mr. Kelly, so let me tell you I've eaten the IRA for breakfast in that city in my time, so you'll know what this means." He rammed the barrel of the Smith & Wesson into the side of Kelly's right knee. "I'll try one, and if that doesn't work, the other."

Kelly, experienced by years of the Irish Troubles, knew a real pro when he saw one. "Michael Quinn, Scamrock Securities, Dublin. I worked under him in Derry in the old days. He called in a favor for a friend. He wanted you to meet with a nasty accident."

"Who was this friend?"

"I asked him if it was anyone I'd know and he said the guy was strictly a middleman. Some kind of broker." There was a pause. "Are you going to shoot me or can I go?"

So Miller did the former, the bullet plowing through the fleshy part of the leg, just behind the kneecap. Kelly groaned and clenched his teeth. "Damn you, it's the truth."

"I think it is. If it wasn't, I'd have really done some damage." He took out a pack of cigarettes, lit one, and put it between Kelly's lips. "Derry in the old days. Better than this. Drugs, prohibition, anything to turn a pound. Where did it all go, Tod?"

"We lost the war and bastards like you won it."

"Did we? I'm not so sure."

"Just fuck off and leave me to call an ambulance."

WHICH MILLER DID, using his Codex to call Holland Park, and was instantly in the hands of Roper.

"Hey, eight o'clock on a dark evening in Washington, I'd say, and raining from the weather report. How are you, Harry?"

"Listen and learn, my friend."

He stood by a tree, his umbrella raised, and gave Roper the details. When he had finished, Roper said, "Here's the thing about Quinn. As head of Scamrock, he's responsible for all security at Belov International, and Volkov's been acting CEO of Belov while Max Chekhov is recovering. So our mystery man, the Broker, has handled the deal, obviously on behalf of Volkov. You've annoyed them, Harry."

"Kosovo?"

"Probably. I'll discuss this with Ferguson. Where exactly are you?"

"Walking along East Executive Avenue."

"Take care. I'll call Blake."

Miller stayed where he was, lighting a cigarette. Volkov? That was interesting. A Russian dimension.

A Chrysler sedan swept up beside him almost noiselessly ten minutes later, and a fit-looking black man in a good suit got out of the passenger seat. Miller noted that the driver had an automatic weapon on his knees.

"Major Miller? I hear you've had some trouble. Clancy Smith. I'm Secret Service, assigned to the President."

"Well, trouble there certainly was. I was foolish enough to walk from the Hay-Adams. Stupid, I suppose, muggers and so on."

"Major Roper indicated there was more to it than that."

"Yes, I did have to shoot somebody."

"So I understand." Way back down the road there was an ambulance by the Ford.

"There's also a man in a bad way in the bushes."

"It's all in hand, Major, not a police matter. If you care to get in, the President's waiting for you. He was quite concerned."

"No need." Miller got into the rear.

"No, Major, I can see that."

Clancy got in the front and nodded to the driver, who carried on to the East Entrance, the best way into the White House if you didn't want to draw attention. They were waved through the gate. From then on, it was smooth sailing. Clancy escorted him through many corridors until Miller finally found himself in the Oval Office, where he discovered the President in his shirtsleeves at his desk, receiving a line of documents to sign from Blake Johnson.

"Great to see you again, Harry," Blake said. "Trouble just seems to follow you around."

IT WAS ALL VERY PRIVATE. Cazalet and Blake sat on one side of the large coffee table, Miller on the other. Nobody else had been allowed in except Clancy, who saw to the drinks.

"The fascinating thing about the whole affair is the involvement of this man, the Broker, and his link with Volkov," said the President.

"And whenever you mention Volkov's name, you include Putin himself," added Blake.

"Your meeting at the UN yesterday—what did you make of it?"

"Russia seems to be everywhere, involved in other countries' affairs."

"Well, we do that," Cazalet told him.

"Not like this. Take that audacious raid by Israeli F-15s on the Syrian target suspected of containing nuclear equipment. Syrian air defenses are pretty formidable and yet the Israelis succeeded in penetrating them. So what are the Russians busy doing? Improving Syrian air defenses for them."

"It's all about things fitting together," Blake put in. "Take our little jaunt in Kosovo, the business of Captain Igor Zorin and the Fifteenth Siberian Storm Guards. Okay, these were only at patrol level, but they were a unit from a crack special forces outfit which shouldn't have been there at all."

"And whose purpose was to stir the pot," Miller put in.

"That's what I mean, just bits and pieces a lot of the time, but it could all be part of a general plan. Putin's proven himself at the sharp end of war, he's a thoroughly able leader, and he's an old-fashioned patriot. I believe he wants to see Russia back where he thinks she deserves to be—as a major power."

"Back to the Cold War?"

"But not with nuclear submarines this time, but oil and gas pipelines. Gas from Siberia now crawls across northern Europe all the way to Scandinavia and Scotland."

Blake said, "Come to depend on it too much and it's a powerful weapon in an argument. All somebody has to do is threaten to turn the tap and switch it off."

There was an even deeper silence. Cazalet said, "Major, how are things in London these days with the Russians?"

"At the moment, they have over sixty diplomats accredited

to the embassy, trade missions and so on. We reckon thirty have an intelligence link. It used to be their interests were only in political or military secrets, but the popularity of London as a destination, even as a residence, has grown so enormously that the oligarchs and Russian millionaires have distorted the housing market as well. The traditional British open-doors policy has also attracted dissidents."

"And, of course, dissidents require investigation by Russia," Blake put in. "In the old days, it would have been KGB, now it's SVR."

"And to a certain extent we have our own problems here in Washington," Cazalet said.

"With the greatest respect, Mr. President, the British situation is unique. We've even had the odd murder or two, notorious dissidents meeting accidental deaths."

"And you think SVR assassins are responsible?" Cazalet said.

"Actually, I don't—because I believe Volkov is behind them, and he's GRU."

"Russian Military Intelligence," Cazalet said.

Miller nodded. "The GRU has six times as many agents operating in foreign countries as the SVR. They even control the activities of the Spetsnaz and they're as good a special forces outfit as you'd find anywhere in the world—Lenin created them, you know."

"Lenin?" Cazalet nodded. "I never knew that. Strange how his name still resonates."

"I did a special study of him when I was at Sandhurst," Miller told him. "The purpose of terrorism is to terrorize, that's what he said—it's the only way in which a small country can take on an empire with any hope. Remember the British being taken on by the original IRA in 1920, led by Michael Collins? It was his favorite saying."

"A bad idea for all of us," Cazalet said. "But it surely tells us something about the world of today. We're fighting a war, gentlemen, a war against terrorism, a war we can't afford to lose, or the whole of civilization faces a return to the Dark Ages."

"Amen to that," Blake said.

"So, Major, I understand you're now corresponding with Charles Ferguson and his people."

"I look forward to it, Mr. President."

"I couldn't be better pleased, because it means coming on board with us from time to time, and working with Blake and the Basement. You're aware of what that is?"

"It's been explained, Mr. President."

Blake said, "Great, Harry, and remember our motto. The rules are that there are no rules. In today's world, if we don't accept that, we might as well give in."

"Enough talk of business for now," Cazalet said. "I understand you came over on Ferguson's Gulfstream. That means his pilots, Squadron Leader Lacey and Flight Lieutenant Parry, are here. I hear they both wear a ribbon for the Air Force Cross these days."

"With a rosette, Mr. President. They're staying at the Hay-Adams, too."

"Wonderful. I have a weakness for heroes. Blake has already booked us a table for late dinner at the Hay-Adams, and Lacey and Parry can join us."

IT WAS A MEMORABLE evening indeed, and the following morning Miller was reading the papers in the plane when Parry entered the cabin.

"If there's anything you want, Major, we have it in the kitchen area. The Yanks are always so generous."

"You enjoyed yourself last night, didn't you?"

"You don't need to ask. Thanks for arranging it all."

"I can't claim credit for that. The President wanted to meet you for himself."

"It was certainly something I'll never forget."

"What's our flight time?"

"There is some dicey weather ahead, but with luck we could manage Farley in, let's say, six hours."

"London time six in the evening. If I have my car waiting at Farley, there could be a decent chance of making my wife's evening performance at the Gielgud."

"With any luck, sir."

Alone again, Miller called his chauffeur, Ellis Vaughan, and found him waiting outside Harrods while Olivia and Monica were inside shopping. Ellis informed him that Olivia had booked him for herself and Monica for the evening performance.

Miller said, "Stick to your arrangement, Ellis, and don't tell her I've spoken to you. There's a chance I could surprise her."

"As you say, Major."

They were well over thirty thousand and climbing high over the Atlantic. Miller found his laptop, put it on the table in front of him, and started on his report for the Prime Minister. An hour later, Ferguson spoke to him.

"I understand you've shot somebody again."

"Couldn't be helped, I'm afraid."

"Is there any chance of a story reaching the press?"

"Absolutely not. The man I shot, and his henchman, were picked up quickly by the Secret Service. The police had no involvement."

"The Prime Minister and Simon Carter are worried about the media getting wind of it."

"They can't possibly. It never happened." He felt strangely impatient. "Listen, Charles, the Prime Minister's all right, but like any politician he worries too much. As for Carter, I've never rated him. He's an old woman fussing at the slightest thing. It's not just that he's the ultimate desk man, he has a problem. Every so often he gets drunk out of his skull, and nothing but venom, poison, and malice oozes out of him. He did it once when I was with him in the Reform Club at a dinner he'd persuaded me to have with him a couple of years ago. He was trying to curry favor because of my position with the Prime Minister. The character assassination he did on you and your organization was unforgivable. I wouldn't repeat it to you. No one was spared—Dillon, the Salters, details of confidential missions. I simply walked out on him."

Ferguson said, "I'm well aware of his hatred for me, always have, but so what? I work with him when I have to. Better the devil you know."

"I suppose so. If there was any leak to the media, it would probably be from here, but I don't think so. I'll see you soon."

He switched off and returned to his report.

AS FOR THE THEATER, he made it with half an hour to spare. He greeted Ellis, who was reading the *Evening Standard* in the Mercedes parked outside, patted Marcus on the head, and with one brisk knock on the dressing room door, he went inside to find Olivia seated at the mirror applying makeup, Monica at her side, just like last time. They both expressed enthusiasm to a certain degree, but it was all rather flat in some indefinable way, and he finally found himself next to Monica in the same seats as the first night. Even the play didn't seem quite what it had been.

At the restaurant afterward, they had champagne and Monica tried to be cheerful. "Come on, what was it like? The UN, then Washington in your own Gulfstream? Tell us about it!"

"I had to sit on a committee meeting on behalf of the Prime Minister—no big deal."

"And Washington? What was that all about? Did you really see the President?

"In the Oval Office in the White House, and we had dinner. He's a great man, everything they say."

"So what was it all about? What happened?"

Miller shrugged. "I can't tell you that—it was confidential."

Olivia, who had been silently toying with her food, suddenly had a minor explosion. "For God's sake, Harry, all of a sudden you're Mr. Big, flying off in your fancy plane to see the President, but we little nobodies, we're nothing, God knows we're not important enough to be told anything! Maybe life as a politician has gone to your head."

"You could be right," he told her calmly, pushed back his chair, stood up, and said to Monica, "You pay, love, when you go, and I'll tell Ellis I'm walking, I could do with the air. I'll use the other spare bedroom for tonight. Get a good night's sleep, Olivia, I think you need it." He walked out.

A COUPLE OF HOURS LATER, after the house was quiet, he went down to the sitting room, poured himself a scotch from the drinks cabinet, lit a cigarette, and sat there in the dark with just the light from the street outside. In a strange way, he felt no emotion about what had happened, none at all.

There was the creak of a floorboard and Monica appeared in a dressing gown. "Do you want a drink?" he asked.

"No, I want you, Harry, my dearest brother, and I don't want what's just happened with Olivia to happen at all."

"The demands of the show, they're probably living on her nerves a bit." He shrugged. "She'll come round."

"Suddenly you're the mystery man, Harry. Where do you go, what do you do? Why this apparent elevation in your status?"

"I just did what the Prime Minister told me to do."

"But no story for us, for Olivia?"

"I'm sorry you and Olivia find my lack of explanation frustrating, but there it is."

"Top secret."

"Yes."

"You always were a bit of a self-dramatist."

"If you say so. I think I'll go back to bed now."

He went out. "Damn you, Harry," she said softly, stood looking at the drinks cabinet for a moment, and then went and poured herself a scotch.

Moscow

London

Beirut

7

QUINN RECEIVED A CODED E-MAIL FROM THE BROKER NOTing that the Gulfstream had landed at Farley Field with a perfectly healthy Harry Miller on board, demanding an explanation. There was no instant reply, and finally, after two days, Quinn phoned him.

"Tod Kelly left his house in Georgetown the night Miller was at the Hay-Adams Hotel," Quinn told him. "He had one of his best hit men with him, Jack Regan. Since then, they've gone missing."

"What is that supposed to mean?"

"Exactly that. They're not in police custody and discreet inquiries by contacts in the police can't find any sign of them. Hospitals, morgues, they've all been tried without success. They've vanished without a trace."

"Which can only mean one thing," the Broker told him. "They've been sorted out in some way."

"This isn't going to look good to Volkov," Quinn said. "I'm supposed to provide security for the whole of Belov International, and this happens."

The Broker surprised him by coming in on his side. "You

did your job. It's Kelly who failed. Miller must have been onto him. I'll tell Volkov that."

Which he did, but Volkov didn't seem as upset as he expected. "Miller can wait until another time. I was going to contact you anyway about something else."

"What's that?"

"Something's just landed on my desk. This is absolute top security. According to a reasonably reliable source, the North Koreans are transporting plutonium-239 to Syria, possibly in some old freighter called the *Valentine*. This could just be a rumor."

"Plain talk here. Are you involved?"

"Absolutely not, and with some delicate international negotiations going on right now, we can't be seen as seeming like we are."

"I can see your point, but the truth is it would suit you very well if this consignment reached Syria."

"Perhaps, but we can't have any direct involvement in the matter, and the Syrians, which means the Iranians, just don't tell us enough. If we know that plutonium had actually gotten through to them, it'd strengthen our hand in the whole nuclear game we're playing. And as for the North Koreans—those awkward sods go their own way and give us the cold shoulder."

"When, in a way, you wish them well and hope the whole thing is a success?"

"Something like that," Volkov admitted. "To be frank, it would be nice to see the plutonium get through, if only because it would give the Israelis a black eye."

"Well, using some battered old freighter to deliver imported goods has worked many times before, the slow-boat ploy," the Broker said.

"Yes, but there are a lot of boats out there from North Africa, passing off the coast of Lebanon, plowing onward to Syria, ending up in Latakia. This *Valentine* will be only one of many."

"So what do you want me to do?" the Broker asked.

"This man of yours, Drecq Khan, he ended up in Beirut, didn't he?"

"Yes."

"Tell Khan to ask around and see what he can turn up. I'll send a couple of GRU agents from our embassy in Beirut to help in any way they can. And remember, we don't want the Israelis getting wind of it."

BEIRUT HAD ONCE been as popular as the South of France, a mecca for the rich, with casinos and hotels as fine as anywhere in the world. The population was a mixture of Christians, Muslims, and Druse, and then emergent Islamic nationalism had entered the equation and fighting had broken out in 1975 between the Christian Phalangist Party and the Muslim militia. In the thirty years since, death and destruction had virtually destroyed a country that had once been the pride of the Middle East, and the recent brief invasion by the Israelis and the battle with the forces of Hezbollah hadn't helped.

But life went on, and Professor Drecq Khan, in exile from London, sat in the study of the old French villa overlooking the harbor from which he ran the affairs of the Army of God and its side organization, the Brotherhood.

Khan had once been very respected in London, a member of all sorts of interfaith committees in Parliament and at the United Nations, but then his terrorist activities had been revealed, and—well, he still shuddered at the thought of Harry Salter's stern warning that if he ever returned to London he'd be dead in a week.

A terrible pity, because he'd liked London better than anywhere else on earth. Now he was here in Beirut, the wreck of a city it had once been, the recent Israeli invasion and war with Hezbollah having made certain of that. So he sat in the old villa with four Muslim servants and hated it. The only thing he wasn't short of was money, Al Qaeda saw to that, so he was able to administer to the various branches of the Army of God, or rather his accountant did.

This was Henri Considine, of French-Lebanese extraction, a Christian from a family once important in the Phalangist

Party who had suffered like many others from one civil war after another. He was in his fifties, his house badly damaged in the Israeli invasion, his wife a victim of the bombing. There seemed little left to live for, then the administration job had come up with Drecq Khan. The pay was poor and his Christianity was just about tolerated, but he was allowed a room downstairs because Khan was hopeless at handling accounts.

Considine was in the next room to Khan now, working away, the door slightly ajar, when the phone rang. Khan had a habit of keeping it on speaker, and Considine heard every word.

"It's the Broker. How are you, Khan?"

It was common for Considine to scribble down what he heard, because often what was said was then put on his plate to handle. He'd learned shorthand in his youth, so it was easy to catch whole conversations.

"How are things there?"

"Dreadful. The place is a wreck, and there's been nothing but killing since. I curse the day General Charles Ferguson and his people entered my life."

"At least you are alive."

"Not if I go back to London. What is this? What do you want?"

"Listen carefully. There is a rumor the North Koreans are transporting plutonium-239 to Syria in some old freighter supposedly called the *Valentine*. Volkov will arrange for a couple of GRU agents from the Embassy to give you any assistance you want. It's important for Volkov to know if there really is such a ship out there."

"But what for? You've said it's only a rumor."

"Rumor is one thing, but this ship actually reaching Latakia with the plutonium is another. If that happens, Volkov wants to know. Anything heading for Syria would be passing through Lebanese waters, so make inquiries, talk to sailors, fishermen. Make it known that you're looking for news of a boat called the *Valentine*. It's important. Put some of Osama's money to good use."

"If you say so." Drecq sat for a moment after he had switched off, then decided to go down into town to the hiring hall used by Army of God headquarters. "I'm going out," he called to Considine, and departed.

Considine sat thinking about it, particularly the reference to London and this General Charles Ferguson, and the dread Osama. And then he remembered something—the Café Albert, where he was still able to afford a drink because his boyhood friend, Alphonse, was the owner. An Englishman always sat in the corner table, according to Alphonse, and he was the military attaché from the British Embassy. Maybe he would find such a story of interest. Perhaps there could even be the chance of a visa to England for Henri Considine? He was almost running as he went out the door.

CAPTAIN DAVID STAGG was in Beirut at the Embassy, and not somewhere like Afghanistan, because that was exactly where he'd been a year before with 3 Para. His leadership of a ferocious charge had sent him home with a bullet in the left hip that had left him with a permanent limp. But his appointment as a military attaché to the Embassy in Beirut had been a blessing. There was plenty going on and he liked the buzz. He was sitting at his usual table in Café Albert, reading a two-day-old copy of the *Times* and enjoying a large gin and tonic, when Henri approached.

Henri's English was excellent, and as he fingered his old Panama, he said, "Excuse me, Captain, but can we talk?"

"Not if you're trying to sell something."

Considine said, "In a strange way, I suppose I am. For what I could tell you, a British visa would be greatly rewarding."

Stagg laughed. "I'm sure it would."

Suddenly, it all seemed futile. "I'm sorry I've bothered you." He sounded incredibly sad, started to turn away, then swung around and said with some violence, "Unless the name of General Charles Ferguson means anything to you."

Stagg had raised his glass and was drinking. Now he put it

down. He had stopped smiling and looked extremely alert. "As it happens, it does. I suggest you sit and tell me what this is all about and who you are."

"You know of Professor Drecq Khan?"

"The Army of God man?"

"I'm his administrator, although I'm not a Muslim. I overheard a strange story on his speakerphone. If I may?"

There was a large wine list on the table. Considine sat down, turned it over, took out his shorthand notebook, and copied out the conversation. Stagg read it, frowning.

"Does it make sense to you, sir?"

"General Charles Ferguson certainly does, and I suspect the rest will to him." He got up. "Come on, I want to get back to the Embassy as soon as possible."

Stagg's call to Ferguson was patched through to the Holland Park safe house, where he was in the computer room with Roper, Miller, and Dillon, discussing what had happened to Miller in Washington and the implications.

"Major Giles Roper speaking. Who is this?"

"Captain David Stagg, Military Attaché at the Beirut Embassy. It's essential I contact General Ferguson."

"Why?" Roper had flicked on the speaker facility anyway.

"Because I've been presented with a story that's so wild I suspect it could actually be true."

The moment Stagg had given Roper his name, his identity had been processed by Roper's computer and it was all there: 3 Para, the Iraq War, the bloody tour in Afghanistan that had effectively ended his army career, albeit with a Military Cross.

"Ferguson speaking," the General said. "How do you know me?"

"Five years ago, my last month at Sandhurst, you gave a lecture in which your thesis was that the forces of terrorism had actually declared war on us and we had to act accordingly."

"I remember it well, and I expect that after 3 Para and Afghanistan, you'll agree with me."

"Totally, sir."

"So get on with it, then, what have you got?"

Stagg told him.

When he was finished, Ferguson said, "You did right. This is an affair of the utmost seriousness. Drecq Khan—do you know him?"

"No, sir, but I've heard of him. The chap I took over from left a file on him, pointing out his London connection, but making it clear he was no longer welcome."

"And Considine's connection with him?"

"To start off with, he's French Lebanese, a Christian, and he's an accountant who does the books for Khan, lost everything in the war, including his wife."

"Right. This is what I want you to do. Call me back in an hour. Have you told the Ambassador about this matter?"

"No, General, he's on two weeks' leave in Switzerland."

"Excellent. Don't say a word to anyone. Carry out your usual duties, but you now belong to me. Considine will be essential to what I have in mind. Make sure he's up for it."

"He's that, all right, sir. He's hoping he might get his English visa out of this."

"Cheap at the price. We'll speak again in an hour."

ROPER SAID, "This old freighter, the *Valentine*—I can put out a search for such a ship, but the problem with vessels like that is false identity. I know cases of these old contraband rust buckets changing their name three or four times over the years."

"I accept that," Ferguson said, "I also accept the rumor could be false, but it's worth finding out because of the connections with Drecq Khan and the Broker."

"In a way, Considine is the most important player," Miller said. "Your eyes and ears."

"As long as he's willing to play spy," Dillon put in. "He's going to have the two GRU agents hanging around the place."

Ferguson nodded. "Obviously, I like to have someone on

the ground." He turned to Dillon. "You're no good, Sean, Drecq Khan knows you too well."

"And that's a fact, and he knows Billy and Harry even better. They were the ones who put Khan through the wringer."

"Which only leaves me," Harry Miller said.

"Impossible." Ferguson shook his head.

"Why not? I'll go as myself, acting for the Prime Minister. In fact, I already did it just after the Israelis withdrew from Lebanon, as part of a United Nations committee."

"I didn't know that," Ferguson said.

"Believe me, Charles, even my wife didn't know. I was supposed to be in Germany. I was only away five days. Even Carter and MI6 didn't know until after it was all over."

"It must have been unpleasant," Dillon said.

"That's one way of describing it. I'm still a member of the committee. We'll both speak to the Prime Minister, Charles, it will work, I promise you."

Roper said, "You really don't have any choice, General. Volkov knows who Harry really is, but nobody can argue with his status."

Miller said, "An under secretary of state on a fact-finding tour representing the British Prime Minister. We could sort out the details today and I'll go tomorrow."

"All right, you're on," Ferguson said. "We'll see the Prime Minister together. And we're in luck—we don't need to have that bastard Simon Carter in on the discussion."

"Why, what's he up to?"

"He sits on the UN Security Committee for Central America. He left yesterday for Honduras. Let's get moving." As they moved out, he said to Roper, "Take Stagg's call and fill him in."

He and Miller went out quickly, and Dillon reached for the scotch and poured a couple, handing one to Roper.

"What do you think?" Roper asked.

"Harry Miller? We've seen what he's capable of."

"But is that enough?"

"I know where we could get a little help. I've been in Beirut twice in past years, and each time I had Mossad backing. There's a man named Cohen, General Arnold Cohen. He's the head of Section One, Activities in Arab Countries."

"Activities in Arab Countries." Roper smiled. "He sounds interesting." And then Stagg came through.

"What's happening, sir?"

"Can you confirm that Considine is willing to be involved all the way on this thing? It could be dangerous."

"Absolutely, sir, that visa is his prize. He'll do anything for it."

"Excellent. If things work according to plan, we're sending an MP tomorrow, Major Harry Miller, who has under secretary of state rank and is a member of a United Nations committee on Lebanon. He's been a troubleshooter for the Prime Minister in the past. His presence won't seem out of place, and you'll do exactly what he tells you."

"Of course, sir."

"He is, shall we say, capable of handling himself in highly charged situations. It brings out the soldier in him."

"I must say I like the sound of that, sir."

"Let me run through the whole thing again with you. . . ."

AN HOUR LATER, General Arnold Cohen was seated at his desk in the study of his Tel Aviv home when the phone rang.

"This is Sean Dillon, you old sod. Shalom."

"The Devil himself." Cohen was delighted, but also alert. "Still working for Charles Ferguson?"

"What else? What about that son of yours, busy as ever?"

He was referring to Lieutenant Colonel Gideon Cohen, a major field agent for Mossad.

"Okay, he's out and about, business as usual. Listen, Dillon, I heard what happened to Hannah Bernstein."

"Sorely missed," Dillon told him. "But I also hope you heard what happened to those responsible for her murder, Arnold. But we have a slight problem. I'm going to pass you over to Major Giles Roper, who you may know runs the Holland Park safe house for us. He'll explain."

"I'll be delighted. Major Roper's fame goes before him. What can I do for him?"

Roper intervened. "Well, this is what we've got, General."

When he was finished, Cohen said, "I'll be honest with you, Major, I know you have something of a genius for what you do, but I have some pretty damn good people working for me, too. I already knew that there was a lot more to Harry Miller than met the eye. This information about Volkov and the *Valentine* is interesting, though. Such rumors are relatively common in our experience, but it's certainly worth checking out."

"Can you assist in Beirut?"

"Yes, I do have someone on the ground."

"Can I have details?"

"No," Cohen said flatly. "My agent will be in touch with Miller when it suits him. We have to take great care these days. Beirut is no place for a Jew."

"I can imagine."

"Leave it with me. I'll be in touch as things happen."

"And I thank you."

LATER, Ferguson came on the speakerphone. "The Prime Minister has authorized it. I've okayed Lacey and Parry for the flight in the morning, using a Gulfstream bearing UN colors."

"Just to make it look official?"

"Of course."

"Something else for you." Roper told him about his conversation with Arnold Cohen.

"He and his people have always been totally reliable. If he says he has a man on the ground, he has a man on the ground. I'll call Harry about this, and you notify Stagg."

"I already have."

"There is one thing," Ferguson added. "Miller wants suitable weaponry supplied. Will you speak to the quartermaster about that?"

"Of course," Dillon said. "Leave it to me."

"And Roper," Ferguson carried on. "Let's keep as low a profile on this as possible. Miller's just making a routine trip for the PM."

"Shouldn't be too difficult." Roper shrugged. "It's pretty uninteresting to most people in the general scheme of things."

"I'll put it on a Code Three at Farley, so the department and destination aren't noted. We can't control the fact of his arrival in Beirut, but it would mean he isn't expected."

THINGS AT DOVER STREET had improved a certain amount. Olivia was deeply ashamed of the events in the restaurant in Shepherd's Market, and Monica had taken advantage of a mid-term vacation at Cambridge to stay on, hoping that her presence might help the situation.

Miller had business at Parliament and returned to Dover Street at about four o'clock, and discovered that Olivia and Monica had gone out in the Mini Cooper. He packed and everything was ready in his room.

Ellis, who was waiting outside, took him back to Downing Street, where he dropped him off. Later, at about five, he phoned Dover Street and Monica answered the phone.

"Are you coming to the play?" she asked.

"Sure, I've told Ellis to pick you up. I'll see you there. I'm busy at the Cabinet Office."

"What's the big flap?" his sister said. "If one's allowed to ask? Are we going to war somewhere else?"

"No, but I'm going to Beirut in the morning. I'll probably be away for a week, perhaps less. I won't know till I get there."

She was shocked. "Beirut? But what on earth for? All they seem to do is shoot each other."

"I'm a member of a UN committee on Lebanon, remember? I missed the last visit." Once again the lies, the deceit. "Anyway, things aren't looking too good and the PM wants me to give him a report."

"Olivia isn't going to like this."

"Monica, my sweet, that's just too bad. She's got her job, I've got mine. I'll see you at the theater and I've booked a restaurant afterwards."

Strange, the feeling of relief that coursed through him. The truth was he actually felt good about going to Beirut. He went and sat at his computer and got on with some work.

IN BEIRUT, two hours on, it was already into the evening, and Drecq Khan sat behind a desk at the hiring hall on the Beirut waterfront with one of the assistants, Abdul Mir. Many men waited patiently, squatting in the hall, seeking work, seamen among them.

"The word has gone out to many people," Abdul said. "It takes time, but there is a problem."

"And what would that be?"

"Captain Stagg, the Military Attaché from the British Embassy. It seems he's been doing the rounds himself, seeking information on a boat named the *Valentine*."

"Is that so?" Khan said.

Earlier in the day, two men in crumpled linen suits had approached him, Bikov and Torin, the GRU men from the Russian Embassy that Volkov had promised. They had slightly worried him, for Khan was meticulous about his appearance, and these were definitely men who preferred the unshaven look. They had been sitting at a street café outside for a couple of hours, and now he went out to them.

"Has something come up?" Torin asked.

"Perhaps. Do you know a man from the British Embassy named Stagg?"

"Sure we do. What's he up to?"

"Apparently, he's also seeking news of the *Valentine*."

"Is that a fact?" Bikov said. "Then we'll have to have words with him."

"Don't kill him," Khan said. "What I really want to know is how he's involved in this *Valentine* business in the first place."

"We'll treat him with all respect," Bikov said.

Torin added, "Then we'll kill him." He stood up and said, "Come on, Boris, I've heard he's at the Café Albert most nights."

They walked away. Khan watched them go, pushing through the crowded streets of the old town, shrugged, and went back inside the hall.

THE CAFÉ ALBERT wasn't crowded, but it would be later when the trio started playing. Stagg stood at one end of the bar, enjoying a large vodka tonic and a cigarette. He could see the door reflected in the mirror on the opposite wall, Torin and Bikov entering. Stagg's Russian was reasonable, thanks to Sandhurst, but he didn't need to use it. Torin and Bikov had served in London, he knew that well.

"Ah, the Brothers Grimm," he said as they approached. "What are you two up to?"

Torin nodded to the bartender, who poured two vodkas without being asked. "At least you drink good vodka, even though you kill it with tonic."

"Never mind that," Bikov said. "We want words, my friend."

"Ah, it's friend, is it?" Stagg asked.

"We're just wasting time here." Bikov gripped Stagg's left arm lightly. "We're taking a little walk outside, where you can tell us why you are so interested in a ship called the *Valentine*."

"So that's what all this is about?"

"Exactly, and you see the hand Ivan has in his pocket? I don't need to tell you he's prepared to put a bullet in your head."

"My arse he is." Stagg was actually laughing as they went out into the crowded street. "What a couple of clowns you are. So you're going to cut me down in a street as crowded as this?"

Torin said, "Life is cheap in Beirut."

"That line is so bad you must have got it from a B movie."

Bikov was enraged and raised his fist to strike, and as Stagg blocked it, an ancient Renault car parked across the street started up and nosed across, scattering people. The driver called, "Your cab, Captain Stagg." The driver got out, came around, and opened the passenger door. He wore a shabby linen suit and looked around fifty, with long black hair, a bush mustache, and olive skin. "Sir?"

"Thank you. Another time, gentlemen." Stagg got in, the cabdriver got behind the wheel, and they moved away. "Home, Captain?" He had a heavy accent, and Stagg couldn't work out what it was.

"Yes, if you know where that is."

"British Embassy compound."

"Are you going to tell me who you are?"

"I'm your cabdriver. Look, people like those Russian bastards carry guns in their pockets."

Stagg raised his right knee to the dashboard, the trouser rolled up revealing the revolver in the ankle holder. "Colt .25?"

The cabdriver nodded. "I might have known." He pulled in outside the embassy gate. "No charge, Captain."

"Well, I'm obliged," Stagg told him. "I'm sure I'll see you again." He nodded to the guards, went in to his quarters, and reported this latest turn of events to Roper at Holland Park.

THAT EVENING IN LONDON, Miller caught up with them, Olivia and Monica in Olivia's dressing room as usual, and found his wife in excellent spirits as she sat applying her makeup. "Monica was telling me about your trip, Harry."

"Yes, sorry about the short notice."

"That's all right. If you've got to go, you've got to go. It must be something to see, the Prime Minister's Rottweiler springing into action."

Monica looked troubled, but Miller laughed. "A thrill a minute. We'll see you later."

ANOTHER WONDERFUL NIGHT, the audience absolutely lapping it up. Monica and Miller waited by the stage door, and she said, "This thing is going to run for months."

"I'm sure Noël Coward would have been delighted." Miller observed. "A pity he's dead."

"What a terrible thing to say," Monica told him. "What's got into you?"

"I haven't the slightest idea, I just feel good." It was Beirut, of course, the prospect of stepping into the War Zone again.

The dinner was superb, Olivia in an excellent mood, Miller at his most charming, Monica grateful that it had all worked so well. Miller paid, and they went to the door and found it raining. There was a pedestrian way through the market; in some places, metal tables and chairs sat outside cafés that had closed for the night. The headwaiter gave the women an umbrella, and they walked together, threading their way through the tables.

A young man was talking loudly in a doorway to a woman, who broke away and ran off. The smell of alcohol was strong, and he swigged it from a bottle, but he was obviously on something. He almost fell over a chair, grabbing at Monica, and he pulled her to him and placed the bottle he'd been drinking from on the nearest table. He smiled at Miller as he fondled her.

"What are you going to do about that, then?"

Miller picked up the bottle by the neck and smashed him across the side of the skull. Surprisingly, the bottle didn't break, but the man released his grip on Monica and fell across the table and down to the pavement.

Miller said, "Come on, girls, let's go," took each of them by the elbow, and urged them around the corner to where Ellis waited.

Monica stayed surprisingly calm. "Are you just going to leave him?"

"Well, I can't think of anything else to do with him, can you? If I called the police in, they'd just say I'd infringed his human rights."

Since he was leaving early in the morning, he slept in the second spare bedroom and found himself downstairs in the sitting room after midnight, having scotch and a cigarette, and it was there that Monica found him.

"The man in the alley—you looked like you'd done that sort of thing before."

No deceit, no lies this time. "Yes, you could say that."

She said softly, "I've never really known you, have I, Harry?"

"My darling sister, what's infinitely worse is that I've never really known me. A bit late in the day to find that out." He got up. "I'm for bed."

WHEN HE ARRIVED at Farley, he found no Ferguson, but Dillon waiting for him with the quartermaster, who took them into his office, where he had a Walther with silencer on his desk, five magazines, and a .25 Colt with hollow-point cartridges. There was an ankle holster.

"An ace in the hole, sir, if you need one. I've found over many years it can make a difference."

"You don't need to tell me, Sergeant Major." Miller put the weapons in his carry bag and said to Dillon, "Thank God for diplomatic status and no security check."

Parry appeared in the doorway. "Ready to go, Major."

They walked to the door, and Miller looked out at the rain. "Ah, well, at least the sun will be shining out there."

"Just remember Drecq Khan is a slippery toad," Dillon said. "Be careful." He watched Miller walk to the Gulfstream and board, then turned and went to his car.

WHEN THEY LANDED at Beirut International Airport late in the day, there was no fuss, for Stagg had arranged it that way. The presence of United Nations troops in the country made a difference from the old days and the facilities for UN traffic were impeccable.

Stagg was waiting when the Gulfstream rolled to a halt, and Miller took to him straightaway as they shook hands. "Good to meet you, Major."

"My pleasure," Miller told him.

Lacey and Parry came down the steps. "The UN provides

crew quarters here at the airport for people like you. They consider it desirable. It's a rough old town out there."

"Oh, we'll get by." Lacey turned to Miller. "Take care—we'd hate to lose you."

"I will," Miller said, and followed Stagg to a waiting taxi, which looked a little the worse for wear.

"Sorry about this," Stagg said as they got in. "A lot of things look a bit rough, but there've been a few wars here."

"I was here for a few days after the recent ones on the Prime Minister's behalf."

"I didn't know that. You're staying at the Al Bustan, which, unlike a lot of other places, has survived. You'll find it thoroughly civilized."

"Excellent." Miller continued in Russian, "How reliable is this driver?"

Stagg replied in the same language. "A Christian Phalangist. What we call a safe driver. How did you know I spoke Russian?"

"Major Roper is rather thorough."

"I spoke to him last night. We're two hours ahead of London here and I had a spot of bother."

"Boris Bikov and Ivan Torin, pride of the GRU? He told me."

"Very bad guys, and capable of quite a lot. The mystery was this taxi driver."

"I don't think so. We have a link with General Arnold Cohen of Mossad, and he said he had a man on the ground."

"And you think that's who it was?" He shook his head. "I don't know. His English was good, but his accent very heavy. I couldn't work out what his background was. You think he'll be in touch?"

"I'm certain of it, but enough for now. I need to settle in and shower, and a late lunch would be nice."

STAGG HAD BEEN RIGHT, the Al Bustan was still everything that could be desired in a good hotel. Stagg sat on the balcony and read that day's copy of the *Times*, which Miller had brought from the plane. Inside in the suite, Miller showered, changed into a khaki bush shirt and jeans, and pulled on ankle boots. Stagg came through and found him fitting the holster to his right ankle.

"Are you carrying?" Miller asked.

"You bet, just like you, and with hollow-points, the Colt is as good as it gets. It's needed in this town, believe me. There are people here who'd kill you for your boots."

"Well, we can't have that." Miller pulled on a linen jacket and reached for his Ray Bans. "Let's go downstairs."

There was a pleasant bar, French windows to the terrace outside and a fine view of the city, although the bombings hadn't helped. The Mediterranean was still there, the harbor crowded with shipping, and far out to sea, ships on the horizon plowed on to other destinations than Beirut. Calls to prayer echoed over the rooftops.

A waiter approached, and Stagg said, "Is lemonade all right, Major? You can't get alcohol until after seven."

Miller laughed. "It's good for us, I suppose." Stagg gave the order. Miller carried on, "Now tell me more about Drecq Khan."

Which Stagg did, at least as much as he was able.

"So, what do you suggest?" said Miller when he was finished.

"We could have a look round the usual haunts, sir. I'll show you the hiring hall, the waterfront. If Khan is away from the villa this afternoon, I could ask Considine to meet us, but I stress it should be brief."

"Have you done this?"

"Once, but frankly, I prefer my mobile phone link with him. One only needs the wrong person to see him and we could be in real trouble."

"Well, let's leave that option for the moment. You call him and find out the latest, while I sample the lemonade."

He sat there, staring out to the harbor, and called Roper on his Codex Four. Roper, as usual seated in front of his screens, greeted him warmly. "How is it?"

"Unusual," Miller said. "It's the sunshine that made it a

millionaires' paradise all those years ago. Stagg's first class, by the way. I don't know why I've called. Sitting here looking out to sea, I find myself wondering what it's all about. Do you ever feel like that?"

"Only seven days a week. Stay well, Harry, and watch those bad guys. Sorry I've not managed to come up with the *Valentine* yet."

Stagg returned. "Khan has had many calls to various Muslim sources regarding the *Valentine*. He seems to be using the muscle of the Army of God to impress the importance of his search."

"And the Broker?"

"Not a word. Khan is at the hiring hall now."

"So let's go and see the sights. Is your safe taxi on hand, or do you have to get another one?"

"He waits."

They went down to the rank and found the driver beside the taxi, checking the wheels. "I can't understand it. Two flat tires, sir. I'll have to get the garage."

There was the sound of an engine starting up and the battered Renault from the previous night drove up. "Taxi, gentlemen?" The driver was smiling. "You said you'd see me again," he said to Stagg.

"Yes, I did, didn't I? I suppose you can guess who this is, sir?"

"I'm sure I can," Miller said. "Let's get in."

They drove away, and the driver said, "Where now? The hiring hall?"

"Who are you?" Miller asked.

"Well, I certainly know who you are." Stagg was astonished. The accent of the night before had been replaced by a perfect English one. "We have something in common, gentlemen."

"And what would that be?" Miller asked.

"We all went to Sandhurst. And, by the way, I outrank you. Lieutenant Colonel Gideon Cohen." He laughed, and his voice changed to the one Stagg had heard the previous night. "Or Walid Khasan, if you like."

"My God, you've got guts," Miller told him. "If they knew you were a Jew, they'd hang you in the street."

"Yes, well, I'm lucky I do a good Muslim." He turned down the hill through a maze of streets, making for the waterfront. "Do either of you speak Arabic?"

"I do," Miller said. "Enough to get by."

"It gave me something to do when I was in therapy," Stagg said.

"Six months in hospital with that wound of yours."

"Why do you ask?" Miller said.

"It helps deal with these people, the fact that you do, because most of the time, they don't expect it. I'll park by the seawall. Have a walk round, get the feel. I've got things to do. Order a whiskey, have a coffee at the Green Parrot by the hiring hall, I'll find you."

They got out and watched where he parked, then moved into the crowd. People milled in and out of the hiring hall. Miller and Stagg, in the press by the door, looked in and saw Drecq Khan on the platform at his desk. Miller recognized him instantly from the material he'd been shown in the Holland Park files.

"That's Khan," Miller said. "Let's get that coffee."

They sat for a while at a table on the railed area in front of the Green Parrot, sampling the thick syrupy coffee, when Torin and Bikov appeared, pushing through the crowd. "Here come the GRU," Stagg said. They exchanged words and came over.

"Why, it's you, Stagg," Torin said. "You just can't stay away from us. Who's your friend?"

Miller stood up and stamped hard on his foot. Torin half fell across the table. "So sorry," Miller said. "Clumsy of me."

He pushed away through the crowd, Stagg following to where Cohen had left the taxi. As they reached it, he approached. "In you get, let's move it."

He threaded his way through the crowd, brushing the Russians aside. "Bad news. Word of your arrival has leaked, Major—the staff at the Al Bustan have a way of doing that."

He turned into one narrow street and then another. Suddenly, Stagg's mobile rang. He answered at once as Cohen pulled over. He listened intently, a hand raised to still the others. "Yes, of course, you must do that to cover yourself. I'll call you back."

"What?" Miller asked.

"Considine. Khan had left his answering machine on. There were two messages. One, an informant leaving word about you, the other from someone called Ali Hassan, who says he has an old man, a sailor named Sharif, who knows something about the *Valentine*. He said he didn't want to bring him to the hiring hall because he's very old and gets confused. He said he'd bring him to the villa by car in an hour and wait for Khan there."

"This could be it," Cohen exclaimed.

"What have you told Considine?"

"We have to consider his safety. Khan frequently calls in to retrieve his calls. Considine can say he was out for his lunch break when the calls were received, but he's bound to tell Khan, if only to cover his back. I've told him to go ahead."

"I agree with you. So what do you suggest now?"

"Just up the hill from the villa is a suburban area pretty well destroyed in the bombing during the war. There's what's left of an old church, St. Mary's Chapel. That's where I met Considine face-to-face. I suggest we take up stations there and await events."

"While Considine sweats it out in the office?"

"We'd better check."

Stagg called back, and Considine said, "I can't stay on. I told Khan, and he's coming straight back."

Stagg quickly briefed him on the plan. "There are three of us up here in the Chapel. We'll be monitoring you all the time. Good luck."

"Maybe I'll need it," Considine said, and switched off.

FROM THE RAVAGED CEMETERY of St. Mary's Chapel, Cohen looked down to the villa with a pair of Zeiss glasses. An old

Peugeot estate car arrived, and Torin and Bikov got out, followed by Khan and Abdul, the hiring hall foreman.

Cohen passed the glasses to Miller, who just managed to catch the men as they walked through the ruined arches at the rear of the villa and went inside.

"The game's afoot," Miller said. "We can only pray."

"Especially for Considine," Cohen said.

•

KHAN SAT AT HIS desk listening to the answering machine, obviously feeling rather pleased with himself, but there was also considerable relief at the prospect of solving the riddle of the *Valentine*. As he had learned to his cost over the years, where the Broker was concerned, failure was not an option. His telephone rang and he flicked on the speakerphone.

"Khan here," he said in Arabic.

The Broker replied in English. "It's me. What's been happening? I'm disappointed not to have heard from you."

At his desk next door, Considine heard every word and, taking advantage of the fact that the Russians were downstairs in the kitchen, moved closer to the door to listen.

"What's happening?" the Broker asked.

"As regards Beirut itself, there's a man named Miller just flown in. It seems he's a member of a UN committee on Lebanon."

The Broker was stunned. "Have you any idea what he's really doing there?"

"He's being looked after by the military attaché at the British Embassy, a man named Stagg. Word has come to me that Stagg has also been trying to discover the whereabouts of the *Valentine*. Anyway, none of this matters. I've had word from a reliable informant who is bringing someone here within the hour who knows all about the *Valentine*."

The Broker said, "This man Miller represents the British Prime Minister and is usually up to no good. His visit must involve the *Valentine* in some way. The fact that Stagg has been asking around speaks for itself. How tight is your security? Is everyone close to you totally reliable?"

Khan was alarmed. "I'm sure they are."

"They'd better be. Contact me when you have real news—and check your people."

He cut off, leaving Khan trembling with fear. Considine was already down the stairs, and he passed the open kitchen door where Torin and Bikov were enjoying coffee. They glanced at him as he went outside and started through the orchard.

Khan called for Considine and, not getting a reply, looked for him in the next room. Finding him gone, he suddenly realized what his absence might imply.

He descended the stairs, shouting, "Considine, where are you?"

Torin stepped out of the kitchen. "He went out a couple of minutes ago."

"Get him," Khan cried. "He's a bloody traitor. I think he's sold me out to Stagg," Which was enough to send Torin out on the run, Bikov at his heels.

Considine got through the orchard and reached the road as Torin fired his first shot. On the hill, it brought the three men to their feet, and Miller glanced through the glasses. "He's in trouble." He turned to Cohen. "You go down in your taxi and block the road. We'll take them on."

He pulled the Colt out of his ankle holster and started down, and Stagg did the same and followed. "We'll need to get close, sir."

"Then we get close."

As they went through the cemetery, both the Russians fired at Considine, who dodged through the gravestones, keeping his head down. Suddenly, he jerked, clutching at his right arm. Torin walked close, taking deliberate aim, and Miller, close now and running fast, shot him in the left shoulder. Torin dropped his weapon, spun around, then fell to the ground. Miller, still on the run, stumbled and Bikov took deliberate aim, his weapon held in both hands. Stagg, running slower than Miller because of his hip, took a snap shot that caught Bikov in the right knee, the hollow-point cartridge doing real damage.

He picked up Bikov's weapon and tossed it away. "I'd say you need a good surgeon. Better phone your embassy and tell them to come running."

"Fuck you," Torin said.

"Well, you would say that, wouldn't you?"

Bikov sat leaning against a gravestone, clutching his shoulder, blood oozing between his fingers. Stagg picked up the gun, a Stechkin. "How is he?" he asked Miller, who was helping Considine stand.

"It could be worse. Arm shot, it's gone straight through." Miller took a handkerchief and bound it as tightly as possible. He looked down, saw Cohen arrive in his taxi and brake, and Khan and Abdul hurriedly went inside the villa. "What happened?" he asked Considine.

"The Broker came on, and when Khan told him of your arrival, he was very angry. He said you represented the British Prime Minister, that you were always up to no good. He said the fact that Captain Stagg had been seeking news of the *Valentine* must mean the story had been leaked by somebody close to Khan and told him to check. That's when I ran for it."

"And the *Valentine* story?"

"He knows an informant exists, but he was more interested in you."

"And I suspect that's our informant arriving right now," Stagg said. An old station wagon was approaching and slowed down, then halted at the sight of Cohen's taxi blocking the road, and he went forward to speak to the two men inside. After a while, he produced a pistol and fired a shot in the air.

"Here we go." Miller gave Considine his arm and they went down through the cemetery.

Stagg rummaged in Torin's pocket, found his mobile, and tapped in a number. He handed it to him. "There you go, Russian Embassy." He went after the others.

Cohen said, "This is Ali Hassan and Sharif, who knows all about the *Valentine,* don't you? I was just demonstrating that I meant business." He'd put the older man in the back and the younger, the driver, with him. "You two go with them, I'll follow with Considine—that's if you've got somewhere to go."

"Yes, I'll call them, a private security facility I have access to," Stagg said.

"Well, while you're arranging that, I'm going inside to speak to Khan," Miller said. "Give me that Stechkin." Stagg handed him Bikov's weapon. "What are you going to do?"

"Have a word with Khan. I won't be long."

He went down through the orchard and entered the rear door. The four domestic servants Khan employed had all cleared off. Miller went straight up the stairs, the Stechkin hanging in his right hand, and kicked open the door of what proved to be Considine's office. Abdul scrambled from behind the door to grab at him, Miller hit him across the face with the Stechkin, and he fell down.

Drecq Khan was gibbering behind the desk, terrified. "You know who I am, you miserable bastard," Miller said.

"Please don't kill me."

"I would, but then you wouldn't be able to tell the Broker I'm going to make it my personal business to destroy him and Volkov. They failed in Washington with Kelly and his chum, and they're going to fail with operation *Valentine*. Do you understand?"

"Yes."

"I've read your file. When the Salters chased you out of London, you left the Brotherhood still intact. You must have left someone in charge. Who is it?"

Khan said desperately, "Please believe me. . ."

Miller fired the Stechkin into the wall, narrowly missing his skull. "If you don't tell me, I'll put the next bullet between your eyes."

And Khan totally believed him. "Ali Hassim—he has a corner shop in Delamere Road in West Hampstead."

"I'd take a shower if I were you. You're beginning to smell bad." Miller walked out.

When he found the others, Cohen said, "You didn't kill him?"

"Of course not. I was squeezing some juice out of him," and he told Cohen what it was.

"Thanks very much. Mossad will be grateful for that

knowledge, even if it is in London. Now let's get going. The boy wonder here has organized entry for us to that private security place he mentioned."

"Excellent." Stagg was driving, and Hassan and Sharif in the rear looked frightened and bewildered. Miller got in.

"Have no fear," he said in Arabic, "I mean you no harm. I want to know about the *Valentine,* that's all. Think about it."

The private security facility was heavily guarded by men in dark uniforms and had obviously been a hotel in earlier times. The guards, as it turned out, were all Lebanese Christians and the captain in charge had a French name, Duval. He had Considine taken away to a medical facility and showed Miller, Stagg, and Cohen, together with the two Arabs, into an interrogation room. It all turned out to be incredibly easy, mainly because Hassan and particularly old Sharif were genuinely frightened and eager to please.

"You take over, Colonel," Miller said to Cohen.

Cohen spoke to them in Arabic. "The *Valentine*—why is there a problem with this ship? Everyone seeks it, and no one knows where it is."

"He knows," Ali Hassan said eagerly, "he knows all about it." Sharif nodded. "It's not called the *Valentine,* not in reality, but the job is."

Miller suddenly saw it. "It's a code, a name for the matter in hand, whatever the contraband is?"

Hassan said, "This is true, and it's a *Valentine* before the real ship is selected. In this case, the real ship is *Circe,* a freighter out of Tripoli, but chartered by North Korean agents. It carries plutonium among a general cargo of machinery. It left Tripoli last week and its destination is Latakia in Syria."

Miller said, "But how in the hell does Sharif know so much?"

The old man plucked at Hassan's arm and muttered to him. Hassan said, "His mind is weak, he is very old. Could he have a cigarette?"

Cohen produced a pack, shook one out and proffered a light, and Sharif took the cigarette with shaking fingers. He sucked at it greedily. Hassan said, "His third wife's brother-in-law has a nephew named Hamid who is a sailor but works only on special runs. Contraband, drugs, arms, that sort of thing. He likes the big money, which is why he took the offer as a crew member of *Circe*."

The old man plucked at his arm again, voice hoarse, and whispered. Hassan nodded. "He says all this is true because *Circe* is only forty miles offshore from Lebanon at the moment, and getting close to what's known as the Careb Shoals."

"And how in the hell does he know that?" Stagg demanded.

Hassan spread his hands. "This is true, gentlemen, you must believe me. Hamid calls Sharif's house on his cell phone every couple of days. He spoke to him this morning." The old man nodded, then took a cell phone from a pocket in his jacket.

There was silence for a moment, then Miller said, "It's so damn simple when you get down to it—the thing that's revolutionized modern times more than anything else. You can ring up from anywhere. You better take his phone, Colonel, and Hassan's, if he's got one." Which Hassan did.

"What do we do now, sir?" Stagg asked.

"That's not a matter for us. I'd say it's a matter for the Colonel." He turned to Cohen. "Isn't that so?"

"I'll contact my people at once. We have a satellite facility over Syria and Iran which can be diverted at short notice to identify such a target. That is all we need, together with the old man's information. I'll leave you now and get on with my job."

"We'll see Hassan and Sharif are held here for a few days," Stagg said, and they went out past a guard outside the door.

"Good. A safe journey home, if I don't see you again. It's been interesting," Cohen said.

He went out, and they followed and asked Captain Duval about Considine. "He's still out from the anesthetic. I'll show you." He led the way down the corridor to the small medical facility. Considine was sleeping, his right arm heavily bandaged. "It could have been worse, but it missed the bone and went straight through. Three or four days and he'll be fine."

"You'll see to him?" Miller said to Stagg as they went out.

"Of course, sir, but what about his visa?"

"No problem, I promise you. So what do we do with Hassan's car, steal it?"

Duval came up behind them. "We'll see to it. I'll have one of my men take you wherever you want to go."

As they got in the car provided, Stagg said, "When are you returning to London?"

"I think I'll leave in the morning, but let's have a last drink together. Café Albert just after seven?"

"You're on."

AT HOLLAND PARK an hour later, Roper was in the computer room as usual, Dillon and Ferguson having coffee in the corner, when Miller came on. "It's me," he told Roper. "Is Ferguson there?"

Roper immediately put him on speaker, and Ferguson called, "I'm here, Harry, what's happening?"

"It's done," Miller said. "It wasn't a ship, it was a code name. The actual ship in question's called *Circe,* and by now Colonel Gideon Cohen will have passed all the relevant information to Mossad."

Ferguson said, "Tell me."

Which Miller did, while Roper recorded it. At the end, Miller said, "I couldn't see the point of killing Khan. I thought you'd prefer him in place. Squeezing the name of his Brotherhood crony was an extra."

"It certainly was. We won't lift this Ali Hassim, of course, it's enough to know who he is. It's an amazing result, Harry. Dammit all, you only flew in this morning."

"Things just fell right," Miller said. "Stagg's a good man, and certainly worth more than military attaché in the mess Beirut has become."

"I'll bear him in mind."

"And Henri Considine? He was the key to the whole thing."

"He'll get his visa within days. I'll put it forward under a Prime Minister's Warrant."

"You can do that?"

"I can do anything, Harry."

"So we leave it to the Israelis now?"

"I think so."

"I'll see you tomorrow. Roper, speak to Lacey at the airport. Make it about a ten o'clock departure. I must go, I'm meeting Stagg for a drink."

Dillon cut in. "Good work, Harry, see you soon."

It was quiet for a moment, and then Ferguson said, "I'll listen to it again later."

"As much as you like," Roper said. "Interesting how shocked the Broker was to find Harry in Beirut."

"Well, the Code Three I authorized obviously had an effect. We know the Russians and others monitor flight details from there. I suppose that includes the Broker. After all, we do the same when we can."

"It's all happened so quickly." Dillon shook his head. "Hot stuff. Harry Miller, you've got to give him credit."

"Oh, I do," Ferguson said. "Now all we have to do is await the final chapter."

STAGG AND MILLER sat at a table against a pillar in Café Albert. Alphonse approached, carrying an ice bucket in which was a bottle of champagne and two glasses, which he set out on the table. He got the bottle open and started to pour.

"Bollinger, just as you asked for, gentlemen. Henri doesn't appear to be coming in tonight. This is unusual."

"He's busy elsewhere," Stagg told him. "But he's well, I assure you."

"I'm relieved to hear it. We live in troubled times in Beirut, only war and then rumors of war. Enjoy your champagne, gentlemen."

Miller raised his glass. "To a job well done. You were first class."

"That's good of you to say so. You were a hard act to follow."

"If you don't mind my asking," Miller said, "why aren't you married? Yes, Roper looked you up on one of his computers."

Stagg's face grew solemn. "I was almost. Engaged. Lovely girl, daughter of family friends, grew up in the same village."

Miller sensed it, that something had gone deeply wrong. "So what happened?"

"Iraq happened. Like everybody else, she saw it all on television. Told me she couldn't marry someone who killed people for a living."

"Life's a bitch sometimes, but if that's how she feels . . ." Miller shrugged. "You know, I like this place. It's straight out of *Casablanca*. Rick's Café."

The trio began to play and the pianist started to sing in French, and Stagg said, "I agree, and there's a taxi driver friend of yours coming in behind you that looks straight out of that movie's cast."

Gideon Cohen, Walid Khasan to the hilt, took off his cap and bowed. "Your taxi, sir. I know I'm early, but I can wait."

"Fine, we'll see you in a little while."

Cohen started to turn away, then smiled. "There's a story going round the waterfront that some ship blew up forty miles out, close to the Careb Shoals."

He went out, and Miller reached for the champagne. "Well, there you are." He emptied it into the two glasses. "What can I say? Those Syrians won't be pleased, or the North Koreans."

"The person I'm sorry for," Stagg said, "is poor old Sharif. He's going to spend a long time waiting for that relative of his to come home."

Miller said, "Well, he shouldn't have joined. Come on, you can drop me at the Al Bustan and I'll say my good-byes to both of you."

AT HOLLAND PARK, Roper sat thinking, phoned Ferguson at Cavendish Place and found him still up, sitting beside the fire, having a whiskey before going to bed.

"I've heard from General Cohen. *Circe* was located about an hour ago by an F-151 of the Israeli Air Force. Two minutes, and it sank like a stone."

"Excellent," Ferguson said. "Volkov is not going to like that piece of news at all. Try and get some sleep, Major."

He cut off and Roper sat there, watching the world of cyberspace ceaselessly turning on his screens.

"Sleep," he murmured. "Who needs sleep?" He reached for the bottle and poured another whiskey.

London

8

When the bad news reached Volkov, he was angrier than he had been in years and contacted the Broker at once. "I presume you've heard about the culmination of this *Valentine* affair?"

"I'm still trying to extract full details from Drecq Khan. I haven't been able to contact him for several hours."

"Miller appears to have gone on the rampage in Beirut, abetted by Stagg, and in the process shooting the two GRU agents I had ordered to assist Khan. From what one of them reports from his hospital bed, it seems that Khan had a traitor in his camp, a man named Considine."

"I suspected such an individual existed, and suggested that Khan explore the possibility when we last spoke. Informants had told him of Miller's arrival, but that meant nothing to him, and then he received word that Stagg had been making inquiries about the *Valentine* matter."

"Ferguson has been clever on this one, I can see that," Volkov said. "He's a devious bastard. When you've found Khan, call me back with his story."

Khan had made himself unavailable for one reason only.

He was truly afraid of what the Broker's reaction was going to be, this man who was Osama's personal representative. But in the end, the Broker had to be faced, there was no getting away from it.

When he finally made the connection, the Broker showed his anger. "Where have you been? Explain yourself!"

"Miller was like a madman, and this Captain Stagg was no better. You were right, there was a traitor in my office itself, the accountant Considine. He made a run for it, Torin and Bikov chased him and managed to wound him, then Miller and Stagg shot both of them."

"I'm surprised Miller didn't finish you off while he was at it."

"Only because he gave me a message. He said you failed in Washington with Kelly, whatever that means, and that you would fail with *Valentine*. He also said he intended to destroy you and General Volkov."

"Really? Was that all?"

Khan lied, for it was impossible for him to admit selling out Ali Hassim in London. The consequences of such treachery in a matter affecting Al Qaeda would have been death.

"Nothing—nothing more, I swear it. What should I do now?"

"Put your house in order or take the consequences."

VOLKOV LISTENED as the Broker went through the whole thing again. "It's not acceptable, any of it," the Russian told him. "First, Quinn's people in Washington disappearing, now this spectacular slap in the face in Beirut. It's going to be very difficult to explain to the President."

"And we must not forget the Zorin affair."

"Don't mention that damn Zorin business. I've had Sergei Zorin imploring my help because his sister, Olga, discovered the truth."

"How did she do that?" the Broker asked.

"Apparently, she's been having her driver take her to her son's grave at Minsky Park every day. Then, a few days ago, her son's sergeant from Kosovo turned up with flowers, spurred on by drunken sentimentality. The drink also made him tell her the truth about her son's death. She immediately spoke to her brother, who saw the sergeant, Stransky, and got the whole story out of him."

"What have you done about this?" the Broker asked.

"Had the sergeant sentenced to a penal battalion. He's already on his way to Siberia."

"And Mrs. Zorin?"

"Inconsolable. Demanding that her brother do something."

"And what does she mean by that?"

"Well, in Moscow it would be quite simple and handled by some Mafia hit man."

"And London? If you really are targeting Miller . . ."

"We haven't been too successful with the London Mafia lately. Max Chekhov is still on sticks and lucky not to have lost a leg. Whatever I decide has to be something special. I want to think about it. I've warned Zorin off, by the way. I can bring the full wrath of the President down on his head if he doesn't behave, in spite of his money. His sister will have to continue wailing, but not for long, as it happens. I understand her heart is a source for anxiety. It appears she's only kept alive with the right pills."

Even the Broker felt a chill at Volkov's words. "You are certain of it?"

"Oh, yes, I've had words with her doctor."

It was enough, and the Broker hurriedly moved on. "I suppose Miller will be back in London around now?"

"Yes, and Ferguson and those bastards who work with him will be over the moon, but not for long," Volkov said. "I swear it."

AT HOLLAND PARK, Miller sat in the computer room with Roper and Dillon and went through everything again. He hadn't seen the Prime Minister. Ferguson had, though, and there was a general feeling of a job well done.

"Watch out, though," Roper said. "Volkov has got to be furious."

"Kosovo, Washington, and now Beirut—that's three times, Harry. That makes you an ace. He must be wondering how long this'll go on," Dillon said.

Roper shook his head. "No, he isn't. He's saying what can I do to stop this guy. You've got to take care."

"It might be an idea to start carrying," Dillon put in.

"A Walther?" Miller laughed. "It's just not possible. I'd never get through House of Commons security, never mind Downing Street. Anyway, nobody's going to shoot me down just yet. Frankly, I feel great. I could even stand another showing of Noël Coward."

"Well, you can count me out," Roper told him. "As Bionic Man, I need plenty of advance warning to prepare for that kind of adventure. Try Dillon—he's an expert in the theater, as we all know."

"Would you join me, Sean?" Miller asked.

"Why not?" Dillon said, and checked his watch. "If we go now, we'll just about make it."

Miller said to Roper, "Curtain down at ten. Do me a favor. See if we can have a table for late supper at the Savoy. They might even have dancing."

"I'll let you know," Roper said, and they went out fast.

At the Gielgud, Miller was greeted by astonishment in his wife's dressing room. He was alone, Dillon having suggested waiting in the bar. Miller had sorted out the extra seat with Marcus, and found Monica, as usual, watching Olivia prepare.

"What on earth happened?" Monica asked. "I thought you were going to be gone for some days."

"So did I, but it was just one of those things. All the people I needed to see were immediately available, it's a quiet time at the moment, very little disruption, but with the situation what it is, you never know—there was certainly no reason to stay. I thought you'd be back at Cambridge."

"As a matter of fact, I'm going up tomorrow," Monica said.

His Codex went and he answered it. "Smooth as silk at the Savoy. The moment I said the name, nothing was too good for you. The fame of the Prime Minister's Rottweiler can achieve anything, it would appear. Enjoy."

"What was that?" Olivia inquired.

"I've arranged supper at the Savoy. We'll send you off in style, darling," he told Monica.

Olivia said, "Actually, Colin Carlton had asked us to dinner."

"Well, that's all right," Miller said. "Make a party of it. I've brought a friend along. He's waiting in the bar."

"Who is it?" she asked with a slight frown. "An MP?"

"Anything but. A chap I've had dealings with lately—Sean Dillon. You'll like him."

She was obviously annoyed for some reason, her plans disrupted. Monica said hastily, "We'll go and have a drink with him in the bar. We'll see you after, Olivia."

They went out of the stage door and walked around to the front of the theater. "She's not pleased," Miller said.

"She wasn't expecting you, Harry. She's got things organized, and then you come roaring back and expect . . ."

Suddenly, she was flustered, and he said, "Expect what?"

"Oh, damn you, Harry, I don't know. In fact, I don't know anything anymore. Now let's see where this friend of yours is and have a drink."

Dillon had managed to find a corner table and had a bottle of Krug champagne open. Monica was charmed. He jumped to his feet, took her hand, and kissed it.

"Lady Starling, it's always a pleasure to meet a truly handsome woman, as Jane Austen would have Darcy say."

She was totally thrown and laughed. "Am I to take that as a compliment?"

"You can take it any way you like, as long as you approve of Krug nonvintage. People of taste and discernment consider it the best in the world. It's the grape mix."

He handed her a glass, then Miller and she sampled it. "I must say that is rather good."

"Then here's to an enjoyable evening."

"I'm Harry's sister, you know that?"

"I know everything about you. University don, Cambridge,

fellow in archaeology, a foremost expert on the Dark Ages, especially in what happened to the Romans in Britain after the collapse of the Empire."

"You are well informed."

"Punch your name into any computer and up you come."

"And you, Mr. Dillon, what do you do?"

"Play a passable barroom piano. I'm also a bit of a linguist, and you can turn a pound or two with that."

"Bit of a linguist," Harry said. "Speaks everything, including Irish."

"I see." She was intrigued. "As you're not an MP, you're some sort of civil servant, I take it?"

"An excellent description of what I do. I serve the Crown." He topped up her glass. "You've just time to finish that, and we'll get to our seats. I'm looking forward to seeing the great Olivia Hunt strutting her stuff."

Harry laughed, and Monica said, "You enjoy theater, do you?"

"Oh, yes, very much." The bell sounded, and the final call to their seats. "Here we go, then," and he gave her his arm.

Afterward, they waited with Ellis for a few moments beside the Mercedes. Olivia and Colin Carlton came out quite quickly, on a high, flushed with triumph. Before being introduced to Dillon, she said, "Oh, what are we going to do? There's one too many for the Merc."

It lacked something certainly, and Dillon made his move quickly. "I've had the pleasure of seeing you many times. Let me say old Noël would have been proud of you tonight, and you, Mr. Carlton." He nodded at Miller. "I'll see you soon, Harry." He gave Monica the most devastating of smiles. "Lady Starling, a sincere sensation."

He simply faded into the passing crowd, leaving Ellis holding the passenger door and a slightly embarrassed silence. "Oh, dear," Olivia said, "have I said the wrong thing?"

Miller said calmly, "We'd better get moving, Ellis, we're

on limited time for the table. I'll sit with you in front." As she brushed past him to get in, Monica gave his hand a brief squeeze.

At the Savoy, as they passed through the tables, Olivia was recognized by many people, and there was a certain amount of applause. The maître d' couldn't have been more obliging and led them to an excellent window table.

Olivia was still on a high. "Champagne, Harry." She pulled Carlton to his feet. "Come on, darling, I want to dance."

Miller waved to the wine waiter. "Krug, nonvintage."

"Are you certain, Major Miller?"

"Absolutely. Best in the world." He glanced at Monica. "It's the grape mix."

The waiter departed, and she laughed. "I did like your new friend, Harry."

"Yes, he is rather special, isn't he?"

"Don't be annoyed with Olivia. You know what actors can be like."

"Of course. Her behavior where Dillon was concerned lacked a certain grace, but it's her loss."

"I really liked that man," Monica said as the Krug arrived. "What does he do?"

"He works for the Prime Minister under General Charles Ferguson. Security work, that sort of thing."

"Some sort of spook, is that what you mean?"

"Why, what did you imagine he might be?"

"I'm not sure. There was something of the soldier about him."

"An interesting observation."

"What is?" Olivia demanded, as she and Carlton sat down and the waiter filled their glasses.

"Oh, we were talking about Harry's new friend, Sean Dillon," Monica told her.

"Strange little man," Carlton said. "What's he do?"

"Started out in your business," Miller said. "A student at

RADA at nineteen. Played Lyngstrand in Ibsen's *Lady from the Sea*."

"Really?" Carlton shook his head. "I always think it's a big mistake allowing students to ruin great plays that are obviously out of their reach."

"Actually, he did it for the National Theatre," Miller told him.

There was a pause, and Monica said, "Well, that's a show-stopper if ever I heard one."

Olivia was slightly bewildered, and Carlton said, "Strange, I've never heard of him."

"He gave it all up way before your time, exchanged the theater of the stage for the theater of the street."

Olivia said, "What on earth is that supposed to mean?"

"Anything you want it to." Miller stood up and gave his hand to Monica. "Let's take a turn round the floor—it's been a long time."

ACROSS THE SEA in the Irish Republic, Michael Quinn was visiting Drumore Place in County Louth, the headquarters of Belov International. It was no hardship to him. He enjoyed everything about it: the small harbor, the villagers who did as they were told, the pub, the Royal George run by Patrick Ryan, whose mother was cook at the big house, Drumore Place, with old Hamilton, the butler. He always felt like a lord of the manor when he visited, and sat now by the fire in the great hall drinking whiskey, when his satellite phone sounded. He answered and found Volkov.

"I thought I'd find you there."

"It's good to hear from you, General. What can I do for you?"

"The mystery of Washington—you still have no news of what happened to Tod Kelly and his underling?"

"Absolutely nothing. They've totally disappeared. Why, have you any?"

"Miller."

Quinn was immediately alert. "What's he done now?"

"Listen and learn," Volkov told him.

When he was finished, Quinn said, "The bastard. Is there no end to him?"

"Apparently not. I've had enough. I want Miller dead. Now. Come to London, take one of the Belov jets."

"But Ferguson—what happens when the news of Miller's death gets out, right in his own backyard?"

"Ferguson will understand. It's all part of the game we play. Remember, last year, when I wanted Ferguson taken out and as many of his people as possible? The *Green Tinker* affair? What a screwup. Four old IRA gun hands and a couple of doped-up hoodlums and Dillon, Salter, and Igor Levin disposed of the lot. But disposed is the operative word, Quinn. It never happened—that's always Ferguson's solution. Nothing ever comes to court—he has a disposal unit which has the use of a crematorium. In accusing you of anything, he would also have to accuse his own people."

"I accept that. I'd also like to point out that in the wrong circumstances, he could dispose of me."

"Not unless he has to."

"That's a great comfort. All right, so tell me what you want to happen to Miller."

"The thing we have to remember about Miller is that there is no public knowledge of his secret side. So I don't want anything to look suspicious. I don't want a bomb in his limousine, or someone on a dark and rainy night shooting him in the back. What I want is his death by accident. The public will accept an accident. Ferguson, Dillon, the Prime Minister, they'll all know the truth, but they won't be able to say so. They won't be able to blame us publicly. We Russians are easily blamed in such matters, but on this occasion . . . ."

"You get away with it."

"Exactly. Think about it for a day or two, then when you are ready to go, I'll fix it for Max Chekhov to order you to London. This is important, you must understand. It will say to Ferguson that *you do not fuck with the Russians.* I'd say you could spend up to fifty thousand pounds for Miller's death."

VOLKOV OBVIOUSLY CALLED the Broker about it, too, because it wasn't much more than half an hour later that Quinn received the Broker's call.

"So we have a situation here?"

"I certainly do," Quinn said. "I don't know about you."

"Perhaps I can be of use. The Brotherhood flourishes in London—it can provide individuals with any kind of skill you might need."

"But Drecq Khan got kicked out."

"But he left somebody in his place, a man named Ali Hassim. He owns a corner shop in Delamere Road in West Hampstead. I will speak to him about you. If there is any way he can help, he will."

"I've got to think about it. There may be someone from the old days, people who used to do this kind of thing, but not regularly."

"Did you know many like that when you were with the IRA?"

"Some. There were people in London who were sleepers, some in respectable middle-class jobs, anything from teaching to banking. They'd turn out sometimes for one job only. In 'seventy-nine, a Member of Parliament was blown up by a car bomb as he drove up the ramp out of the underground car park at the House of Commons. They never got anybody for that, and the word always was that the people involved only did the one job ever."

"Interesting that there could be individuals like that still in London. The man next door, as it were."

"Why not? There are thousands of Irish born in London. Anyway, here's one thing you could do. If this Ali Hassim has people who can help, it would be useful to get a report on the comings and goings at Miller's house, wherever that is."

"I already know where it is. The family has owned a townhouse in Mayfair for many years. Excellent area, good address, 15 Dover Street. I'll see Hassim gets it."

He was away then, and Quinn poured himself a large whiskey, went and stirred the fire, sat down and thought about it.

ALI HASSIM found that with his age he slept lightly, and frequently dozed on his couch beside the fire in the back room of his shop, which is where the Broker found him when he called.

"Are you awake, my brother?" he said in Arabic.

"Who is it?"

"The Broker."

"Blessings on you."

"And you. I hear your wife died since we last talked."

"A heart attack. It was her time. What can I do for you?"

"Do things go well for the Army?"

"Oh, yes, thanks to the money Osama provides. We do obvious good, provide soup kitchens for the unbelievers, hostels for the poor, that sort of thing. Too much good to be bad."

"Which must make it difficult for people like Charles Ferguson."

"That's the whole idea. The Army cloaks the activities of the Brotherhood, but I have severely curtailed those in the present climate. I have no wish to draw the attention of the authorities to our activities, but it would be difficult for Ferguson to actually prove anything."

"Do you hear from Khan these days?"

"Very seldom. His task in Beirut must be demanding."

"And brings its own troubles. Listen to me well." The Broker proceeded to tell him everything.

Afterward, Ali Hassim said, "Truly, something should be done about all this. The death of this man Miller would not bother me in the slightest. As you know, it was Ferguson and his people who were responsible for the disappearance of my nephew, Abu. You can rely on me and my people to assist you in this matter."

"Excellent. I knew I could rely on you. I'll leave it with you."

Ali Hassim sat there, thinking. Suddenly, he was no longer tired but quite alert. He went to his laptop and soon produced Miller's details on the screen, read them with interest, then had the copier throw up a few photos. He got his mobile out and inserted a number.

"Abdul? I'm putting a photo through to your laptop. The client is a politician, Harry Miller, the address 15 Dover Street. Basic surveillance. Background, daily pattern, comings and goings. Low-key, but priority."

So—life got interesting again, and he went and made coffee in his small kitchen.

THE MORNING AFTER the Savoy, Olivia was sleeping late, as was her usual practice after the previous night's performance. Miller had slept in the spare bedroom so that he didn't disturb her. He and Monica had breakfast together. "Are you coming down to Stokely this weekend?"

"It's very sweet of you, Harry, but it's time I got back to work, and then there's my book."

"Still at it after four years."

"It's very complicated stuff."

"Yes, well, the Romans were very complicated people. Come on, Ellis is due about now. We'll take you to Kings Cross for the train."

She was finishing her coffee. "I was thinking of Dillon. He is a spook, isn't he, Harry?"

Miller said, "He'll roar with laughter when I tell him you said that. Actually, he was a top enforcer with the Provisional IRA."

She almost choked on her coffee, she laughed so much. "Honestly, Harry, you are an idiot sometimes."

"Okay, I give up. Come on, let's get going."

THEY DROPPED HER OFF, he kissed her good-bye, then Ellis took him to Downing Street. He didn't have an appointment with the Prime Minister, but walked into him by chance as the great man was coming out of his office. He pulled Miller to one side and said in little more than a whisper, "Bloody good work. My God, it's given the bastards a black eye."

As he rushed away and went downstairs, Simon Carter emerged. "There you are, Miller. Been up to your tricks again while I've been away."

"Well, the tricks got a result," Miller told him. "Doesn't that please you?"

"There's a way of doing things, a proper way, sensible diplomatic overtures. Not Ferguson's way and not your way. You're going too far. For God's sake, man, it could be the death of you, can't you see that?"

Miller sometimes called him Simon because he knew it annoyed him. "My dear Simon, I didn't know you cared."

"What's the point?" Carter said. "Carry on like this and see where your stupidity gets you." He went downstairs.

Miller checked a few things, then called Ellis, went outside and got into the Mercedes when it arrived, and told Ellis to make it the House of Commons. He went in at the St. Stephens Entrance, went through the central lobby to his office, then down to the House and passed the bar. The debate was about some aspect of housing policy, the speeches very partisan, and suddenly he was so bored he couldn't stand it anymore. He went to the Whip's Office, said he had something to do for the Prime Minister for three days, a common occurrence, and left the House, calling Ellis on his Codex.

He told him to take him to Dover Street, but when he got there, there was no Olivia, so he phoned and found her at the hairdresser's. "Do you fancy lunch?" he asked. "A run out into the country, perhaps?"

"Good God no," she said. "I've got a working lunch with Colin, then the whole afternoon I have a run-through with my new understudy. Francine's been offered a play at the West Riding Playhouse. Management has told her she can go."

So that was that. "I'm going away for a day or two. I'll leave you Ellis full time. I'll take the Mini Cooper. Is that okay?"

"I suppose so. Where are you going?"

"I haven't been to Folly's End for ages. I feel like getting away for a day or two. It's time I checked the place out."

She sounded perfectly cheerful. "If that's what you've got to do, that's what you've got to do. Tell Ellis where I am. He can pick me up from here."

He changed into casual clothes—black velvet cords, black shirt, bomber jacket—and threw a few things in an old duffel bag, found a trench coat, and went downstairs. The Mini Cooper was parked at the curb, covered by a resident's parking permit like many townhouses in Mayfair. Ellis was pulled in farther along, waiting for him, sitting behind the wheel, reading the *Mail*.

Close by was a man in a yellow oilskin jacket with a yellow handcart. He was sweeping the pavement with slow, deliberate strokes.

Miller said, "Change of plan, Ellis. Madame is at the hairdresser's. That's Joe Hansford."

"What are you going to do, Major?"

"I think I'm going to go down to West Sussex, Folly's End, for a couple of days. I'll have a check on how things are at the cottage."

"We haven't been there for a year at least."

"I know, Ellis, time I did. On your way now." He closed the door and Ellis drove off. Miller nodded cheerfully to the sweeper, went back to the Mini Cooper, got inside, and drove away. Within minutes, he was driving out into Park Lane and turning up toward Marble Arch.

His intended destination was a few miles along the coast from Bognor Regis, not even a proper village, just an inlet where there was room for half a dozen boats to anchor, a scattering of cottages, and a pub called Smugglers', and behind it what was left of the grass runways of a Battle of Britain fighter station, Haddon Field. His father had bought one of the cottages after the Second World War for five hundred pounds. The times spent there had been some of the most cherished memories of childhood. He couldn't wait to get there.

• • •

ABDUL, THE SWEEPERS' FOREMAN, had done Dover Street himself and reported what he had overheard to Ali Hassim on his mobile.

"You've done well," Ali told him. "It doesn't need to be a full-time operation. Just tell your boys to keep an eye out generally and report anything of interest."

He searched a shelf above his desk that contained a series of travel handbooks covering most parts of the country, and found what he was looking for, an area map of West Sussex, and soon located Folly's End. He thought about it, then phoned a member of the Brotherhood, who worked for a financial house in the City.

"Are you available?" he asked.

"Since my promotion, I'm in charge of my own destiny. What is it you want?"

"Come round to the shop and I'll tell you."

SAM BOLTON was actually Selim. His story was simple. His mother was Muslim and despised by her people for marrying his English father, who raised him in a totally Christian culture. His father had died during his first year studying accountancy at London University, and his mother had returned to her Islamic faith. There had been those who had seen distinct possibilities in a handsome young man in a good suit who seemed English and had an excellent background in the City. The truth was that Bolton wasn't in the slightest religious and accepted his sleeper role in the movement more out of a sense of adventure than anything else. The other truth was that Ali, wise in the way of the world, was perfectly aware of the situation.

Ali didn't think Bolton had any need to know what the mission was really about, nor who Miller really was. Bolton looked puzzled when Ali gave him the name, and checked him out on the laptop.

"So why him?" he asked, looking at the laptop on his knees. "He seems a typically pin-striped MP, except for his patch in the Falklands, and enjoyed a totally deskbound career."

"Appearances can be deceptive."

"Do you know more than you're telling me?"

"See what you make of him."

"If that's a challenge, you're on." Bolton closed his laptop. "You do realize I haven't had breakfast. I'll stop at a Little Chef on the way."

"You intend to go as you are?"

"You mean dressed like this, an accountant from one of the best investment firms in the City, on his way to Bognor Regis in his Audi and lost in the labyrinth of country roads that is West Sussex?"

"Go with my blessing, you rogue, and Allah protect you." Ali patted him on the cheek as Bolton went out.

MILLER HAD A GOOD fast run from London through Guildford all the way to Chichester and down to the best of West Sussex, into a complex of country roads that he remembered well. It was a two-and-a-half-hour run, so he was at Folly's End about half past one.

There were sailing boats anchored in the inlet, a solitary motor cruiser, four cars outside the pub. He parked the Mini Cooper, walked down to the shingle beach, smelling the same salt smell from childhood, then turned to Smugglers'. When he went into the bar, two couples were sitting in separate booths, working their way through ham salads, beer on the tables.

Behind the bar, polishing a glass, was the publican, Lizzie Arnold, a widow for seven years now, one son away in the Army, a paratrooper. She was forty-five and comely, a local farmer's daughter. Miller had known her forever.

"My God, look what the cat's brought in." She leaned over the bar and kissed him. "It's been too long. Where have you been?"

He held her hands across the bar. "Oh, here, there, and everywhere. You wouldn't want to know. Everything okay at the cottage?"

Stepping in through the door, Sam Bolton had heard all

this and did an excellent impersonation of someone who didn't have the slightest idea where he was.

"Excuse me."

Lizzie took a key from one of many hanging on a board behind the bar. "Everything's in apple pie order, Harry." He started to move out, and she said to Bolton, "What's your problem, my love?"

"I'm down from London, managed to hit Chichester, and as it's Bognor Regis I'm making for, I thought I'd find a scenic route, cut into the country, and I seem to have got thoroughly lost."

Miller said from the door, "You certainly have, but she'll put you straight. I'll be back, Lizzie."

He went out, and Bolton said, "I suppose I could do with some lunch while I'm here, and a pint of beer. But just the one, I'm driving."

He really was a handsome devil, she thought, and pumped his beer.

"I'll just lock my car."

"No need round here, love, believe me."

"I've got some really important papers in there for the client I'm seeing in Bognor."

He slid behind the wheel of the Audi, reached under the dashboard, and dropped a flap that held a Walther PPK. He slipped it into the briefcase he was carrying as he returned to the pub. He was probably being foolish, but the pin-striped MP in the laptop was one thing and the man in black cords and bomber jacket wearing Ray-Ban Wayfarers was something entirely different. He was now perfectly certain that Ali had not been honest with him, had involved him in something that was more than it seemed.

She had his beer waiting at a corner table. "My trade is mainly in the evening these days, so I'm finished for lunch. Steak-and-ale pie, and fries out of the microwave. Any good?"

"Just bring it on," he said, and started to drink his beer.

• • •

THE COTTAGE was in first-rate condition, not a trace of damp, the smell of polish everywhere, the kitchen spotless. Miller picked up the photo of his mother. She'd been the most important thing in his life for the first five years and then tragically died in childbirth with Monica. He kissed the photo as he always did, replaced it on the sideboard, then took out his Codex and contacted Roper.

"It's Harry. I've taken the day off. I've come down to a hamlet called Folly's End on the West Sussex coast. We've had a cottage here for years."

"And—?"

"Roper, the only reason I'm still here at forty-five is because all those years in and out of Northern Ireland branded me. When I see some individual who's out of the ordinary, I know him instinctively and beyond doubt to be suspicious. Some guy just appeared in the small pub of this tiny hamlet, claiming to have lost his way to Bognor Regis. No name, but I have the number of a silver Audi coupe."

"Then give it to me," which Miller did. He was back in seconds. "Samuel Bolton. Has a flat in Belsize Park. M.B.A. from London University, investment manager with Goldman-Greene in the City. Does that help?"

"I didn't know his name when I asked you, so I'll have to go and check. Is that it? Nothing else?"

"Except the fact that his mother was a Muslim and Iranian. She's dead, by the way, heart attack five years ago, his father last year. It's all here. These finance houses are very thorough. What is this, Harry?"

"I left my place in Dover Street this morning. I was giving my chauffeur from the Cabinet Offices his orders for the day, telling him I was coming down here in the Mini Cooper, and I saw something I'd never seen before."

"What was that?"

"A man in a yellow oilskin jacket with a yellow trolley, and he was sweeping the street. He was a Muslim from his appearance, and he was close enough to hear me."

"Army of God," Roper said. "The sweepers, the Brotherhood. What are you going to do?"

"I told you in my Beirut report about Drecq Khan confessing that a man named Ali Hassim ran the Brotherhood. I'll see what Bolton thinks about that."

"Take care, Harry. The Brotherhood isn't supposed to exist. However, if this guy Sam Bolton is an agent of such an organization, have you considered his purpose in being there?"

"Well, I could always ask him."

A LITTLE EARLIER, a speedboat had arrived in the inlet and Lizzie had come to the window and groaned. "Not him again."

Bolton glanced out and saw the man at the wheel push the prow into the shingle of the beach, scramble over the side, and wade out of the water. He was big and powerful, wore a fisherman's smock, and had tangled hair and was badly in need of a shave. The youth who scrambled out behind him looked about eighteen and was a younger version.

One of the couples on the other side of the bar glanced out, there was a hurried exchange, and they got up and left. The other couple looked distinctly worried.

"Trouble?" Bolton asked.

"Nothing but trouble. Seth Harker. He likes the fisherman look, but he's a retired property millionaire from London who made it by walking all over people. Drunk as a lord most of the time, and the other idiot is his son, Claude, who's permanently on something. I tried barring them, but it's difficult. And there's no man around the place until this evening."

Harker came in laughing, followed by the youth, and the remaining couple who had been having lunch got up to go.

"Leaving, are you?" Harker roared, and as the young couple passed, his son patted the woman's bottom.

"Nice arse on her, Dad."

The couple hurriedly left and Lizzie came straight around the bar. "I'm not having that kind of conduct in my pub. I'm telling you for the last time, you're barred, so get out."

Claude Harker came up behind her, grabbed her close, and ran a hand up her skirt. "That's nice," he leered, absolutely coked up to the eyeballs from the look of him. "I like that."

Lizzie Arnold was helpless, crying with rage as she struggled in his grasp, and Harker went behind the bar, laughing his head off, and helped himself to whiskey. Sam Bolton got to his feet and moved in.

"She doesn't like that, you little toad, hadn't you noticed?" He pulled Claude around, slapped him across the face and simply threw him away, then turned to Lizzie. "Are you all right?"

Seth Harker, moving surprisingly fast for such a big man, was through the bar flap instantly, had one arm round Bolton's neck, and grabbed a wrist.

"Trouble is it, you bastard? You've come to the right place. Go on, Claude, do him up."

Lizzie cried out in indignation. Claude Harker got one good punch in, and Miller arrived on the run behind him and punched him in the kidneys. Young Harker howled in agony, and Miller simply dragged him away to fall over a table.

Seth Harker seemed transfixed, staring at Miller in a kind of wonder. He released Bolton, who staggered away, blood on his mouth. Claude, pulling himself together, swung a wild punch at Bolton, who blocked it easily and punched him in the face.

Harker said, "I'll have you for that, but first, I'm going to break your friend's arms, both of them."

He launched his full weight at Miller, hands reaching. Miller simply deflected the left arm, grabbed the wrist, and twisted, running Harker into a display of bottles at the end of the bar. The arm for the moment was rigid, and his clenched right fist descended in a hammer blow.

Harker's cry of agony was very real, and Miller said to him, "You mentioned two broken arms. I've let you off with one this time. If you ever show your face here again, I'll break the other."

Harker was clutching his broken arm. Miller grabbed him by the scruff of the neck and called to Bolton, "Bring that nasty little sod, will you?"

He urged Harker down through the shingle to the speedboat. "In you get," he said, and heaved him headfirst. Bolton brought up the rear with Claude Harker and thrust him over behind the wheel, where he sat, blood on his face, looking distinctly the worse for wear.

"Use your brain, if you've got one left, turn the key and the engine should start, then just go away. Come back and you know what to expect." Miller turned to Bolton. "The bastards are going to need a shove."

They gave the speedboat a push. It drifted out into the waters of the inlet, the engine started, and the boat moved away. Miller said, "I think I could do with a drink. How about you?"

"I'm driving, but I could kill for a cup of tea." Bolton had a handkerchief out and was trying to stem the blood from the punch in the mouth he'd received.

"Nasty," Miller told him.

"Nothing like as nasty as what you did to Seth Harker. Is he always like that?"

"I wouldn't know," Miller said. "My family's owned a holiday cottage here since I was a kid, but it's been a year since I was here. Harker, you say?"

"That's what the lady called him."

They went in the pub and found Lizzie picking up bottles that had been knocked off the bar. She turned and threw her arms around Miller and kissed him. There was a kind of awe on her face. "My God, Harry Miller, I've known you since we were kids together." She shook her head. "It was as if I'd never known you as I watched what you did to that rotter."

"Oh, he made me angry," Miller told her. "Enough said, Lizzie. If he bothers you again, I can arrange for pressure to be applied from the right people to assist him in mending his ways."

She turned to Bolton and held out her hand. "Lizzie Arnold. When that slimy little article put his hand up my skirt, I felt sick, but you came roaring in." She kissed him on the cheek. "You're another hero in my book. Can I have your name?"

"You can have my card, if you like." Bolton extracted one from his wallet and gave it to her.

"Harry Miller." He held out his hand. "Can I have one, too?"

"Certainly." Bolton found another, and Miller read it.

"Goldman-Greene Investments. You're a long way from the City."

"Making for Bognor—we've got clients there. Actually, I think I'd better make a move."

"Well, God bless you, love, and you're welcome anytime," Lizzie told him.

"I'll see you off," Miller said, and they went out.

They walked a little way on to the beach, the shingle crunching under their feet. Sam Bolton felt calm, better in himself than he had in a long time. "This is a really special place. I envy you." He simulated hesitation. "You know, I feel in some strange way that I know you or that I've seen you somewhere."

Miller was amused but didn't show it. "I've been on television on the odd occasion. I'm a Member of Parliament."

"Of course." Bolton laughed. "Well, if you don't mind me saying so, you're like no Member of Parliament I ever knew."

"Sometimes I lose my temper. Did you get what you came for?"

Bolton answered instinctively, his big mistake. "Yes, I think so."

He froze for a moment, and Miller smiled. "Well, that's good. Safe journey, and thanks for stepping in. There's still a brotherhood of men of goodwill who're willing to step in when the going gets rough in this wicked old world. I like that." He turned and went into the pub.

What had been said, the use of the word "brotherhood," could only have one meaning, and Bolton got in the Audi and drove away, and for some reason found himself laughing, because he'd liked Miller, liked him a lot.

"He knows," he said aloud. "The bastard actually knows. I wonder how."

Fifteen minutes later, he found the main road and started back to London.

WHILE LIZZIE was making him ham sandwiches in the kitchen, he Codexed Roper. "Call off the cavalry," he said, and gave him a brief account of what had happened.

"Dammit all, Harry, you seem to have a flair for turning everything into the Gunfight at the OK Corral."

"Not quite true this time. It was Sam Bolton who stepped in first, to protect a lady's honor, as it were. He didn't hesitate, even though there were two of them. He didn't know I was going to arrive through the door to back him up. Anyway, he could handle himself and he was prepared to have a go. He wasn't your average guy next door, but the most significant thing was that instinctive reply he made when I asked him had he got what he'd come for."

"And he said I think so."

"And what do you think he'd come for?"

"To suss you out, Harry, something like that. I must say he must have found you interesting."

"He did say I was like no Member of Parliament he ever knew."

"Don't worry, old lad, you're definitely a one-off. Perhaps that's what he needed to find out. We'll speak again."

In London, Bolton went straight to Hampstead when he arrived, and found the corner shop still open, a young girl in a head scarf working behind the counter. Bolton asked for Hassim, she went in the back, returned and held the door open for him, and he passed through.

Hassim was sitting behind his desk and glanced up. "How did it go?"

Bolton took a chair by the fire. "He's a very exceptional man."

"I had become aware of that. Tell me what happened. Obviously, something out of the ordinary did."

"You could say that." Bolton proceeded to give an account. "This is a very dangerous individual. His image, the Reform Club member, the MP in a pin-striped suit, gives a totally false idea of who he is."

"No, of *what* he is would be more accurate." Ali Hassim sighed. "Of course, it is a pity that your actions called into question your own credentials. You are convinced that he was onto you?"

"Why use that reference to 'brotherhood'? But there was more than that, I sensed it. It was as if he knew me."

"Which is unfortunate," Ali Hassim told him. "You were in your own car and the number plate alone would open a wealth of information about you and your identity."

"As a sleeper, my usefulness is the genuineness of my identity. I gave him my card because I am who I say I am, an investment manager with an important City firm. We live in the world of the instant check. Mine would prove at once, even to the police, that I am totally respectable."

"But yet you say he suspects you of being a member of the Brotherhood?"

"That is true, and if I am right, there must be more going on in the background than even you know. Has it ever occurred to you that your enemies are perfectly well aware that under the respectable religious cloak of the Army of God, the Brotherhood exists? Perhaps the situation suits them." Bolton got up. "So I've done my bit. I must get back to earning a living."

He went out and Ali Hassim sat there, thinking. Bolton was right in what he had said, the implication that people like Ferguson were happy to allow the activities of an organization like the Brotherhood to continue because they were able to monitor it. A slightly depressing thought, but even more depressing was the fact that Bolton was beginning to query things. The trouble was, he wasn't religious at all, so no control was possible because it meant he was not to be trusted. So, in future, he would have to be treated with caution. On the other hand, he was so useful to the cause, totally accepted as one of their own by the enemy, hugely intelligent. Too valuable to let go. In any case, he had made his vows to serve Allah to the death. If he ever attempted to go back on that, there would only be one possible outcome. He sighed, went into the kitchen, and made a cup of tea.

9

Two days later, Miller returned to London to an exceptionally busy time in politics, debate after debate in Parliament, crucial votes necessary again and again. Add Cabinet Office business to that, and he saw little of Olivia. He also saw little of Ferguson.

But he himself was not forgotten, certainly not by Quinn, who was thinking a lot about the old days and about one man in particular. He'd been not only a top bomb maker, but a mechanical genius, and his name was Sean Fahy. Born in Kilburn, the Irish quarter of London, he'd lived there all his life, a problem solver of the first water. Quinn wondered . . . He went to his laptop and soon found a number and an address: Derry Street Garage. He phoned a special number from the old days and waited. It seemed to ring forever—and then, unbelievably, it was picked up.

Fahy was sixty-five and looked older, with sallow cheeks and a kind of eternal sadness to him, the general look of a man who had found life more disappointing than he had hoped.

He wore an old raincoat over a dark suit, a shirt so old-fashioned it lacked a collar, and a battered tweed cap, touched with oil from too much time spent under automobiles. He had been out in the yard, about to leave his premises, when he'd heard the sound of the old telephone, the one someone in the Movement had fitted illegally for him in the pantry. He hadn't answered a call in years, because there hadn't been one. He slumped on a stool, breathing hard from his rush to get in, and put the phone to his ear.

"Who is this?"

"Michael Quinn, you old sod. How are you?"

"Mother Mary, after all these years. Quinn! What in the hell do you want?"

"A kind word would be welcome, especially as I have work for you that would be right up your street. Take my number. I'm calling from County Louth. Go on, take it. You won't regret it." There was an old pencil in a jar beside the phone, so reluctantly he used it to write on the whitewashed pantry wall. He was slightly incredulous, and in any case didn't feel well.

"For God's sake, Quinn, it's over, the whole bloody game. Peace in Ireland and all that shite. I was your best bomb maker and that's a fact, but the days of the bomb are over, except for the damned Muslims."

"Never mind the bombs, you were also a mechanical genius, you knew more about car engines than any man I knew. Remember that judge who was killed in his car in County Down when you came over from London special? That was no bomb, just your touch with the engines."

"I remember him well enough, and also the wife that was with him and left in a wheelchair for the rest of her life. No, whatever it is, I'm not interested. Now I'm due at a nursing home to see my wife, so I'll say good-bye."

"Fifty thousand pounds."

Fahy stood there for a moment clutching the phone. "For what?"

"For what you've done many times before—helping someone out of this wicked old world into the next."

"You must be mad. Leave me alone, and I mean that. Don't call again."

QUINN THOUGHT ABOUT IT and then spoke to the Broker. "I've got a prospect who could be of use to me residing in Kilburn. His name is Sean Fahy, at a place called Derry Street Garage. He has a flat above it. See if this Ali Hassim of yours can have somebody give him the once-over to see what the situation is. It could be important."

"I'll see what I can do. Something stirring?"

"I think so."

FAHY WAS WALKING through dark rain, head down, in a turmoil, and the pain in his gut that had started only a couple of weeks earlier was really hurting. He would be late for Maggie and he hated that, but when Doc Smith's secretary had phoned about the X-ray results from the hospital, she'd been abrupt with him. The doctor needed to see him and that was that. Ten minutes later, he walked into the surgery and the receptionist told him to go straight in.

He knew it was bad news, you could see it on Smith's face; he had the X-rays up on the screen and the report from the hospital. Fahy made it easy for him. "It's bad, isn't it?"

"Cancer of the pancreas. We've known each other a long time."

"Serviced your bloody car for years. How long have I got?"

"Three months tops."

"Can't anything help? Chemotherapy or drugs?"

"Not with this." Smith hesitated. "I know it presents you with a difficulty regarding your wife."

Fahy got up, surprisingly calm. "Not now, Doc."

AT SAINT JOSEPH'S HOSPICE, he sat holding her hand while she lay propped up in bed, unaware of his presence, and it struck him again how cruel Alzheimer's could be, to destroy the real person she had been for forty years and leave only a vacant shell.

Sister Ursula looked in. "I think that's enough for today, Sean."

He kissed Maggie's hands and followed the young nun out, thinking how good the nuns were and that at least Maggie had the loving-kindness of the hospice.

In the entrance hall, Sister Ursula said, "Sit down a minute, Sean." He did and she carried on. "The local hospital trust wants to move her. I did warn you it might happen. They say their facility is perfectly adequate and at their price."

"I want her to stay with you. I'll find the extra."

"That isn't the point. We're private, and they don't like that. We'd be happy to keep her on at the rate they charge, but they're going to refuse to pay it if she stays here, and they'll get away with it because they've got room for her there."

"It's no better than a madhouse, Victorian style. I wouldn't keep a dog in there."

"But can you afford it here, Sean? It would be a great burden."

He stood. "Not to worry, Sister, I've come into a bit of money. I'll just need a week or two to sort things out."

Her smile of relief filled the room. "I'm so relieved."

"To tell you the truth, so am I."

Fahy let himself in the main door. The garage was huge, extending all the way into the back of the property. It smelled of petrol and oil. There was a big white Ford van with *Vehicle Recovery* painted on the side and an old Triumph roadster that went back a few years. He patted its roof as he went by and reached the kitchen through a small door. He found himself a pen and pad just in case and sat on the stool in the pantry and phoned.

"You're back," Quinn said. "That's wonderful. Good on you, Sean."

"Don't stroke me. First of all, before you say another word, these are my terms."

"Go on," Quinn said.

"You'll arrange a bank draft for fifty thousand pounds within the next twenty-four hours."

"You want payment in advance?"

"No, I want the first installment in advance. Successful completion costs you another twenty-five."

Quinn laughed. "You old bastard. You thought I'd quibble? Your money is in the bag. First thing in the morning."

"So who are we going to ease into the next world?"

"A Major Harry Miller. He's a Member of Parliament and an under secretary of state. Does that scare you off? He put plenty of your comrades in their graves in the old days, believe me."

"I'm not worried in the slightest. So what are the specific details?"

"Do you have a computer?"

"I have for years. It's old, but it seems to do the job."

"I'll pass a load of stuff to you now. When we were talking earlier, you said you had to get off to see your wife in a nursing home. Maggie, as I remember. Is there a problem?"

"Not at all," Fahy told him. "A woman's thing."

"That's good. Just give me your e-mail address."

BY THE TIME he got to the computer in his office, the attachments were there and he printed them out, three sheets in all, then sat down, took a bottle of Bushmills out of a drawer, poured another one, and started reading. It was just like the old days: details of the target, family, general circumstances, Miller's wife, his sister, and then Miller himself. He sat looking at the photos and the material collated by Ali Hassim's people, photos of Dover Street. The whiskey he'd taken had killed most of the pain now, so he sat back and smoked a cigarette and allowed all the information to come together. One thing was essential. He needed to check out Dover Street for himself, so he went downstairs, opened the garage, and drove away in the Triumph roadster.

• • •

He liked Mayfair, always had, the network of streets lined with fine properties, some from as early as the eighteenth century. Dover Street was no exception. Most townhouses didn't have garages, but that was common enough and parking was at the curb when available. Fahy noted the Mini Cooper outside Miller's house. He'd already seen that on a surreptitious photo taken by a sweeper.

Fahy reversed into the cul-de-sac now. There were two other cars there, and when he checked, they each had a residential parking permit. He went out into Dorset Street and checked Chico's. There were a couple of tables with chairs in the wide doorway. For the moment, the café was quiet, just one girl behind the bar. He went in and asked for a coffee, then sat in the doorway, looking along the street.

It was luck, of course, but it wasn't long before a black limousine turned into the end of the street, not a Mercedes, but an Amara. It halted next to the Mini Cooper, and a driver got out and held the passenger door open. Miller had a bundle of files under one arm and carried a briefcase. Fahy knew all about the Amara, a luxury vehicle and yet still a performance car. The engine was in the rear, which could make access easier for what Fahy intended. On the other hand, he'd no means of knowing if the change of vehicle was permanent. Miller talked for a minute, then the driver got back behind the wheel and drove away, passing Chico's. Fahy watched as Miller struggled to get his key out, but he finally managed it and entered the house. Curious how close you could face your intended victim; he'd forgotten how that felt. Still, it was all beginning to make sense. As he got up to go, he noticed a street-sweeper in yellow turn the corner. It struck him he'd have to do something about that, and he returned to his Triumph and looked around. There was a manhole cover close to the wall with *London Water* engraved on it. It was like a sign from heaven. He got behind the wheel of the Triumph and drove away.

• • •

BACK AT THE GARAGE, Fahy sat at his desk and had another Bushmills. He'd have to watch it, but it was a genuine relief from the pain for a while. He phoned Quinn.

"Is the money arranged?"

"Yes. It's coming from Ali Hassim's people, a man they call the Broker."

"I don't care who it's from, as long as it's money."

"I've arranged for them to speak with you in a little while."

"That's okay by me."

"Can I ask you how you are going to do this thing?"

"You said you wanted it to be a car accident."

"And you can do that?"

"I think so. But there's always an element of uncertainty. Take Princess Diana in Paris. Four of them in the limousine, three dead, and yet her bodyguard survived. Very badly injured, mind you, but you get my point."

"We'll have to take our chances with that. What help do you need?"

"The stuff from this Ali Hassim was useful. I've got a question about the street-sweepers, though."

"Tell you what, why don't you talk to the Broker about it when he calls."

"Fine by me."

IT WAS ONLY half an hour later that the phone rang as Fahy was making a sandwich. "This is the Broker, Mr. Fahy. Quinn is quite hopeful about things after you spoke to him." He was warm and courteous, very English in an old-fashioned way. Fahy pretty well repeated what he had told Quinn.

When he was finished, the Broker said, "You make good sense. After all, there is risk in everything in this life. Wasn't there supposed to be a murderer in Victorian London who survived three attempts to hang him?"

"So they say."

"Quinn says you were pleased with the material Hassim's sweepers obtained?"

"Yes, good stuff. But I was in Dover Street earlier, checking things out, and a sweeper turned up at the end of the street. They look a bit conspicuous in that yellow gear. Hassim can get his hands on all sorts of people?"

"Absolutely."

"Well, eliminate the sweeper and let's have a traffic warden. They're much less conspicuous."

"Consider it done."

"And see what Hassim's connections are with the Water Board. They have those small green maintenance vans. I'd like one delivered to my garage tomorrow. I'll leave the door unlocked."

"Consider that done also. I've heard details of your record with the IRA. Very impressive."

"Yes. I've killed a Member of Parliament before."

"Do you really think you can make Harry Miller kill himself in a car accident?"

"You've got the wrong end of the stick. I'm hoping I can make his chauffeur kill him. Now, what about the money? If it's not here in the morning, I'm done with you."

The Broker said, "At precisely noon tomorrow, my messenger will arrive at your garage. He'll give you an envelope containing a key to a locker at an establishment in Camden. That's not far from you."

"Just down the road. What kind of establishment?"

"Once the messenger has departed, I'll phone you with the name and number of the locker and in it will be a manila envelope containing an open bank draft with the Bank of Geneva behind it. Will that satisfy you?"

"Isn't that a roundabout way of doing it?"

"A safe way, Mr. Fahy. We'll speak again."

NEXT, the Broker spoke to Ali Hassim and told him to do exactly what Fahy wanted. Then he spoke to Volkov in Moscow. Volkov listened patiently, and when the Broker was finished, said, "I can see what Fahy is getting at. Let's face it, you could break your neck stepping off the pavement on the wrong foot. Let's see what the Irishman comes up with. His record's admittedly a long time ago, but it's impressive."

"Even Miller in a wheelchair would be worth it," the Broker said. "Just one more thing. Quinn was supposed to come to London. You told him you felt that Ferguson wouldn't dare arrest him. But he greatly fears that Ferguson might not be able to resist."

"In other words, he's lost his nerve."

"So it would appear. He hasn't returned to his Dublin office. He's staying on at Drumore Place, well-guarded by old associates."

"Oh, dear." Volkov laughed harshly. "Well, first things first. We'll let Fahy go about his business. Then I'll deal with Quinn afterwards."

FOR FAHY there were the painkillers that Dr. Smith had originally given him, and coupled with the Bushmills, he had a better night than he had expected. He rose at eight, went down to a café in the next street and tried the comfort of a full English breakfast, returned to the garage and waited, slightly aimless, and then it happened. At noon on the dot, a special deliveryman in black helmet and leathers and riding a BMW motorcycle appeared. The garage door was up, Fahy waiting. He was offered an envelope.

"Do I sign?"

"No." The messenger rode away.

There was a Yale key inside and a blue plastic card in the name of Smith & Co. and the notation *Full Membership*. It didn't say where for, but before Fahy could think about it, the phone rang and the Broker said, "You have it?"

"Yes, and a bit of useless plastic."

"A group membership card to a place called The Turkish Rooms in Hoxley Grove off Camden High Street. You simply walk in with the card, go through an archway, turn right, and you'll find the locker room, wood-paneled, very friendly. The lockers are for clothes. Your key fits locker seven. You'll find what you want in there, lock it again, and leave."

• • •

No more than a couple of miles down the road to Camden, Fahy found an old Victorian building with a sign that said *The Turkish Rooms,* and parked outside. He went in through the marbled entrance hall, found an empty reception desk and a button that said *Ring for Attention.* He ignored it, turned right, and found the locker room. There was no one there, but beyond, through another archway, came sounds of voices, showers behind metal doors.

He had locker seven open in an instant, found a manila envelope, and there was the draft. He locked up again, went straight out, the desk still unattended, got in the Triumph, and drove to Kilburn to the branch of HSBC where he had his account.

He asked for the duty manager, waited until he had confirmation that the money was credited to his account, and drove straight to St. Joseph's Hospice, where he saw his wife.

She was much as usual, pale and wan, but her hair had been neatly arranged and her nightgown and robe were clean and fresh. The nuns were wonderful at that. Truly caring. She lay propped up by pillows, staring vacantly into her own private world.

Sister Ursula found him there. "She's a little better this morning, Sean." He forgave her the lie.

"A bit of an inheritance has come through, Sister. She'll end her days in your care."

"Are you sure, Sean?"

"Just work out the cost, Sister. I'll make you out a check for a year in advance if you like."

"Oh, that's wonderful." She was obviously thrilled.

"Have it down on paper for me to see the next time I'm in."

"I will, Sean, I will."

He left, got in the Triumph, and sat there for a moment and thought about Miller. "Well, I'm sorry, me auld son, but I'd no choice, you see. You'll just have to take your chances."

• • •

WHEN HE GOT BACK to the garage, a green old Morris van with *London Water Board* painted on the side stood inside. He checked it out quickly. An ignition key was in place, and a neatly folded green boiler suit lay on the passenger seat, with *London Water Board* printed on the back. When he opened the rear door, he unveiled a small workshop and the wooden bollards necessary to guard an open manhole.

All this would be the cover for him to appear to be working down the manhole at the end of the cul-de-sac. In the best of all possible worlds, Miller's chauffeur would park the limousine, whichever it was, and go to Chico's for his coffee while waiting for Miller. That would give Fahy time to place underneath the engine a lethal contraption he was about to make involving electronics and nitric acid. Once in place, within fifteen minutes of starting, the car would experience a catastrophic loss of fluid, leaving its brakes totally useless. It had worked before, a long time ago, resulting in the death of an Army colonel on leave from Ulster, the long hand of the IRA reaching out to punish, even in London. Of course, it might be that the chauffeur didn't have time to visit the café. That was all right. If it didn't work one day, it would another.

PRESSURES AT WORK had kept Miller busy and he hadn't seen much of his wife. Relations between them were perfectly pleasant, and yet she seemed to have developed a kind of studied indifference to their relationship. He had seen photos of her in the media with Colin Carlton. Miller wasn't aware of any feeling of jealousy on his part, although remarks in the gossip columns were already hinting that there could be more to it.

He was changing his shirt in the spare bedroom when she opened the door and glanced in. "There you are. Are you coming tonight?"

"It's not possible, I'm afraid. Important debate on Kosovo. There might be trouble again, and a lot of people want to make sure we don't go poking our nose in. The PM wants me to do my bit."

"What a bore," she said. "The producers are throwing a hell of a good party at Annabel's. I'll just have to go with Colin."

"It's the price of fame, my love. The paparazzi and the gossip columns will love it. You might even make *Hello* magazine. It's a damn sight more entertaining than a debate on Britain's foreign policy in countries about which the average voter doesn't have the slightest interest."

She sat on the edge of the bed and watched him fix his tie and pull on the jacket of a navy blue suit.

"I haven't seen that."

"No, I was passing through Harrods and they were having a sale. I thought it might give me a serious man-of-purpose look coupled with a crisp white shirt with good cuffs, regimental tie. I'm performing tonight, too, remember."

"You old fool. On the other hand, you do look seriously good, Harry. The Prime Minister might have you in the cabinet yet."

"Over my dead body." He combed his hair and glanced in the mirror. "Not bad."

She got a white handkerchief and arranged it in his breast pocket. "What's happened to us, Harry?" There was a slight edge of despair there, and he smiled, put his hands on her shoulders, and kissed her forehead.

"It's called marriage, love. You think it's going to last forever, but nothing does. Nothing stays the same. Take you. You've been acting your head off since you emerged from drama school thirteen years ago, and now you've given a performance that's made you the toast of the London stage." He shook her lightly. "It's all happening, you cuckoo, Hollywood beckons. Enjoy it, you've earned it."

"And where does that leave you?"

"Boring old me, you mean?"

She shook her head. "I was speaking to Monica. She's got the idea that Dillon is a spook. She said you fobbed her off, but when she raised it again, you said he'd been a top enforcer with the IRA."

"Which gave her a good laugh."

She looked at him searchingly. "I've shared my bed with

you, Harry Miller. If I know anyone it should be you, and you don't make fun. You're a dour, serious man. I think what you said to Monica about Dillon must be true."

He took her hands and held them tight. "Sean Dillon is probably one of the most remarkable men I've met in my entire life." He was gripped by the desire to tell the truth to the only woman he had ever truly loved, and he thought, yes, now was the moment. "You've always thought I was a desk man, a Whitehall Warrior. Isn't that right?"

"And that wasn't true?"

"In 1985, aged twenty-three, I was sent undercover to Belfast to seek out a particularly obnoxious murdering piece of scum. I came across a priest named Father Sharkey. We killed together, fled through the sewers of Belfast. *That* man, I've discovered of late, is the Sean Dillon now working for the Prime Minister's security team."

"Killed? You killed?" There was a troubled look on her face. "After we were married, those trips you always went away on . . . ?"

"To Northern Ireland. I was never away for long, you recall? Just a few days, a week at the most."

"And what happened in those few days—that's what you were doing?" She pulled her right hand free and punched him in the chest. "That terrible man in Shepherd's Market, the one you hit with the bottle. It makes sense now. Good Lord, Harry, I've never known you at all."

"So where does that leave us?"

"I don't know." She was angry and more than a little frightened. "Just go, Harry, go. I need to think this through."

"I'm sorry it's upset you. I've wanted to be honest for a long, long time."

"Honest?" She really was angry now. "You don't know the meaning of the word. You were living a lie when we got married. What kind of love was that? You deceived me totally, and what kind of trust did it show?"

"I was afraid you wouldn't approve."

"You were right, I don't." She pulled open the door and walked out.

Miller stood there, saddened, but it was done now and could not be taken back. He took out his phone and alerted Ellis that he was ready and went down.

LATER, MUCH LATER, when he'd had enough of Parliament, he left and walked aimlessly through the streets. He'd sent Ellis back to Dover Street earlier to pick up Olivia, told him to stay with her. Finally, with nowhere else to go, he hailed a cab and told the driver to take him to Holland Park, where he found Roper in the computer room.

"You got bored with the debate, I see," Roper said. "I watched if for a while on television, caught your short speech, succinct and very practical. 'Serbs like to butcher Muslims, so Muslims understandably would prefer Kosovo to be independent. Let's face up to that, gentlemen.' "

"If only it was that easy," Miller said. "Can I sample your whiskey?"

"Only if you pour one for me, too." Which Miller did. "You seem rather depressed."

"I'm that, all right. I'm also in the doghouse."

"Well, if you want to share, here I am."

So Miller told him all about it.

Afterward, Roper poured him another drink. "You've dug yourself into a real hole there."

"Dug myself into my own grave, in a manner of speaking. I can see now that she's unlikely to forgive me."

"Why on earth did you come clean after so long?"

"A mad impulse. Love, a proper relationship, of its very nature implies total honesty between people. In her eyes, I've acted as badly as if I'd been having an affair with another woman."

Roper felt desperately sorry for him. "Look, you're a decent man, Harry, an honorable man. Remember Derry all those years ago? You went into harm's way to pull out that young officer, took on four IRA guns. Soldiers take care of those things which ordinary folk can't. You've been a great one. I take my hat off to you."

"God bless you for saying that, Roper, but it doesn't help, unfortunately. I'll be on my way. I'll get Sergeant Doyle to call in a taxi for me."

He left, and Dillon entered the room. Roper said, "I didn't get a chance to tell him you were in the house. He just poured it all out. How much did you hear?"

"Enough. He's a good man."

"But racked with guilt now."

"And who needs that?" Dillon said.

"Maybe she'll come round."

"Yes, maybe, but somehow I doubt it. Come on, let's go down to the Dark Man. You need a break."

IN KILBURN, Fahy sat at his workbench, filling the vial of acid linked to the electronic circuit, the whole enclosed in a plastic box with grip clips that could be fitted to the brake fluid tube in seconds. It was painstaking work performed under a large magnifying glass, but in the end he was satisfied, particularly with the tiny watch battery that would act as a trembler underneath once the engine was turned on. Twenty minutes after his gadget was set in motion by the car starting, the vial would rupture and the acid would do its work virtually instantly.

He was tired, eyes sore, and now his pain started again. He got the Bushmills out and had a large one, for he intended to go to bed soon. His phone rang, and when he answered it, he found the Broker on the other end.

"Is everything proceeding smoothly?"

"Does anything in this life? The device is prepared."

"Will there be any trace of it after the accident if the wreck is inspected by experts?"

"It's so small that it's extremely doubtful. Years ago, when I used the same thing for the Army colonel in London, the coroner recorded a verdict of death by misadventure."

"I like that."

"The sweeper reports say Miller's chauffeur is never there before eight-thirty, but I'll be in the cul-de-sac by seven-thirty, just in case. What about the traffic warden?"

"Hassim has found you a real one. He's named Abdul and he's been told the minimum he needs to know." A lie, of course, for Abdul was Hassim's enforcer.

"That's good. I'm going to go to bed now."

The Broker said with great sympathy, "I get the feeling you're not well, my friend."

"Well enough to see this through. Good night." Fahy turned off the phone.

THE BROKER sat thinking about it and debating whether to speak to Volkov, but decided against it. He would leave it until the morning when, hopefully, the news would be good. What a triumph it would be, seeing off Miller. There were four decanters on his desk: gin, whiskey, brandy, and port. He decided on port, poured a glass, and said, "Here's to you, Miller, and may you rot in hell." In the distance, Big Ben started to strike.

AT DOVER STREET, Miller sat by the bow window in the dark, smoking a cigarette and enjoying a glass of whiskey. His wife had not returned yet, not that it bothered him, and then his phone rang and it was Monica.

"Harry?"

"Yes, old girl, where are you?"

"New Hall, my rooms. Olivia spoke to me earlier, told me this astonishing news about you. Is it true?"

"The short reply is yes."

"I don't know what to say."

"Well, you could try 'Harry, I still love you,' I suppose."

"I always will, you know that. It's just such a shock."

"What, having a killer in the family? I've managed to get by with that knowledge since 1985, and I'm sure she's told you that was when I first came across Dillon. You told me you liked him. Do you like him less now you know something of his past?"

There was a pause, and she murmured, "I don't know what to say."

"Actually, that's the second time you've said that. My advice is say nothing, love. Night, bless."

He put his phone away and heard a car, looked down outside, and saw a black cab draw up. Olivia got out, laughing, obviously on a high, and Colin Carlton stepped out behind her.

"Thanks a lot, darling," she said. "It was marvelous. I'll see you at the BBC tomorrow morning."

She reached to kiss his cheek, his arms went around her, she dropped her bag and her arms went around him, and the kiss was long and obviously fruitful. It was almost funny.

"Ah, well," Miller murmured. "That's show business."

He turned, got out of the dark room fast, was upstairs and into the spare bedroom before she got the front door open. He undressed quickly and slid into bed, switching off the light.

He heard her come up the stairs, walk along the corridor, pause, then continue to the main suite. He said softly, "That's that, then." He closed his eyes and went to sleep.

10

FAHY ARRIVED AT DOVER STREET AT SEVEN-THIRTY. IT WAS raining steadily. The traffic warden was already there in uniform and cap, wearing a mackintosh that almost reached his ankles and holding an umbrella over his head, clutching a clipboard, his ticket machine hanging from his shoulder.

There were no cars in the cul-de-sac, and the warden approached as Fahy got out of the van. "The people who usually park here, so they told me, have gone to work. I'm Abdul."

"Anyone else tries to park, move them on, except for the chauffeur in the Amara."

"Leave it with me."

The traffic warden went and stood on the corner, and Fahy opened the rear of the van, got two levers out, and raised the manhole cover. There was a very short ladder, pipes down there, no nasty smells. He brought the bollards from the van and circled a small fence around the opening, then brought a stool he'd found, a bag full of tools, and a shabby old black umbrella. Obviously, the Water Board maintenance people were used to rain.

Miller's chauffeur appeared at the end of Dover Street at

eight-fifteen and Abdul, standing on the corner beside Chico's, turned and waved briefly to Fahy, who prepared himself to look busy. What he didn't know was that Ellis Vaughan had already checked in with Miller, who had told him he wouldn't need him for half an hour at least and to go to Chico's and have breakfast.

The Amara passed the cul-de-sac, then reversed in. Vaughan got out, looked toward Fahy, then walked to the end and said to Abdul, "I'm going in the café for twenty minutes. My governor isn't ready yet."

He kept on going and moved into the café. Abdul turned toward Fahy and nodded. After almost forty years of dealing with cars, Fahy had a small leather case of master keys that between them would unlock any car. The third one he tried got the engine cover open, and he took the plastic box out of his pocket. The grips fit perfectly over their target. He placed the engine cover back down and locked it again. He nodded to Abdul and went straight back down on the stool.

Fifteen minutes later, Miller went downstairs and found Olivia wearing a raincoat over a trouser suit, finishing a cup of coffee fast. "Oh, there you are," she said. "I was coming to look for you. Colin and I have been asked to go on the BBC lunchtime television show. It'll be marvelous publicity for the play."

"I shouldn't think you need it, but I hope you do great."

She smiled. "Look, Harry, I've phoned the hairdresser's, and as a special favor, they'll take me early if I can get there as soon as possible. I'm asking you as a favor—please, can I have Ellis?"

"Of course you can." Miller took out his phone and called Vaughan, who replied at once. "It's me, Ellis, we need you now. Mrs. Miller's going on television and wants you to get her to the hairdresser's as quickly as possible."

"On my way, Major."

Vaughan switched off, and Miller smiled at her. "Your carriage awaits, Madame."

There was a slight sadness there when she said, "You are good to me, Harry," but she didn't kiss him, simply opened the front door and went out and down the steps, as Vaughan appeared.

In the cul-de-sac, Fahy was surprised by Vaughan's sudden departure, but he assumed it was Miller in the car. Abdul came toward him. "I understood his passenger would be a man."

"What in the hell do you mean?"

"It was a woman, a good looker, came down the steps fast and he was away with her."

It took only seconds for the implication to strike home to Sean Fahy. "Dear God, no, not that."

He went back up the cul-de-sac and, in a frenzy of activity, replaced the manhole cover and put everything back in the van. His stomach was burning, the pain terrible, and he turned against the wall and was very sick indeed.

Abdul moved in behind him. "Are you okay, man?"

"No, I'm not."

"What do I do now?"

"Whatever the hell you want."

He was in despair as he got in the van, reversed, and turned into Dover Street and passed the house. He didn't know what to do, but the truth was there was nothing he could do, and he continued to drive slowly through Mayfair.

SHORTLY AFTERWARD, Ellis Vaughan drove to the end of a street leading into Park Lane. As he approached, the lights changed to green, so he put his foot on the accelerator to catch the light, braking as he encountered heavy traffic, and in a few desperate and horrific minutes, discovered his brakes no longer worked. It was like gliding on the rain-wet road, and he bounced one car to his left, spun in a half-circle, and ended up pointing the wrong way in the fast lane. The driver of the bus hurtling toward him could do nothing in the heavy traffic conditions of the morning rush hour. The bus plowed into the Amara, hurling it to one side like a toy. Olivia Hunt had barely time to cry out, but Vaughan heard her and then he heard nothing.

• • •

CONGESTION AND THE ENORMOUS buildup of traffic led Fahy in the right direction. He left his van in a courtyard and proceeded on foot. The police were there in force, had closed that side of the dual carriageway. There were three ambulances already, a Fire Service recovery vehicle, men working on the wreckage. Fahy joined the onlookers on the pavement and watched as what looked like the driver was pulled out. There was more work going on at the back of the car.

A police motorcyclist in black leathers came across. "Come on, folks, you're blocking the pavement, keep moving."

"Anyone dead?" a middle-aged woman asked.

"Don't know. They've pulled out a chauffeur and he's on his way to hospital. There's a woman in the back, and getting her out is awkward. If you want to know any more, you'll have to buy an *Evening Standard*."

People started to move, but Fahy lingered, watching, as they finally got Olivia Hunt out and onto a board and into an ambulance. He turned away slowly and went back to the van, left it where it was, and returned to Kilburn.

MILLER DECIDED to stay home for a while that morning. He'd brought plenty of papers home from the Cabinet Office. It was just nine forty-five when the front doorbell sounded. He was whistling cheerfully as he moved along the hall, dodged into the sitting room, and glanced out through the window to see who it was. A police car was parked beside the Mini Cooper, and two officers, a man and a woman sergeant, were at the door. He frowned and opened the door.

"Major Miller, sir?" the sergeant asked. "I wonder if we could speak to you?"

"Yes, what's it about?"

At the same moment, his phone rang. "Excuse me," he said to the police. "Do come in."

It was Henry Frankel, the Cabinet Secretary, at the other

end. "My God, Harry, this is so terrible. I don't know how to tell you."

"What's so terrible, Henry, what on earth are you talking about?" And then he saw the distress on the woman police sergeant's face and she put a hand on his arm.

"Please sit down, sir. I really think it would be best."

And somehow he knew; the police always sent a man and a woman when it was the worst of bad news. He stepped into the sitting room and sat on a chair very carefully, and she took his phone and said, "Sergeant Bell here, sir, we're just breaking the bad news to Major Miller now. Yes, I'll tell him that."

She put the phone on the small table beside Miller and nodded to her colleague. "George?"

He went to the drinks sideboard, poured a brandy, handed it to Miller. "It was Mr. Frankel from Downing Street, sir. He said the Prime Minister is devastated."

"About what?" Miller asked with a strange kind of patience.

"Your wife. I'm afraid there's been a dreadful accident on Park Lane."

"How bad?" Miller asked.

The sergeant was actually crying. "She was dead when they took her out."

Miller's face was wiped clean of any kind of emotion. "And the chauffeur?"

"He's still with us, but dreadfully injured. They've taken them both to Guy's Hospital." Miller took the brandy down in one swallow. "Tell me, is it five hours backward to American time or six?" he asked.

"I think you'll find it's six, sir." She hesitated. "Can we take you to the hospital?"

"That's very kind, but I've just got a couple of calls to make. Why don't you and your friend make a nice cup of tea in the kitchen."

She nodded and they went out. It was four o'clock in the morning in Washington, but what were friends for?

Blake Johnson was aroused from a deep sleep by the call.

Codex orientated, he knew it must be important, but he was totally shocked by Miller's news and was instantly fully alert.

"What can I do, Harry? Anything!"

"Her father, Senator George Hunt, lives in Georgetown. The President said he knew him."

"We all do."

"He lives alone, a widower. Olivia was his only child, the apple of his eye. It's an imposition, but could you possibly find it in yourself to be the one to break the news? I would just be a voice on the phone, and I think he's going to need more."

"I'll handle it, I promise, and I'll make sure he has an early flight."

"I'll be in touch."

Next he phoned Roper. "Have you heard?" he asked when Roper answered.

"I've just been watching the morning program on television. There's been a news flash. What can I say? I'm very sorry. Ellis Vaughan seems to be in a coma. And you know about Olivia?"

"Yes. What happens now?"

"There'll be an autopsy, that's the law, Harry."

"Of course. It's unpleasant to think about what that means. I'm going to Guy's now. I'll let you know when I have more information."

He phoned Monica but got only her housekeeper. "She's lecturing, Major. Was it important?"

"Yes, Mrs. Jones. My wife has just been killed in London in a car accident. Tell her to contact me when she can."

He took the mug the sergeant offered and drank about half. He forced a smile. "You've been very kind. Let's go now."

And at Cambridge, Mrs. Jones ventured onto the stage where Monica stood at the lectern addressing a hundred students. To those watching, Monica seemed to stagger, then held on to the lectern tightly.

"My dear friends," she said. "I've just received the most distressing family news. I'm afraid I'm needed elsewhere."

• • •

At Guy's Hospital, Miller was taken through to a private reception area, where he discovered Ferguson and Dillon.

Ferguson said, "A terrible business, Harry."

Dillon simply gripped his hand tightly for a moment, and Miller said, "What's happening?"

"We've got the best two men in London here," Ferguson told him. "Professor Henry Bellamy, a great surgeon, who was here to meet the arrival of both ambulances. Also, Professor George Langley, our foremost forensic pathologist. They'll be with us soon."

At that moment, Henry Bellamy came in wearing theater greens. "Major Miller, I'm so dreadfully sorry, but there was absolutely nothing we could do to save your wife."

Miller took a deep breath. "Can you be more specific?"

"She had massive internal injuries, a huge shock to the heart." He paused. "The scan shows a broken neck. If it's of any comfort to you at all, it all would have killed her instantly. There would have been no pain."

Miller said calmly, "May I see her?"

"Of course, she's being prepared now for autopsy. You do realize we need to do that?"

"Certainly. I've been familiar with the death business for some years now."

"I'll mention it to my colleague, Professor Langley." At that moment, the man in question entered reception. He wore a tweed suit, an open-necked shirt. "Here he is," Bellamy said. "Henry, you know Ferguson and Dillon, of course. This is Major Harry Miller."

"Sorry for the delay," Langley said, and shook Miller's hand. "I've been visiting the site in Park Lane. This must be a coroner's inquest, of course, and an autopsy. A dreadful business for you, Major."

"I would like to see my wife as soon as possible."

"You shall."

"How long?"

"An hour to an hour and a half."

"I think I'd like to look at the accident site myself." He turned to Ferguson. "Charles?"

"Of course. We'll go with you."

Miller nodded. "And how is Ellis Vaughan?"

"Massive internal injuries, fractured pelvis, fractured skull. I will be commencing serious surgery soon," Bellamy told him. "He is unconscious, and I suspect traumatic coma."

"So there's no chance of us knowing what went wrong?"

"Certainly not at the moment."

"Thank you. I'll see you again later."

STRANGE HOW QUICKLY life moved on in a great city. There was virtually no sign of what had happened. Ferguson, Dillon, and Miller got out and stood on the curb.

"You'd never know anything had happened," Miller said. "Were there any casualties on the bus?"

"I spoke to the superintendent at Traffic," Ferguson said. "People were thrown from their seats, five had to be taken to A and E. I believe a woman had a broken arm. The bus, of course, is in a traffic impound, along with the Amara, or what's left of it."

"Could we go there?"

"Of course. You know where, don't you, Hawkins?"

"I certainly do, General."

THERE WAS AN ENORMOUS GARAGE, many vehicles there and all the worse for wear. A police sergeant in an oil-stained white overall took them to the Amara. They stood looking at it in silence. Finally, Miller said, "It's difficult to imagine anyone surviving."

The limousine was an absolute wreck, the engine cover torn away, the engine itself smashed to pieces, oil, petrol, and brake fluid everywhere.

"How can you ever tell what happened when you look at a mess like that?"

"With great difficulty, sir, and possibly never. We have

another problem. With the chauffeur in the state he is, we've no means of knowing what went wrong. Statements from many people say that he emerged from the side street at some speed into the congestion of the morning rush hour."

"It baffles me, Sergeant. He's been my chauffeur for some time. A thoroughly competent driver, an ex-paratrooper."

"Well, only he can tell us. We'll just have to pray he pulls through."

Miller's phone sounded and he answered. "Dreadful, Harry, dreadful, what can I say?" It was the director of the play. "Colin Carlton is distraught, positively suicidal."

"I expect he'll get over it," Miller commented. "Did you want something?"

"Just to say we're going dark for the rest of the week as a mark of respect. We'll spend the time bringing the understudy up to speed and open again next week."

"Well, you know what they say, Roger, the show must go on."

He cut him off and turned to the others. "I've seen enough. Thanks a lot, Sergeant."

"I'll do my best, sir, terrible business."

And to that there was no answer, for it would be said by one person after another as a constant.

BACK ON DERRY STREET, Fahy sat at the desk in the garage, stomach burning, and poured the Bushmills down, as close to despair as he had ever been. Strange when one considered the deaths at his hands over the years, and yet this was different and he knew why. Maggie was a part of it. Her new situation had been bought at a terrible price.

The phone rang and the Broker said, "What went wrong?"

"Not a thing. Everything worked perfectly, except for the woman coming out of the front door and jumping in the Amara. One minute, the chauffeur was having breakfast and waiting for Miller, the next it was all hurry."

"Are you certain a police examination of the wreckage won't discover the cause?"

"Nothing's absolute in this life, but it's very unlikely."

"I hear the chauffeur is doing very poorly, may never come out of his coma. We'll just have to hope he dies."

"My God," Fahy said. "What kind of man are we? You'll be suggesting next that we'll send someone in the hospital to pull out his tubes or something."

"It's a thought. Desperate measures are sometimes necessary, my friend. You would do well to remember that."

SAM BOLTON caught it on television in his office and phoned Hassim angrily.

"You bastard," he said. "I knew there was more to this when you sent me to Folly's End to check on Miller. You were planning a contract on him then."

"Careful what you say," Hassim told him.

"Obviously, whatever happened was intended for him. His wife was just in the car at the wrong time."

"Keep your tongue still, Selim," Hassim told him. "It can easily be cut off."

"Why don't you go and fuck yourself," Bolton told him, and slammed the phone down.

BACK AT THE HOSPITAL, they found Monica waiting, looking terrible, quite distraught. She ran into Miller's arms. "What are we going to do, Harry? It's unbelievable. I was only on the phone with her yesterday."

"Nothing to be done, love, except lay her to rest as best we can."

At that moment, George Langley appeared in green theater overalls. "There you are, Major. I've had things prepared, now I'm ready to proceed. Do you still wish to come in?"

"Yes, I think I would. This is my sister, Lady Starling."

"Would you care to join your brother?" Langley asked.

She turned to Miller, crying. "I can't, Harry, I'm such a coward."

"No, you're not." He turned to Dillon. "Sean?"

Dillon moved in and put an arm around her. "You get on with it, Harry."

Langley led him into a white-tiled room with fluorescent lights. There was a row of stainless-steel operating tables and Olivia Hunt lay on one of them. She was completely naked, obviously injured, although the body had been cleaned as much as possible. There was the Y cut of the preliminary, the top of her head covered by a rubber skullcap, blood seeping through, and the neck was terribly bruised.

Two nurses waited, and one of them pulled surgical gloves on Langley's hands. Nearby was a cart with the instruments of the trade and a video recorder. One of the nurses switched it on, and Langley said: "Resuming postmortem, Mrs. Olivia Hunt Miller, 15 Dover Street, London." He paused. "And do you, Major Harry Miller of the same address, confirm this is your wife?"

"I do."

Langley nodded to one of the nurses, who switched off the video. He said, "Major, in a moment I will request a DeSoutter saw to take off the top of the skull so that your wife's brain may be removed to be weighed. I will then have to break her ribs and open her up for the removal of bodily organs. You don't want to see this, believe me. Better, by far, to remember her as she was."

Miller's eyes seemed to be burning. He took the deepest breath he had ever taken in his life and then nodded. "Very civil of you, Professor, sound advice," and he went out.

THE BROKER CAUGHT VOLKOV at the Kremlin and broke the news. Volkov received it wearily. "It seems to me impossible to complete an operation against these people with any kind of success."

"With the greatest respect, you're missing the point," the Broker told him. "Fahy's attempt was totally successful—it just couldn't have been foreseen that Miller would let his wife have the car."

"I suppose so," Volkov said grudgingly. "What about Quinn? Have you told him?"

"No."

"He'll be warier than ever of turning up in London now. After all, what if Miller thinks the accident too much of a coincidence? What if it leads him to ask questions?"

"He can ask. An accident is an accident, and there's no proof to the contrary. If the chauffeur was able to say that his brakes failed, that might cause a question, but it's unlikely he'll survive the coma he's in."

"How do you know?"

"Hassim's Brotherhood has many members who are nurses. Trust me. I'll speak to Quinn."

"And keep an eye on this Fahy."

"He won't cause any trouble, why should he? If he does, I'll have him killed."

At Drumore Place, Quinn listened in horror to the Broker's account. "What in the hell are we going to do? If Miller finds out what really happened, he'll be after the lot of us."

"You give him too much credit. He's not invincible. I've spoken to Volkov, by the way, who's not happy you still haven't gone to London."

"Maybe so, but I think I'll just stay where I am until we see which way the wind's blowing."

"Surrounded by your old comrades from the glory days? At the end of the day, you're just a coward, Quinn," and the Broker cut him off.

At the hospital, Ferguson took a call from Downing Street. "The Prime Minister would like to see you, Harry."

"All right, I'll come."

Monica said, "I'd rather go to Dover Street, but I'm not sure I can be on my own."

"You won't be," Dillon told her. "You two go. I'll take Monica to your place and stay with her."

"Speak to Aunt Mary," Miller told Monica. "She must be told, and the vicar, Mark Bond. She's going to need him."

So it was resolved. Hawkins delivered Miller and Ferguson to Downing Street, where they were met by Henry Frankel coming out of the Cabinet Office. He was very distressed.

"I don't know what to say, Harry."

"Then best to say nothing, old lad."

"Is the PM busy?" Ferguson asked.

"He called Simon Carter for a quick chat, something that came in about these wretched voting problems in Kosovo. Anything I can do, Harry, just say the word. I've spoken to your secretary at the party office in Stokely, told her the worst. She was very upset and said she would go straight round to your aunt."

"That was kind of you."

The door of the Prime Minister's study opened and Simon Carter emerged and saw them immediately and looked wary. "Look, Miller, we've had our differences in the past, God knows, but I wouldn't wish what's happened to you on any man's shoulders." He was stiff and uncertain, his gray face tight, and in a way, Miller felt sorry for him.

"That's damn nice of you. I appreciate it." He walked into the Prime Minister's study, followed by Ferguson.

"A rotten business, Harry." The PM gave him a hug. "You'll need some time off. You'll bury her at Stokely?"

"Of course. Her father, Senator George Hunt, is on his way."

"I'd be privileged to attend the funeral with my wife."

"You'll be more than welcome, Prime Minister."

"Fine, so just do what you have to do for the next few days."

"Of course."

OUTSIDE, Henry Frankel appeared again with a couple of typed sheets. "Some stuff from the Cabinet Office on what to do. Legal requirements, a few good funeral directors. I'm sorry to sound so horribly practical."

"Not a bit of it, Henry, you're a star. Could you choose the funeral director for me? I've a lot to sort out. We'll bury her at Stokely Parish Church. The vicar is Mark Bond. I'm Catholic, of course, but she wasn't."

"I'll see to all that for you."

Ferguson looked at his watch. "So much has happened and yet it's only two o'clock. We could still catch a decent pub lunch. We'll go to the Dark Man. You need friends at a time like this."

Driving along in the Daimler, Miller got a call from Dillon. "Your father-in-law has turned up. I feel I'm in the way. They're crying all over each other."

"Get a taxi and meet us at the Dark Man," Miller said.

"I'll see you there."

They found Harry and Billy with their heads together in the corner booth, looking grim. Joe Baxter and Sam Hall were at the bar, with Ruby on the other side.

"Major, what can I say?" Harry Salter spread his arms. "It's a vale of tears sometimes."

Ruby came across, dabbing her eyes, and kissed Miller on the cheek. "It's so cruel. What can I do?"

"Open a bottle of champagne so we can toast a great lady, and then give us some shepherd's pie," Ferguson told her. "We've still got to eat."

Everyone had a drink, then two. Gradually there was less awkwardness, the food came, and then Dillon turned up. "Everything okay at Dover Street?" Miller asked.

"Oh, yes, the Senator's a nice guy. He's looking forward to meeting with you. The champagne looks good, and the pie. I'll have both."

AT GUY'S HOSPITAL, Ellis Vaughan jerked a little, his head moved, and there was a strange hoarse sigh. A nurse, who had just checked his many tubes and was about to leave, was nearest as the alarm sounded. Within seconds, the entire crash team swung into action, Bellamy appearing no more than two minutes later to join in the fight. None of it was any good, and Bellamy's face was sad as they switched off.

"Time of death three-fifteen, is everyone agreed?" They all nodded. "I'd better call Major Miller."

THE PARTY at the Dark Man sank into depression again at the news, and Ferguson shook his head. "No way of finding out what went wrong for him now."

"He was a good man," Miller said. "Survived the Iraq War and two tours in Afghanistan."

"And dies after being hit by a London bus," Billy Salter said. "It doesn't seem right, does it?"

IN DR. SMITH'S OFFICE, Fahy was dressing behind a screen after a searching examination. The pain had become unbearable and he had to accept that simply pouring Bushmills down him was not the answer. He'd come in the hope of finding some really powerful painkillers. He put on his jacket and went and sat opposite the doctor.

Smith looked grave. "I won't beat about the bush. There's a marked deterioration in your condition. You're obviously drinking a great deal, you reek of it."

"It helps, Doctor, it really does."

"But only for a while, so you have to take another and another."

"Haven't you got some really strong pills?"

"It's gone too far for that."

"So what are you saying?"

"I want you admitted today. Only in hospital can the pain therapy you need be administered."

"So that I can die easier." Fahy shook his head. "That would mean I couldn't see my Maggie. She's not fit to visit me, nobody knows that better than you."

"I'm truly sorry, but you've progressed faster than we thought you would. I can only suggest what I have."

"No way, Doc." Fahy got up. "I've come into money, so I'm in the middle of arranging Maggie's future at St. Joseph's.

Things to do, you see, as well as dying." He gave Smith a ghastly smile. "Thank you for your time."

He went around the corner to the City of Derry, sat in the corner of the bar, forced himself to eat a hot Cornish pastry, and washed it down with a double Bushmills, when he got a call on his mobile. It was the Broker.

"I've just had news that the chauffeur, Vaughan, has died."

"So what are you saying?"

"Obviously, anything he knew has died with him. I thought you'd be pleased."

"Not really. I've got other things to worry about."

"Anything I can help with?" Once again, the Broker sounded kind and considerate, and for some reason Fahy responded. "My wife's in the local hospice, St. Joseph's—Alzheimer's."

"My dear chap, I'm so sorry." The Broker sounded genuine.

Fahy said, "Nothing to be done. At least I can now afford to keep her going with the nuns instead of some National Health Service dump."

"Is there anything I can do?" the other man said again.

"You've done enough helping to put me back to work again. I'll go now. I've got to visit."

The Broker sat at his desk, thinking about it. He liked to know everything he could about people, and he savored the irony of two deaths paying for the support of Fahy's ailing wife, who wouldn't know what was going on around her anyway.

He called Quinn at Drumore Place and told him about Vaughan. "So, you see, any worries you have about Miller finding out have been taken care of."

"Well, that's good to hear. When is the funeral?"

"Wednesday."

"I'll be a lot happier when it's all over, and that's a fact."

"My dear Quinn, we all will. Keep in touch."

Finally, he called Ali Hassim. "You've heard about the chauffeur?"

"Yes."

"Which wraps it up nicely."

"I have one anxiety."

"Tell me."

"My most important sleeper, Selim Bolton."

"The one who works in the City? The man you sent down to this Folly's End place to see what he could find out about Miller?"

"Yes. I told him I only wished for general information, didn't hint there was more to my interest in Miller."

"So?"

"He's been to see me, has worked out the whole plot. A very clever young man. We had words and he left very angry. He doesn't approve of his part in what he sees as the accidental death of the woman."

"It's not worth arguing about," the Broker said. "Kill him before his conscience gets the better of him."

"I've already put a Brotherhood member as an agency temp in his offices. She may come up with something useful."

WHICH SHE DID. As with most high-powered financial houses, people worked staggered hours. The girl in question was a young Muslim named Ayesha, and keeping an eye on Bolton, she noticed the desk behind him had been vacated early, so she moved to it and made herself look busy. It was close to seven and darkness falling, still many people working away at their desks. Bolton had made the odd business call and she had heard him clearly.

Finally, he sat there for a while, as if thinking, then made another call, obviously got an answering machine, and started to speak. "Major Miller, I'm sorry to hear about your wife. This is Sam Bolton calling. I gave you my card when we met at Folly's End. I'll speak to you again. There's something you need to know about this morning's events."

She kept her head down as he got up and moved away, then followed him, calling Ali Hassim as she did so on her mobile, repeating the message she had heard Bolton deliver.

Hassim said, "Don't lose him. At this time of the evening, he'll probably go for a meal."

Next, he called Abdul in the garage at the back of the shop. "Get ready quickly, motorcycle and leathers. I've got a hit for you, top priority."

BOLTON TURNED into a one-way street between old buildings and went into a simple café called The Kitchen. He took a corner table, ordered a glass of red wine and a ham salad, and outside, Ayesha stood in a shadowed doorway and called Hassim.

"The Kitchen, Brook Street, quite close to the office."

"Can vehicles negotiate it?"

"It's one-way."

"Wait until a motorcycle passes you, then go away."

She did exactly as she was told, staying in the shadowed doorway. She could see Bolton through the window eating, and then a BMW coasted past her, stopped at the end of the street, and pulled into an entrance. The driver dismounted, supremely menacing in his leathers and black helmet, and she stepped out of the doorway and darted away.

BOLTON FINISHED HIS SALAD and drank his wine, thinking about what he intended. That there was some connection between what he had been sent to do at Folly's End and the events of the morning leading to the death of Miller's wife seemed obvious. He tried calling again, and once more got the answering machine and repeated his message. He got up, paid his bill, and went out, deeply disturbed about the whole thing. What had he been thinking about to get so involved with Hassim and his people in the first place? he asked himself as he walked down the street. He wasn't a religious fanatic. In fact, he wasn't religious at all.

He passed a dark doorway, sensed someone move in behind him and then the needle point of a knife nudging through his clothes. He'd been mugged before, it went with the territory in London, so he raised his hands.

"Okay, okay. Wallet and cards inside my left pocket, a hundred and ten pounds inside right. Seiko watch, left wrist. Mobile phone, left trouser pocket. Is that enough?"

"Not for offending Allah so grossly," Abdul told him, and the knife sliced up expertly and found the heart.

Bolton died instantly, and Abdul cleared his pockets and took the watch and left him in the doorway, another crime statistic, another mugging. A moment later, he rode off and, some distance away, stopped and called Hassim.

"It's done."

"Excellent. Come home."

He had Miller's home number listed and called it now. It was still on the answering machine, which meant that all Miller had to go on was the message Bolton had left, which told him absolutely nothing. All in all, very satisfactory. A pity about Bolton, though, who had obviously had more of a conscience than he had realized.

MILLER HAD SPENT that part of the evening at the French restaurant in Shepherd's Market with Monica and his father-in-law. He'd always got on with the Senator, who was not only a distinguished attorney in Boston but as a young man had been in the infantry in the Vietnam War.

They had a pleasant, but sad, evening reminiscing about Olivia, each one of them with his or her stories. It was obvious to Miller that Olivia's untimely death was a blow from which the Senator would probably never truly recover. He kept gripping Monica's hand, and there was an anxious and hunted look on his face.

Speaking now, he said, "It was a kind thought, Harry, to ask Blake Johnson to break the bad news to me. To have another human being with me, and a friend, was a wonderful support. I'd no idea you knew him."

"He's a good man," Miller said.

"And then the President coming on the phone. So kind, and authorizing the Gulfstream like that."

"Yes, well, there are some good people in the world," Harry told him. "But you need a decent night's sleep, George, so let's get you home."

MONICA SAW the Senator up to his room and Miller went into the sitting room and punched the phone for messages. They were numerous, expressions of sympathy and so forth, and then Bolton, and it wasn't just what he'd said that was interesting, but that he'd called twice. He was listening again, a frown on his face, when Monica entered.

"Poor old boy, he's shattered."

"I know. I doubt whether he'll ever get over it."

"Or me. I could do with a stiff drink and bed. How about you?"

"I'd join you, but actually I've got to go out."

"Have you, Harry? I mean, after everything?"

"It could be important." He took the tape out of the answering machine and put it in his pocket, and then went into the kitchen and called Roper on the extension.

"Something interesting's come up. Can you send Sergeant Doyle to get me? I've been drinking."

"Of course. What's up?"

"I'll tell you when I see you."

He went back to the sitting room and joined Monica, who had his drink ready. "Well, here's to us, my love."

"What's left of us."

"Stokely tomorrow afternoon. Did you phone Aunt Mary again?"

Monica nodded. "I doubt whether she'll ever recover also."

The front doorbell rang. She said, "Is it important, Harry?"

"What I'm doing now? Yes—very." He kissed her cheek. "Get a good night's sleep."

He let himself out, got in beside Doyle and was driven away, and what he didn't know was that almost three miles away in the City, two police officers were examining Sam Bolton's body, having been alerted by a member of the public.

"Cleaned out totally," one policeman said. "Wallet, credit cards, watch, mobile phone, all gone. Typical mugging. No identity."

"I'll give you a little tip," his friend said. "The handkerchief pocket. Amazing what people slip in there." He tried his luck and held up a business card. "There you go. All you have to do is live right."

WHEN MILLER went into the computer room at Holland Park, Roper said, "You've saved me phoning you. Ferguson's just been on. The inquest is at the coroner's court in Westminster tomorrow by special arrangement with the Lord Chancellor's Office. They're going to do Ellis Vaughan at the same time."

"Why would they do that?"

"Because it's sensible and practical, and you're who you are and you've got friends in high places. It's the great and the good doing what's fitting and looking after each other in the process. Ten o'clock in the morning. There's a jury because that's the law, but it should go through without fuss. Now, what's the mystery?"

"Listen to that. It's the tape from my answering machine. The two most recent ones are the same."

Roper listened, then said, " 'There's something you need to know about this morning's events.' That's the intriguing phrase."

Miller looked in a pocket in his wallet and found the business card that Bolton had given him at Folly's End. "There you are. I was convinced he was involved with Army of God. It was your check which told us he was half-Muslim. Run him through again, put a general trace on the name, see if anything comes up."

Which Roper did, and the screen rippled and Metropolitan Police came on and various statistics, and it was still rattling through before their eyes.

"What the hell is going on?" Miller asked.

"Give me a chance." Roper worked at his keyboard and came up with *London Area, Serious Crime* and there it was. "Samuel Bolton, 5 Belsize Park Mansions, dead on arrival at Kensington Mortuary."

"It can't be him," Miller said. "Look at the arrival time. The body was only received there an hour or so ago."

"Murdered, knife wound in the heart, and pointing to a street mugging," Roper said. "God knows that's common enough these days. Everything of value taken. Identity confirmed by a business card found in his hanky pocket." A facsimile of the card was shown.

"Exactly the same as this." Miller held up the card Bolton had given him. "The first call on my tape was six forty-five, the second at seven thirty-five."

"He was found in Martins Lane at eight-thirty by a passerby who called in the police."

"So what do we have here? A guy with some sort of connection to the Army of God, which could mean the Brotherhood?"

"Of which you don't have the slightest proof," Roper said. "Say you tried to pull in the organizer, this Ali Hassim—he'd be out so fast you'd be reeling. Crown Prosecution Service wouldn't touch it with a bargepole. The usual organizations would be screaming human rights instantly."

"There's something you need to know about this morning's events." Miller was quite calm, totally in control. "This morning's events, the death of my wife and my chauffeur in a car crash, were so unusual, we can't work out how it happened. Now, you are one of the most intelligent people I've ever met in my life. What's your opinion?"

"I'd say it's fairly obvious. The Amara was rigged in some way, an accident waiting to happen, but meant to happen to you, Harry. Olivia just got in the way, wrong place at the wrong time."

"Exactly." Miller was still incredibly calm. "I'll find who was responsible if it's the last thing I do."

"The man who did it would be a pro. The more important

question is who paid him." Roper's face contorted, and he grasped his arm and then reached for the whiskey. "Sorry, Harry, I hurt like hell tonight. This is all that helps."

"I'll have one, too." Miller took one himself.

"Let's see who we're dealing with." Roper's fingers danced over the keys. "The Russians, for starters." Vladimir Putin appeared on the screen; Volkov joined him, and then Max Chekhov. "All three controlling Belov International."

"So?"

The screen changed and Michael Quinn appeared. "I can't say the IRA, because we're at peace and it isn't supposed to be a problem anymore, but that bastard isn't at peace."

The screen changed again, to Osama Bin Laden. "I only show him because he invented Al Qaeda, and the movers and shakers in this thing seem to be Drecq Khan, who founded Army of God with Al Qaeda money, and his organizer Ali Hassim." Miller looked up at both of them.

"So?"

"You want the assassin, and I can't show you his face, because we don't know who the hell he is. There's someone else I can't show, too—in my opinion, the most important of the lot."

"The Broker?"

"Exactly."

Miller nodded. "One way or another, I'll have them all. But there's the inquest first, and then Stokely, to see to my wife in the most fitting way possible."

Roper nodded. "I'll be there, old son, we all will."

11

The Cabinet Office had arranged a limousine for Miller, a Mercedes, with a driver named Arthur Fox, also an ex-soldier, Blues & Royals this time. Miller sat up front with him, and Monica and Senator Hunt were in the rear.

A scattering of people were sitting on the benches outside the inquest room, along with police officers, the odd person in legal robes passing through. A woman in her thirties, from the look of her, got up and came forward uncertainly.

"Major Miller? It is you, isn't it? I'm Ellis Vaughan's sister, Jean." She had obviously been crying.

"Of course," Miller said. "I arranged for you to go to the Buckingham Palace garden party two years ago. This is my sister, Lady Starling."

Monica came and put an arm around her. Jean burst into tears. "I don't know what I'm going to do without him. My husband, Tony, was killed in Iraq last year. My mother married again and lives in New Zealand."

Monica sat her down and tried to comfort her, and at that moment the double doors opened and an usher called, "Court now in session."

They filed in, along with half a dozen members of the public, and took seats. Already present were two or three people in legal gowns, a burly police sergeant, and the clerk of the court at a desk below the bench. George Langley walked in and reported to him.

Miller said to Senator Hunt, "That's the pathologist, the one who did the autopsy."

The clerk of the court called, "Rise for Her Majesty's coroner," and the coroner came in, looking about seventy with white hair. A little later, an official opened a door and the jury entered and took their seats.

The coroner said, "This hearing is a little unusual. Mrs. Olivia Miller and her chauffeur, Mr. Ellis Vaughan, died in the same unfortunate accident. The Lord Chancellor's Office has given me permission to consider the cases together. Police evidence, please."

A police sergeant read a long statement, pointing out the facts in the matter, and entered in five sworn statements from witnesses to the fact that the Amara had jumped the lights. The coroner had them accepted by his clerk and said, "Could there have been any mechanical reason for what happened?"

The sergeant produced another sworn statement from the police sergeant who had examined the Amara at the pound. So badly had the engine been damaged that there was no possibility of reaching a conclusion. The coroner ordered his clerk to accept that statement also.

The clerk then called George Langley, who took the stand under oath. The coroner said, "Professor Langley, I have the two autopsy reports on the matter. Did you perform them yourself?"

The clerk of the court passed copies to the jury, as Langley said, "Yes."

"Have you any particular observation to make?"

"Both of the deceased had massive injuries sustained in the crash, which I've detailed in my reports. If you will permit me, there is one thing worth mentioning regarding the point that the vehicle was driven at speed through lights into rush-hour traffic?"

"Please, Professor."

"There was no evidence of alcohol in the driver's system, nor the slightest trace of drugs of any description."

There was a slight pause, then the coroner said, "Over a long and distinguished career, you've had experience of similar cases?"

"Yes, many times."

"So what conclusion would you draw?"

"That some kind of mechanical failure took place beyond the driver's control, although I have no hard evidence to support that view."

"Please accept the court's thanks and step down, Professor."

The coroner shuffled his papers, then started his address to the jury. "Ladies and gentlemen, facts are what we must consider, not conjecture, facts alone. The tragedy speaks for itself. A brilliant and talented lady at the height of her powers cruelly snatched away, as well as a young man with a gallant service record behind him."

He put his fingers together as if thinking. "I appreciate the point Professor Langley makes and thank him for it, but we cannot say it is factual, only supposition. He is right, however, to point to the fact that Vaughan was not driving under the influence. We have a mystery here. In the circumstances, I would suggest an open verdict. You are, of course, at liberty to retire."

They muttered to each other, heads bobbed, and the foreman stood. "The open verdict seems sensible to us."

"Let it be so entered. Now we come to the question of next of kin. If Jean Marlowe is in court, please stand." Jean, sitting next to Monica, did. The coroner said, "I will now issue you with a burial order as Ellis Vaughan's sister. You have my sympathy. You may retrieve the body at your convenience."

Jean slumped down, and Monica put an arm around her.

"Major Harry Miller." Miller stood. "I will issue you with a burial order. You also have my sympathy."

The clerk cried, "The court will rise for Her Majesty's coroner."

Everything was suddenly in motion; the jury shuffled out and the court started to clear. Miller went to the clerk of the court's desk and Jean followed him, bewildered. They were each given a burial order. They walked out and paused beside the Mercedes.

"What are you going to do now?" Miller asked.

"I'll be fine. I'm a nursing sister at Guy's Hospital—isn't it strange he should end up there? My consultant and matron have been very good. They've already arranged an undertaker. I'll just have a few friends at the crematorium. Day after tomorrow. You'll be going to Stokely, I suppose?"

"Later today. The funeral's tomorrow," Monica said.

"Ellis loved it at Stokely. It's a funny old life, isn't it?" She turned suddenly and walked away.

"Poor girl," Monica said. "Now what?"

Miller held up the burial order. "We'll deliver this to the undertakers Henry Frankel arranged for me. Ten Vine Street, Arthur." They all got in the Mercedes.

HOWARD AND SON it was called, an imposing Victorian townhouse, like another world once you stepped inside—a world of polished mahogany-paneled walls, an abiding smell of lilies, just a hint of music. They were greeted by a well-shaved, dark-haired man named Jarvis, wearing a black suit. "Would you carc to view the deceased?" he inquired.

It was Senator Hunt who suddenly came to life, having hardly said a word all morning and nothing in court. "Oh, yes, most definitely."

They were led to an arcade, chapels on each side and several occupied. Olivia was in the third. She lay at rest, garbed in a white robe, her hair neatly arranged, her face a mask of makeup.

"Our embalmer, Joseph Bilton, has done his very best with Mrs. Miller, Major. She required careful work, I'm afraid. There was damage."

Miller looked down at her for only a moment or so, but

this wasn't his wife, not Olivia at all. The Senator said, "She looks lovely. She could be sleeping."

Miller turned to the door, and Jarvis followed him and took the burial order he was offered. "You've been in touch with the vicar at Stokely, Mark Bond?"

"Yes, Major, we're taking her down early tomorrow morning. The service will be at noon. Mr. Frankel from Downing Street arranged everything. He assumed that as a Catholic you would not want cremation?"

"Excellent." Miller didn't argue. "Anything else you need, deal with my sister, Lady Starling. I'll be in my car."

"Yes, Major, of course." He turned back into the chapel, where Monica was hugging a very disturbed man indeed.

THE DRIVE DOWN to Stokely was a miserable affair, mainly because Senator Hunt was really grieving, despair finally breaking through. Monica did her best to comfort him.

"How can life be so cruel?" he demanded, and there were tears on his face. "Everything to live for and the kind of success she'd always dreamed of finally achieved." He shook his head. "All snatched away. It doesn't make sense."

Which it didn't. He couldn't be told the blunt truth. His heart was not good at the best of times; he'd already had one bypass. The knowledge that his daughter had met her death as the innocent victim of an assassination plot to kill her husband could well be enough to push him over the edge.

The very idea of having to tell Monica filled Miller with horror, and yet at some stage it would have to be done. He was here being driven through the Kent countryside, and his wife was in her coffin, and the truth was it should have been the other way around. He had chosen a way of life with great risks inherent to it, and it was Olivia who'd paid the price.

AUNT MARY WAS like a ghost, drifting around the house, her voice a whisper. She and Hunt sat by the fire, totally at a loss. Fergus Grant and Sarah were deeply touched by events, already in mourning. They saw to Arthur Fox, giving him the second spare bedroom at the cottage, leaving the one Ellis had occupied locked out of respect.

Miller was having a cup of tea in the kitchen and Monica came in. "So, Badger's End has been booked for the whole day." It was a country hotel close to the church. "They'll do a buffet for a hundred and fifty."

"A lot of people will drive up from London, I suppose."

"Of course they will, and many of her theater friends."

"Have you spoken to the vicar?"

"He's been very good. Managed to get Cooper's to rush out an order of service. He's choosing the hymns, because he said he knew what she'd like. I'll go round and check the hotel. What about you?"

"I thought I'd look in at the constituency office. If there's nothing doing there, I'll drop in at the pub, get a sandwich, show my face."

"Maybe I'll see you there."

"Why not?"

THE CONSTITUENCY OFFICE was closed. The notice on the door said *Out of Respect* and there was a black-ribboned mourning wreath with it. People passed to say how sorry they were, some actually dodged out of the way as if embarrassed; older women were the most upset, many of whom had known Miller since boyhood. He wandered into the churchyard of St. Michael's. It was quite beautiful and dated from the fifteenth century. St. Michael's was Church of England, not Catholic, but Olivia had always loved the place, had regularly put flowers on the family plot by the far wall, an old cypress tree extending over it. His father's and mother's remains were there by special dispensation, and the church verger was there with the local gravedigger. Everything was obviously ready, neatly covered with a green tarpaulin.

"Thank you," he said.

The vicar, Mark Bond, came out of the side entrance,

wearing a black cassock. He was bound for the rectory, but saw Miller and threaded his way through the stones, his face grave. He shook hands warmly.

"Are you coping?"

"Just about. We had the coroner's inquest this morning on both of them. I presume you heard that the chauffeur died?"

"Yes, I heard from Howard's in Westminster."

"You realize the Prime Minister will be here, and that means the press?"

"It had come to my notice. A full house, Harry, she was greatly liked in Stokely. They'll all turn out."

"Obviously, Monica was at the court this morning, and Olivia's father, Senator George Hunt."

"Whom I met a couple of years ago. I'll call round later on if I may?"

"Of course you can." Miller shook his head. "I don't know how you cope, Mark. The death business is a constant in your profession."

"True."

"But then, you have faith to support you."

"And you don't, Harry?"

"Lost it during the Falklands War, when the wind blew the mist away at Tumbledown and I saw the dead and wounded, heard the cries from both sides. I think that wind blew away my faith, too. Strange, as I'd been raised a Catholic, but I found I couldn't pray anymore."

Bond put a hand on his shoulder. "Then I'll have to pray for you. I'll come round later."

He walked away and Miller stayed there, thinking, aware of the rooks calling to each other in the trees above, and he walked across to the Stokely Arms. Holly Green, the publican's wife, another childhood friend, was behind the bar, it being the quiet half of the afternoon. She came around instantly and put her arms around him.

"God bless you, Harry," she said, and that was all.

"I'll have a large scotch."

"Go and sit down, and I'll bring it."

There were perhaps a half a dozen people scattered around

the ancient bar, a fire smoldering in the open hearth. He sat in the old oak booth in the corner and she brought the whiskey and Monica came in.

"That looks good, I could punish one. How are you, Holly?"

They embraced and Holly went to get another, and to Miller, everything seemed to be happening in slow motion. Monica received her drink. "Everything's organized. What about you?"

"I've seen Mark Bond. It's all in hand, he's even got God on his side."

"And you, Harry, are you all right?"

"I don't think I ever will be again, but that isn't the point. You're still my dearly loved sister, even though you heard something about me from Olivia that truly shocked you. Now I'm going to shock you again, but it has to be done."

"Then tell me."

"It wasn't an accident. The Amara was interfered with. The crash was an assassination attempt on my life in revenge for my success in doing away with some very bad people."

There was horror on her face. "Oh, dear God."

"There is no God, not for me. The Amara was waiting for me, but Olivia wanted to get to the hairdresser's fast to prepare for her television appearance, and she asked me if she could have it. It was as simple as that."

She took a breath. "Do you know who?"

"There are several possibilities, but it doesn't matter. I'm going to get the lot if I can. It's all my fault, you see that? If I hadn't hurt them so badly, they wouldn't have tried to get me. The guilt is on my head and not to be shared, but I'll make them pay."

"What about the Senator?"

"I'm not trying to avoid anything, I've proved that by confessing to you, but I don't think it would help to tell him."

"I agree." She was quite calm now. "Tell me something. Is your friend Sean Dillon included in this business?"

"Well, he usually is. Does that bother you?"

"Not at all. If you're going to war, you need the right

troops." She got up. "Don't worry, love, whatever else, I'm your sister and I'm on your side. Now let's get back."

THE CORTEGE ARRIVED at the house in good time and parked in the grounds, the great and the good arrived steadily from London, and in the unusual circumstances, Miller left Monica in charge at the hall and headed a reception committee at the church comprising a team of local men supplied by the constituency office.

Cars parked all over the place as people flooded in, so many from London. The cast of the play headed by the director, Colin Carlton looking pale and drawn, Ferguson, Roper in his wheelchair, Dillon, Harry and Billy Salter, a number of MPs, and Simon Carter, of all people, who shook Miller's hand and said, "I had to pay my respects, and the PM offered me a lift."

"Kind of you to come." They touched hands, and then the Prime Minister arrived with his wife and several photographers stepped forward.

The ushers packed them in until it was standing room only and then the moment came; Mark Bond emerged from the door in his robes and stood waiting. Miller joined him, and the cortege came down the hill, and the men from London, headed by Jarvis, took over.

Monica, Aunt Mary, and the Senator got out of the front funeral Rolls and came forward. Miller gave Aunt Mary his arm, Monica and Hunt joined together, and they walked in behind Bond as the organ burst into sound.

WHEN IT WAS OVER in the church, and the interment took place, the weather still held up. Standing with Monica at the graveside, Miller murmured, "They say it always rains at funerals, and especially with bad March weather. I was certain it would."

She squeezed his hand. "Well, it didn't, God rest her. Now

let's allow others to pay their respects and go and put a brave face on it."

Which they did. The Prime Minister stayed for half an hour at the reception, then put an arm around Miller and kissed Monica. "So glad we could come. Sorry to rush off, but duty calls."

Carter nodded, and looked a little frosty as Ferguson appeared and followed the Prime Minister and his wife to their limousine and the small entourage of security people and they were driven away.

Miller turned to Ferguson, who had been joined by Roper, the Salters, and Dillon. "Well, at least he came. Carter, I mean."

"Come on, it would have looked bleeding bad if he hadn't," Harry Salter said.

Monica had joined them. "Succinct as usual, Harry." Miller turned to Monica. "These are friends of mine you haven't met, General Charles Ferguson and associates."

"Lady Starling," Ferguson said. "Your fame precedes you. I expect you know my cousin, another archaeologist, Professor Hal Stone of Corpus Christi?"

"Of course I do, the biggest rogue in Cambridge. Somebody shot him last year and—" She stopped, looked at them all, and said to Miller, "Are all of these people spooks?"

"No, the other Harry there used to be a gangster and then discovered it was just as easy to be rich in the business world."

"Well, I can't argue with that." Monica suddenly discovered she was enjoying herself. "Is somebody going to offer me a glass of champagne?"

"That's my pleasure." Dillon took her arm and walked her away.

Ferguson nodded to Miller. "A word, Harry."

He moved out into a large sun lounge and they followed, joining him when he sat in a corner. "Roper's spread the word about what happened to this chap Bolton. It's something we've all got to take on board."

"I'd say it's obvious what's gone on," Harry Salter said.

Billy nodded. "I agree. So what to do about it? It's time we sorted the Army of God people and Ali Hassim."

"Hold your horses." Ferguson turned to Miller. "You made an assumption about Bolton at Folly's End, that he was Army of God?"

"True, and I baited him by making a reference to the Brotherhood."

"But you didn't have any substantial proof that he was a member?"

"No, but Roper discovered his mother was Muslim."

"So what? That wouldn't have any significance legally. Legally, the Army of God is a registered religious charity that happens to be Islamic, and the Brotherhood is just a rumor. So I don't want anybody going kicking any doors in."

"That's a pity," Harry Salter said. "Last year when we had trouble with that worm Drecq Khan, he shot his mouth off big-time when we dangled him from the hoist over the stern of the *Lynda Jones* and dumped him in the Thames."

"I want none of that," Ferguson said. "And that's an order. We need something more positive, a real breakthrough. I've got a feeling we'll get one. We'll have to wait."

Monica, enjoying her glass of champagne on the patio with Dillon beside a half-open French window, had heard most of what they'd said, even though Dillon had tried to guide her away. Ferguson and company rose and followed Roper into the hotel, where the call to lunch had just been made.

"What a bunch," Monica said to Dillon. "I can't believe it. Villains, the lot of you."

"Young Billy Salter's an agent of Her Majesty's Secret Security Services. Roper was the greatest bomb-disposal expert in the British Army till he tried to defuse one too many and got a wheelchair and the George Cross out of it. Good old Charlie Ferguson has a DSO and the Prime Minister's full confidence, just like your brother. They help keep people out of harm's way in a world gone mad. They are soldiers who take care of those things ordinary folk can't."

"And you?" she demanded. "The pride of the IRA?"

"Peace in Ireland, Monica, that's what we've got now." He reached to a passing waiter's tray, took two fresh glasses, and offered her one. "I'm simply along for the ride."

"I just bet you are." She sipped her champagne, more excited than she'd been for years.

AT DERRY STREET later that day, Fahy was much worse. The pain was indescribable, the shot of whiskey each time it got bad, unsustainable. He felt himself to be groggy, the whiskey going to his head, and finally put his phone over to the answering machine and fell on the couch and blacked out. One hour later, it rang and a message was received, but he didn't respond. In fact, it rang three or four times, but nothing could break through that fog of alcohol and he continued to sleep.

EARLY EVENING at Stokely. The guests departed, Aunt Mary retired some time later, and the Senator followed her. Miller and Monica sat in the drawing room, having a coffee.

"I'm bushed," she said. "A hard day."

"What did you think of my friends?"

"I don't know what they do to the Queen's enemies, but they scare me."

"I thought you got on rather well with Sean Dillon. There's hope for you there, Monica."

"What nonsense. He probably sleeps with a gun under his pillow. You've got yourself mixed up with a strange crowd. Where is it going to lead?"

"Hopefully to whoever was behind the plot to finish me off." He got up. "I'm restless, love, I'm not going to stay on here longer than I have to. Do me a favor. Comfort Aunt Mary and encourage the Senator to stay on for as long as he wants. I think he needs to."

"And you?"

"I'm going to call Arthur and tell him I'm going back to Dover Street."

"Are you sure?"

"Absolutely." He reached for the phone.

She saw him off at the door fifteen minutes later, hugged him fiercely. "Take care, promise me?"

"I always do."

She stood there, listening to the Mercedes fade into the distance, and as she turned to go back inside, she was afraid.

FAHY CAME BACK to life, his head aching. The liquor was by the phone, so he poured another and went in the kitchen, turned on the cold tap in the sink, and splashed water on his face.

Behind him Sister Ursula's voice said, "Mr. Fahy, this is most urgent. Maggie isn't well. Please come at once." It cut off and he toweled his head vigorously and the machine came alive again with the same message, and then a third time as he struggled into his coat. As he made for the door, the phone itself rang and he grabbed it.

"My dear chap," the Broker said, "I was wondering how you are."

"I've no bloody time," Fahy said "An emergency with my wife." He slammed the phone down and ran out into the garage, raised the door, and got in the Triumph and drove away.

The Broker, at his desk, then dialed the number of St. Joseph's Hospice, which he had already obtained. When a nun on reception answered, he said, "I'm inquiring about a Mrs. Margaret Fahy, a patient."

"Are you a relative?"

"Yes, her brother-in-law." The lie came smoothly.

"I'm afraid the news is bad. She passed away a couple of hours ago. A stroke."

"I see. How unfortunate."

A little later, Fahy parked the Triumph outside and staggered in. "My wife," he demanded. "I'm Sean Fahy. I want to see my wife and now."

The nun rang the alarm bell.

• • •

IT TOOK TWO NIGHT PORTERS to handle him while Sister Ursula was sent for and managed to calm him. They took him through to a small white-tiled mortuary where his wife lay on a gurney covered with a white sheet. Ursula pulled it back so he could see the pale, waxen face.

"It was very quick, she died in a few seconds. A massive stroke. A kindness really, God's kindness."

Fahy slumped down on a metal chair. "I never did her a kindness, I was nothing but a worry to her for years, until the end, when I thought I could buy her a bit of happiness for a while. I couldn't even get that right, so it cost another woman her life."

"I don't understand," Sister Ursula said, and thought him rambling. "Go home and get a good night's sleep. Come back in the morning, and Father Doyle will be here to help you make the arrangements."

"Yes." He nodded vaguely, brushed past the porters, and left.

He made it back, parked the Triumph inside the garage, left the door open, and went upstairs. He sat there numb and the pain started again, and he found the Bushmills and was drinking from the bottle when the phone went.

The Broker said, "I was worried about you. I checked on your wife's condition at the Hospice and discovered the bad news."

"That's right. She's dead, cursed by God, a punishment to me for murdering an innocent woman, because that's what I did. I took the job for your stinking money to see to my wife's future, and do you want to know why? I've got cancer of the pancreas. I've got days to live, that's all, and if I could put right what I've done, I would, so to hell with you." He slammed down the phone.

The Broker contacted Ali Hassim and quickly explained the situation. "This man is clearly unbalanced. He must be eliminated. There is no knowing what he might do."

"You're right. Leave it to me. I'll send Abdul to deal with him."

• • •

FAHY WAS SITTING THERE, feeling strangely alert. He'd had another swig from the bottle. Time had no meaning, the whiskey now seemed to have no effect on him, and then he heard the rumble of an engine through the floor and he got up and went downstairs to the garage. There was a BMW motorcycle parked beside the Triumph. He examined it, puzzled, then turned and Abdul moved in, the knife cutting into the left side of the stomach as Fahy faced him.

"For Christ's sake," he cried, and staggered back into what had once been a fireplace in Victorian times.

"No, for Allah's sake." Abdul stood there, staring at him, knife in hand.

Fahy said, "Listen, you stupid bastard, I served the IRA well for years in London and the police never rumbled me, but if they did, I always had my ace in the hole ready, and it's still there."

He put his hand up inside the chimney, grasped the Smith & Wesson .38 revolver hanging from a nail, and shot Abdul between the eyes.

IT STARTED TO rain again, quite hard. Fahy went to the door and listened. No one appeared to have been disturbed, but then, it was the kind of area where people minded their business, and with crime at the level it was in London these days, shootings and knifings not uncommon, it didn't pay to go looking for trouble.

His left hand was covered in blood, and he sat down at the desk again and opened a deep drawer. There were useful items from the old IRA days, some British Army field service wound packs and various medicines. He took the cover off one of the packs, opened a bottle of Dettol, and poured it all over the wound, not caring. He tightened the linen holding straps as hard as he could, then found a plastic pack of morphine ampules, snapped the end of one, and stuck it in.

"Daft idiot, you've had it, the bastards have done for you, Ali Hassim, the Army of God and this bugger." He stirred Abdul's body with his foot. "Muslim terrorists, Al Qaeda, so the Broker must be a Muslim in spite of his fancy talk." He swayed in the chair but pulled himself together. "You can't die yet, you old sod. Got to pay the bastards off, and there's only one man who can do that for you."

He opened the drawer, took out the notes he'd made to help him plan the whole Dover Street operation, and found the telephone number he needed.

ARTHUR FOX dropped Miller off after receiving instructions about the following day, and Miller let himself into the house that seemed curiously quiet, as if it knew that nothing would ever be the same again. He listened to the stillness, then went into the kitchen, made a cup of tea, returned to the sitting room, looked out at the bow window, and the phone rang.

He picked it up, and the first thing he heard were the words "Christ, it hurts!" followed by a terrible groan.

There was a pause, and Miller said, "Who's there? What's wrong with you?"

"I'm dying, that's what's wrong with me. Muslim fella from the Army of God stuck a knife in me. I've shot the bastard. Just let me take another pull at this Bushmills." There was a gurgle. "That's better."

"Who are you?"

"If you're Miller, I'm the man who tried to kill you, only it all went wrong, as you know better than anyone. My name's Sean Fahy."

There was that feeling of everything easing into a different time frame again, and yet Miller felt totally in control. "Just take your time and tell me where you are."

"You've got to promise me first. No police, no ambulance, and I mean that. I've a pistol in the desk, and if I hear sirens approaching, I'll finish myself off. Now, do you want to hear about Quinn, a man called the Broker, Ali Hassim and his Brotherhood? I've even got Russians in the plot."

Miller said, "Just tell me where you are."

"Your word, Major, that you'll just let me die."

"Your dying gives me no problem at all."

"Derry Street Garage, Kilburn. I'll hang on for you, I swear." He laughed hoarsely. "Let's hope the Bushmills lasts out."

MILLER GRABBED a raincoat, slipped a Walther and silencer into a pocket, and went out to the Mini Cooper. He drove carefully through empty, rain-soaked streets, calling Roper on his phone. Roper had been sleeping in his chair as he often did, but came awake as Miller's voice boomed over the speakers.

"What's up?" Roper asked, and Miller told him.

When he was finished, Roper said, "You'll need backup."

"What I need is no interference. Fahy wants to unload and I believe it's genuine, so I don't want anything to interfere."

"Would Dillon be okay?"

"Nobody else. I need to hear what Fahy has to say more than I've ever needed anything in my life."

"Good luck, that's all I can say. I'll alert the others."

DERRY STREET was dark and still, and in his lights Miller saw that many of the houses were boarded up, obviously awaiting the attention of the developers. There was a narrow cul-de-sac beside the garage, and he coasted the Mini Cooper in and switched off. The garage door was partially down, rain pouring over in a kind of waterfall. He ducked under and found it quite dark. The only light was at the far end, where Fahy sat behind the desk.

"Is it yourself, Major? Come in. A terrible time in the morning, one o'clock."

Miller moved past the Triumph, noted the BMW and Abdul on his back, also the pistol that Fahy raised in his bloody left hand. "Would you be having one of these in your pocket, Major?"

"Different model."

"Yes, it would be. This was hanging from a nail in the fireplace. The bastard stuck me and got the last surprise of his life. One between the eyes. I was never big with the handgun, the bomb was my specialty."

"So?" Miller waited, hands in pocket.

"I used to work for Quinn in the glory days, but I haven't been active for years. He phoned me from this Drumore Place in Louth and offered me fifty grand to top you and said he was in charge of security for Belov International and that people wanted you dead. I told him to get stuffed."

"But you changed your mind?"

"My wife was in a hospice near here, Alzheimer's. The nuns were wonderful, but the National Health people said they wouldn't pay for her there anymore. They were going to put her in some dump. I couldn't have that. All I gave her was trouble for years, and I wanted to make it up to her."

"With fifty thousand pounds?"

"Something like that. Quinn told me you knocked off a few of the boys during the Troubles so it was tit-for-tat."

"What did you do to the Amara?"

"I designed a gadget I'd used in the old days. Twenty minutes after starting, the brake fluid system was burned out. I fitted it while he was in the café. In your street. He didn't have any brakes when he tried to stop at those lights." His voice was fading a little. "It was meant for you. Quinn and his Russian bosses wanted it and the Broker man wanted it. He represented Al Qaeda and took over my payment with Osama money. Ali Hassim and his people are controlled by the Broker."

"Did you ever see the Broker?"

"Never. Only spoke on the phone. He sounded English and very top drawer. A messenger delivered an envelope with a key in it at noon. He went off at once, and the Broker phoned a few minutes later to say it was the key to locker seven at a place called The Turkish Rooms in Camden."

"Explain," Miller said.

Fahy did, and ended, "The envelope I found contained an open bank draft for fifty thousand pounds, one of those untraceable Swiss jobs. HSBC accepted it in my account without hesitation."

"When was this?"

"The day before the accident." His head lolled and he sagged across the desk and pushed himself up, leaving a bloody handprint. "I never even saw your wife get in the car. I'd no idea, but she did, and you haven't heard the best bit. My wife died, Major, died of a stroke. It's all been for nothing. She's lying in the morgue up there in St. Joseph's. I'm supposed to see Father Doyle, and he'll sort things out later today."

His eyes were sunken, there was sweat on his face, and he was trembling now as Miller said, "So that's it, you've told me everything?"

"I think so. I'm sorry about your wife. Is there any chance you could forgive me?"

"Not really. I can't even forgive myself."

Fahy gave him a ghastly smile. "Somehow I thought you'd say that." He went down in a kind of slow motion, his head to one side and eyes staring. Sean Dillon stepped out of the darkness, leaned over, and searched for a pulse. "Dead," he said, closed Fahy's eyes, and lifted him out of the chair and down to the floor.

"Did you hear any of that?" Miller asked.

"Just about everything." He called Roper and got an instant reply. "Two disposals. Utmost dispatch. I'll wait for the team. Derry Street Garage, Kilburn. I'll report details later."

"What happens now?" Miller asked.

"Years ago, Ferguson got tired of a system where you bag the bad guys and then clever lawyers get them off. If you accept that a bullet is a more efficient answer, you need the disposal team to clean up. Those two will be six pounds of ash around two hours from now."

"And you can do that?"

"Ferguson can do anything. Blake Johnson does roughly the same thing for the President. Would you quarrel with that? Take Abdul here." He bent down and picked up the knife still in Abdul's hand. "You heard how he was part of the plot in Dover Street that ended in the death of your wife, acting on orders from the Army of God. And Fahy? Did he really deserve pity because of his wife?"

"Do I?" Miller asked.

"Now you're being stupid. Sam Bolton wanted to give you information about your wife and ended up stabbed to death, probably by Abdul here with that same knife and on Ali Hassim's orders."

"Then shouldn't we dispose of him while we're at it?"

"We very well may, but Ferguson has to make the decision."

"She was my wife," Miller said bleakly.

"I know, old son, I know." There was a quiet rumble outside and then silence. "Here they are."

Dillon pulled the door right up and a large black van drove straight in. Four men in black overalls got out and the one obviously in charge nodded to them. "Gentlemen." He walked over and examined Abdul and then Fahy. The other three produced body bags, eased the corpses in, and put them in the back of the van. Then two of them produced cleaning equipment and went to work.

"The Muslim in leathers obviously owned the BMW?" the one in charge asked.

"That's right, Mr. Teague," Dillon said. "The white van and the Triumph are Sean Fahy's, the owner of the garage."

"We'll remove them. Leave the place orderly, but an implication that Fahy has departed for pastures new."

"What about the BMW?"

"One of my people will leave it in a multistory car park. It will languish until someone moves it to a police pound. I'd go if I were you, gentlemen, leave us to tidy up."

Miller followed Dillon outside. "What did you come in?"

"That ancient Mini is mine."

"Are you going home?"

"No, I'll make for Holland Park and give Roper the gory details. We've got good staff quarters. Always useful."

"I might see you there, then."

"You wouldn't be going to do anything you shouldn't?"

"Now, do I look like that kind of chap?"

"Yes, you do," Dillon said, and got in his Mini and drove away.

MILLER KNEW WHERE Ali Hassim lived from discussions with Roper about the Army of God, especially when he'd reported back on events at Folly's End when he had met Bolton. The corner shop, Delamere Road, Hampstead. He drove there through increasing rain. By then, it was about three o'clock in the morning. The shop was in darkness, but when he circled round to the rear, there was a yard with a garage and steps up to a back door and a dim light at the window.

He drove some distance away, sat in the Mini for a moment, screwing the silencer on the Walther, then he got out, locked the car, and walked back. There wasn't a soul about, not even any traffic. He went up the back steps and stood on the porch, holding the Walther against his leg. There was a bell push and he tried it.

Ali Hassim had found that with age he slept lightly, and he rested on the couch by the fire, having awakened from a doze half an hour earlier, and been disturbed to find no sign of Abdul or the BMW, which meant that when the bell sounded, he went to the door at once and opened it on the chain.

"Abdul, is that you?"

He had spoken in Arabic, and Miller replied in the same language. "There has been a problem. I must speak with you."

Almost as a reflex, Hassim undid the chain. Miller stepped in, kicked the door closed behind him, slapped Hassim across the face and sent him staggering back against the wall.

He carried on in English. "Harry Miller. I'm sure you're familiar with my face since you've taken an interest in me. Abdul sends his regards. He knifed Fahy, only Fahy shot him dead in return. You know what the Irish are like—unpredictable." Hassim tried to scramble away, and Miller grabbed him and threw him back into the hall.

"Leave me alone," Hassim cried, totally terrified.

"I can't do that till you've heard the rest. Fahy bled to death, but not before he'd invited me round to hear his confession. I know everything. Quinn at Drumore Place, Volkov and company—and the Broker, we mustn't forget him. I suppose you're going to tell me you've never met?"

Ali Hassim grabbed at the question as if it offered him some chance. "No one has, I swear it, not even General Volkov or any of the Russians. He's a voice. He chooses the people he deals with, he serves Osama. When he first spoke in Arabic, I thought him an Arab, but his English is perfect."

"Tell me about Bolton." He pushed the end of the silencer into Hassim's stomach. "Who killed him? He was murdered in the City. It's been on the police reports on television. I know you sent him to spy on me at Folly's End, so speak the truth or I'll kill you."

"Abdul did it. He didn't like Bolton, envied him his job in the City, his success."

"And you had nothing to do with it and didn't send Abdul to Dover Street posing as a traffic warden?"

"No, I swear it."

"You'd swear to anything, you bastard." The Walther swung up, coughed once, the bullet hitting Ali Hassim between the eyes, killing him instantly. There was blood on the wall as he slid down, and Miller turned, opened the door, switched off the light, and went out. Fifteen minutes later, he reached the Mini, got behind the wheel, and drove away.

He felt nothing; what was done, was done. Someone the system couldn't touch, a man obviously responsible for many deaths, had been eradicated and he didn't feel the slightest regret.

He was admitted to Holland Park by Sergeant Doyle on night shift twenty minutes later, left the Cooper for the sergeant to park, and went and found Roper and Dillon in the computer room.

"What did you do?" Dillon asked.

"Disposed of him. They'll find him when whoever works for him turns up in the morning. People involved in extreme

Islamic groups not only argue, they kill each other all the time." He turned to Roper. "That he sent Abdul to waste Fahy was a fact, but he denied having given Abdul orders to kill Bolton. He said that had been an act of jealousy on Abdul's part."

"Anything else?"

"To Fahy, the Broker was a voice on the phone. A toff, as he described it. Hassim said his English was perfect, but he thought he was an Arab at first, he spoke the language so well. He swore to me that even Volkov and his Russian chums have only heard the voice, and I must say I believed him."

"And shot him," Dillon said. "And Ferguson isn't going to like that."

"Too bad. Now, who's going to join me in a drink?"

12

Ali Hassim's body was discovered at seven o'clock that morning by the young woman who worked for him behind the counter, so it was quickly in the hands of the police. A detective inspector had a look and told his sergeant to get Forensics in.

"Some Muslim religious thing, I suppose. They'll all keep mum about it, but we'll have to go through the motions."

The word spread rapidly through the Army of God community, so within hours of the discovery, the Broker was on the phone to Moscow. Volkov was stunned by the news.

"Unbelievable. Who was responsible? Could it be some other Islamic faction?"

"In my opinion, no. Everyone knows Al Qaeda supports the Army of God. To attack us would obviously be unwise."

"Ferguson's people—Miller perhaps?"

"There's no evidence they knew about Hassim. And wait, that's not all. Let me tell you about Fahy."

When he was done, Volkov said, "It's like a bad novel. His wretched wife dies, he's consumed by guilt, and goes over the edge. Hassim told you he'd send Abdul to take care of him? Did he?"

"I checked out Fahy's garage personally. The back door was unlocked, the flat was empty, and the garage had no vehicles in it, totally deserted."

"So he's moved on. And Abdul?"

"Lived at the back of Hassim's shop. He's disappeared, too, with his BMW motorcycle, that's the word among the Brotherhood."

Volkov said, "To say I have a bad feeling about this would be an understatement. Many long and violent years in this business tells me that Fahy and Abdul have met the same fate as Ali Hassim."

"What do you want to do?"

"I'll have to speak to the President. I'll be in touch with you again quite soon."

PUTIN LISTENED without any evidence of emotion, and Volkov ended rather lamely, "It seems to be a mystery."

"Don't be absurd, it's perfectly obvious. It's been organized in some way by Ferguson, and Miller's decided to join in, seeking revenge for his wife."

"So what do we do?"

"Stand back for a bit, let this play out. I'm getting disillusioned by the Broker, though—too many failures. In fact, this whole hidden-identity thing has become an absurdity. Tell him if he isn't willing to disclose his identity, then I don't want anything more to do with him. And for now, I think it's best if everybody keeps their distance from him. Tell Chekhov, too.

"As for Fahy, he was hired by Quinn, and I'm getting tired of Quinn. Dispose of him as you see fit." The secret door opened and closed again, and he was gone.

CHEKHOV, on the phone, received all the news and said glumly, "It's like a bad Saturday night in Moscow with the

Mafia on the loose. It's certainly not what I came to London for."

"Don't be stupid. You didn't *come* to London, you were *sent* there, and as far as the President is concerned, you signed up for life. There are ways he could stamp on that bank account of yours. Do you want that?"

"Of course not." Privately, Chekhov didn't think it likely, but he couldn't afford to take the chance.

"So don't rock the boat, and remember—if the Broker phones, you aren't interested."

"What about Quinn?"

"I'm going to pay him a visit. I'm taking Yuri Makeev with me, and Grigorin."

"The executioners?" Chekhov shuddered. "God help him."

"Naturally, you will not tell him. It would distress me to find that you had."

"Of course not," Chekhov said hastily.

"Good. I want this to be a real surprise for Michael Quinn."

QUINN WAS NEXT on his list, and Volkov gave him the same message about the Broker but told him not to worry. "I'll be over to see you in a few days. We'll be able to talk and sort things out."

He switched off, leaving Quinn sitting beside the fire in the great hall at Drumore Place and wondering nervously what "sort things out" meant.

FINALLY, THE BROKER. In a strange way, it gave Volkov a certain satisfaction, waiting for him to answer the phone. "It's me again," Volkov told him.

"What did the President say?"

"He wasn't too pleased. Basically, he wants us to stand back now, keep a low profile. But he did make one point concerning you. He's tired of the voice-on-the-phone business. He wants to know who you are."

There was a short pause. The Broker said, "I can't do that."

"Is that your final answer?"

"Absolutely."

"Then he's instructed me to inform you that he doesn't want anything to do with you anymore. Don't call me, don't call Chekhov, don't call Quinn."

The Broker's voice was calm as usual. "General Volkov, you are aware I speak for Al Qaeda? Osama will not be pleased."

"The President couldn't care less, my friend. He has other fish to fry."

The Broker was still calm. "He may come to regret this."

"A word of advice, my friend. Don't try to threaten him. He is more powerful than Osama, more powerful than you."

"Let us hope his confidence is not misplaced."

SHORTLY AFTERWARD, Quinn answered the phone, still beside the fire, but now drinking a large Irish whiskey. "Who is this?"

"The Broker."

Quinn, thoroughly angry, said, "Piss off and don't call again."

"But you could be in great danger, my friend."

"I've been in great danger for the last thirty years of my life. Now bugger off."

He looked at the phone, the special one with which he'd always answered the Broker's calls, then tossed it into the log fire.

CHEKHOV WAS STANDING on his terrace, looking across Park Lane to Hyde Park, remembering what Volkov had said. He had the special mobile in his pocket because one hand held his walking stick, the other a drink, so he knew who it would be when it sounded.

He put the drink on a ledge, took out the phone, and heard the Broker say, "My dear Chekhov."

"Never again."

Chekhov dropped the phone, stamped on it with his good left foot, and picked up his drink, gazing out at Hyde Park, aware of a strange feeling of freedom.

At Holland Park, they had all assembled: the Salters, Dillon, and Miller, distributed around the computer room, Sergeants Doyle and Henderson stiffly military in spite of their ties and navy blue blazers.

Ferguson was calmly stern. "In spite of the way we do business, there has to be a method to our madness. You went off the reservation, Harry, with Ali Hassim. I appreciate how you feel, we all do. But you can't do anything like that again." He relented slightly. "For one thing, you were taking a chance on acting alone, and we wouldn't like to lose you."

"I take your point."

"He's right," Dillon said. "Remember what Father Sharkey told you?"

"I always have," Miller said. "That's why I'm still here."

"So what happens now?" Billy asked.

"We still can't do anything about the Broker, since we don't know who he is. Quinn, though, that's another matter."

Bill perked up. "We've had a bit of experience with that place he's holed up, Drumore. Had a little bit of a shoot-up there a while ago." He grinned. "There're some villains who won't be bothering anybody anymore. Wouldn't mind trying it again."

Roper said to Ferguson, "Moscow might not appreciate it. How far do you want to go?"

"Quinn's got away with murder for years, and he's certainly an accessory to the murder of Olivia and Vaughan. He should pay for that."

"I'd like to see the bleeder in court at the Old Bailey," Harry Salter said.

Ferguson said, "I'm thinking of something much simpler."

"And definitely more certain," Miller said.

"If you want to end it once and for all, a frontal attack would be needed." That was Dillon.

"We'd need more information on Quinn's situation there," Roper said.

Billy looked at his uncle and grinned. "And I know just who could fill us in. Max Chekhov. And I know where he lives."

Harry Salter stood up. "Make an old man happy, General, and let Billy and me go and lift him."

Ferguson smiled. "Dammit, why not? No rough stuff, mind you."

"Hardly likely. We put him on sticks, didn't we? We'll be back in no time."

They went out, and a few minutes later, Miller's phone sounded. "Hello, love, where are you?" It was Monica.

"Oh, with General Ferguson and the crew. How are things at Stokely?"

"Excellent when I left. Aunt Mary's suddenly come to life, and it's had quite an effect on the Senator. They're getting on famously. Since they've got the Grants to look after them, I thought I'd join you for a few days. I'm on the train just about to coast into Kings Cross. Don't worry about me, I'll get a taxi. I've got my key. By any chance . . . is Sean Dillon there?"

Miller grinned. "Sean? A friend of yours." He handed the phone to him. "Monica."

Dillon was genuinely pleased and retired to a corner to talk. Ferguson said, "What's this development? Dillon moving into the aristocracy?"

Miller shrugged and said a surprising thing. "She could do worse. She's been a widow too long."

"Well, God help us, but Dillon would certainly turn her life around."

MAX CHEKHOV DECIDED to cheer himself up, and what better venue than the bar at the Dorchester Hotel, a favorite for many of his friends and only a short distance away. The walk would do him good, exercise his right leg, so savagely kneecapped by a hit man delivering flowers on behalf of the Salters. Of course, even Chekhov had to admit he'd asked for it. He plodded along, stick tapping, and a scarlet Alfa Romeo pulled in at the curb and Harry Salter stepped out.

"Max, my old friend," he said. "Nice to see you. No need to walk, we'll give you a lift."

Chekhov panicked. "Get away from me!"

Harry pulled open the passenger door and stepped behind him. "Of course, I could say I'll blow your spine in two if you don't do as you are told, but I'm sure that won't be necessary." He shoved his head down and pushed him in the back of the car and climbed in after him. "There you go. An old friend just waiting to have a chat."

"And who would that be?"

"General Charles Ferguson. Only the best for you, Maxie boy."

Chekhov groaned. "Oh my God."

Billy said, "Nice to see you again, Max." He drove away.

BILLY LED CHEKHOV in and they all assembled. Ferguson said, "So, Mr. Chekhov, how are you?"

"How do you expect me to be? This is illegal, you know it is. What are you going to do?"

"What do you expect? A flight to Egypt to some very small concrete room where the torturers get to work on you? We don't do things like that."

"What about your friend, Dillon? I seem to remember his favorite parlor trick is shooting off half of somebody's ear if they won't talk."

"I've given that up for Lent, Max," Dillon told him. "Be sensible and just answer a few questions. Allow me to introduce you to Major Harry Miller here. He was a target for Volkov, the Broker, and the Army of God, and they were so inefficient they managed between them to kill his wife and his chauffeur. It's not surprising he isn't pleased with you."

"Okay, so there was a mistake, but there was no mistake

on his part when he shot dead Captain Igor Zorin of the Fifteenth Siberian Storm Guards in Kosovo."

Roper broke in. "So you know about that? Of course, the fact that Zorin was going to rape a few young girls and burn a mosque doesn't matter to you?"

"Look, I don't know what you want. I don't know anything about the death of the Major's wife. I didn't have any thing to do with the death of the man Fahy or this Hassim."

He stopped suddenly, aware that he had said too much. "Who said anything about the death of a man called Fahy?" Miller asked. "The man you're referring to doesn't exist. In fact, there's no report of his death, no body, so where does your information come from?"

No one spoke until Ferguson said, "This is a safe house under my command. I can hold you here for as long as I like and I don't need to tell anyone that you are here. Our version of a cell is extremely comfortable but a hundred percent secure. The food is excellent, I eat it myself. Books, a television, it's all yours, but there you stay until you tell me what I want to know, and if that means till Christmas, you'll be here for the next ten months. Sergeants Doyle and Henderson will be responsible for you. Take over, gentlemen."

Chekhov suddenly had had enough, and that meant enough of everyone—the President and the Russian Federation, General Ivan Volkov, the Broker, Quinn, the whole business.

"General Ferguson," he said wearily. "I'm tired, and the pain in my right knee, thanks to the Salters' generosity, is almost killing, so I'll make a bargain with you. Give me a very large vodka, followed by another, and then I'll answer any question you care to put to me if I can."

"Done." Ferguson smiled. "In fact, you can have a whole ruddy bottle if you like."

He sang like a bird and, by the end of it, was thoroughly drunk. "Is that it?"

"Absolutely," Ferguson said. "You've been very informative. You'll have to stay with us for a week, though, just until we've got things sorted."

"Anything you say. Can I go to bed now?"

"Of course. Have a good night." Doyle and Henderson took him away.

"SO THE BROKER is thoroughly shafted," Roper said.

"Interesting, Putin playing hardball in spite of Al Qaeda," Dillon said.

"And now we have Quinn's setup at Drumore Place, along with the number of guards," Ferguson said.

"You'd like to snatch him?" Miller asked.

"Or something." Ferguson nodded. "The day after tomorrow, Volkov arrives."

"You wouldn't be thinking of snatching him also?"

"No—but he could always happen to be in the line of fire."

"If there was a line of fire."

They all waited. Ferguson said, "I've had enough of these people and the incredible harm they do. Quinn and any of his old comrades who are foolish enough to back him up, deserve anything they get. If Volkov happens to be there, so much the better."

Excitement stirred. "What are you thinking about?" Billy demanded.

"The other year, we attacked in an old motor launch called the *Highlander* and sailed from Oban, remember?"

Dillon smiled. "How could we forget? But getting close to that tiny port, especially during the day, would be impossible, the way things are now. Quinn would be certainly well-prepared."

"Not if you were in the right kind of boat," said Ferguson. "The kind of thing only multimillionaires can afford."

They looked at him.

"You mean some sort of gin palace?" Billy said.

"A vulgar term, but yes. An appallingly wealthy friend of mine owns quite a nice, large yacht. As you may be aware, I'm something of a sailor, did the Atlantic crossing single-handed in my time. A boat like that demands attention, especially with a handsome woman on the stern deck drinking a cocktail. Nobody could imagine it being there for anything else but pleasure, a cruise off the Irish coast."

They were stunned. Harry Salter said, "Genius! That handsome woman, though—a bird like that would be putting herself in harm's way."

"You've got someone in mind?" Dillon asked.

"Helen Black."

"The sergeant major? I remember her well," Billy said. "What a woman."

"But first, I need to secure the loan of the boat, so have a drink or something while I speak to my friend. I'll use the office." He went away.

Miller said, "The sergeant major?"

"Military police," Harry Salter said. "Used to run this place for Ferguson."

"Got the Military Cross for shooting a member of the IRA in Derry who was leaving a van with Semtex on board outside a nurses' hostel," Dillon said. "Took a bullet in the left thigh, got the guy who did it, then sat up and shot his friend in the back as he ran away. Went to Oxford, but refused a commission every time one was offered. Her husband was an officer in the Household Cavalry. Killed in Iraq the other year."

"Well, I'm sorry about that, but I must say she sounds impressive," Miller said.

"A handsome lady. Never had any children. About the same age as Monica."

"Really?" Miller said. "I look forward to meeting her."

Ferguson came back. "The boat is mine. Wait till you see it. Avenger Class Ten. If you thought you knew what a motorboat was, think again. It's in the Isle of Wight at the moment, and my friend will have it rushed up to Oban, delivered by two of his men. It will be waiting for us by the afternoon."

"Good God, can it get there in time?" Billy said.

"Believe me, this boat is sensational. Wait till you see the wheelhouse, and there's a flybridge up top."

"Who's going?" Miller asked.

"Me, to give things authority. You, Harry. Dillon, Billy, and Helen Black. Sorry," he told Harry Salter, "not this time."

"Never mind, my bleeding arthritis wouldn't stand up to it. I was sorry to hear Mrs. Black's husband bought it in Iraq, I didn't know."

"About two years ago. She's over it now. Writes children's books these days. All I've told her is the job is fairly similar to what she helped us on three years or so ago. She's quite a sailor in her own right. She accepted without question. I've invited her to dinner tonight at Quantinos. Harry," he said to Miller, "I'd like you to meet her. You can come too, Sean," he added to Dillon.

"Actually, as you heard, my sister has just arrived from Stokely. Perhaps she could join us?" Miller said.

"Make up the party?" Ferguson thought about it. "Yes. Why not? Now there are things to do. We'll all meet later, gentlemen."

MILLER FOLLOWED FERGUSON out to where their cars were waiting. Ferguson said, "Tell me, Harry, how much does Lady Starling know about everything?"

"Keep calling her that, Charles, and she'll brain you. Monica she is, and that's what she expects. The answer is, she's recently had to face up to my murky past, because I've told her. When you were discussing things with us after the funeral, she was outside on the patio with Dillon. She heard a lot of what was said."

"Bloody fool should have tried to move her on."

"He did, but she's a determined woman. I discussed things with her before returning to London. I told her I'd make them pay."

"Does she know about recent events?"

"No, but she will do when I get back to Dover Street."

"Good. Then I can make the whole situation clear to Helen Black when we meet tonight."

MILLER CALLED IN at the Cabinet Office to thank Henry Frankel for all his help with the funeral. "The least I could do, old man," Frankel said. "You didn't want the Prime Minister, did you?"

"As it happens, no. Why do you ask?"

"He's hosting at Chequers for three days, the French and Dutch foreign secretaries. The usual thing, trying to make sense of the EU."

"Well, that should provide an entertaining weekend."

"What about you, Harry?"

"Nothing too exciting. I might go back to Stokely and take it easy for a while. If anything comes up, you can always get me on my phone." He left, and Arthur drove him back to Dorset Street.

It was late afternoon now and he found Monica in the sitting room reading *Country Life*. She tossed it to one side. "What's happening?"

"For one thing, I intend to have an early-evening drink, and you might care to join me. After that, you'll want to have a shower and find a decent frock, because we're going out to dinner."

"That sounds nice. Anywhere special?"

"Quantinos at seven. It's early, but we have a big day tomorrow. And it has to do with what I'm about to tell you. I've been honest with you about my past, and after you overheard Ferguson at the funeral, you asked me if I knew who was responsible for the assassination attempt. I said there were several possibilities, but I intended to get the lot of them."

"And have you?"

Miller went to the sideboard and poured a brandy and ginger ale. "Horse's Neck?"

He handed it to her and poured another. "I think I'm going to need it."

"Sean Fahy, once a bomb maker, was given the contract and carried it through," he told her. "He's now dead and disposed of."

"Did you kill him?"

"No, he was murdered by other people connected with the plot who wanted him silenced. I heard his confession as he was dying, and so did Dillon."

She drank some of her brandy and steeled herself. "Go on."

"If that's what you want. Just listen. The full story."

Afterward, she said, "I think I need another of these." She gave him her glass. He got her the drink and she carried on. "This Ali Hassim, a dreadful man, a terrorist, I can see that, responsible for so much, but didn't it bother you killing him?"

"Not in the slightest."

She nodded and swallowed her drink straight down. "So Charles Ferguson is aware that you're telling me all this?"

"Yes."

"So what's the next move?"

"Michael Quinn is sitting in Drumore Place, well protected, and General Volkov is flying in for who knows what purpose, but he intends to surprise Quinn."

"And you want to do something about that?"

"That's it. You'll hear more at Quantinos, where Charles Ferguson and Sean Dillon will bring Helen Black up to speed."

"Come to think about it, I shall enjoy meeting your sergeant major." She got up. "I'd better go and sort some glad rags out. You know what we women are like when we're in competition."

She left him and went upstairs.

AT QUANTINOS, Ferguson and Dillon had a drink in the bar, and it was there that Helen Black found them. She had streaked blond hair and an unlined face and was elegant in a deceptively simple little black dress and a short black diamante evening coat.

She kissed Dillon on the cheek. "Sean, you old devil." She turned to Ferguson. "Indestructible as ever, Charles?" She put an arm around him.

"Sorry, my dear, about Terry." He was referring to her husband.

"Old history now, Charles. Gone are the days when House Cavalrymen were chocolate soldiers riding around London in breastplates. Ireland, Bosnia, Kosovo, Iraq, Afghanistan—

nothing but casualties these days, and their gallantry awards speak for themselves. Never mind that. Give me a scotch and soda and tell me about Harry Miller. Just another politician, I thought, and then you told me of another side to him. Can it be true?"

"Well, he shot somebody dead last night," Dillon told her.

"To be accurate, it was in the early hours of the morning, but the person concerned richly deserved it," Ferguson said. "Here he comes now."

"The good-looking woman on his arm is his sister, Lady Starling. She's a Cambridge don and a widow," Dillon murmured.

"And it's an open secret that Dillon fancies her." Ferguson smiled. "The Salters have great hopes for him."

Miller and Monica forced their way through. He took Helen's hand. "Harry Miller."

"And you're Monica," Helen said. "Dillon's told me wonderful things."

"You're mischief making, woman," Dillon said. "Will you stop it?"

Helen laughed. "He's blushing. I can't believe it. You're at Cambridge, I hear. Which college?"

"New Hall."

"I was at Oxford myself, St. Hughes."

"Well, that's not your fault."

"No Oxbridge wrangling, if you please. Let's get to the table," Ferguson ordered, and took Helen's arm.

THEY STARTED WITH champagne, Dillon insisting on the usual Krug. "So what's the plan?" Helen Black asked.

"Well, it isn't to play patty-fingers. I remember last time out on the old *Highlander* you wore paratroop boots."

"I still do when I'm gardening. They're so comfortable."

"You had a Colt .25 hollow-point stuffed into the right-hand one. When the opposition took over the boat, you shot a man named Kelly at the wheel and ended up in the water in the darkness, with Billy Salter and me facing death on deck."

"And how in the hell did you get out of that?" Miller asked.

"Billy jackknifed under the keel, scrambled up the other side to the wheelhouse, and got the Walther concealed in a flap."

"I remember it was bloody cold," Helen said.

"Well, I should imagine it would be." Monica was trying to take it all in. "I must say this is the most remarkable dinner party I can remember. Could we order now?"

THE MEAL, as always, was excellent and afterward they had brandy and coffee, except for Dillon, who insisted on tea. Helen said, "So tell me about the motorboat."

"Avenger Class Ten. You need to be seriously rich to own one. It's the ultimate, every kind of luxury. It's in the Isle of Wight, but a scratch crew of two men will rush it up to Scotland. It will be at Oban in the harbor waiting for us tomorrow afternoon."

"May I ask why Oban?" Monica inquired.

"It suits my purposes. There's an RAF air sea rescue base, so we can land there in my Gulfstream. The run down to Louth goes past Islay and down through the North Channel to the Irish Sea. It'll be nothing to a boat with the speed the Avenger is capable of. An interesting trip."

"So tell me fully now how you intend to handle it?"

"It's simple enough. We'll dress in what my friend's sending—sailing gear that make us look like the crew of such a boat. You can appear on either the stern deck or on the flybridge up top, with dark glasses and champagne."

"In other words, I'm a rich bitch?"

"Exactly. Touring the coast on the way down south. No need to hide. Then we drop anchor off their excuse for a port."

"And get up to skulduggery under cover of darkness?"

"Something like that. Our general appearance and your cavorting around will keep the envious natives curious but happy, and that should include Quinn's people."

"Sounds good." Helen nodded.

Monica took a deep breath. "But it would be even better with two."

"Two what?" Ferguson asked.

"Two rich bitches cavorting around the deck."

"My dear Monica, you can't be serious."

"Why not? I think it would make perfect sense, don't you, Harry?"

Miller said, "It would be something of a departure, love. I mean, the academic life . . ."

"Don't give me all that stuff about gleaming spires, dinners at high table, Oxbridge dons living a life so separate from the lives of others that it's devoid of humanity. I not only admired my sister-in-law as a fine and talented actress, I also loved her as a human being. If I can help bring down rotten people who were responsible for her murder by lounging around on deck on this boat of yours, then I'd like to do it." She turned to Helen Black. "I'm afraid I'd have to leave the gun stuffed into the boot to you, Helen. I don't think I'd be very good at that."

"You're certain about this?" Ferguson said. "It's a big step."

"One I'm prepared to take, so can we agree that it's settled?" She turned to Dillon, who was smiling slightly. "Don't you say a word except to ask me to dance. There's some perfectly good music going to waste here."

She got up, and Dillon followed. "My pleasure, Lady Starling."

"Don't you dare start that," she said, and they moved into the crowd of dancers.

The others watched. Helen Black said, "That's one heck of a lady. She's welcome aboard, as far as I'm concerned."

Ferguson turned to Miller. "Harry?"

"I've found that it never pays to argue with Monica."

"So, six of us it is, and Farley Field for that Gulfstream at noon tomorrow."

"Suits me." Miller turned to Helen Black. "Would you care to take a turn around the floor?" She smiled, and they joined the others.

Ferguson watched them, feeling quite paternal, took out his Codex and contacted Roper. "Slight change of plan. Six of us tomorrow for the Oban flight. Lady Starling's decided two rich bitches on show on the flybridge would be better than one."

"Good God. And Miller's agreed?"

"He'd no choice, that lady's her own woman. She's dancing with Dillon at the moment. 'Our love is here to stay.' Isn't that Cole Porter?"

"There's hope for him yet. I'll let Billy know the change. I've spoken to the quartermaster, explained the type of operation, and he'll have suitable weaponry on board for you."

"Nothing else to report."

"Not really. I've confirmed there's a flight plan for a Belov International Falcon leaving Moscow the day after tomorrow, checked through to Dublin with advance permission to land at their base in County Louth. The two pilots are mentioned as Yeltsin and Sono, and guess what?"

"Surprise me."

"Chekhov was telling us the truth. Three passengers, including Grigorin and Makeev, pride of the GRU."

"And the third?"

"Ivan Petrovsky, listed as a security expert."

"Petrovsky, eh? That's Ivan Volkov, trying to pretend he isn't there," Ferguson said. "A certain danger in that. It titillates."

"It certainly does." Roper laughed. "I'm on all night, so if you need me. . . ."

He cleared the line just as the dancers returned to the table. Ferguson glanced at his watch. "Almost ten. I think it's settle-the-bill time. A big day tomorrow. I'll drop you off, if that suits, Helen?"

"Thanks very much."

"We're fine," Miller said. "Big Arthur's at the wheel of my Mercedes."

"The fruits of office." Ferguson kissed Monica's hand. "Glad to have you aboard. Till tomorrow." He gave Helen his arm.

Miller and Monica followed them, and found Arthur waiting across the street. "Home, Arthur," Miller said, and kissed Monica on the cheek. "Did you enjoy it?"

"What do you think?" She smiled. "The only problem it leaves me with is what to wear. I'll have to go through my wardrobes the minute we get back to Dover Street."

"Women," he said. "How wonderfully practical you all are about the essentials in life."

AT DOVER STREET, she went straight in while Miller paused to explain the situation to Arthur and how it was going to affect him for the next few days. He arranged for him to be on standby in the morning, bade him goodnight, and followed Monica inside, hurrying as rain started to fall. Monica had gone straight upstairs, he could hear her racketing around. He smiled, then walked into the sitting room and noticed the red light on the answering machine.

He paused at the sideboard, pouring a scotch, picked up the phone as he drank it, and listened to the recorded message. Then he had to sit down. He was stunned. It was a man speaking in Arabic.

"It is ten o'clock and you are obviously out, Major Miller. If you have any interest at all in the identity of the Broker, a messenger will be waiting very close to you in the graveyard of St. Mary's Church, Coin Street, until eleven o'clock. All your questions will be answered."

The Arabic was clear and fluent, he recognized that. He checked his watch. It was twenty minutes to eleven, and Coin Street was just down the road on the near side of St. Mary's Square.

Time was of the essence. He pulled open the middle drawer of the sideboard, produced a silenced Walther, dropped it in his raincoat pocket, and made for the front door. As he got it open, Monica appeared at the top of the stairs.

"Harry, where on earth are you going?"

"Business, love, in a hurry."

He went down the steps and started to rush along Dover

Street in the rain, his Codex to his ear as he called Roper, who answered instantly.

"Who is this?"

"It's Harry." He was running across the square now. "Had a message from some Arab. Told me there'd be a messenger waiting for me in the graveyard of St. Mary's, Coin Street."

"What the hell is going on?"

"Someone who can reveal the identity of the Broker."

Roper was shocked. "Dammit, Harry, it could be a trap. You need backup."

"No time. The messenger will only wait until eleven, and this is Mayfair, Giles, not Beirut. I'm just coming up to St. Mary's now. I'll be back."

Roper was already doing a conference call that took in Dillon, Billy Salter, and Ferguson at the same time.

THERE WERE LIGHTS at the heavy iron gates of the churchyard, a couple on a wall of the church itself, and the gravel patch from the gate was shadowed as it wound its way through a forest of Gothic monuments and gravestones. His shoulders were soaked in the heavy rain, and he put his Codex in his pocket and gripped the Walther without taking it out.

He saw an Angel of Death, common enough in Victorian times, a mausoleum with a couple of marble figures at the entrance, then something stirred and a young woman stepped out of the shadows clutching a small umbrella in her left hand. In the half-light from the church wall, he could see at once that she was Muslim. He couldn't make out if she had on a full chador, because she was wearing a raincoat over her garments, but certainly her head was covered and part of her face. When she spoke, her English was excellent.

"You are Major Miller?"

Miller glanced beyond her and around. "Are you alone?"

"Yes."

She couldn't have been more than sixteen or seventeen, with great luminous eyes. The scarf had slipped from her face and she was beautiful.

"Who sent you?" he said. "I was told there would be a messenger, but who from?"

"I am that messenger," she said. "I am from the Army of God, who serve only Allah as the Broker ordains."

"You know the Broker?" Miller was instantly eager beyond caution. "Who is he?" He put a hand on her shoulder. "Tell me, child."

"He is the voice of Allah who speaks to me on the telephone, who speaks to many. He has told me what must be done." She added in Arabic, "You are accursed in the sight of Allah."

He was close, a hand on her shoulder now, and as she still gripped the umbrella, he was not aware of her right hand with the knife, thrusting it into his left side. He cried out in pain, trying to push her away, half turning, and now she stabbed him under the left shoulder so deeply that the knife stuck for a moment. He pulled away, his hand scrabbling in his pocket and finding the Walther.

As he pulled it out, his leg collapsed so that he fell on his back and tried to scramble up, an arm raised to ward her off. She was a demon that could not be satisfied, and as she stabbed again and again, he pushed the end of the silencer against her heart and fired, only the once, but that was all it took, and she was hurled back against the doors of the mausoleum and slid down.

He crawled over to her, slipping the Walther into his pocket with a bloodstained hand. He was racked with pain, blood oozing from so many places, but the only important thing was her and what the half-light from the church revealed. The young face gravely peaceful, eyes half open in death.

He was aware of a strange buzzing from inside the other pocket and realized it was his Codex. Roper's voice was urgent. "Are you all right, Harry? Dillon and Billy are on their way."

"Bleeding like a stuck pig, but then maybe that's what I am. I kill kids now." A kind of weeping possessed him.

"What is it, old son? What's wrong?"

"It was the Broker himself who made that call. The bastard

sent a young disciple, a lovely girl of sixteen or so. I wasn't expecting it and tried to talk to her." He was fading now. "She told me I was accursed in the sight of Allah and she stabbed and stabbed and stabbed. In the end, I shot her." He took a deep breath. "So Dillon and Billy are coming?"

"They sure are."

"And you've alerted the disposal team? We mustn't forget them." He tried to laugh. "What bastards we are, Roper."

"It's the world we live in, old son."

And then Billy Salter's red Alfa Romeo pulled inside the entrance and Dillon was out and running, dropping to one knee.

Miller opened his eyes. "Who's that coming in behind the car?"

"It's what we call the dark ambulance. We have a very private hospital called Rosedene. Absolute total security and privacy, and the finest general surgeon in London, Professor Henry Bellamy."

The paramedics hurrying up the park were all in black tracksuits. "It's bloody funny, really," Miller said. "It's getting more like a funeral every minute." He lost consciousness.

At Rosedene, Dillon sat with a very stressed Monica and Ferguson. They were subdued, waiting for news, and the matron, Maggie Duncan, looked in. "Before you ask me, he's been stabbed several times, so it's taking ages doing the necessary repair work. He's lost a lot of blood, but that's being taken care of. I'll have one of the girls bring more tea and coffee. If you want anything stronger, Sean, you know where the medicinal whiskey is kept in Professor Bellamy's office." She turned to Monica. "Lady Starling, he isn't going to die, so stop worrying. He's in a mess, yes, but it will heal in time. I'm an expert. We specialize in people who end up in here badly knocked about. It's the name of the game."

Monica jumped up and went across and kissed her. "Thank you so much."

Maggie smiled and went out, and a moment later Roper entered in his wheelchair, Billy and Harry Salter with him. Roper said, "Has Bellamy given the good word yet?"

"No, but Maggie Duncan's been helpful," Ferguson said.

Monica put in, "She said he's in a mess, but it will heal in time."

"But there's the other side to this business," Roper told her. "The Broker set Harry up. The girl was very high on coke and a couple of other things that are worse. A blood test showed it. The Broker used her as a weapon, it's as simple as that. She told Harry she knew he was accursed in the sight of Allah. She'd been turned into a religious zombie by a truly evil man. Harry was weeping as he spoke to me. He said: 'I kill kids now.'"

"That's bleeding nonsense," Harry Salter said. "There's only one guy bad in this business, and Gawd help him if I ever get my hands on him."

"Join the queue," Ferguson said. "It would be a long one." He turned to Roper. "That poor girl?"

"The disposal team took care of it an hour ago." He sighed. "Billy and I attended."

Billy was embarrassed. "I didn't feel comfortable about her being alone. All she had with her was the knife, so there's no means of knowing her identity. The Broker was covering his back in case anything went wrong."

Harry Salter said, "There'll be a judgment day, you'll see."

Shortly afterward, Bellamy came in straight from the operating theater. "A nasty business, and it's taken some fancy embroidery, as they say in the trade. One thrust could have cost a kidney, but missed by a whisker. There were many wounds, but the trench coat he was wearing helped stop full penetration of most."

"Can I see him?" Monica asked.

"Not for some time. He's still under. If you'd care to stay with us, Matron can find you a room, no problem."

"Yes, I think I'd like that very much."

Bellamy turned to Ferguson. "He'll need a couple of weeks

to pull round to a reasonable level. We'll say he's got pneumonia, that's to cover him with the Whips in Parliament. He hasn't a cut on the face, and the rest of him will be covered one way or another."

"Sounds reasonable." Bellamy left, and Ferguson said to Monica, "I'm damned sorry things have turned out this way, but it makes me more determined than ever to push the Irish trip through. We'll leave you now to see how he gets on." He glanced at his watch. "One o'clock."

Monica managed a faint smile. "Good luck to you all." She went out to Maggie Duncan's office.

Ferguson said, "Yes, I know it's early in the morning, but I suggest we adjourn to Holland Park to discuss matters."

"ALL RIGHT, what's changed?" he said later.

"Harry Miller and his sister won't be coming," Billy said. "That's Dillon, Helen Black, me and you, General. Can it be done?"

"Well, I could say stuff the arthritis," Harry said.

"All very well," Dillon said, "but I've had an idea. We pick up the boat at Oban tomorrow afternoon, leave that night or early the following morning. We sail through the North Channel into the Irish Sea and skirt the coast of County Down and the Mourne Mountains."

"Is this a geography lesson?" Ferguson asked.

"My uncle on my mother's side, Mickeen Oge Flynn, has a garage in a place called Collyban. A mile round the point is a disused quarry in the cliff and a rather nice Victorian jetty. You'll drop me off. I'll walk a mile or two and call in on Mickeen, who'll have a car waiting for me. I'll wear a black suit and trilby hat, a clerical collar, a pair of Zeiss tinted glasses, the kind that change color, a slight disguise if you like."

"And what the hell do we do?"

"Anchor off the harbor at Drumore as planned. Volkov and his heavies will drive down the coast road to Drumore when they get off their plane. I'll see what they get up to."

"What you get up to, you mean," Ferguson said.

"If I can do myself a bit of good with the Russians, it would make up for Harry being in a bed at Rosedene, and it would just leave Quinn and company to deal with."

"Crackers," Billy told him. "You can't do much with the Russkies on your own."

"Ah, but it won't be me. Father Martin Sharkey, that's the name."

"Well, I'm against it," Billy said.

Ferguson shook his head. "Harry Miller is a significant loss to the operation. Dillon's right. Anything he can do to even things up could prove crucial." He turned to Dillon. "Okay, you get your way." He stood up. "I don't know what the rest of you are going to do, but I'm going to bed for a few hours. Staff accommodation will be fine. I suggest you do the same."

He left, and Harry Salter said, "We'll go back to the Dark Man, Billy and me, and save him a trip in the morning. Farley Field at noon. We'll see you there, Dillon." He led the way out.

Roper said, "Are you staying or going, Sean?"

"I might as well get off to Stable Mews and get my disguise together. Mickeen Oge Flynn wouldn't thank me for phoning him at this time."

"You never know."

"That's true. He was always up for it during the Troubles." He took his Codex out and thumbed the number. "There you are, transfer to your system and we can both listen."

The number rang for a couple of minutes and then there was a drowsy, slightly drunken voice. "Who the Christ is calling at this fuggin hour?"

"It's your nephew, you ould sod."

The other voice changed, came to life. "Sean, is it yourself?"

"And no other. I'll be dropping in to see you early in the morning, not today, tomorrow."

"Where from?"

"The sea, you daft idiot. You'll have a motorcar waiting for me, and I'll have one thousand pounds in fifty-pound notes to slap in your hand."

"What is it, Sean, what are ye up to? Is it back to the great days?"

"Gone forever, *avic,* but there are still those who need sorting out down Drumore way. Are you sound on this?"

"Would you insult your old uncle? I'll be here, and your car." He chuckled. "But bring the cash!"

He went, and Dillon turned to Roper. "You see, all you have to do is live right."

"So it would appear. Anything else you need?"

"Yes, ask the quartermaster to get me a twelve-bore double-barreled shotgun, sawn off, naturally. I'll see you in the morning."

He went out and Roper lit a cigarette, poured whiskey into a paper cup, and started to probe cyberspace.

Scotland

Ireland

13

Monica followed Maggie Duncan's advice and took a sleeping pill so that it was nine o'clock before she stirred, Maggie's hand on her shoulder.

"How is he?" Monica swung her legs to the floor.

"Believe it or not, but he's just had a cup of tea, with my assistance. Have a shower, shake yourself up, and you can see him."

When she went in his room, he was gaunter than she had ever seen him, eyes sunken. They had raised the bed behind him, he was on two drips, and a loose clinical smock covered his bandaged wounds.

"Hello, love, sorry to put you through it again."

She kissed him fondly. "Don't talk nonsense."

"That poor girl. She was like a demon, stabbing, stabbing." He was very emotional. "I was desperate, and there was the gun in my pocket."

She sat on a chair beside the bed and tried to soothe him. "It wasn't your fault. The Broker used that girl abominably, made sure she was on drugs, persuaded her she would be doing Allah's bidding. I don't accept that for a moment. The

Prophet himself would damn him. The true evil of this man was to persuade the girl to do *his* bidding."

The door had opened quietly, and Dillon entered. "I couldn't agree more." He said to Miller, "The lady's right. You're as much a victim in this as anyone. How do you feel?"

"Bloody awful, but the morphine's kicked in. What's happening, Sean?"

"We leave at noon as planned."

"But without me, and that leaves you short. Could Harry Salter take my place?"

"He's not really up to that sort of thing anymore, but we're determined to go through with it. I've spoken to Helen and she's still with us. I've rearranged the plan just to try and even things up."

"And how would you do that?"

"Resurrect Father Martin Sharkey."

WHEN HE WAS FINISHED, Miller nodded. "I can see what you're getting at and it's a bold plan, Sean, but you'll be on your own."

"Sure, and I've been on my own for most of my life, and I'm still here. I'll be fine."

"Makeev and Grigorin are the best the GRU can provide, and that means damn good."

Monica looked troubled. "Don't worry about me, love," Dillon told her. "Let me tell you how I got into all this in the first place. Charles Ferguson got me out of a Serb prison, where I was awaiting a firing squad, but only on condition that I agreed to work for him. He said he had so many bad guys to handle, he wanted someone on his side who was worse than they were."

She was angry. "That's so stupid."

"Not really. He saw me for what I was, and so should you." He turned to Harry. "I'll be in touch, you can count on it."

Monica didn't stand up. "What about me, can I count on it?"

"There's an old Irish poem. 'She turned my head not once,

but twice.' " He smiled. "And that's the kind of woman you are, Lady Starling. So let me get away out of this before I find myself in trouble. God bless all here."

The door closed behind him and Harry caught Monica smiling. "You like him, don't you?" he said.

"He's an easy man to like." There was sweat on Miller's face, and she wiped it dry with a paper towel.

"But frightening, I suppose?"

She paused, frowning slightly. "But I don't find you frightening, not in the slightest. Why would I feel differently about Dillon?"

Miller smiled. "Maybe he finds you frightening?"

"I very much doubt it, and I'm a woman, we know these things. God created us with moral superiority, which is a good thing because, without us, man would have wrecked the planet years ago."

"Forget the slick Oxbridge talk, Monica, those Russian bastards he intends to have a go at on his own really are bad news." He was angry now and sweating again. "And here I am lying on my back."

"I know what you mean. Now calm down." She pressed a button and, when a nurse glanced in, said, "Could you ask Matron to check on my brother's morphine situation? I believe he's in pain again. And tea for two, if that's possible."

The nurse went out, and Miller said, "You're a cool one."

"Not really, but I know you're in good hands here. As for Sean Dillon, it's the GRU who would worry if they knew he was on his way. And as far as I'm concerned, it's all hands to the pumps."

The nurse hurried in with the tea. "I've spoken to Matron and she's seeing to the pain relief."

She went out, and Monica poured. "My God," Miller said, "You're going to go with them."

"Perhaps I can be useful. I'll damn well try. Three days, at the most. You'll be well looked after here."

He held the plastic cup of tea awkwardly with the uninjured fingers of his left hand. "What's happened to you? You're a different person. It's as if I never knew you."

She laughed. "My darling Harry, I must say that's a bit rich coming from you."

The door opened again and Maggie Duncan entered, a nurse carrying a hypodermic and morphine on a tray. "Not feeling too good, are we?"

Monica stood up. "I've got something very important to take care of for the next few days, Matron, so look after him for me." She leaned over and kissed Miller on the forehead. "God bless, darling, see you soon."

"Mad," Miller said. "Out of her mind," but Monica was away, the door closed firmly behind her.

Maggie Duncan found a patch on his right arm that hadn't been bandaged and the nurse passed her the hypodermic.

"This will help, Major, then you can have a nice sleep."

AT FARLEY, just before noon, Harry Salter delivered Billy. The quartermaster and Parry were handling a box into the plane between them, Dillon supervising. Ferguson was standing outside the office, talking to Lacey, with Monica and Helen to one side, heads together. Harry Salter joined them, and Billy went to Dillon.

"What's Monica doing here?"

"She's decided to go for it, wants to help pay the bastards back for Harry. He'll be okay at Rosedene for a few days."

"If you say so. What have we got?"

The quartermaster said, "Uzi machine pistols with silencers, five Walthers with silencers, Colt .25s with silencers, stun grenades, some of the fragmentation variety. It's all close-quarter stuff, so I've left out rifles. You're going to war, Mr. Dillon?"

"We could be, Sergeant Major."

"More than twenty years ago, I was chasing you in South Armagh."

"And never caught the bugger," Billy remarked.

"Well, I don't hold it against you, Mr. Dillon, best forgotten. Bring back what you can and I'll put it in store. Oh, by the way, you'll find a double-barreled sawn-off as you requested, steel-ball shot."

He walked back toward the office, paused by the women, and said to Helen, "Nice to see you again. I remember you from Derry."

"A long time ago, Sergeant Major."

He went inside, and Ferguson said, "Let's get moving, then."

They walked toward the Gulfstream, and Harry Salter called, "Bring him back in one piece, Dillon."

"Don't I always!"

"No, actually."

He waited, watching them go up the steps and Parry close the Airstairs door. Lacey had already started up, so there was no delay. They taxied across to the runway and roared along it and lifted into a leaden gray March sky.

"Give the bastards hell," Harry murmured. "That's what I say." He went back to his Bentley, got in, and drove away.

LACEY HAD THE CONTROLS, but half an hour into the flight, Parry took over and the squadron leader came back. "Everyone okay?" he said. "Sandwiches, salad in the fridges, plus everything from champagne on down. Coffee and tea makers in the cupboard. Getting on for four hundred miles from Farley to Oban. Allowing for adverse wind on occasion, we'll still manage it in this plane in a couple of hours."

"That's good," Ferguson said. "Have you arranged quarters for yourselves with the CO at RAF, Oban?"

"Oh, yes, they'll look after us."

He went back to the cockpit, and Helen made coffee. Dillon was already opening a half-bottle of scotch from the bar.

Billy, sitting across from him, said, "Amazing differences in people. I was a streetwise young bastard, even though Harry sent me to St. Paul's School."

"Some might say the best in London," Dillon said.

"Well, he wanted to make a toff out of me. Anyway, I

remember a guy producing half a bottle of rum he'd nicked from somewhere. There were four of us and it was a test-of-manhood thing. One sip, Dillon, that's all I took, one little sip. Alcohol was the worst thing I'd ever tasted in my life. It's never touched my lips again, and I mean not ever."

"What about your chums?"

"Finished the bottle, and sick as pigs for it. It was in the games room. The sports master found them and they all got a flogging." He smiled back into the past. "Served the buggers right. But you, Dillon. Ever since I've known you, you put that stuff away like nobody I ever knew—and I've never seen you drunk."

"It's my liver, you see, Billy." Dillon grinned. "We're on very good terms."

Ferguson was in front of them, drinking the coffee that Helen had passed to him, and Dillon moved to sit across from him.

"Has it ever occurred to you that you're possibly getting a little too old for this kind of game?" he asked Ferguson.

"Frequently, but then it's a wicked old world we live in, and getting worse. I can't stop it, the curse of the suicide bomber, ordered by people like Al Qaeda to commit mass murder. What upsets me about it is the lack of any moral viewpoint. In other times, people at least tried to devise rules for the way wars were fought. There was a concept of honor, but all that changed when revolutionaries discarded the idea of uniform, and suddenly, you couldn't recognize who your enemy was, just like your lot in Ulster."

"The IRA didn't invent it," Dillon pointed out. "What about the Boers?"

"Yes, but it was Michael Collins in 1920 who created the concept of assassins in civilian clothes operating on a regular basis."

"You have a point, but then, as I've pointed out before, his favorite saying was: The purpose of terrorism is to terrorize. It's the only way a small country can take on a larger one with any hope of success."

"Lenin said that first, and a hard prospect it's been for the world for years," Ferguson said. "And still is."

"Then let's have a drink and cheer ourselves up," Dillon suggested.

"An excellent idea."

Helen leaned across and murmured to Monica, "Funny people you meet on a plane sometimes, don't you agree?"

"Absolutely."

They started to laugh.

IN LONDON, the Broker sat at his desk, finally facing the fact that his scheme of the night before had obviously failed. It had been a crazy idea, and ill thought out, as he now acknowledged to himself, a symptom of his increasing desperation at the way his fortunes had sunk so low. It was silly to leave a message hoping it would tempt Miller to investigate. After all, such a man, a proven killer, backed by political power and supported by Charles Ferguson's people, had to be treated with care. It was for this reason he hadn't ordered sweepers to spy on the house or follow Miller. With a man like that, it could be suicide.

On the other hand, it appeared that the wretched girl he had selected so carefully, brainwashed over time, and supplied with drugs, had vanished. Such was the information he had received from Army of God sources.

So all it proved was his desperation, he who had been so powerful. He switched on his computer and checked the *Serious Crime* data for the Central London area, hoping against hope, but the cupboard was bare.

As he had done many times in the past, he called in details of Belov International plane departures in Moscow and noted the slot booked by the Falcon, but the names meant nothing to him, and the Belov facility in Louth was often used on Belov general business. He moved to Farley, but nothing there. What he didn't know was that Ferguson had put a block on any report of the Gulfstream's movements.

He switched off and sat there morosely, the man who had once had everything, power in every country in the world, even to the level of Putin himself, and now kicked out, denied any contact at all. The truth was he was afraid—afraid what this might mean to him when the news reached Al Qaeda and, through them, Osama.

MARCH IN OBAN and the Scottish Highlands meant rain, and rain it was. They landed a little later than Lacey had envisaged, transferred to a van driven by an RAF sergeant, and left Lacey and Parry in the aircraft.

The sergeant said, "General Ferguson, sir?"

"That's me."

"Duty officer's compliments, and I'm to take you straight down to the harbor, where you'll find your boat waiting. It was delivered by two gentlemen a couple of hours ago, who phoned in as ordered and just managed to catch the Glasgow train. The boat is anchored out in the harbor, and they've left a large inflatable at the jetty. It's stenciled *Tender to Avenger.*"

"Excellent, Sergeant." Ferguson settled back to view the scenery.

"A trifle grim, I would have thought," Helen said.

"Well, it is the Highlands in March," Monica told her. "I've done archaeological digs in the islands when it's been something else. On the other hand, it's not exactly the weather for cocktails on the flybridge."

Billy laughed. "Too right, Lady Starling."

Ferguson said testily, "No need to be a spoilsport at this stage. The rain falls just as much on the rich as the poor. It won't make the slightest difference to our plans. The Avenger will still look as imposing as it is, even if the heavens open on it at Drumore."

"I'll believe that when I see it."

In fact, she soon changed her tune when they passed through Oban town and along the waterfront backed by houses and buildings in Highland granite, and turned onto the jetty.

It was obvious which craft was the Avenger. She was anchored two hundred yards out, and Billy said, "That's got to be it. It certainly makes an impression."

"You can say that again," Dillon said. "Look at the lines on her."

She was snow white with a navy blue trim, and breathed style, beauty, and class. The sergeant said, "By God, that's a thoroughbred, sir."

"It certainly is," Ferguson agreed. "But we're going to get soaked getting out to her."

"I can help there, sir. I've got a couple of big golfing umbrellas in the luggage compartment. I'll leave them with you."

So it was that the two women went down the steps to the tender first, Billy in front to hold the line. They stepped in and each got an umbrella up. They waited, and Ferguson said good-bye to the sergeant and found them. Dillon and Billy handled the weapons box and the luggage and were soon on board. Ferguson tried the outboard, which fired instantly, took the tiller, and they were on their way.

They bumped alongside the stern. Billy scrambled to the deck, held out his hand, and had Helen and Monica aboard into the shelter of the stern canopy. They folded the umbrellas and went through a door into the saloon. Ferguson followed, and Billy and Dillon wrested the weapons box and luggage up. Eventually, they joined the others.

"Magnificent," Ferguson said. The saloon was mahogany, with a center table, swivel chairs on either side. There was a fully equipped kitchen at one end, a stairway dropping down to a shower room and toilet, and a long corridor linking several cabins.

A companionway led into the wheelhouse, although it was like no wheelhouse Ferguson had ever been in. Again, mahogany everywhere, wraparound vision, a very futuristic control panel, and double leather swing seats in front of the wheel.

"It must feel like you're driving a racing car," Billy said. He and Dillon moved in to examine everything, but now

Dillon went up another companionway and called from above, "It's fantastic up here, but get me one of the umbrellas, it's pouring."

Billy passed one, and Dillon had it up when he joined him. "This is amazing," Dillon said. "The flybridge—you can drive the boat from here if you want, and what a place to entertain. It's perfection, but not today." He huddled under the umbrella.

"Look at it," Billy told him. "Just the same as the first time you brought me here. Bleeding awful."

Oban was enveloped in mist and rain, wind pushing across the water of the harbor. Above on the land, the clouds draped across the mountains, and the waters of the Firth of Lorn looked troubled.

"What a place," Billy said. "I'm going below and see what there is to eat."

AT HOLLAND PARK, Roper listened to Ferguson's description of the boat and noted his obvious enthusiasm. "Ah, what it is to be rich," he said.

"That's my friend, not me," Ferguson reminded him.

"The same thing, since you're getting the benefit. I've checked the weather forecast for the next few days, and I hope the ladies appreciate that any hope of an Irish version of Monaco is out."

"It's been discussed," Ferguson told him. "The boat is still what it appears to be, a rich man's toy, and that's the impression it will give, whatever the weather. Anything to report from your end?"

"I'm still trying searching for the Broker, to no avail. I've also checked with Maggie Duncan. Harry is fine, but heavily sedated."

"I'll tell Monica. She can speak to Rosedene a little later. Of course, we know from Chekhov that all contact with the Broker has been banned—"

Roper interrupted, "And apparently by Volkov, speaking under Putin's orders."

"A president who seems to be making it plain he's no longer willing to be swayed by Al Qaeda." Ferguson chuckled. "Wonderful what Harry Salter's offer to pick up Max Chekhov has produced. Such useful information."

"Always accepting that Quinn does as he's told and cuts all contact with the Broker. The most important thing Chekhov told us was Volkov's strict instruction not to warn Quinn of Volkov's arrival. I presume that if he feels like that, he'll order the people at the controls to keep quiet as well."

"Interesting to see how that works, Quinn caught on the hop, as it were," Ferguson said.

"And with the Avenger homing in, he's between a rock and a hard place. If he only knew what's coming from our side: two gorgeous ladies, one a decorated war hero with a penchant for carrying a pistol in her right boot, an East End gangster who's Billy the Kid for real, and a crusty old warrior."

"And Monica?"

"She'll find something to do, I've every faith."

"Just like I do in a certain man of the cloth who was once the most feared enforcer in the Provisional IRA. Though God alone knows what he'll get up to."

"One thing's certain," Roper said. "He'll preach one hell of a sermon."

SOME OF THE CLOTHING the owner had left on board was being examined in the saloon. There were crew jerseys in navy blue, three-quarter-length yellow oilskin coats with *Avenger* stamped across the back. Monica and Helen tried one each.

"Very fetching," Ferguson told them. "You'll do nicely. Those crew jerseys for the men will make us look very professional."

"Well, I'm all for showing ourselves off," Monica said. "We've checked the kitchen and there's enough food in there for an Atlantic crossing."

"And the booze would keep you drunk for a year," said Dillon. "But I don't feel like eating on board tonight. I can't see how the rain is going to do us any harm in all this wonderful gear, so why don't we go ashore and find a decent meal?"

"Why not?" Ferguson said. "A splendid idea."

HALF AN HOUR LATER, they coasted into the jetty in the tender, tied up, and went ashore, choosing a nearby pub that turned out to boast an extensive restaurant. There weren't many customers, it was the wrong time of year for that, but the wine flowed and the food was magnificent and a good time was had by all. It was Helen who tried to get down to business.

"Have you worked out a plan of action yet, Charles?"

"A frontal attack."

"Which could lead to a rather heavy exchange of fire."

"Not could, *will* lead to a rather heavy exchange of fire," Dillon said.

"And kill them all?"

"Quinn knows the game, he's been playing it for long enough," Billy said. "The other year, he put me and Dillon and a good friend of ours in harm's way down the London Dockland, brokered a deal for a group of old IRA hands to knock off the General here, among other things."

"I presume they didn't, as the General is obviously with us."

"Floating downriver last I saw of them, but Quinn got away with it."

"But not this time," Dillon said.

"You're that certain?"

"As the coffin lid closing."

There seemed a sudden chill in the air. Monica seemed a little thrown. Ferguson called for the bill. "Back we go, people, early start in the morning." They started to move.

LATER, MUCH LATER, when it was really dark, the Avenger swayed at anchor, the tide flooding in from the harbor entrance, only her deck lights on, and it was time to retire for the night. Dillon, restless, found himself alone and went out on the stern deck, where the canopy offered shelter from the rain, silver in the yellow light. Way beyond the harbor entrance, he saw the red and green navigating lights of a ship passing down the Firth of Lorn. He was suddenly aware of one of those what's-it-all-about feelings, sat down, produced his silver case, and lit a cigarette.

The door behind him creaked, and Monica said, "Could I have one of those?"

"Bad for your health, girl." He passed his cigarette to her and lit another. She sat in one of the swivel chairs, and he found her.

"It's nice like this," she said. "The rain, the sea, ships at anchor with riding lights. Are you a rain man?"

"It's bred in the bones if you're from Northern Ireland. I'm a rain walker, yes, and I've always liked it, the city at night, wet streets stretching into autumnal darkness as you walk enclosed in your own private world, a feeling that something absolutely marvelous is going to come round the next corner."

"I would have thought it would most likely be a mugger these days."

"It's a cynic you are, but maybe you're right, perhaps I see it through the eyes of youth. London by night, I loved that."

"But you're Irish."

"My mother passed away when I was born, so after a few years my father came to London for the work. We lived in Kilburn. I went to a school with a good drama department, and that led me to trying for a scholarship at RADA, as you've heard."

"But you moved on quickly. What happened, Sean?"

"I'd managed to ignore the first few years of the Troubles. Then my father went home to Belfast on a trip, got caught in a firefight, and was killed by British paratroopers."

"And you went back and joined the glorious cause?"

"That's it. Was sent to Algeria to a training camp that processed young idealists like me who needed to know how to kill people successfully."

There was silence for a moment. Finally, she said, "It's what you would expect from a young boy, his father killed and so on."

He lit another cigarette. "I turned out to be too good at it. Don't have any illusions about me, Monica. As someone once said, Wyatt Earp killed seventeen men. I haven't the slightest idea what my score is, except that it's more. Don't make me a hero figure with an Irish tricolor in one hand and a pistol in the other, like some Easter Rising painting on the wall of a Dublin bar. When I tried to blow up John Major and the War Cabinet in February 1991, I was being well paid, just as I was when I worked for the Israelis and also the PLO. I'm very even-handed. That's what Ferguson liked about me when he blackmailed me into joining him."

"No redeeming features at all?"

"An acceptable barroom piano, I suppose."

They sat in silence in the yellow light, rain dripping from the roof. "You can't make me hate you, Sean, because of what you've done. It would mean I'd have to hate my brother, and I can't do that. You're a good man, Sean Dillon, in spite of yourself, I think."

The pain he felt was intense, for it was one of the last things that Hannah Bernstein, Ferguson's strong right hand, had said to him as she lay close to death in Rosedene. He struggled for breath for a moment.

Monica grabbed his arm. "What is it?"

"Someone very close who could never forgive me the past said the same words before her death. It was at Rosedene, and painful to discuss."

"I'm sorry."

He pulled himself together. "Nonsense, girl, I'm fine. Let me give you a lesson." Between them was a flap on the cabin wall. "Watch me." He pulled a ring and opened it to reveal a battery of fuses. He produced a pistol from his pocket. "Walther PPK and ready to serve you. Just point and pull the trigger." It fitted in beside the fuses, and he closed the flap. "Useful if someone tries to climb over the rail to get at you."

"Thanks very much."

"Naturally, I'll do exactly the same in the wheelhouse. I'll show you." He pulled her up. "You're in the death business now, love."

"Really?" Suddenly, she slipped her right hand round his neck and kissed him fiercely and for a long moment, then pulled away. "And that, Mr. Dillon, is life. Think about it."

"I certainly will."

"Good. I'm tired now, so you can take me to the bar, get me a nightcap, and I'll go to bed for a while, only don't keep telling me what a terrible man you are. It gets boring."

She opened the door and went in. He hesitated, then followed, more surprised than he had been in years.

LATER, Dillon occupied himself checking the weaponry, particularly the sawn-off, loading it with two shells, seeing that everything worked. It had been a long time since he'd had a shotgun, a murderous weapon, especially with steel-ball shot. The *Lupara,* Sicilians called it, and much favored by the Mafia.

Ferguson appeared in the saloon. "My word, that should do the job."

"It's been known to. Everything else in stock. You'll know it like the back of your hand."

"You've got your nylon-and-titanium waistcoat?"

"Wouldn't be without it. I brought two, gave Monica the other, just in case she was anywhere near the odd angry shot. We had a nightcap. She's gone to bed."

"Very decent of you. She's a lovely lady." He hesitated, as if about to say something, but changed his mind. "I'm going to check the wheelhouse. The others all seem to have their heads down."

"I'll join you, but I'm going to have a drink first. Can I get you anything?"

"Coffee." Ferguson grinned. "With a touch of whiskey in it."

• • •

DILLON JOINED HIM a little later and found him in one of the two swing seats close to the steering wheel, checking the controls. Dillon passed a mug to him and sat down. Ferguson was more than satisfied, sat back, and sipped his coffee.

"Try the bottom flat. Full of fuses." Ferguson did so and found a Walther.

"You?" he said.

"Yes. All the comforts of home. Monica joined me up here for a nightcap, was here when I put it in place. I'd already shown her the Walther in the similar flap on the stern deck next to the chairs."

"Useful information, I suppose, but you'd never expect her to be able to use one, a Cambridge don."

"Well, the only other Cambridge don I know is your cousin, Hal Stone, who's been up to scratch for you on several occasions."

"True." Ferguson sipped his coffee, and Dillon decided to put him out of his misery.

"I know what you're trying to say, Charles. She's gone through hell of late, including discovering incredible things about her brother. She has enough trouble coming to terms with all that without a wretch like me entering her life."

"You have a way with the words, Dillon, something I've always admired."

"I should also point out that all those doctorates indicate a lady with the kind of intellect that enables her to see through any false romantic image attached to a man like me."

He swallowed his whiskey, and Ferguson said, "Good God, I always thought you a man of intelligence, but I see now I was wrong in my assumption. You obviously know nothing at all about women." He shook his head. "Let's turn in. We've got a long day tomorrow."

So they did just that.

THEY DIDN'T LEAVE until seven, and Ferguson was at the wheel as they moved out of the harbor. A gray, bitter morning, a headwind pushing rain toward them, and once out of the harbor entrance, the sea started to heave, and he throttled back the powerful engines, enjoying the whole business.

Helen and Monica had found him, while Dillon and Billy stayed below, checking each weapon carefully, loading the pistols and Uzi machine pistols. The Colt .25 hollow-points weren't forgotten, laid out with their ankle holsters on the saloon table with the other weapons. Billy examined the sawn-off.

"A real killer, this one."

"It's supposed to be," Dillon said.

Billy shook his head. "We're really going to war this time."

"I thought that was the idea."

Monica appeared and sat down, watching. Billy said, "What are you taking for yourself?"

Dillon lifted up an old-fashioned carpetbag and opened it. He held up a Bible and a violet stole. "In case I have to hear confession. Black shirt, white clerical collar, and how about this?" He produced a soft black trilby hat in velour and put it on. Then he took out a pair of Zeiss-tinted glasses and put them on also. "Very popular item at the Vatican this year. What do you think?"

Monica cut in. "Put all that together with a black suit and you'll look like the devil himself."

"Now you wound me, but I'll be in Ireland, remember, where a priest receives instant respect more than anywhere else in the world." He produced a manila envelope. "One thousand pounds in fifties for Mickeen Oge Flynn. I was forgetting."

She said, "Just look at you. Acting again. It's meat and drink to you, isn't it?"

"So you've found me out?" It was as if they were alone. "Very clever, but the performance isn't on stage, love, it's for real."

"And don't you think I know that?" She shook her head. "To hell with it. I'll see what's happening on deck."

She went out, and Billy said, "I don't think she's happy."

"I can see that."

"You might be getting in a bit deep here."

"Oh, really?" Dillon said. "Well, thanks for telling me. I'm going to my cabin to check my suit and things."

He took the carpetbag and went out, and Billy said softly, "I can't believe it—Dillon in love?"

A moment later, Monica returned. "Has he gone?"

"Yes."

"Good. I wonder if you'd do me a favor." She picked up a Walther from the table. "Could you show me how to handle one of these?"

Billy smiled. "My pleasure, Lady Starling."

IN THE WHEELHOUSE, things were getting interesting. Ferguson started to increase speed, racing the heavy weather that threatened from the east, and the waves grew rougher. Helen Black had had considerable experience of yachting in her time.

"Is it hard going?"

"Not at all, handles like a dream." He got up, still holding the wheel. "Take over. I'm going to get a coffee. Just put your foot down and let's see some speed."

She did just that, and the Avenger surged forward suddenly into a curtain of mist and rain until she saw, to her astonishment, that they were racing ahead at forty-five knots. Suddenly she was happy, really happy, for the first time since her husband's death.

SHE STAYED at the wheel for an hour and a half, then handed it back to Ferguson and went below and joined Monica in the kitchen, where they devised a prelunch break together timed for ten o'clock. There was minestrone soup direct from the can, a selection of sandwiches ranging from salad, to ham, corned beef, and a cheese, tomato and onion pizza. Everything was laid out at one end of the saloon table.

"Marvelous," Billy said. "I'm hungry already."

"Amazing what you can do with a microwave," Helen told him. "God knows how they got on round the Horn."

Dillon had his soup, then took a plate of sandwiches and joined Ferguson in the wheelhouse. "We're really cracking on. When should we make Collyban?"

"About eleven-thirty. This thing flies. I've never known anything like it."

"Excellent. Not much more than forty miles to the Belov complex and airstrip."

"Always supposing that Roper's prediction for when Volkov's Falcon lands is accurate."

"It's been my experience that he's never wrong." Dillon's plate was empty now, and he put it down. "Away you go and get yourself something to eat, and I'll spell you for a while."

Which Ferguson did, and Dillon sat, his hands on the wheel. Monica came in with a mug. "Tea," she said. "And whiskey in it. I took a chance."

"What a woman. I suspect you may turn out to be a treasure." He drank some of the tea and put the mug on the ledge. "How are you doing? Seasick, by any chance?"

"Helen gave me a pill last night, and I've rung Rosedene on the Codex that Charles got me. The news is good, Sean, Harry's stirring already." Sitting beside him, she took his left hand in her two. "It's such a relief, I can't tell you."

"You just did. I'm glad for you, and glad for Harry." He stood up. "Slide into this seat and take the wheel. I'm going to say hello to Roper."

She did as she was told and it proved easier than she thought. Dillon opened his old silver case, put two cigarettes in his mouth, lit them, and put one between her lips.

"So I'm Bette Davis and it's *Now, Voyager.* What are you up to?"

"The last of the great romantics, that's me."

"That'll be the day." She sat there, one hand on the wheel, absurdly happy, as she smoked a cigarette in the company of this extraordinary man who had come into her life, this thoroughly dangerous man.

Dillon said to Roper, "How are you?"

"I'd rather be you out there on that boat like a bullfighter, moving into the circle of danger, and I'd rather you be me, squatting beside a bomb in a Belfast street, but that was then, this is now."

"Ah, one of those days, is it? Hang in there. There's an old Spanish saying: 'It's not the same to talk of bulls as to be in the bullring.' "

"And what the hell is that supposed to mean?"

"It's an existentialist kind of thing. Seek for it too hard and it won't happen, but somewhere up ahead, something totally marvelous might come round the corner."

"What in the hell's got into you? Okay, you've even got Billy tuned into moral philosophy, but this is ridiculous. What are you doing right now?"

"I'm on what passes for a bridge in this boat, and letting Monica have a trick at the wheel."

"I don't believe it. She's really touched a nerve, hasn't she? You can't afford it, not with what you've got on your plate. Volkov would be easy, but Grigorin and Makeev are Spetsnaz. What in the hell are you going to do about them?"

"Kill them," Dillon told him.

"And you think that's going to be easy?"

"I've got Holy Mother Church on my side and Father Martin Sharkey. There's a saying where I come from: If you can't trust a priest in Ireland, where can you trust him?"

"And what's that pearl of wisdom supposed to mean?"

"That for Volkov and his minders, I'm just a priest, someone not to be taken seriously. Keep the faith, old lad, call me closer to the arrival time for the Falcon." He switched off.

Monica shook her head. "Totally crazy."

"Well, I'm from County Down, and we're all supposed to be a little mad there." He started to thumb a number.

"Who are you calling now?"

"My uncle at Collyban." The phone was picked up instantly, and Dillon said, "It's me, Mickeen, Sean. Are you ready for me?"

Mickeen had obviously been on the drink already. "Sean, me boy. I can't believe it, but ready I am, plus a Ford saloon car."

"An old saloon car, I imagine."

"For one thousand pounds, what do you expect, but it's a good runner, my word on it. When are ye arriving?"

"I said noon, and with luck, should keep my word. Is there anyone else at your place?"

"I only keep the one mechanic, Paddy O'Rourke, him who's serviced the car, but I'll give him the afternoon off."

"Good man yourself, and don't be too shocked by my appearance. I don't want you dying on me."

"So everything's set?" Monica asked.

"It looks like it, and not long to go." He held up the Codex. "The brilliance of these things is that nothing fazes them. I'm always there in a matter of seconds, and you'll hear my voice. Once I leave the boat, you'll move on to Drumore, anchor off the harbor, and wait."

"For you to do what you have to do?"

"Something like that. Ferguson will sort things out, Billy is outstanding, believe me, and Helen is all soldier."

She kept her right hand on the wheel and produced a Walther from the left-hand pocket of the yellow oilskin coat she was wearing. "I got Billy to give me a quick lesson in what to do with this."

He was angry again. "He shouldn't have done that, damn him, it's not expected of you. I won't have it."

Her smile was instant, an inner glow that was remarkable. "Poor old Sean, I've caught you out, you do care."

There was an edge of desperation in his voice. "This has gone too far, love, I'm not right for a woman like you, never could be."

"You can be anything you want, so don't talk nonsense. Go and change and tell Charles to come up and take the wheel."

Her calmness, her certainty, totally defeated him. "I'll do that and see you later."

It was like the acting, preparing for a performance. Black trousers and shoes, black shirt, the snow white band of the clerical collar. He put his right foot up on a stool, fastened the soft leather holster around his ankle, and slipped the Colt .25 hollow-point in place. His black jacket with wallet, a false passport in the name of Father Martin Sharkey, born in Banbridge, County Down, Northern Ireland, a wallet with two hundred pounds in it plus a false credit card from the Catholic Guild. The Zeiss glasses completed a satisfactory image; the velour trilby was just right and the black raincoat perfect. It certainly wasn't the Dillon anyone could have seen on any previous visits to Drumore.

In the carpetbag was his violet stole, the Bible, Mickeen's money, and on the narrow bed was an Uzi machine pistol, the stock folded, the sawn-off and a Walther PPK with silencer, and a fragmentation hand grenade. The door opened and Monica slipped in. She stood looking at him.

"My God." She shook her head in disbelief. "We're close."

He put the Uzi and the sawn-off in the carpetbag with ammunition and slipped the Walther into his right raincoat pocket. "Will I do?"

"Well, I don't know what they'd say at the National, but Hollywood would love you."

He pulled on a pair of thin black gloves and picked up the bag. "That's it, then. Let's go."

Her arms were around his neck in a moment. "You really *are* a bloody madman, aren't you?"

"Of course."

She reached up and kissed him for a moment. "If you don't come back, I'll never forgive you. Now let's go." She opened the door and led the way out.

THEY WERE ALL in the wheelhouse when Monica led Dillon in. Billy said, "Even Harry would be impressed."

"Just right, Sean," Ferguson told him. "And on time. Lots of rain and nicely misty. Collyban over to starboard, but can't see it. Mountains of Mourne running down to the sea, or whatever the damn song says. I'm going to move in closer because, in spite of the weather, by the wonders of modern technology, the navigating screen gives a perfect picture. We're easing in beside the point now, and there's the disused workings in the cliff face and the stone jetty. I think we can ease in alongside, so no need to use the tender. Helen, you know the ropes, so take Billy with you. A few minutes only, mind you."

Helen was already on her way, Billy behind her. A moment later, she was in the prow, a line in one hand and a folded umbrella in the other, ready to jump, and Billy was amidships. The jetty loomed out of the mist, great granite stones from another age. Helen already had bulky yellow fenders over the side, Billy the same, and then they touched close and both of them were across with their lines.

"God bless," Monica called, but Dillon was out and making his way down to the deck.

He brushed past Helen, who said, "Take care." She handed him the umbrella.

Billy called, "Look after yourself."

They were back on board a moment later, and the Avenger moved away, increased power, faded into the rain. The only company he had were disturbed seagulls circling above him, calling angrily.

"Oh, get stuffed, why don't you?" Dillon called, raised the umbrella, and moved along the jetty to the track curving up toward the clifftops.

Drumore Place

14

FLYNN'S GARAGE, AS THE SIGN SAID, WAS ON THE EDGE OF Collyban, had been home to Mickeen Oge these forty years, and the ancient pumps that stood in front of it bore witness to that fact. The garage doors were down, giving the place a rather desolate look, and the cottage that went with it and stood slightly up the hill behind looked a couple of hundred years old and had a small barn with the door open, two goats standing patiently looking out at the rain.

Mickeen Oge was in the office inside the garage, a small gnarled man of seventy-eight in a very old tweed suit, long gray hair falling almost to his collar. He was impatient and considerably excited, had taken to drink and decided to have another, sloshing Irish whiskey into a glass. He went to the window, peering out as he drank it, and swore at the sight of the priest with an umbrella turning in to the forecourt.

He opened the Judas gate in the main door and stepped out. "I'm closed, Father, you'll have to go to Malone's down by the church."

Dillon paused and stood for a moment looking at him,

umbrella in one hand, carpetbag in the other, and the strange tint of the glasses under the velour hat.

"You're not closed, you ould bastard, just stupid to be standing out here in the rain. It's enough to give a man of your years pneumonia."

Mickeen was astonished. "Sean, is that you?"

"No, it's Father Martin Sharkey, so get in with you."

The old man turned, stepped inside the Judas gate, and Dillon followed.

THERE WAS THE USUAL garage smell, oil and petrol, and vehicles of one kind or another parked here and there. The office was an untidy clutter. Dillon sat on a chair by the desk and Mickeen took one on the other side, found a second glass, and poured for him.

"May you die in Ireland."

"An excellent sentiment, and I very well might in the next few hours."

"That bad?" Mickeen shook his head. "I mind well in the old days, twenty years or more ago, when you played Father Sharkey, it was always the hard time. You mentioned Drumore and those there who needed seeing to?"

"Remember Michael Quinn?"

"The one who was Chief of Staff in his day?"

"He runs security for Belov International, from Drumore Place in Louth."

"Not much more than forty-five miles from here over the border. Look, Sean, is the Provisional IRA in this?"

"Those days are gone, Mickeen. Having said that, Quinn tried to have me and friends killed in London last year and failed. He also supplied an ex-Provo to knock off a friend of mine in London a few days ago."

"And did he succeed?"

"The job turned sour, and my friend's wife was killed by mistake."

"Jesus, Sean."

"So Quinn must pay for that, and the man who ordered

Quinn, he must pay, and it's never-ending. Didn't we find that in the Troubles?"

"We surely did."

Dillon reached for the whiskey and poured another. "I know, I shouldn't, as I'm driving, but this is Ireland, and whoever heard of a policeman stopping a priest in his car to check if he'd been drinking?"

"I'll remember that and start wearing a priest's collar myself." Mickeen drank it down. "To business."

"Always that." Dillon put the carpetbag on the table, produced the manila envelope, and took out the wad of notes. "One thousand pounds, ould son, in crisp fifties. Don't spend it all at once."

"Sure, and what would I spend it on? I was joking, Sean, this is family, after all. It'd be a blot on my soul to take a penny, so don't argue with me."

Dillon gave him a brief hug, put the money back in the envelope, and returned it to the carpetbag. "You sentimental old bastard."

"Exactly," Mickeen Oge said. "So now for your car."

He led the way into the garage, pressed a button, and the door opened, creaking away, disclosing the pumps. He turned and walked to one of the cars and slapped it on the roof. It had recently been cleaned and was black as night.

"What is it?" Dillon asked.

"A Ford Anglia."

"Did you find it on the Ark or what?"

"Don't ask. Old but trustworthy. An excellent drive, Sean, my word on it, and it suits your disguise as a simple man of God. The tank's full."

Dillon put his carpetbag on the backseat and embraced Mickeen. "It's been good to see you. At the end of the day, family's everything, as you said."

"Are you trying to make me cry? Go on, fug off."

Dillon got behind the wheel and switched on the engine. He leaned out of the window. "Sounds perfect."

"And didn't I tell you? Away with you, and God help Michael Quinn."

"So you still have faith in Father Sharkey?"

"In Sean Dillon, you idiot. If I didn't, I wouldn't have sold you the car. Now, bugger off and do what must be done."

THE FALCON, well out of Russian air space, was climbing up over north Germany and leveling out at forty thousand feet. Volkov sat alone in the rear cabin and looked through the archway to the forward cabin, where he could see Makeev and Grigorin sitting on either side of the aisle. The cockpit door opened and the senior pilot, Captain Sono, emerged and came down the aisle.

"A great pleasure to be flying you again, General. Is there anything I can do for you?"

"Yes, try and remember the name is Ivan Petrovsky, I thought I'd made that clear. No mention of me at all in any conversation you have with Control."

"I understand perfectly. Your orders in the matter have been strictly adhered to, and so it will continue. It's just that when dealing with you personally. . ." Here, he hesitated. "It's difficult when I know who you are."

Volkov was human enough to be rather pleased. "Nice to discover at my age that I'm such a great man." He smiled. "Go on, go away and fly the plane."

"Any further orders, sir?"

"Make sure there's a limousine waiting for us. No driver is needed. Tell Captain Makeev and Grigorin to join me."

They came at once, hard, intelligent young men with considerable battle experience. "General," Makeev, the senior one, said. "How can we serve you?"

"By getting out the vodka you'll find in the icebox behind me and filling three glasses." Makeev smiled and Grigorin did as ordered. Volkov raised his glass. "To President Putin, to the Motherland." He emptied his glass at one swallow, and so did they. "Once more." He pushed his glass forward. "And then we talk."

• • •

HE TOLD THEM EVERYTHING, including about Miller in Kosovo and Beirut, and the activities of Ferguson, Dillon, and the Salters. He was quite open about the Russian connection and the various failures of the London Mafia because of the Salters, and acknowledged his own connection with Al Qaeda through the Broker and his dealings with the IRA over many years. When he was ended, of course, he flattered them totally.

"Everything I've mentioned is known to our President, a man already making the Russian Federation great in the eyes of the world again."

"And succeeding, Comrade General," Grigorin said, eyes blazing.

"I'm glad you called me that," Volkov told him. "That we are all comrades together just like the old days is as it should be—and our mission is ordered by the President himself." He reached for the bottle and filled the glasses again himself. "I welcome your comments."

"Well, Al Qaeda and the whole Muslim thing can rot in hell. We both served in Afghanistan and Chechnya," Makeev reminded him.

Grigorin said, "So General Ferguson and these gangster people he employs have made monkeys of the Moscow Mafia in London. These oligarchs and the people who work for them disgrace the name of all Russians."

"They're rubbish," Makeev said. "So the Salter people don't particularly impress me, and neither do these Provisional IRA people."

"Not even the man Sean Dillon?" Volkov asked.

The two men looked at each other inquiringly, and Makeev shrugged. "Not particularly."

"So if I assigned each of you to the Embassy in London, you would be willing to serve?"

"In what capacity, General?" Makeev asked.

"I'm sure we could find something suitable to your talents, but that lies in the future. Now we must consider the situation which lies before us, the question of Michael Quinn."

"And what exactly would the General like us to do in the matter?" Grigorin asked.

"Kill him. Of course he has bodyguards, old IRA hands who could prove a problem."

Makeev turned to Grigorin and they both smiled. He turned back to Volkov. "Oh, we've handled bodyguards before, Comrade General."

"Excellent," Volkov said. "Our arrival will be something of a surprise, a pleasant one, I hope. No need to alarm him. I always think the smiler with the knife is the sensible way. Now go and eat, I've got work to do."

"Of course." Makeev nodded to Grigorin and they returned to their cabin.

Volkov opened his briefcase, took out a file, and started to go through it.

DILLON HAD PASSED through Warrenpoint, the scene of one of the worst disasters suffered by the British Army at the hands of the IRA in the entire history of the Troubles. He crossed the border into County Louth in the Irish Republic north of Dundalk with no trouble or hindrance, pausing for a few moments, remembering the old days at the crossings, the police, the soldiers. It was as if it had never been. Sitting there in the Ford at the side of a windswept road, he felt a sense of desolation, wondering what it had all been about.

He got out of the Ford, lit a cigarette, and stood there smoking it, thinking back, but that was stupid and he remembered a fine writer who had made an obvious point. The past was a distant country and people did things differently there. He took out his Codex and called Roper. "Just checking in."

"Where are you?"

"Well on the way. I came round Warrenpoint by Carlingford Loch and I've just crossed the border. Rotten weather and very depressing."

"You'll pass through Dundalk next?"

"That's it. Any news from the Avenger?"

"Not at the moment. Everything went well with Mickeen?"

"Perfect. He turned sentimental on me and refused the thousand pounds, but got me a twenty-year-old black Ford

Anglia in first-class mechanical condition. I think you'd make money out of it in London. Can you tell me anything about the Falcon flight?"

"Yes, I'm hacked into the Dublin control system. It's still got an arrival time of three o'clock."

"That's fine."

"One thing. Bad March weather isn't the only problem in that part of the world. It gets dark pretty early. I suppose what I mean is it gets damn gloomy."

"I'll bear it in mind." Dillon got back in the Ford and followed the road down to Dundalk.

ON BOARD THE AVENGER, Ferguson had the wheel, Monica and Helen standing in the rain on the flybridge, each wearing the yellow oilskins stamped with *Avenger* on the back. They'd also discovered a couple of naval-style peaked caps and wore one each.

Ferguson had already punched in Drumore as his destination, and now full details of the small harbor appeared on the screen. There were only five fishing boats lying off a stone jetty, and the area indicated for visitors at anchorage was a hundred yards out. There was nothing there. Two or three inflatables were pulled up on the small beach area at the bottom of the harbor pilings, but not much else.

"Not exactly the thrill of your life," Monica said.

"When I was last here, it was all action by night," Helen said. "Way beyond the village is the big house, Drumore Place, on the hill. There are only about thirty cottages, and over there where you see a low stone wall, that's a car park in front of the pub, the Royal George."

"But I thought they were all Republicans hereabouts, so why call a pub after an English king?"

"It's a very old pub, and only the Irish could explain it to you."

Ferguson's voice came over the speaker beside the flybridge wheel. "This is the designated area for visitors, so I'm anchoring here, ladies."

He pressed a button on the wheelhouse control box and the anchor dropped automatically. He turned to Billy. "I'll call Roper."

Which he did, and the reply was instant. "Where are you?"

"Just anchored at Drumore. The weather is as you forecast—terrible."

"Well, I had heard it rained a lot in Ireland. Just two o'clock. You've done well."

"This is an incredible boat. Two great-looking ladies in yellow oilskins and navy caps up on the flybridge, but I doubt whether anyone would be looking. What about Dillon?"

"Everything went perfectly, and his uncle furnished him with a rather old Ford Anglia."

"I didn't know they still did them."

"I said old, didn't I? The Falcon's still on course for an arrival time of three."

"I wonder if I should call him—Dillon I mean."

"I'd leave it. You never know where he could be. He'll call you when it suits."

HELEN AND MONICA stayed on the flybridge for a little longer. A man with an umbrella and a dog on a lead walked along the jetty and paused, obviously admiring the boat, then turned and went away. A couple of men emerged from a wheelhouse on a fishing boat and stared across, then retreated out of the rain.

"We're not having much of an impact," Monica said. "Let's go down and have a word with Charles."

In fact, Patrick Ryan, the publican up at the Royal George, had been more than interested. His mother, Mary, who was cook at Drumore Place, was sitting in the lounge bar enjoying a drink with Hamilton, the butler from the house. Sitting at a table by the window were three of Quinn's security men, all wearing navy blue reefer jackets and jeans like a uniform. Nolan, Tone, and Logan were their names and they were eating Irish stew. Ryan had got a digital camera, a pair of Zeiss glasses from behind the bar, went to the large front door, and opened it. He took a couple of photos, then focused the Zeiss glasses on the two women.

"My God, a couple of crackers there," he said.

Nolan, a hard brute of a man with tangled hair and unshaven chin, got up, came across, and grabbed the glasses. "Let's have a look." He focused them and whistled. "Look what we've got here, boys. I wouldn't mind one of those."

He was joined by Logan and passed the glasses to him. "Jesus," Logan said, "I could go for either of them."

"Or both," Nolan said, and at that point, Helen and Monica went below and found Ferguson and Billy enjoying a coffee in the kitchen.

"I was wondering," Monica said. "We don't appear to be attracting a great deal of notice. What if Helen and I went ashore and descended on the pub?"

"I'd consider that most unwise."

"What if I went with them?" Billy said.

"I wouldn't imagine a crew member would do that." Monica shook her head. "He'd take you in on the tender, that's what crew members do."

Billy laughed. "I can see the logic, and it gets the message across to the natives. I'll take them and wait for them like an obedient deckhand."

"Half an hour," Ferguson said. "That's all, so get on with it."

On the Falcon fast approaching its destination, Volkov was approached by Captain Sono. "I'm sorry to bother you, General, but may I inquire how long you intend to stay in Drumore? It wasn't made clear."

"Two days, three at the most. Why?"

"There is a certain irregularity in the port engine. Don't be alarmed. We can land safely, but I wouldn't want to try to fly back to Moscow without a proper check, and we can't do that at our destination."

"So what do you suggest?"

"I've checked with the Belov facility at Dublin. If I drop

you off and carry straight on to Dublin Airport, they're confident they can handle the problem in two days at the most."

"Then that's what you must do. How long to landing?"

"Half an hour."

"Excellent."

AT ABOUT THAT TIME, Dillon called Ferguson. "How are things?"

"Safely in port, which looks thoroughly miserable. Nothing but bloody rain. The two girls have gone ashore in their finery to sample the delights of the Royal George. Billy's taken them in the tender. I can see him from here at the harbor steps, waiting for them."

"Well, they should certainly stun the occupants of the bar."

"Where are you?"

"There's a Catholic chapel just off the road by the Belov complex. It provides an excellent view of the airstrip. I'll be able to see the landing."

"And then?"

"I don't know, Charles. From here, the most direct approach to Drumore is the road along the cliffs, dropping down to the village and onwards to the big house. I'll wait and see. There's a way inland, but it's longer. Leave it to me, and don't call."

"If that's what you want."

AND DILLON had been right about the effect Helen and Monica would have on the Royal George. It was Mrs. Ryan who had borrowed the glasses to observe the boat who saw them coming. "Oh, my Lord," She said. "There are two women off the boat and coming up here."

Ryan came around the bar and snapped away over his mother's shoulder. Nolan and Logan were up fast, Nolan grabbing for the glasses from the old woman, but he didn't need them, for Helen and Monica were already halfway there.

Mrs. Ryan went behind the bar, and Ryan went into his office and got on the telephone to Drumore Place.

When he was answered, he said, "We've had an event, Mr. Quinn, a strange boat in the harbor."

Quinn was immediately on edge. "What kind of strange boat? Who is it? Can you tell?"

"The kind of boat that must have cost a million, and I don't mean euros, and there's two women come ashore like something out of a magazine. Your mother's here, and Hamilton. Oh, and Nolan and Logan and Tone."

"I can just imagine what those three would be like with a couple of rich bitches to slaver over. I don't want any trouble now."

"Jesus, your mother's here, I told you."

"Well, you keep a hand on things."

Ryan peered into the bar. Helen and Monica were sitting at a small round table. They'd taken their caps off, and Hamilton was delivering two large gin and tonics to them on a tray. Ryan snapped them twice, his lens in the close-up mode.

"Isn't this marvelous, darling?" Monica said. "Such fun."

"Absolutely," Helen told her. "Drink up."

"Oh, I will, darling—believe me, I need it. That bloody voyage. I'd give anything for a cigarette, but I believe you can no longer smoke in an Irish pub."

The three security men had gazed at them in awe and then whispered to each other, but now Nolan was on his feet and across with a packet of cigarettes in his hand. He opened it. "Sure, you can have one of mine and bugger the law. Ryan won't mind."

"How sweet." Monica took one and the light that followed.

He looked at his friends and winked, then pulled a chair across, sat down, and put a hand on her leg. "A couple more drinks and I think you and I will get along fine."

There was a hush from all there. "I don't think so," Helen said, and turned to Monica. "Do you, darling?"

"Definitely not. In fact, we should be going."

Nolan exploded. "You'll stay where you are, you fancy

bitches." He banged a fist on the table, knocking over a glass. "Coming in here, you and your rich friend, laughing at us. Time you were taught a lesson."

"Now, Nolan, leave off," Ryan ordered. "Mr. Quinn won't be pleased."

"Go and fuck yourself," Nolan said, and Monica's hand rose above the table holding a silenced Colt .25 hollow-point, with which she touched the side of his face.

"Just stand up, back off, and sit down with your friends like a good boy."

She stood herself, pulling on her cap with her left hand, and Helen rose, too. "We're going now, so everybody stay nice and calm."

Nolan suddenly moved and stood with his back to the door, legs apart. "You aren't going anywhere, and you aren't going to fire that popgun. Who do you think you're kidding?"

There was a vase with artificial flowers on a stand to his left. When Monica fired, the silenced Colt made only a dull thud, but the vase disintegrated. Mrs. Ryan screamed, Nolan darted out the door fast, head down, and his two friends stood up, disbelief on their faces.

"So sorry, everyone," Helen said.

They went straight out together. As they went down toward the harbor, Monica started to shake.

"Are you all right?" Helen asked.

"I can't believe I did that."

"Well, you did, and Charles is going to be furious."

They reached the tender and scrambled in. "Everything all right?" Billy asked as he started the outboard.

"Not exactly," Monica said. "I think the roof just fell in."

FERGUSON WAS CALM, but still angry. "So what do we do now? I knew it was a mistake."

"If I may make a point, Charles," Helen said, "Monica and I were simply acting out your plan of campaign. A couple of rich bitches from a millionaire's boat showing themselves off in the local pub. Nobody could have foreseen what happened.

After fifteen years in the military police, I know villains when I see them, and that's exactly what they were."

Monica said, "It was interesting that the publican tried to put them down by reminding them that Quinn would be displeased."

Billy, the streetwise gangster, summed it up. "Of course, she could have just sat there while the goon tried to feel her up, and God knows what else with the booze flowing." He turned to Monica. "It was the Walther, I explained to you when you asked me. Where did the Colt .25 come from?"

"That was me," Helen said. "Actually, I had one in my boot as usual."

"Marvelous," Ferguson said. "Gunfight in the Last Chance Saloon. The point is, Quinn can only draw one conclusion from this. That all is not what it seems on board the Avenger and that we're up to no good." He turned to Billy. "We might have to repel boarders at some point, especially when it gets darker. Have the right weapons available at strategic points, and you two had better familiarize yourselves with what he arranges," he added to Monica and Helen.

"One point intrigues me," Monica said. "I know the village is rather small, but there must be a few people around. What do they make of all this?"

"Simple. They stay indoors and keep their heads down. There's an old republican tradition, Monica. Say nothing and then say nothing. It has a powerful effect on these people."

"And the police. There must be a local station?"

"Closed by now, I should imagine." Billy smiled. "Somebody's rustled some cows fifteen miles away up the coast, something like that. This is still an IRA area, peace or no peace."

Ferguson's Codex buzzed, and when he answered, it was Dillon. "Just to let you know, the Falcon's arriving, I can hear it in the distance. Everything okay with you?"

"I'm afraid not." Ferguson gave him the bad news in a few brief words.

"And Monica did that?" Dillon was astounded. "Who does she think she is, Annie Oakley?"

"Not her fault, it just happened, but it changes the game."

"Completely. I must go. The Falcon is getting very close."

THE FALCON came in to a perfect landing and Grigorin and Makeev, alerted to the situation, were ready as the aircraft turned along the runway and paused outside the small office block. The second pilot, Yeltsin, opened the Airstairs door, the steps dropped, and Volkov went down, followed by Grigorin and Makeev with the bags. A man rushed forward with a black umbrella as the steps were raised and the Airstairs door closed again. The Falcon moved away at once.

"You are?" Volkov asked the man with the umbrella in English.

"Pushkin, Mr. Petrovsky." The man hesitated and said in Russian, "But I know who you are. I'm the traffic controller. I've seen you in the past at the Moscow complex."

"So, a Russian, and I hadn't expected that. Very remiss of me. Let's go inside." Which they did. "You have a car for us?"

"A Mercedes, General, parked outside."

"You followed your instructions about me?"

"To the letter, General. No mention of your arrival at all."

Outside, the Falcon roared along the runway and took off. "Yes, Captains Makeev and Grigorin are GRU and take matters concerning my security seriously. This is a matter of state security, on behalf of President Putin, and I particularly wish to announce my arrival to Michael Quinn myself."

"Of course," Pushkin said, completely overawed, and at that moment his mobile sounded. He looked hunted, then answered. "Pushkin here." He glanced at Volkov. "Oh, yes, Mr. Quinn, it was just a Belov Falcon touching down with a package of drugs for the nun's hospital. It took off again for Dublin. Yes, sir, thank you."

"Good man," Volkov said in Russian, and patted him on the shoulder. "We'll go now. Of course, if we discover we are expected, then my friends here will obviously be back to find out how such a misunderstanding could have occurred."

Pushkin took one look at Makeev and Grigorin's threatening faces and almost had a bowel movement. "Everything is as I've said, Comrade General, I swear it."

"I'm sure it is."

Pushkin led the way out to the Mercedes, held the rear door open for Volkov, and closed the door on him, half bowing. Grigorin took the wheel, Makeev sat beside him, and they drove away. Dillon, standing beside the Ford, was watching, for what happened next would be crucial. If they turned left out of the gate, it would mean the inland route; if right, the coast road. They turned right, and at two hundred yards' distance he had plenty of time to get behind the wheel of the Ford, turn into the coast road, and drive away in front of them.

HE DROVE VERY FAST, the Ford Anglia responding superbly. Mickeen Oge had certainly been right in the performance he had promised with the engine. He pushed it to seventy-five, the coast road skirting clifftops, the rain and mist driving in from a turbulent sea. There was no sign of the Mercedes in the rearview mirror, but then, he had been driving dangerously fast.

Ahead, there was a rock face to his right, and opposite on the left, a lay-by, a place that could take perhaps three cars, a wooden fence on the edge. He pulled in nose first, leapt out, and went to the fence. It was an overhang, a drop of over a hundred feet into the sea. He turned, got back into the Ford, took the sawn-off out of the carpetbag and laid it within reach of his left hand, and sat there, the engine running.

What he intended had to be savage and brutal and without mercy. He took off the Zeiss glasses, put them in his pocket, and waited, looking through his windows to the left, aware of the Mercedes rounding the bend and rushing toward him. Dillon hung on till the last possible moment, then rammed the gear stick into reverse and exploded into the road.

Volkov cried out in alarm. Grigorin, at the wheel of the Mercedes, cursed and slammed his foot on the brake. The car skidded, turning in a half-circle, finishing up on the lay-by only a yard or so from the fence.

Makeev leapt out of the passenger seat and stood up, shouting in English, "What the hell's going on?" Grigorin had his window down, rage on his face.

Dillon took Makeev first, firing the sawn-off across the top of the Ford, blowing him away, then gave the next shot to Grigorin full in the face as he sat there. The sound was very loud, echoing through the rain, seagulls calling angrily. Dillon pumped two more steel-ball shot in place and wrenched open the rear passenger door.

Volkov crouched back in his seat with nowhere to go, looked death in the face and knew it. "Welcome to Ireland. Dillon's the name. If you've got a pistol, give it to me or I'll blow your head off."

"This is madness. Kill me and President Putin will stop at nothing to avenge me, and I'm not armed. This is murder."

"But you're not here," Dillon said. "That's the beauty of it. Just some guy named Petrovsky. This is for a lot of things in the past, but let's just make it for Major Harry Miller's lovely wife."

He opened the driver's door, stretched across Grigorin's body and released the hand brake, then slammed the rear passenger door. A quick heave and the Mercedes, helped by a slight slope, fractured the wooden rail, Volkov trying to open the door, and then it was over. The rear of the car tilted and Dillon went to the edge and saw it fall the hundred feet down to the sea below. He watched it explode in a great gout of water and start to sink.

Which left Makeev lying on his side. Dillon turned the body over, got him by the belt, hauled him to the edge of the cliff, and simply let go. The body bumped once against the cliff and dropped through space, hitting the water where the Mercedes had already sunk.

HE DIDN'T GO DOWN to Drumore, but turned the Ford and drove back to the chapel close to the Belov complex, parked, and went in. There was a washroom, and he checked his clothing. The right-hand sleeve of his raincoat had some blood on it, received when he'd reached over Grigorin's body to release the hand brake. The place was decent and well looked after and there were plenty of paper towels and warm water available, and he managed to do an acceptable job on his sleeve.

He went out into the chapel. There was a sanctuary light at the altar, the virgin and child in the darkness at one side, candles guttering. It took him back to childhood, candles, incense, and holy water, but there was no way back to that. He went outside to the porch, and it was gloomy. No wonder it had been dark in the chapel.

He phoned Roper. "It's done," he said simply.

"Volkov?" Roper sounded incredulous. "His plane landed at Dublin. It's due back the day after tomorrow."

"And the two GRU goons. I did some shooting with the sawn-off and put their Mercedes over a cliff. Volkov was still alive in the back."

"Not a nice way to go."

"I didn't feel nice. Anyway, as they would say in Sicily, Ivan Volkov is asleep with the fishes."

"Have you told Ferguson?"

"No, but I'll speak to him."

"What happens now?"

"It's going to be dark quite soon. I think I'll leave it until it's time to board. A strange priest might cause comment in the village, but I'm out of the way at the moment. I can always go for a drive round the surrounding countryside for an hour. How's Harry?"

"Improving, but still very weak. Do you want me to tell him?"

"That's up to you."

Then he called Ferguson, who answered at once. "What's happening?"

"It's done, Volkov and his minders all taken care of."

"Putin won't be pleased."

"He'll never know what happened. Volkov's Falcon is due

back from Dublin the day after tomorrow, to find no Volkov. The pilots know he was delivered here, but with a false identity. A problem, that, for Putin, whichever way you look at it."

"Are you coming in?"

"I don't think so. I've just been passing the good news to Roper. As I told him, I think I should drive around for an hour until it's good and dark, then I'll join you."

"What do you think we should do?"

"Why don't you give that some thought, General. I've just killed three people, so I've been busy."

He cut off, and Ferguson turned to three anxious faces. "It was Dillon. He's taken care of Volkov and his men."

"All three?" Billy said. "Christ Almighty."

"He's all right, though, he's coming back?" Monica demanded.

"Yes, he's going for a drive to keep out of the way until it's nice and dark, and then he'll board."

"So what comes next?" Monica asked.

"To be honest, I'm not sure. The way Volkov had it planned, Quinn wasn't to know he was arriving. That means Quinn won't be agitated about his death, because he didn't even know he was here."

"An interesting situation," Helen said.

"To put it mildly. We'll wait and see what Dillon thinks."

BUT UP AT Drumore Place, things were happening. Quinn sat by the fire in the great hall, drinking whiskey, his mother on the sofa on the other side of a glass table. "Terrible it was," she said. "When she pulled that gun out and fired at the vase, the heart nearly stopped in me."

Nolan, Tone, and Logan were ranged along the back of the sofa, and Quinn said, "Has the world gone bloody mad? What would the kind of woman you mention be doing with a gun? It doesn't make sense."

Ryan came in from the study. "I took some snaps with that new digital camera of mine. State of the art. You put them into the computer, then use the printer and out come the pictures just like this, Mr. Quinn."

Quinn looked at them, the boat, the two women walking up to the pub, the close-ups of them at the table with their drinks, caps off. He exploded and jumped to his feet.

"I know one of them, for Christ's sake. Lady bloody Starling, sister to that damn Harry Miller and no friend of ours."

"But how do you know her, Mr. Quinn?" Nolan asked.

"From the television, you idiot. There was a funeral the other day, Miller's wife. It was a big do. The Prime Minister was there. This woman here was mentioned by the TV reporter as Monica, Lady Starling, and he said she was Miller's sister."

Nolan said, "That's the one who fired the pistol. What would she be doing here?"

"God knows. I don't know who the other one is, but this is definitely Miller's sister."

Nolan said, "But what are they here for?"

"Up to no good, that's for sure."

"Did you recognize anyone else in that TV report?"

"It was only a minute on the evening news. They didn't trawl the crowd."

"The thing is, they aren't going to be on that boat on their own," Nolan said. "Perhaps we should take a look?"

Quinn nodded. "See what you can do, you three, and I'll alert a couple more of the boys. Make sure you're armed to the teeth, but if you could get your hands on that particular woman, it could be more than useful. There could be a big bonus for you. Let's say five thousand."

"Okay, I'll get my hands on her, all right," Nolan said. "Come on, boys."

They went out, and Quinn rang a bell and the butler entered. "What can I get you, sir?"

"Not a bloody thing. I want you to take my mother right now to my aunt Kitty's for the night." She started to protest, and he said, "Shut up. I've enough on my mind and I want you out of it." He gave her a shove toward the door, and they departed.

He went to the sideboard, opened a drawer, and found an old Browning pistol. It was loaded, of course, and it made him feel secure just to hold it. Whom did he have to fear? That bastard Ferguson, and Dillon, who was a good comrade in the old days. Who could it be with the women on the boat? He suddenly thought of the obvious and searched for Volkov on his coded mobile, but there was nothing, no helping hand or reassurance, just a resounding silence as he went to the door and called for Riley at the top of his voice.

A small, energetic man with red hair came from the kitchen on the run. "Mr. Quinn, what is it?"

"Nolan, Tone, and Logan are away down to the harbor. We could have trouble. I want you, Hagen, McGuire, and Brown, back door, front, terrace, French windows. No messing, AK-47s, so get moving."

Riley went out on the run and Quinn went to the sideboard. When he poured another very large whiskey, his hand shook.

THE AVENGER WAS A PLACE of shadows as darkness fell. Billy was on the flybridge, had discarded the yellow oilskin coat as being too good a target. In fact, they all had, scouring the boat for anything darker and more sensible. Ferguson was in the wheelhouse with an Uzi machine pistol, Helen and Monica on the stern deck. There was the riding light, but nothing more.

"I can't see much," Monica said.

"At least the shadows give some kind of protection."

In fact, Nolan, a veteran of the Iraq War, had night glasses through which he could see a kind of green world, Billy on the flybridge, a vague impression of Ferguson in the wheelhouse, but the two women in the stern deck were plain.

"Right," he said, and passed the glasses to the others. "The two women should be available without much trouble. We'll use the two small inflatables and paddle. You take one, Tone and Logan and I will use the other. Nice and quiet from the side of the jetty and just drift in."

• • •

DILLON WAS JUST OUTSIDE Drumore, close to a garage that was closed, a few parking places free in the forecourt. He eased into one of them, got out with his carpetbag, and called Ferguson. "Everything all right with you?"

"So it would appear. Where are you?"

"On the edge of the village. I've parked at a garage that's closed. I'll walk down to join you. I'll call in when I'm there."

"Good man. We'll be expecting you."

TONE DRIFTED IN amidships, bumped silently against the boat, and slipped up under the rail. He stood up, a Smith & Wesson in his hand, and stumbled. In the stern, Helen turned at once and shot him with her silenced Walther. He fell backward over the rail, alerting Billy on the flybridge.

Monica, Walther in hand, standing by the stern rail, turned to see what was happening, but behind her, Logan and Nolan had drifted in silently and Logan reached up and caught her leg. She struggled frantically, half turning and firing down into him, the silenced Walther making a dull thud, but as he released her and fell back, Nolan reached up and pulled her.

"Get down here, you bitch."

She catapulted over into the inflatable beside him, Logan half in the water, and Nolan tossed him out and punched her on the side of the jaw.

"That should settle you," he told her, and pushed the inflatable away, swallowed by the darkness, as Helen peered over and Billy arrived too late.

Ferguson switched on the wheelhouse searchlight and swept the harbor, but there was nothing, because Nolan, suspecting something of the sort would take place, had paddled into the shelter of the fishing boats moored for the night, emerging on the beach side where there were steps up to the seawall. Monica had fainted. He had her over his left shoulder, carrying her through the streets easily enough. Logan and Tone dead, so that five thousand pounds would be all his. Once he had that, there was also the question of what happened to the woman. He was filled with excitement as he went up the hill.

DILLON HAD JUST REACHED the harbor when the tender came out of the darkness and nosed onto the beach. Billy closed down the outboard and climbed out after Ferguson and Helen. They each had an Uzi on display.

Dillon said, "What's happened?"

So Ferguson told him. "It must be Quinn's people, has to be."

"I agree." Dillon nodded. "And two down already? That's a good start."

"What do you suggest?" Helen asked. "We can't just go walking in."

"I can," Dillon said calmly. "But you three would be better employed elsewhere."

"What the hell do you mean?" Ferguson demanded.

"I presume Monica had her Codex with her?"

"Yes, she did," Helen said. "I was with her when we changed into dark clothes. She had it in her left shirt pocket."

"Good. If I punch in the return code, her number will come up automatically."

"Yes, but if she's in Quinn's hands, he'll have found the phone or hear it if he hasn't."

"That's exactly what I want. Come on, we're wasting time." He led the way as they went up the hill. "I'll tell Quinn I want a deal, any deal to get her safely back, I'll come alone."

"He'll kill you," Billy said.

"Not straightaway. He'll want something out of it, anything that's going, so he'll want to know what I'm up to."

"So you go straight in the front door?" Ferguson said.

"Bag in hand, yes. I'll tell him I'm there to make him an offer he can't refuse, if I might steal the phrase."

"And us?" Helen demanded.

"Billy here knows the house and grounds like the back of his hand. He and myself went through it like a dose of salts the other year and even saw off the great Josef Belov himself on that occasion. You remember, Billy, get to it, and fast as you can." He thumbed in the right signal, and in a few seconds it was received and Helen, Ferguson, and Billy rushed away.

IN THE GREAT HALL, Monica, pale and wan, sat on the sofa wrapped in a gray blanket. Nolan stood behind her, and Riley to one side of Quinn with an AK-47. Monica was shaking, her face swollen, a glass of brandy in her hands.

"Drink it up, Lady Starling, it'll stop you getting pneumonia."

Nolan said, "You promised five thousand, Mr. Quinn. Now Tone and Logan are gone, by rights I should get the lot."

"All right, I hear you," Quinn said.

"And her?"

"God, you're like some bloody great dog straining at the leash. So, what's going on?" he demanded of Monica. "Who are the men in the boat?"

"I've got nothing to say to you except that you're a murdering swine, responsible as much as anybody for the death of my sister-in-law."

"Jesus, woman, that was a mistake. It was intended for your brother, that business, and he richly deserved it."

The Codex he'd taken from her pocket was impervious to water and was on the table. Suddenly, it sounded. "Now, there's a thing." Quinn switched it on.

Dillon said, "Would that be you, Quinn?"

"That's right, and who might you be?"

"Sean Dillon. We once crawled through a sewer together in Derry to get away from Brit paratroops."

"Happy days, Sean, and what would you be wanting?"

"Lady Starling, and don't tell me you haven't got her."

"Ah, you mean Monica? Yes, she's here, very wet, but wrapped in a blanket and sitting on my sofa. What do you want with her?"

"A deal, that's what I want."

"A deal?"

Monica shouted, "Don't do it, Sean."

Quinn said, "Now, what could you possibly offer me that I'd want? I've got Lady Starling, I hold all the cards."

"We're wasting time here. When there's a knock on the front door, you'll find me standing there. What you do is up to you." Dillon started to walk up to the house.

AT THE SAME MOMENT, the kitchen door at the rear opened and McGuire stepped out and looked around the courtyard. All was quiet. He turned to go back, and Billy Salter shot him with the silenced Uzi, driving him inside. He stepped over the body, closing the door behind him, went out and, remembering the back stairs, ascended cautiously.

Ferguson went through shrubbery, crouching, Helen by his side. "I'm getting too bloody old for this," he whispered.

French windows extended to the left; one of them was open and a velvet curtain stirred in the wind. They could hear voices faintly.

"I'll go in. You stay here and cover me," Ferguson said.

He moved up some steps to the terrace and started toward the open window. Brown came around the corner on the left, holding his AK across his body. Helen stood up and shot him with the Uzi several times in the silenced mode, and he lurched back over the balustrade.

Ferguson returned and whispered, "How many more, God alone knows. We'll check down to the conservatory, covering each other. Dillon must be inside now."

"If they let him in at all," Helen whispered, and they moved into the shrubbery again.

BUT DILLON had rung the bell at the front door a good ten minutes before, bringing Quinn to his feet. "That must be the bastard now," he said. "Answer the door, Riley, and you watch the woman," he said to Nolan, walked to the sideboard, and picked up the Browning.

"Oh, I will." Nolan ran his hand over Monica's head, and she tried to pull away.

Quinn had slopped whiskey into a glass, tossed it down, and crossed to the archway leading into the great hall. He could see the outside door wide open, Dillon framed in the entrance on the other side of Riley, the carpetbag in his left hand.

"Hands up, damn you." Riley thrust the end of the AK into his stomach. "Hand over your gun."

"Which one?" Dillon said, playing one of the greatest bluffs of his life.

"Is that you, Sean?" Quinn called.

"As ever was, Michael, and if it's guns your man here wants, he can take his choice. There's an Uzi for starters." He took it from the carpetbag, pushed Riley's AK to one side, and thrust the Uzi at him. "And a PPK complete with silencer. Will that do to be going on with?"

He elbowed Riley away and walked straight to Quinn and held up the bag. "And plenty of other goodies in here. You'd be surprised, so let's go in and see if the lady's in one piece."

There was astonishment on Quinn's face, but he was frowning also and followed, the Browning ready. "No tricks now, I know you of old." Dillon walked to the table and put the bag down on it.

Monica tried to stand, and Nolan, a revolver in one hand now, shoved her down and she was angry in a strange kind of way. "You bloody fool. They'll kill you, Sean."

"Not Michael, my love, curiosity always got the better of him. Before he kills me, he'll want to know what I'm doing here committing suicide like this, and he'll want me to tell him before I go."

Billy from the top of the back stairs had made his way along to the gallery above the great hall. It was dark up there and he was perfectly concealed, but there was Riley, who had discarded his AK for the Uzi, Quinn with the Browning, and

Nolan, now holding Monica up on her feet and back against him, his left hand on her face, the barrel of his revolver resting on her shoulder. It was too risky to attempt a shot, certainly from her point of view, and he knew Dillon and waited.

"For my next trick, see what we've got here." Dillon produced the manila envelope containing the cash intended for Mickeen Oge Flynn, took out the wad, tore off the paper band around it, and tossed the notes high in the air in a shower. "Did you ever see the like? Fifty pounds each, every one."

As was intended, it was a considerable shock. Riley said, "Mother Mary," and took several steps forward, dropping to one knee, trying to pick up notes in his right hand, still clutching the Uzi in his left.

"Here there, none of that." Quinn stepped close, reached down and picked a fifty up himself, and looked at it. "What's your game?"

Outside, Ferguson had reached the end of the terrace and peered through the window of the conservatory. Satisfied, he turned away and Hagen came around the back of the conservatory, AK raised. Helen erupted from the bushes firing her Uzi and he fell back, discharging the AK, which was not silenced.

In the great hall, the sound was clearly heard. Quinn turned and glanced at the archway leading to the hall. "What in the hell was that?"

"I haven't the slightest idea." Quinn was standing so close that Dillon was able to slide his right hand over his shoulder to pull him close. At the same moment, he put his left into the carpetbag and took out the fragmentation grenade. "But I know what this is." He pulled the pin with his teeth and held the lever tight, the pin bouncing on the table.

Riley raised the Uzi threateningly and Nolan pointed the revolver. "I wouldn't," Dillon said. "Because I release this lever, it not only kills Quinn and myself obviously, but most people in a radius of twelve yards."

"Don't be a fool," Quinn said desperately. "You'll kill the woman, too."

"You intended to do that anyway, didn't you, and probably after having your way with her."

Quinn took a chance. "I don't believe any of this. Shoot her, Nolan."

On the balcony, Billy didn't even wait to see what Nolan would do, shooting him through the head. Monica dodged away, and Dillon called, "Run for it, out to the garden."

It was Riley who ran, turning and darting out into the hall, running headlong into Ferguson, who shot him instantly. In the confusion, Quinn suddenly wrenched himself free of Dillon, ran to Monica, got an arm around her neck, and held his Browning to her side. He started to walk backward, dragging her roughly.

"Now, I don't know what you're going to do with that thing, Sean, but I'm out of here with the lady, and that's a fact."

He'd reached the French window behind him and kicked it open, keeping well behind Monica, as they all stood watching.

"And so's this." Dillon dropped down on his left knee and pulled a Colt .25 hollow-point from the holster on his right ankle and shot Michael Quinn between the eyes without hesitation.

Quinn went backward, crashing through French windows to the terrace, and Monica darted to one side as Dillon continued through. He stood looking down at Quinn, remembering Derry a long, long time ago with something like regret, and then he turned and went back in, still holding the grenade in his left hand, the Colt in his right.

"I'm sorry," he said to Monica. "I must have scared you."

He walked across the room, putting the Colt in his pocket, picked up the pin from the table and fit it back in the grenade, which he then dropped into his carpetbag. Billy and Helen had been picking up the fifty-pound notes, and she put them all back into the manila envelope, which she dropped into the carpetbag.

"How kind," Dillon said.

"Waste not, want not."

"It's over, then?" Billy said.

"There's an old saying that nothing ever is, but one thing's for sure. I think we should get the hell out of here." He turned to Ferguson. "Wouldn't you agree?"

"While we can." Ferguson looked around him. "God knows what our Russian friends are going to make of all this. Let's go, people."

He led the way out, pausing at the front door, turning all the lights out, leaving the charred house that had been Drumore Place in the darkness behind them.

THEY WERE HEADING OUT to sea twenty minutes later, Ferguson at the wheel, and he put the Avenger up to top speed, racing through the night as if trying to put what had happened at Drumore Place behind them as quickly as possible. Dillon called in to Roper from his cabin.

"It's finished," he said.

"You mean Quinn?"

"And seven of his men."

"That's quite a score."

"Eleven in all when you count Volkov and his minders."

"I wonder what Putin will make of it?"

"Not much, I expect. He doesn't like messes. Volkov and the GRU guys have gone for the deep six and it's doubtful if anyone will ever find them. They'll remain a permanent mystery. I think GRU security will clear up the mess at Drumore House quickly and wind down the activities locally of Belov International."

"So Volkov, Quinn, Fahy, and Ali Hassim, all responsible in some way for the death of Harry Miller's wife, and all have paid the price."

"Which leaves only the Broker."

"Well, I can't help you there, Sean. All my vaunted expertise in the fields of computers, the ins and outs of cyberspace, all my wizardry has failed."

"Picasso said computers only give answers."

"Well, mine isn't giving me an answer on this."

"Perhaps it's too complicated—for the computer, I mean. Maybe there's a simpler solution."

Roper said, "Well, I'll take that on board."

"How's Harry?"

"I had a brief word. He's hoarse and slow, but Maggie said he's been propped up and is managing to do a little reading."

"That's encouraging. I'll go now. See you soon."

HE LOOKED IN at the saloon, found Monica and Helen having a glass of wine, Billy green tea. There was the remains of a meal on the table.

"Did you want something to eat?" Monica asked.

"Not really, but Ferguson might. I'll join him in the wheelhouse."

He found Ferguson listening to the radio weather forecast. "Winds five to six," he said. "Could be worse. How are you?"

"Winding down. I've spoken to Roper. He tells me Harry is improving. I'll spell you if you like."

"Yes, I would. What are the others doing?"

"They've eaten. Now they're having a drink."

"A satisfactory result. The Russians won't be pleased, it's put a dent in things for them, but they won't do anything about it, just clean up the mess. That's all they can do for the moment."

"And pay us back next time?"

"Of course. The name of the game, Sean."

He went out and Dillon sat there, the wheel on automatic, and lit a cigarette. After a while, the door opened and Monica found him. She reached for the cigarette between his lips, smoked it herself for a moment, and then gave it back.

He said, "I had to take that chance with Quinn."

"I never doubted you."

"They tell me you had to shoot somebody."

"A very objectionable man, Nolan's pal, who was helping abduct me."

"Does that give you a problem?"

"I haven't had time to sort out whether it does. My life has totally changed in just a few weeks—everything is different, and I'm different with it. I don't know what that means."

"It could be you take a deep breath and go back to the gleaming spires of Cambridge University and dinner at high table. You'd be a sensation with the students if they knew what you've been up to."

"Well, they won't, will they?" She took his left hand and held it firmly. "But you do."

They sat there together, the Avenger plowing on into the night.

London

End Game

15

Two o'clock of that same morning at Holland Park, Roper sat in front of his screens, a glass of whiskey in his hand, running through the computer the material he had put together concerning the Miller affair, everything that he considered to be of any significance, even matters before Miller's time that had in any way related to the Broker.

The link with Al Qaeda, with Drecq Khan, who had been empowered to organize the Army of God, the involvement with the Provisional IRA during the final years of the Troubles, Volkov, the Russian factor, so important. A man of a certain international stature, the Broker had to be. From his voice, a Westerner, although no one had ever suggested he might be an American. Upper-class English, because as one person had described him, he sounded posh.

Roper reached for the whiskey, drank a little, and said softly, "But then, the bugger also speaks rather good Arabic." He laughed. "So does Dillon, so does Harry Miller, so what does that prove?"

Sergeant Doyle appeared. "Here you are again, Major Roper, overdoing it. What am I going to do with you?"

"I've had the good word from both Dillon and General Ferguson. They're on their way back from the Irish venture, and it's been a total success. They'll be in Oban in the morning, where Lacey and Parry are waiting. Probably here around noon."

"Well, that's good, sir. Can I get you anything?"

"Answer a riddle for me that I can't answer myself."

"And what would that be?"

"Who the bloody Broker is. You've been involved enough around here and long enough to have heard him mentioned in a number of important matters."

"That's true, sir, so what's the problem?"

"Identity, Sergeant. You've been a military policeman for long enough to know that's the first order of priority in any crime, knowing who you're looking for, and in this case, all we have is a voice on the phone. To everyone he's been involved with, even at the level of General Ivan Volkov, President Putin's personal security man, he's always been a voice on the phone. One person after another in this affair has described him that way, someone reminiscent of an Oxford professor but who speaks Arabic."

Doyle said, "Well, begging your pardon, Major, but maybe he *is* an Oxford professor who speaks Arabic. There were some funny buggers in our business produced by the Cambridge system, weren't there?"

"You're quite right. Burgess, Maclean, Kim Philby, all worked for the KGB. I've put some of the relevant facts together like a documentary, and it's not long. I'll show it again and see what you think. Run your copper's eye over it."

He lit a cigarette and leaned back in his wheelchair. Doyle, genuinely interested, watched instantly. When it was over, he said, "You've got some really good stuff there. In fact, you've built a hell of a case against him to which no court in the world could deny a guilty verdict."

"Guilty, the anonymous man," Roper said.

"Where did you get those photos of Fahy?"

"That was Teague and his disposal team. They found them when they cleared the flat and garage."

"What I found particularly interesting was Fahy's dying confession. I felt a certain sympathy for the poor sod, but that was only because of his wife."

"So you're a decent guy."

"The statements that made up his confession, given to you by Dillon and Major Miller, don't vary an inch. The business of the motorcycle deliveryman in leathers giving him the envelope containing the key was so bizarre it had to be true."

"Do you think he was the Broker?"

"God, no."

"Why are you so sure?"

"A copper's nose, Major Roper. After years of practice, you learn to go with your instinct. First suspicions are right most of the time."

"And yours tells you the guy on the motorbike wasn't the Broker?"

"It just doesn't seem probable. He was compelled by Fahy to make that bank draft an open one. As I understand it, anyone who had it in their possession could have used it. That's why the messenger was delivering an envelope with just a key. He didn't know it was for a locker at this Turkish bath place. The Broker told Fahy that over the phone."

"You're right, that's an interesting point.

"I accessed the place's membership list. There's no card in the name of Smith and Company, and it's impossible to check all the Smiths in London. It's a dead end there."

"I suppose so. Think it has anything to do with the gay subculture?"

"I doubt it. That was long ago. All kinds of people come and go now. No fuss."

Doyle said, "I suppose that's why he chose it. Nice and quiet. People minding their own business."

"When you say he, you mean the Broker?"

"Who else? The bike messenger delivered a key and had no means of knowing where it fitted. If the Broker was that cautious, he'd never risk anyone else delivering the envelope to the locker. He'd do it himself." He shook his head. "He put the bank draft in the locker, then gave the key to the messenger somewhere else."

Roper poured another whiskey and drank it. "So simple—so bloody obvious, so why didn't I see it before?"

"You were expecting the computer to think for itself, and they don't. We're still a long way from conceptual thought with those things."

Roper's fingers danced over the keys, and he produced the Web site for The Turkish Rooms on the screen. "There you go, Tony—a steam room, marble slab massage, an ice-cold pool. You'll love it."

"I see." Doyle grinned. "You want me to look the place over?"

"After you've provided me with a bacon sandwich and a cup of tea. It opens at nine-thirty." He reached for a cigarette. "London has more CCTV cameras in place than anywhere else in the world, did you know that?" He grinned. "Maybe we'll get lucky."

AFTER DOYLE had left, Roper stayed by his screens. Pain, as usual, was ever present in his bomb-ravaged body, but he held off taking the most effective of his pills, poured another large whiskey, and sat there reviewing the situation. Perhaps the Broker was doing exactly the same thing somewhere, considering what to do, wondering what might happen.

Roper went out through the corridor to the entrance hall, opened the front door, wheeled his chair onto the porch, and lit a cigarette, staring out at the rainswept courtyard, feeling himself at the end of something in a way he never had before. Doyle found him there when he drove into the yard and got out of the car.

"Are you okay, sir?"

"I've been better, Tony. How did you get on?"

"Fine. Geezer called Harvey in a tracksuit was on duty. Grenadier Guards in his day. I flashed my ID card and he was very civil. Guided tour, cup of coffee in the café. Ten percent off as a serving soldier."

"And the security aspects, what about that?"

"CCTV cameras in the entrance and inside. He was joking about that and the lack of privacy in the changing rooms, but he said it's all these health and safety laws they have to observe these days."

"But sometimes useful," Roper said.

"Do you think you'd be able to access them, sir?"

"If the CIA can infiltrate the London railway stations, I should be able to penetrate The Turkish Rooms."

But he hesitated, and Doyle said, "You're worried about this, aren't you? What exactly are you looking for, sir?"

"You mean who, don't you? Now that we may be close to identifying the Broker . . . I wonder if I want to know."

He shook himself. "Make sure I'm not disturbed, Sergeant," he said, and he glided back into the computer room.

GETTING INTO THE SYSTEM turned out to be as easy as he thought. Once in, he found a choice of cameras, but it was the one covering the locker room that he wanted. He fast-forwarded it to the right date, then slowed it down after the time code indicated noon. He watched intently, going into close-up. No one was in the locker room, as Fahy had said, and then as the time code indicated twelve-twenty, a man in a fawn raincoat appeared. Roper could see only his back as he moved in quickly from the right. He unlocked number seven, took out a manila envelope, and turned, pausing to open it and to take out what was obviously the bank draft. Roper recognized Sean Fahy clearly, it was without doubt the man on the three or four photos Teague had supplied from the garage. Fahy didn't even smile, simply locked up as ordered and walked away.

Roper moved back to just before the moment Fahy had arrived and put the episode into his copying system. When he was satisfied with what he had, he took the whole thing back to nine-thirty, opening time, and started to work his way through. It was ten-fifteen before two aging men came in talking, opened a locker each, and removed a terry-cloth robe. They undressed, talking amicably, put on the robes, and hung their clothes up in their lockers. They closed and locked them and vanished to elsewhere in the building, still talking. After that, there was nothing, and Roper pushed it on. Eleven o'clock and still nothing, eleven-fifteen, and he was beginning to wonder, and then it happened, just as he'd hoped it would. A man in a navy blue raincoat came into view, as Fahy had, moving in quickly from the right so Roper could only see his back. He had two manila envelopes ready in his left hand, placed one in the locker, then took out the key and dropped it in the other. He turned, sealing it, so ordinary, a furled umbrella hanging from his wrist, and walked away. Roper pulled back to enlarge the picture and watched him walk away through the door, knowing beyond any shadow of a doubt that he had finally found the Broker.

BAD WEATHER CONDITIONS had delayed takeoff at Oban, and it was three in the afternoon when it finally landed at Farley. Ferguson decided to go straight to his flat at Cavendish Place and offered to drop Helen Black off at her house in his Daimler.

She kissed Dillon and Billy on the cheek and hugged Monica hard. "A remarkable few days. I won't say we must do it again sometime, it doesn't seem appropriate."

"Exactly," Monica said.

Harry arrived at that very moment in the Bentley in answer to Billy's call. He got out and embraced his nephew. "Been a naughty boy again, have you?"

"We all have," Dillon told him. "But we won't go into that now. Billy will fill you in on the juicy bits. If you could drop Monica off at Rosedene, that would help. They'll drop me at Stable Mews in a Farley car."

"Could you come with me, Sean, to Rosedene?" she asked.

"If you'd like me to."

"I would." She took his hand lightly for a moment.

"Then of course I will."

"We'll catch up later," Ferguson called, and they all dispersed.

• • •

AT ROSEDENE, Maggie Duncan emerged from her office and greeted them in reception. "I'm glad you're back. He'll be pleased to see you."

"He's well, is he?" Monica asked eagerly.

"The truth is he's still very poorly. The viciousness of the stabbing has not helped at all, but he'll be so pleased to see you."

Dillon said to Monica, "You go, have a bit of quiet time with him. I'll avail myself of the facilities and have a good shower. I'll see you in a while."

She kissed him briefly and went along the corridor.

Maggie Duncan said, "That I should see the day."

"And you won't." He shook his head. "Maggie, you know the man I am and the life I live. You've been patching me up for years. She's a wonderful woman, and it may sound corny to say she's far too good for me, but it's the truth."

"And have you told her that?" Maggie smiled. "I don't know men. Go and have your shower, Sean." She went back into her office.

MUCH LATER, and having borrowed a fresh shirt from laundry, Dillon appeared at Miller's room and found him sitting up and leaning against a recliner, his face quite haggard. Monica sat beside him, holding his hand and looking worried.

"There you are," he said. "Up to your old tricks, it seems. I've just made Monica tell me all about it. No more Volkov? And Quinn." Miller shook his head. "One thing you can say about you and me, Sean, the body count is remarkable. Lying here feeling lousy and rather sorry for myself, I begin to query the point. It won't bring Olivia back."

His distress was obvious, and it was at that point that Dillon realized how deeply damaged he was. "All we're missing is the Broker."

"Suddenly, I'm not interested. Having just discovered that my sister's joined the club by killing her first man at Drumore, I wonder where it's all going to end and whether it's worth it."

He was racked by coughing. Monica rang for the nurse, who came in, followed by Maggie Duncan. Dillon said, "I'll get out of the way."

He went into reception, walked out into the porch of the front door, and smoked a cigarette, looking out at the rain. After a while, Monica joined him and stood beside him, her left arm around his waist as if seeking security.

"He's not good, Sean."

"I can see that."

"Not just in body, but in spirit." They turned to go in and met Bellamy coming out of his office.

"Ah, there you are. I'm glad you're here. I need a word."

"I'd imagine you would," Monica said.

"First, his physical health isn't at all good. Some pretty serious infection of the wounds haven't helped. To be frank, I've a nasty suspicion that the knife supplied to the young woman was poisoned, certainly contaminated in some way. I'm having checks done on that now, so we'll see. The other thing is his mental state. He feels an enormous personal guilt because he had to kill that girl. He also feels a terrible guilt because his wife died in his place when he was the target. No reasonable argument is possible with him on that matter at the moment. If you don't object, Lady Starling, I'd like to call in a colleague, one of the finest psychiatrists in London, as soon as possible to examine him and suggest proper therapy."

"I'd welcome it." She turned to Dillon. "He's just told me he feels he should resign his seat."

Dillon flared with anger. "Don't let him do that, he was a good guy in all this. Volkov, Hassim, Fahy, and Quinn were bad people, the lot of them, responsible for so much evil and by intention."

"I know," she said. "And the damn Broker still out there." She was half crying. "I must go back to him, Sean. I'll stay the night." She gave him a brief hug and departed.

"There it is," Bellamy said. "Most unfortunate. I'll speak to my colleague now. I'll see you later, Sean."

He went to his office and Dillon went out onto the porch,

and Harry Salter's Bentley drew up, Billy at the wheel. They both looked serious, and Harry leaned out of the window. "Glad you're here. Get in and quick."

Dillon didn't argue, only saying as Billy drove away, "Where's the fire?"

"Ferguson called me at the Dark Man," Harry told him. "Said he wanted me and Billy to pick you up here and join him and Roper at Holland Park."

"What for?"

"He said we'd find out when we got there, but nothing had ever been more important."

"Then put your foot down, Billy," Dillon said.

AT HOLLAND PARK in the computer room, the Salters, Dillon, and Ferguson watched the events at The Turkish Rooms unfold. At the last moment, as the Broker turned to walk away, Roper froze the image. There was a strange stillness for a moment, and then Ferguson spoke.

"It's so totally damning that it's breathtaking."

"Not much to say, really." Dillon shrugged. "So what do we do about it?"

"I know what I want to do," Harry said. "Bury the bastard, and alive if possible."

Billy nodded. "I'd second that."

There was another long pause, and Roper said, "So how are you going to handle it, General, confrontational or what?"

Ferguson turned to Harry Salter. "You still have those pleasure boats on the Thames, don't you?"

"That's right. There's the *River Queen* and the *Bluebell*."

"Westminster Pier. Let's say seven o'clock" He turned to Dillon. "Would that suit you—the *River Queen*?"

"Fair enough, but would he come?"

"He will if I make it seem important enough."

"And what happens?" Dillon asked. "That's the thing."

"I haven't the slightest idea, the implications are too enormous, we simply go with the flow." Ferguson stood and said to Roper, "I think you should be there with this." He gestured at the frozen image and turned to Harry. "Do you have a television set on board?"

"In the lounge."

"I'll manage," Roper said. "Billy and Harry will help."

"No one else," Ferguson said. "This is very personal for all of us. I'll go off now and make contact. If it isn't going to work, I'll let you know and we'll decide on something else."

He went out. Harry said, "You could always wait for a wet Saturday night when the bastard is walking home and simply give him a bullet in the head."

"If only life were that perfect," Dillon said. "But let's get started. There's a lot to sort out."

Westminster Pier at around half past six. The rain had increased with force as darkness fell. Harry and Dillon had been on board the *River Queen* for some time, organizing things, and now Billy arrived in the van with Roper. He got him out, hurried ahead, went on board, and opened a section of the rail that allowed wheelchair access to the deck. He made sure that Roper had negotiated safely and once more moved ahead. He opened the door of the lower-deck saloon and Roper followed him in.

There was a television high up in a corner. Dillon and Harry were standing at the small bar, having a drink. "There's your television," Harry said, "and it does DVDs."

"And I've made one. Put it in for me, Billy, and give me a drink, Harry. No sign of Ferguson?"

There was the sound of a car. "That'll be him now."

He went out on deck to put up the rail again and saw Ferguson paying off a taxi. It drove away, and Ferguson came toward him as Billy put up a sign that said: *Private Party Only.*

Ferguson came up the gangway. "A taxi seemed the sensible thing to do."

"I wonder if he'll think so, too."

"Who knows? Join the others and get moving as soon as he arrives."

Billy went and Ferguson turned, waiting. It was quite still, just traffic sounds in the distance, and then a small man, holding a large black umbrella over his head, simply emerged from the darkness. He stood there, looking up at Ferguson, his face yellow in the jetty lights, his hair still obviously white: Simon Carter, Deputy Director of the Secret Security Services.

"There you are," Ferguson called. "No taxi?"

"Walked along from the Houses of Parliament. What's it all about? I thought all this kind of cloak-and-dagger stuff went out with the Cold War. What's so important that we have to meet like this?"

He came up the gangway and boarded. Ferguson unhooked it. There was a line coil dropped over a deck post. Ferguson slipped it off, strode to another amidships, and did the same. The *River Queen* started to edge away at once on the current and the engine rumbled, started by Billy up in the wheelhouse.

"What in the hell is this?" Carter demanded.

"Evening cruise on the river, Simon, maybe as far as Chelsea while we discuss business. Sorry about the rain. It turns up everywhere when you least expect it. Raining on the coast road in Louth when Dillon ambushed Volkov and two GRU hard men and killed them, raining in Drumore last night when we finished off Michael Quinn and company at Drumore Place."

Carter was dumbfounded. "What in the hell are you talking about?"

The saloon door opened and Sean Dillon said, "Come in, Mr. Carter."

And Carter, urged forward by Ferguson's hand in his back, had no option but to go.

THE FILM ENDED with the frozen image of the Broker, turning to walk away. Billy, in the wheelhouse, had the windows open as they proceeded upriver toward Chelsea in spite of the rain, and had the rear door of the wheelhouse open at the top of the steps leading down to the saloon so that he could hear what went on.

"So what have you to say?" Ferguson demanded. "That screen damns you. Your guilt is absolute."

"Don't be so stupid. Guilty of what? A voice on the phone to everybody for years, that's all."

"To Volkov, and through him the President of the Russian Confederation himself," Roper said. "High treason."

"Even Kim Philby or Guy Burgess couldn't compare with what you've done," Ferguson said. "The links with Al Qaeda and the international implications alone are unbelievable, and the fact that it was all passing through Volkov's hands."

"I say again, even there, I was just a voice and I never met one of them. How do you prove a voice? Your people have always operated outside the law. Look at the things you do, your cavalier attitude toward the legal system, which is, why try a suspect when you can kill them and have your disposal unit handle the consequences? Yes, I know all about you."

"You missed on Miller in Beirut, but you were away, as I recall, and I put a stop on any mention of his flight from Farley. I did that when we flew up to Oban the day before yesterday and foxed you again. Dillon got Volkov, we all finished off Quinn and his people. In case it hasn't got through to you, Abdul, sent by Hassim, stabbed Fahy on your behalf, but Fahy shot him dead. He then made a dying confession to Dillon and Miller. Both he and Abdul went for disposal. Miller executed Hassim later that night."

Carter's face was contorted. "Miller's not with you, I see. Could it be a certain young girl got to him with her knife? Disposed of, was she? Thank you, Ferguson, I only have to look at your face. Her knife was treated with a particularly virulent poison. If Miller isn't dead, he soon will be."

"You fucking bastard," Harry Salter said.

"My God, it can talk, just look at it." Carter's contempt was total. "You never liked me, Ferguson, just because I was a desk man and never served in the field, but at least my job took brains. How else would I have come to be Deputy Director of the Security Services? I never liked you or this nonsense about heading the Prime Minister's private army, or your IRA gun hand."

"God save your honor," Dillon said. "It's a blessing such a great man as yourself would allow me in the room."

"You murdering Irish dog." Carter laughed harshly. "I'll tell you how I started, though it won't help you one bit, Ferguson. Professor Drecq Khan. The other year, MI6 heard from Pakistan sources that he'd met Osama in Afghanistan and was bedazzled. Naturally, the news landed on my desk and I seized on it. You were having bad trouble with British Muslims at the time, so I couldn't resist stirring the pot. I invented the Broker, phoned Drecq Khan and said I represented Osama and Al Qaeda, passed privileged information to him that helped the cause. Khan believed me, the man of mystery, the voice on the phone, because I could also speak Arabic, thanks to Oxford. It so amused me that I did the same thing to Volkov when he entered the game."

"And you couldn't stop?"

"I wasn't allowed to. After a while, a message came from Osama himself direct to me. My cover was blown—I've never been able to find out how, but it was."

Dillon said, "So your instructions were to keep the Broker going or else?"

"Something like that, and it was so easy to protect my back. Take Miller's escapade in Washington. I knew exactly what had happened because I'd been with the Prime Minister when Ferguson reported the facts, but I couldn't tell Quinn or Volkov in that case, for obvious reasons."

"Very clever," Ferguson said.

"I always was, so what are you going to do? Send for Scotland Yard? Stand me up in the Old Bailey? Do, and I'll sing so loudly they'll hear me in China. I'll expose everything you've put your hands to, all of you, and we'll include all your dealings in Washington on behalf of the American President by Blake Johnson. I'll bring it all out. You can't afford it, Ferguson, neither can the government or the Prime Minister, so why don't you go to hell, the lot of you? You mentioned Chelsea. I'll get off there."

He turned, opened the door and went out, paused to raise his umbrella, and went up the six steps to the foredeck, lit by deck lights, where Billy stood in the wheelhouse, the window open. Carter paused and glanced in. "Oh, it's you, you swine. Don't worry, you'll go the way of the rest of them."

Billy shouted, "Collision course, hard aport." He spun the wheel, and as the *River Queen* veered around, Dillon, Ferguson, and Harry in the saloon staggered and fell over, the deck tilted, and Roper in his wheelchair ran into the table.

On the foredeck, Carter was thrown violently to the side and attempted to hang on to his umbrella, losing it and falling on his front as the deck inclined more, slipping backward under the lower rail, a situation in which his small size did him no favors. His head was raised as he grabbed at the rail, Billy caught a flash of the desperate face in the desk light, then he was gone into the darkness. He spun the wheel again, bringing the *River Queen* back on course, and as things calmed, Dillon came up the steps from the saloon behind him.

"What was all that about?"

"I thought we were going to hit something, but I got it wrong. Darkness, rain, you know how it is? Unfortunately, Carter fell down and slipped under the rail. I'll turn and take us back to Westminster." He smiled savagely. "At least that's my story, Officer, and I'm sticking to it."

Dillon returned to the saloon. "When Billy spun the wheel, Carter lost it, slipped under the rail into the river."

"A likely story." Harry said. "But he got what was coming and no one put a finger on his. I don't know about you, but I could do with a drink. Do we report it?"

Ferguson said, "You're the original river rat."

"It's a known fact that more than half of those who go in never get found, the tide takes them out to sea. Another thing, he didn't arrive by taxi, he walked—so nobody knows he was here."

"We'll leave it to the river, then. I'll join you in a scotch."

"I'll have one, too, as Carter was wrong about one thing," Roper said.

"What was that?" Ferguson asked.

"The Muslim girl's knife, the poison. Monica phoned me

just before Billy picked me up. Bellamy has a report from the pathology lab. They've discovered what the poison is and they've got an antidote, which has already been delivered to Rosedene."

"Why do I feel like cheering?" Ferguson said.

"Because we all should be," Dillon told him, and he walked outside and stood on deck, feeling absurdly happy as Billy took the *River Queen* into Westminster Pier.

LATER, MUCH LATER, with everyone dispersed, he got out of a taxi at Rosedene and went in. Ferguson had given him the task of telling Monica and Miller everything that had happened. Reception was quiet, no sign of Maggie Duncan, just a young probationer on night duty, but she knew him.

"How's the Major?"

"A wee bit better. He's on new medication. Lady Starling's with him now." She was from Northern Ireland and fond of Dillon. "I'm sure they'd love to see you. I heard them talking only minutes ago."

"You're a grand girl, Molly, so I'll do as you suggest."

He moved along the corridor, knocked on the door, and went in. Miller did look a little better, leaning back on the recliner, but Monica was delighted. Jumped up and reached for his hand.

"I left a message for you with Roper. Such good news. Did he give it to you?"

"Not right away. We had serious business to deal with, but I know now and I'm delighted for you, Harry, it's great news. How are you up to hearing mine?"

"It's that important, is it?"

"It's closure for you as regards the matter of Olivia's death. Roper finally found out who the Broker was, someone you know well."

"Who?"

"Simon Carter."

There was total shock on Miller's face, and it was as if life stirred in him again. "What nonsense is this? The Deputy Director of the Secret Security Services, the Broker? It's impossible."

"We have him on CCTV film taken at a Turkish bath putting the envelope with the bank draft for Fahy into locker seven. Confronted by Ferguson and the Salters, me and Roper, he admitted everything."

"Confessed?"

"Boasted. Defied us to do anything about it. He was going to ruin the lot of us, including the government, if he ended up in court, and had already finished you because he'd been responsible for the Muslim girl and her poisoned knife. He's dead now."

"You killed him?" Monica asked.

"Never touched him. Let me go over the whole thing."

When he was finished, Miller shook his head. "The bastard came to Olivia's funeral, remember, with the Prime Minister. He offered his condolences, gave me his hand." He shook his head. "Deputy Head of the Secret Security Services. How did that happen?"

"Well, they'll need a new one, and I know where the Prime Minister should be looking, and maybe he will. Of course, you'd have to resign your seat in Parliament."

"You must be crazy."

"Think about it. Night, love," he told Monica. "I'll get off."

On the porch at the front door, he phoned for a taxi and stood staring out at the rain. He took out a cigarette, and as he was lighting it, Monica appeared from behind and took it from him.

"I'm pleased for you," he said. "Harry, I mean."

"So am I, pleased for all sorts of reasons. Do I see you again?"

"I think I'd be seriously silly not to."

"Sensible man. One day at a time." She passed him his cigarette back, took his arm, and together they waited for his taxi.